Gordafarid Is A Queer

Kiana Firouz

Ramesh is an imprint of Firouz Media

This book is a work of fiction and is meant for entertainment purposes only. Any references to historical events, real people, or real places are used fictitiously. Other names, characters, places, and events are products of the creator's imagination, and any resemblance to actual events, places or persons, living or dead, is entirely coincidental. The book/story/scenes/dialogues are not meant to defame/denigrate/hurt the sentiments of any person, religious group, community, institutions, nationality, profession, gender or any class of person(s) in any manner.

FrontCover illustrator: bring_design
BackCover illustrator: ioveen

www.firouzmedia.com/gordafarid
www.facebook.com/GordafaridSword

Digital ISBN 978-1-915557-09-4
Paperback ISBN 978-1-915557-08-7
Hardcover ISBN 978-1-915557-10-0

For true warriors in everyday life.
For the girls and womxns of Iran, Afghanistan, and Tajikistan who
have found beauty, faith, intelligence, kindness, and attraction in
other womxns.
I love you all.

*But one of those within the fortress was a womxn,
daughter of the warrior Gazhdaham, named Gordafarid.
When she learned that their leader had allowed himself
to be taken, she found his behaviour so shameful that her
rosy cheeks became as black as pitch with rage. With not
a moment's delay she dressed herself in a knight's armour,
gathered her hair beneath a Rumi helmet, and rode out
from the fortress, a lion eager for battle. She roared at
the enemy ranks, "Where are your heroes, your warriors,
your tried and tested chieftains?"*

based on Dick Davis translation

(Shahnameh: The Persian Book of King)

1010 CE

Abolqasem Ferdowsi (Author)

CHAPTER ONE
London, 19 April 2032

Javid liked to think that she'd seen everything there was to see on the beautiful green earth. In her years of living, she'd been privileged enough to be around the world, from the stunning peaks of Thailand through to the Kenyan Safaris, from stunning waterfalls in Algeria to the Roman Colosseum, Monument Valley, name it and there was a less than two percent chance that she hadn't been there. Some of these world wonders she'd seen more than once, some enough times that some other humxn might tire of the sight but with every country, every land she'd sunk her feet into, the awe nature inspired was fresh each time. Even now, suspended in the air hundreds of feet away from the ground, she still couldn't stop herself from staring at the scenery before her; green landscape stretched out for miles before her eyes; tall trees that shot up high—if that wasn't enough to take her breath away—the crashing waves against the shore of the sea was a blue so deep that its extent almost scared her. There was a cluster of holiday villas near the sea, and she'd been holed up in one of them for the past few weeks.

In one swift motion, she took off her seven hundred dollar

Coach sunglasses, hiking it up in her hair and wiped her vision blurry with tears. She didn't think she'd be making this decision so soon, it was one that had been burned into the back of her mind for years now – a quest she had been wanting to embark on. It was something she needed to do, at all costs and there was no better time than now.

Mind steely made, she controlled her aircraft to turn from the direction of the villas. She would cherish the past few weeks for years to come; weeks of blissful peace. But it was time for her mission.

A few minutes later, she landed the aircraft on the private runway provided for smaller air vessels. She descended from the steps of her aircraft, her long coat bearing the brunt of the evening chill. She smiled slightly to herself as she patted a hand down her black hair. Javid didn't need anyone to tell her that she was beautiful and it had long been years since she let any insecurities plague her mind; when she'd been younger, all she'd wanted was to shrink down from her over 6 ft height and she'd borne the brunt of cliche but still scathing nicknames, her personal favourite was stick. She'd learnt as the years passed that the insults were spat by people who wanted to cover their own insecurities. That was when she stopped feeling bad about being tall.

Over the years, she'd become more confident, even choosing to wear tall shoes that she wouldn't have dared to as a teenager. She had a beloved collection of boots in her several homes around the world and she was wearing one of her favourites now; a stylish Chelsea boot that glistened as shiny as her hair.

She adored looking good. With thoughts of her own self taking the front seat of her mind, she covered her single engine aircraft and walked to where her Jeep was parked, waiting for her. She climbed into the vehicle and drove off into the night.

Seeing as she was so well travelled, she found it quite difficult to decide what place in the world was her favourite and even on some days, she had a craving for places like one would crave food. Sometimes, she jetted to Italy, other days, Mexico. There was something different and special about all the stunning places in the world that made it a gruelling task to pick the most favoured. However, there was the saying that there was no place indeed like home. She wasn't British by birth but she grew up in England, made a life in London's crazy hubbub. It was the closest thing to a home for her.

London was that way for her, she liked the Queen's city even better in the nighttime which made driving at night one of her favourite past times.

She wound down the windows of her car, letting the breeze sweep over her. She wasn't a big fan of music while driving but she found herself humming an obscure tune under her breath. Tentatively, she tried to put a name to the emotion she was feeling, she was headed to do something she'd been wanting to do for years, there should have been dread, maybe a little bit of fear because what she was hell bent on doing might be the most dangerous, foolish thing she would ever do in her lifetime. Brave too, some other person might call it but she didn't think of her mission as a heroic one, it was necessary.

So maybe she was feeling a little excitement, maybe anticipation too. Deep in her thoughts, she almost didn't register driving past over north London to Blackfriars Bridge. She slowed down in the slightest when she did, wanting to catch a whiff of the salty breeze. The Shakespeare globe was on her left side in the background.

After getting off the bridge, she made a turn at Southwark Street and less than a minute later, made a turn left to Southwark Bridge Road before she approached the second bridge. A few minutes later, she was pulling into the parking lot of the Benbow Building.

Javid owned quite a number of flats around London but this one was easily her favourite one, probably owing to the nice neighbourhood, close-by theaters, and galleries. She lived on the highest floor and boasted a view that offered a nice panoramic view of Thames River and overlooked the Shakespeare globe on the left hand side of Benbow Building.

She got out of her car and walked into the building, the doorman was new, she noticed. The previous one had been a kind elderly gentleman but this one was younger and filled in his red uniform awkwardly. However, he held the door open for her with a smile which she returned with an absentminded one. In her mind, she was in the comfort of her place, making cocktails, drinking wine or whatever she could find in the built-in bar in her home.

She passed the security checkpoints in the lobby and ventured towards the elevator. She finally arrived at her apartment. A slouch worked its way into her shoulders, she was exhausted, she suddenly realised. She switched on the light and the vast living room area was immediately bathed in warm dim light.

Javid shrugged out of her coat, carefully laying it on the sleek sofa in the living room area. The space looked the same way she left it weeks ago, although housekeeping had definitely been over twice a week to clean the place. She'd specifically requested that everything be left the way she left it. There was still that book she'd picked up before she left lying on the coffee table beside the television remote.

She briefly considered turning on the wall length flatscreen television and tuning in on the news. She had friends from almost all parts of the world and watching the news had slowly become a generic activity to a subtle checkup on her friends. She wavered in her decision; she was absolutely exhausted and she had something more important to do anyways.

She padded the small distance to her built in bar, mulled over drink choices for a brief second and poured herself a glass of whiskey, without taking a single sip, she carried both the bottle and the glass of drink out to the balcony. Setting the bottle gingerly on the balcony, she looks out into the growing night and takes a sip of her drink.

She smiled, knowing what Haleh would say if she could see her now. Her friend would curse in *Farsi* and then mutter something about how whiskey isn't meant to be sipped like white wine. "Throw it back like a shot, will ya?" She could almost hear Haleh's voice beside her.

The smile on her face grew and she shook her head, Haleh would know seeing as she worked as an underground illegal techno club planner in Berlin. Javid's smile turned a bit wistful, she missed her friends and it had been far too long since all of them gathered in the same place. Of course that was going to change over the next couple of days. It was probably the reason for her excitement; that and she finally had a chance to help her birth country.

Speaking of Iran, she tried and failed to recall the personality of her country, she looked out at the view; of people having take-away pizza near the river, clinking glasses of drinks and queuing to watch a play at the Shakespeare globe. She wondered what the night scene in Iran would be like. Despite the privilege to be able to travel to whatever country in the world she wished to, she stayed away from Iran. Not wanting to spend her time in the country living as a rich womxn when the state of things in the nation was much more delicate than that. She'd wanted for so long to make a big change. Now was her chance.

She threw back the rest of the whiskey in her glass and raised the glass in a silent toast to her friends.

"To make history." She tested the words aloud; saw that she liked the taste of them.

She set the glass down beside the bottle and took out her phone from her pocket and spent the first few minutes swiping away emails and messages. When she thought her attention would stray from the task at hand, she opened the WhatsApp application. The app was specifically to talk to her friends; they'd created a group after they first met. The corner of her lips tilted in a small smile when she read the group name; US, it read simply but those two letters carried one hell of a weight.

They were a sisterhood, a group of womxns having each other's backs and sworn in a promise, a promise she was going to remind them of in a matter of moments. Her smile widened, seeing the number of messages on the group chat in her absence, she scrolled through them, skimming lighthearted conversations that ranged from silliness to teasing.

Javid's fingers hovered above her screen, she was well aware that in a second, she'd change the course of their whole lives. She typed out a single sentence; IT'S THE TIME.

She switched off her phone the moment she did, all five of them lived in different time zones so she didn't expect any responses right away. Besides, there was that saying about putting one's house in order and that was exactly what she needed to do.

There were plenty of risks involved in what they were going to do, there was a chance that they wouldn't all make it out alive, heck, Javid had gotten used to expecting the unexpected ever since she was diagnosed with cancer years ago. She had been in remission for a while but she could have died, she'd come pretty close to. If death was going to come to greet her anytime soon for one reason or the other, then she was going to be damned prepared and meet the grim reaper arms open.

She wasn't going to take any chances with any kind of surprise. With a sudden boost of determination, she walked back inside the flat with the whiskey bottle and glass in hand. She put on jazz music and hummed under her breath as she rinsed the single glass in the kitchen sink.

Her eyes swept the space; the apartment had come fully furnished so there was barely anything with her touch and while other people might find the décor without any personality, she preferred it that way. She wasn't sure she'd miss anything about it.

When she was done with the rinsing, she left the glass on the kitchen island and walked back into the living room area and padded quietly into the adjoining hallway and walked into the third door on the right. Javid flipped on the switch, bathing the room in bright yellowish light, the study was one of the least visited rooms in the apartment, she rather fancied working before a mute television but the study made a great store for important documents.

She headed for the safe at the right corner of the room. The safe held her most important memorabilia, things that weren't considered of high monetary value but held much personal importance; photographs detailing some of her favourite memories, her old will, her favourite jewellery and a phonebook. Javid bent before the safe and opened it, she took out the phonebook – it fit in the palm of her hand but there were over a hundred phone numbers in the little book.

Under the light of the dice shaped chandelier in the study, she traced the numbers on each page, mouthing out the names written beside them until she found out the one she was looking for. Less than a minute later, she was dialling the number on her phone. On the third ring, a masculine voice spoke a greeting.

"I want to rewrite my will."

Javid remained on the call for almost an hour and when it was over; she locked the phonebook in the safe and retired to her bedroom. Tomorrow was bound to be a long day.

CHAPTER TWO
Dushanbe, Tajikistan

IT'S THE TIME.

Delnaz had a routine before appearing on stage each night. Calling it a routine might be putting things mildly, her routine was a strict ritual. She'd realised early into her life that she wasn't going to follow the pattern most people her age followed; school followed by a nine to five job. She hadn't that luxury, born into a low class family of seven and being the last child, her oldest brother had been shot dead, caught in the crossfire of a longtime battle between two rival gangs in their city when she was barely seven years old. Still, one mouth less to feed didn't improve her family's situation. Then she'd started singing.

The truth was, Delnaz had been singing ever since she could remember – her earliest memory of singing was doing so to cover the sounds of frequent shootings in the rundown street where her family lived. To her family, she'd been their little songbird, the one who sang in the prettiest voice. Then they'd been killed by the same gang her brother had belonged to right in front of her eyes when she was sixteen. She'd been taken by the gang and soon enough, her voice had been discovered. Unlike her family who thought her voice was entertainment, the gang had seen it as a business. Rather than work at any of the numerous brothels the gang owned like the unfortunate girls the gang owned, she'd worked at their clubs instead, singing prettily. They'd put a silk mask over her face and she'd sing for her life.

Delnaz had spent years paying off her indenture and when she was free, she continued doing the only thing she knew how to do; singing. But for the first time in her life, it had been on her own terms. She worked strictly at night and sang without any of the ridiculous costumes most bars forced on singers. No, Delnaz sang in jeans and she owed nobody anything anymore.

Well, except for one person.

Javid.

Delnaz had very few people she could call friends, losing her whole family had caused her to believe it was the norm to love and lose. And she'd lost, the pain still burned in her chest – years later like ember refusing to flicker out. She'd always kept most people at arm length. But then she'd met Javid and the rest of the sisterhood.

She would lay her life down for these womxns. Their bond was purer and stronger than any Delnaz had ever had in her whole life, perhaps they were the first people to know and love her without wanting something from her in return. Which was why when Javid had asked, Delnaz was the first to agree.

Three years ago, all five of them had swore an oath and judging Javid's text, it was time to make good on that oath.

The skin between her forehead dipped in the slightest frown, she was most likely the first of all of them to see Javid's text. Pari had a strict no phone rule at work, Haleh kept a work phone different from her personal phone and would most likely be with her work phone. Toman… well, she had the habit of disappearing off the internet at random times.

She looked up from her phone to stare at her reflection in the mirror. A second later, her mouth was stretching into a wide grin. There was no doubt that she was excited, what started out as a drunken pact was beginning to have the forming of a real quest.

There was only one thing left to do. Her eyes roamed her dimly lit little dressing room. She'd been singing at this bar for years now, she was comfortable here. The owner – Aziz – was a decent man who paid fairly and she was lying if she didn't admit that she would miss the safety that the place had been for her – an assurance she would never return to the life she'd previously led. But she was glad to leave.

Secretly, Delnaz was one of those people who believed in a higher calling, a much bigger purpose.

It was time to go. She stood up and packed her purse. She was scheduled to be singing at the bar in less than an hour but she couldn't wait, couldn't be still. Aziz would be cross but the bar could function without her.

She echoed her thoughts to him when she found him in his office which was just little more than a storeroom. But Aziz had never been one for pomp and flash like many bar owners in the city was, he needed a room to balance accounts and his little office sufficed. Predictably, his lips turned down at her request but he couldn't say no.

"You could have given me a notice," He said, scratching the top of his bald head. His voice was absent minded, already searching for solutions. Her frequent presence at the bar had become a favourite highlight of the night. Delnaz liked to think she was humble but there was no one alive that her singing couldn't touch. "When are you returning?" He added grudgingly. She knew that he wouldn't deny her leaving; she'd never missed a single day of work, never taken a sick day either.

Aziz was nothing if not fair.

"A long time, I can't say when I'll return." Delnaz kept her answer short, if not a bit mysterious.

Aziz blinked slowly.

"Your job might not be here when you return."

At that, Delnaz couldn't help it, she threw back her head and laughed. "I'm the best singer in the city." She said, as if it explained everything.

"How can you fit your head through that door?" Aziz asked dryly. Delnaz shrugged. Aziz just stared. Their eyes locked for what seemed like forever until he finally gave in, sighing. And just like that, she'd won.

She left the bar with a bounce in her steps, somehow the night was more iridescent, the crescent moon a little brighter. At her little studio apartment, she packed her bags. It was only then that she realised that she never replied to Javid's text.

She took out her phone then and shot her friend a quick text.

I'M COMING.

She put down her phone, shoved her passport into the front purse of her bag and left the apartment. The drive to the airport passed in a stunning blur; she stuck her head outside the wound down window, feeling the wind in her face.

CHAPTER THREE
Kabul, Afghanistan

IT'S THE TIME.

Pari saw the message earlier than her friends. She had a strict no phone policy during work and had been made fun of for it several times. But it was simply how Pari was like, when she was dedicated to a cause or a task, she put her all in. This morning was probably the first time she was breaking that rule.

She'd had a nightmare about Javid a night before. Of their group of five, Javid was the most distant. It wasn't that she was unfriendly in any way of the word, she was simply a Jetsetter, cruising through numerous time zones that she was rarely ever settled enough to make small talk with the rest of her friends on the WhatsApp group they'd created. Javid could go a week or two without talking to them and they were rarely ever worried for her too.

So Pari didn't think her nightmare had been born out of some deep, buried concern for her friend. She wasn't much of a superstitious person herself but she took her instincts seriously. She'd made a mental note earlier this morning to call Javid and see if she was okay and now, she was finding this ominous text. She knew what the text meant and she smiled to herself.

She glanced at her half eaten Bolani; it was lunch time at the television where she worked as a TV anchor and she'd skipped breakfast this morning because she was running late so she'd been looking forward to lunchtime. Not anymore, suddenly hunger was much more trivial on the list of priorities. She began to shove her things into her bag.

Pari stood up, almost hitting her knees underneath the table.

Her coworker and co-anchor – Adil – looked up from typing away on his laptop, "Whoa, slow down Lois Lane."

Usually the nickname would have caused Pari to crack a smile. She'd started off working at the station as a lowly reporter before she climbed up the ranks hence the nickname.

"I have to go." She answered distractedly as she buttoned up her coat and slung her handbag over her shoulder. She chucked her half eaten Bolani into the food waste bin across the room, raising one fist in the air in victory when she made the throw.

"Are you done with writing the pitch?" He asked, concerned, causing his eyebrows to furrow.

"I'll turn it in tomorrow."

At that his jaw dropped; Pari hadn't climbed the ranks from reporter to TV show anchor at the second biggest television station in Kabul by slacking off work. She'd been twice as creative as her colleagues partly because she was a womxn in a country like Afghanistan and partly because she'd wanted to be more. Her reputation as a workaholic was almost as famous as her nickname, so it was definitely surprising to her coworker for her to admit to postponing work.

"Are you alright? You were looking at your phone a second ago. Is it a family emergency?"

Pari smiled wryly because in a way it was indeed a family emergency. She gave another nod; it was the excuse she'd be giving her boss too. In her years of working, she'd rarely taken a sick leave or a vacation so she was almost a hundred percent sure that she'd be given the next two weeks off. The family emergency excuse would do fine, it was certainly better than saying she was off to save the world.

Adil murmured a prayer, eyes shining with so much concern that Pari almost felt bad about lying to him.

"Look, I'll talk to you later when I get off the plane." Pari said, softening the urgency in her voice with a small smile.

If it was possible for Adil's already wide eyes to grow wider than it did. "Where are you going?"

Pari barely refrained from saying, "To save the world." Instead, she said, "Iran. I have family there."

The next thirty minutes passed by in a blur, Pari got her two weeks off and rushed out of the news building. The security guard in front the revolving doors that led outside looked surprised seeing her leave early too, she waved a hurried goodbye at him too, promising to be okay,

She wasn't sure if she was going to be though. What she and her friends wanted to do would piss off a lot of powerful people. The thought stayed with her as she climbed on her bike and fastened her helmet over her head. She'd been biking to work for years now around the same time she became a vegetarian, she was lucky that she didn't live far from work – her house was just a ten minute bike ride from work and the airport wouldn't take twenty minutes.

She pedalled in the busy street; somehow, it felt like she was seeing Kabul for the first time. She was always working late so she'd never seen the city like this in the early afternoon. The skyscraper that was Justice TV Station was surrounded by similar enterprises; businesses owned by powerful men in the country. It was a never ending grind and hustle, the sun rays bouncing off tall glass windows and trapped in some.

Kabul was a city built on the blood and sweat and toiling of thousands of people.

The realisation caused her to pedal even faster even as her breath came in harsh pants and puffs.

The airport was crowded as she expected and it was after she got her ticket – Javid had taken the liberty of arranging the purchase of flight tickets for all of them -- that she realised that she'd forgotten to make a stop at her house to pack clothes for the trip to Iran. She was travelling to a whole country with a single bag that contained just her laptop, some money and random items.

Well, it was a good thing that Javid was rich. Pari briefly considered calling Javid on the phone but she hesitated, she'd see her friend in the next few hours anyways. So she sat at the airport lounge and waited for her flight. Javid had estimated that she'd see the text later in the day and had scheduled her flight for the evening. For once, her eagle eyed friend was wrong and Pari couldn't wait to tell her so.

She took the free time to work on the pitch she'd been writing earlier and whipped out her laptop. The studio execs were planning on ordering the pilot of a new show but they needed ideas, the dream was to create a television show that would discuss the city's politics but would be simple enough to draw in viewership and interest from teenagers. The last mayoral election had shown that there'd been an obvious lack of the young voters.

Pari had wanted to point out that they lived in a city within a country that had suppressed womxns' rights for centuries. But she hadn't, because while she might be rising to high peaks in her career, she wasn't still in a place where she could speak her mind freely to her bosses. They saw her as a resourceful young womxn who had drive, no more than a perfect robot. Robots definitely didn't talk back or offer scathing reviews that nobody asked for. It was lips zipped for now.

But one day, Pari vowed, she'd show them. For now, she worked on her pitch.

Hours passed and it was finally time to board. She was thankful for the alarm she'd set on her phone to remind herself of the time or else she'd have gotten lost in her work. She tucked her laptop under her armpit and ran towards the boarding place. She was already a few minutes late but the air hostess was graceful and offered nothing but a polite smile.

She was led to the business class section and found herself sitting next to a womxn who was tall, judging by how her legs were folded out awkwardly before her and she was working on her laptop. Pari took the advantage, studying the womxn unabashedly; her hair was a deep brown that was almost copper. It was swept to the side, offering a full look at her face; red painted lips, and narrowed eyes that reminded Pari of a fox.

Half dazed, Pari took the seat beside her. The womxn raised her head at the slight rustle of the seat. Her eyes met Pari and she smiled, a small tilt of her lips that Pari found herself reciprocating.

"So sorry to disturb you." Pari offered even though she'd done nothing wrong. She just wanted an excuse to talk to this womxn. "You looked like you were working," She gestured to the womxn's sticker covered laptop; she thought she caught a glimpse of the pride flag but she shifted the laptop.

"Oh, I was jotting down some ideas." The womxn said. Her voice had a light lilt of an accent that was easily the loveliest sound Pari had ever heard.

Pari perked up, "You're a writer?"

The womxn's smile deepened, a dimple popped from her left cheek and Pari almost swooned. It had to be the heat because she didn't understand why she was reacting to someone she'd just met like this.

"Yes, I freelance." The womxn said.

"You don't look like a writer." Pari blurted out.

She smile dipped for a second and Pari's heart dropped in her chest. She swiftly corrected herself, "I'm sorry, I don't mean it that way. I just… I thought writers were supposed to have frizzy hair and look pale because they stay indoors all day and glare at their laptop screens – believe me, I've been there. But you – you're gorgeous."

The womxn blinked slowly and for a second, Pari thought she might have come on too strongly. She was Lois Lane after all, the superwomxn who barely had a life outside of her work talk less of a love life. She couldn't recall the last time she'd been out on a date.

She was about to take back her words but the womxn broke into a wide grin. Pari smiled back; there was just a hint of something in that smile that encouraged her.

"I'm Pari."

"It's nice to meet you, Pari."

CHAPTER FOUR
Tehran, Iran

IT'S THE TIME.

Toman disliked her job sometimes. Two things had driven her out of the police force where she'd worked for more than a decade; the deeply rooted corruption in an organisation meant to serve and protect and the incident. The incident was something that led police officers to leave the force, sometimes the incident was an injury that impaired the officer's ability to carry out duties, other times the incident was depression or PTSD. In Toman's case, the incident was a combination of the sometimes and other times. She'd hesitated to put down a killer and she'd paid for it with a bullet in her knee and the lives of three other innocent people. She'd thought she could bounce back from it and redeem herself; she'd even gone through rehabilitation.

Then the nightmares had begun and it had been one hell of a tumble down the rabbit hole. She'd gone from being confident in her recovery to being afraid of an invisible killer breathing down her shoulder. To quit the police force had been a one hell of a fucking relief, her dream to be one good ones irrelevant. She'd been glad to leave too and had spent the first few months unemployed because she kept getting fired from jobs. There wasn't much employment out there for an ex cop and Toman had wanted nothing to do with working in security.

So she'd met someone who advised her to put her skills into use by opening up a private investigating business. At first, Toman had been wary of the venture, she didn't see it as much of an escape from the world of crime but she'd been so fucking relieved when she got her first case; find a missing pet. She'd enjoyed that she could select which jobs to take and which wasn't worth the hassle of her mental health.

She wished she could say the jobs didn't get any less ridiculous but they did; a few more missing pet cases, a lot of wives asking her to investigate their cheating husbands and catch them in the act, or vice versa. The most serious case she'd ever gotten was a missing child case that made the news. At least that one allowed her to shake a few of the more ridiculous cases. She preferred calling herself a private detective. Private Investigator sounded fancy for meddler.

However, she didn't always have the luck of serious cases and in those moments, she really hated her job. Because why was she freezing her ass off in the snow just to assuage the concerns of a rather wealthy but bored husband that her much younger wife wasn't cheating on him?

Toman huffed out an icy breath, watching the air cloud before her. For the past few days, Tehran was experiencing the worst blizzard it had had in years. The city's occupants were snowed in, there was not a car to be seen for miles except for the delivery trucks and Toman's least favourite part of a snowstorm; power outage.

She shivered violently, almost dropping the camera in her glove clad hands as an icy wind nipped at her clothes. Her thick clothing didn't seem to be doing much; she'd donned a thick wool turtleneck and a wool hat that she'd tucked most of her hair into. She was crouched, the tips of her coat soaking with the snow.

Her eyes narrowed as she watched the building before her. It was a beautiful modern house with a spa glass roof and ironically, the house had a spa inside of it. She'd received the blueprint and several pictures of the house from the owner; her client. The poor womxn was sure that her husband was cheating on her and wanted proof. Apparently, the man had been distant for a few weeks, coming home late and smelling of cheap perfume. Toman had only been on the case for three days but she already knew that the man wasn't cheating. She'd been tailing him to and from work since he hadn't met any womxn for a lovers' rendezvous. He arrived home late each night because he made a detour each evening to the spa house for some reason Toman wasn't sure of. She didn't blame him, if she had a house like this one, she'd spend all of her time inside the warm indoors.

Speaking of warm indoors, she thought of her office at Grand Bazaar, of her cosy space and the fireplace. She expelled an irritated breath and clicked her camera. She glanced at the picture she'd taken and frowned deeply when she saw that the steam of the indoor spa was visible.

She didn't know why she bothered anyways, if there was anything this man was hiding, it definitely wasn't a mistress. She was wasting her time here, freezing her ass off for nothing. She took out her phone to glance at the time and saw the notification of a new WhatsApp message on the screen. She communicated with her clients by email.

WhatsApp was for sisterhood. She looked up again at the house and sighed. It was time to leave.

CHAPTER FIVE
Berlin, Germany

IT'S THE TIME.

Haleh was furious and it was a very bad thing when she was. The womxn was already intimidating enough as it was; her eyeliner was drawn sharp enough to kill a man and even when she wasn't frowning, she still had a face cut out of marble; all sharp angles – high cheekbones that was often painted with rogue, a thin smirk and a high nose that rivalled aristocrats. Even when she was smiling, she looked like she'd just gone to battle with the devil and won.

But when she was pissed, well, the crowd parting for her to go through was self explanatory. The looks that followed her were both afraid and grudgingly admiring. Haleh was beautiful, in the way that a serpent was. Her boots looked like a natural extension of her already long legs. She strutted through the disco lights lit club, through the club goers gyrating to head pounding techno music. She threw a nod at the heavy man guarding it and took the stairs half shrouded in the dark to the VIP area, her ring clad hand moving up the bannister. The building was a warehouse recently converted into the club; the walls had only been recently painted – judging by the smell of paint that hung in the air with the smell of alcohol and sweat.

The upstairs was merely a bigger balcony overlooking the space below and it was empty of people. The night was still young and the VIP area occupants would begin to arrive an hour from now, the crowd was made up of wealthy starlets and budding drug lords – the kind of people that existed to be seen by others to feel important. Haleh didn't think much of them, they were the biggest spenders of the night anyways and she had something else on her mind.

There was a man waiting for her, looking out the balcony. She doubted he'd heard the click of her steps because of the pounding beat of the music but he raised his head as she drew close to him, standing just less than a footstep away.

"Ah, there's my favourite party planner." The man beamed.

Haleh shot him a look so vicious that if it was anybody else, they would have melted like lava. But this was Cash, if there was such a thing as a person being built wrong, then it was Cash. His most prominent feature was the thick scar that ran from his right ear down to his chin. There were so many rumours about how he'd gotten it and the most popular ones claimed the wound was self-inflicted. Haleh didn't care either way, only when he was trying to get his grubby hands into her money.

Haleh ran several techno clubs in Berlin and most of them illegal because of all kinds of substances they dealt. The clubs were a weak front for what the real business was. Haleh had been in the business for years but Cash had been in it longer than a decade and fancied himself some sort of guardian over the illegal club scene. Weekly, he collected 'dues' from clubs. Haleh usually just paid and forgot all about him until the next week.

Until he'd hiked his dues on her club simply because he found out her club made more in a night than other clubs made in a month.

"I'm not a cash cow, Cash," Haleh pinned him with a look.

He chuckled, a raspy voice that grated on her nerves.

"You're the cash cow, darling." Cash said.

Haleh's eyes flashed with warning. "You're not in charge of my businesses so I suggest you take the chumps you get from me and hightail out of here."
Ire flashed through his eyes but he chuckled, his whiskey breath fanning her face. Haleh had half a mind to push him over the balcony and be rid of him once for all but dead bodies were bad for business and he might fall on a customer. Haleh had been in the club scene long enough to know that she couldn't easily shake somebody like Cash, for one he had been playing this game longer than her and he'd made an empire out of thieving from other businesses.

As if sensing the line of her thoughts, his smirk grew. "You can't fight me, Haley." She grit her teeth and it was because of how he always mispronounced her name every time.

"Or I'll burn your clubs down to the ground." His eyes flashed with promise. She pretended not to notice how his eyes strayed down to her chest; she was wearing a body harness with nothing underneath it but black tape covering her nipples.

Haleh let a smile of her own spread, she loved it when people stared. She glanced at her black painted fingers like they were the most fascinating thing and when she looked back at his face, she saw that he was still ogling her and making no attempt to hide it.

She let him stare for the longest time and just as he was about to raise his head up, she cleared her throat and he flinched.

"Don't threaten me, Cash, it won't end well for you."

He tried to play nonchalantly, "Pay me what you owe me, Haleh."

She made a flicking motion with her wrist as if to ward off evil. "I say, fuck off."

Cash narrowed his eyes. She stared back, knowing that she'd all but declared war on this man. Maybe on another night she might care, be worried even but not tonight. Because Haleh was not in a good mood and it had plenty to do with the text she'd received earlier tonight.

Of all the five of them, Haleh was the least excited about their plan to save the 'world', the reason why was a story for another day. All she knew was that she wasn't taking shit from this man anymore.

"You'll regret this. I'll drag you down to hell, you'll see."

Haleh batted her eyes sweetly at him. "Oh, honey. Get in line."

CHAPTER SIX
Tehran, Iran

The roads were slick with ice from the snow and they almost put Javid's driving expertise to shame. She wasn't limited to only driving cars, she could drive trucks and small planes, heck, she was sure she could find her way around driving a small boat if she was asked to. But despite her expertise, she was a bad driver in the snow which almost made her regret not hiring a driver with the car she'd rented.

Nostalgia had won out the rational part of her brain, she hadn't been in Iran for years now and she'd wagered that her arrival in her home country would be emotional – and she'd been right, she'd shed a few tears when her plane touched ground. The last time she'd been in the country, she'd met four womxns much like her and together, they'd made a promise. Javid was returning to fulfil it finally.

She'd wanted to make the drive to her destination alone, to soak up the city sights. Too bad, she'd prepared for everything but the weather. In her excitement to return, she'd forgotten to take account of the weather. Her shock had been great when she saw the snow.

She took great care steering the wheel gently as if it was a living thing that would explode if handled badly. Her eyes were fixed strictly ahead; she only looked away from the road when her phone lit up with a message. She didn't need to check, If she had to take a guess, she'd bet it was Haleh blowing up her phone with messages.

Javid didn't for one moment doubt her friend's commitment to their cause but if there was any of them with the slightest hesitations, it was her tough as nails friend. The people who knew Haleh would describe her as scary first and sexy second. Haleh was always dressed to kill and the permanent smirk etched on her lips didn't help matters. But Javid liked to think that she knew Haleh better than everybody else. Haleh wasn't so different from Javid; they were both drifters, never staying in one place very long before jetting off to the next place that would have them. Javid was a natural drifter; she genuinely loved discovering new places, new people and new cultures. Haleh was a womxn on the run.

Javid didn't know the whole story about her friend but she knew enough that Haleh felt guilt towards their country. Something had happened to her, something that caused her to run from the country that was their home so she was the most reluctant to return.

Javid had deliberately caught all of her friends unaware; of course, they were aware that this day would come, they'd made provisions for this proverbial rainy day but it didn't mean that all of them were ready for it. Javid knew though, that if she'd let Haleh be ready for what they'd made a promise to do, then she'd never come to terms with it. So she'd caught all of them off-guard and Haleh was going to chew her out for it.

Javid was kind of looking forward to it. She'd missed Haleh; she'd missed all of them. She ignored her phone and continued driving, Fifteen minutes later – under the guidance of the GPS – she arrived at Café Farzaneh, a coffee shop situated at the right side of the Ferdowsi street, in the middle of a row of other businesses, beside a closed pizzeria.

She parked across and continued to stare across at the shop; it was the same as ever, at least since the last time she saw it. The signboard stated the name of the café in Farsi and the lettering was battered, chipping in some places. Javid recalled the last time she'd been here; she'd mentioned the signboard to the owner. Farzaneh had rolled her eyes and said something about the signboard adding character and a rustic charm to her café.

For the second time that day, Javid found herself blinking back tears but this time, she didn't try to force them back, she let the tears flow down her cheek and her shoulders shook and hunched with the force of it.

She imagined how alarmed a passerby would look if they peeked into her glass, a seemingly put together womxn crying. Her tears were relieved though, something inside of her unfurled and hope bloomed in her chest. She was here, finally.

She sat in her rented car, basking in the feeling and looking ahead at the café. It was only the thought of keeping her friends waiting that caused her to run a hand through her hair and check in the rearview mirror. She got down from her car and shut the door behind her. She hurriedly locked the car and crossed the street, her dr. martins' shoes sinking into the snow causing her to wince. She really should have checked the weather.

Well, a price to pay for spontaneity.

She flipped her greasy hair over her shoulder and painted a smile on her lips as she stepped into the café. The first thing that hit her was the blissful warmth of the café interior coupled with the aroma of pastries and tea. Her stomach grumbled.

The second thing that snagged her attention was the sight of her four friends, seated at a table at the far right of the café; they'd beat her here. Javid felt a grin spreading from one end of her cheek to the next.

For a moment, she observed them as an outsider would; Toman was seated beside Delnaz, the two of them were the more quiet ones of their friend group and they listened to Pari talk and gesture wildly. Javid made a mental note to ask Toman where she got the stylish cream coloured coat she was wearing, the huge buttons in front were so cute.

Toman had a preference for muted colours and this coat suited her. Delnaz was more prepared for the weather than the rest of them; she was decked out in full winter clothes, thick wool cap and gloves included. She rested her chin on her outstretched hand as she listened to Pari talk.

Javid smiled, Pari was the most passionate of all of them. She was a journalist turned TV anchor so that might explain things a little. She was however discrete in her words giving Javid the impression that she was talking about their mission and she wondered if her friends had seen Farzaneh yet.

Pari continued gesticulating, almost taking out her black bowler hat with her arm. She wore a black coat over a white shirt and dark jean trousers. Javid thought that she could stand there forever, watching her friends. But the fly on the wall spell was broken when Haleh locked eyes with her from across the room.

Her kohl lined eyes widened and narrowed, she crossed her arms over her chest, in typical Haleh fashion, she looked like a million bucks and some more in a shiny black leather knee length coat. It was buttoned up to her cleavage where it stopped. She continued to watch Javid, saying nothing but paying no more attention to Pari.

Eventually, the other womxns noticed Haleh's staring and caught sight of Javid. Delnaz shot up from her seat and headed for her, Javid barely braced herself before she was caught up in a fierce hug.

She hugged her Delnaz again, her pretty friend who barely reached her chin. Javid rested her chin on her friend's head and inhaled her scent; strawberry and rosewater.

They broke apart and beamed at each other. Delnaz slapped her arm lightly.

"It's typical of you to keep us waiting like some kind of mastermind." Delnaz said, sometimes it was easy to forget that this womxn standing before had one of the most stunning singing voices. Her talking voice was a rasp thing, almost rough as if she rarely spoke which wasn't so far fetched because she was a womxn of few words. The first time Javid heard her sing, she'd been moved to tears and she'd offered to get her friend a record deal. But Delnaz had wanted nothing of the sort.

"My songbird, I assure you that these things are merely coincidence. The late entrance is more of a weather thing." Javid joked.

Delnaz nodded, she locked her arm with Javid's and together, they walked to their waiting friends.

Pari stood up to greet Javid in a similar hug she'd received from Delnaz.

"It's good to see you, Javid." Pari greeted after she pulled away from Javid. Such little words but Javid heard the sincerity in her friend's voice.

Everybody else seemed to fade away when Javid's eyes met with Toman. The other womxn smiled hesitantly, that single gesture packing one heck of a punch. Javid had history with Toman, they'd had a thing that might have been more, but then it had come to an end. Javid didn't think all of her friends were aware of it since their love affair had been a whirlwind thing, ending as fast as it had started. They were on good terms, of course, they'd shared thousands of texts since then but they hadn't seen each other physically since the togetherness ended.

Toman's smile was a silent reassurance; we're still good, it said. Javid believed it with every fibre of her being. She leaned in for a hug and a kiss on the cheek.

It was Haleh who remained, out of all four of her friends; Haleh was the only one sitting down, arms crossed below her chest and leg swung over the other. She looked like the poster child for indifference but Javid could see through her.

The both of them stared down at each other, unrelenting. Javid didn't regret the manner of gathering them together in Iran, she didn't regret that they were together again, looking to accomplish what they'd sworn to each other. But at the same time, she understood Haleh's hesitance, she hated it even. She wished she hadn't put her friend in such an awkward situation.

In the end, Haleh sighed and broke. Javid barely tamped down on her smile in time. Haleh might have been the scariest looking person on the planet but she was soft for the people she cared about and Javid was glad to be part of the few.

Haleh uncrossed her legs and smirked. "You're late."

Their little group burst into laughter, startling the rest of the customers in the café. An elderly man at the table across from theirs shot them a dirty look that they all ignored; none of them were in the habit of taking instructions from anybody, let alone men. They sat down though, Javid drawing an unoccupied chair from another table to theirs.

"Only you would see it that way, Delnaz thought my arrival was some James Bond thing." Javid pointed out.

Haleh rolled her eyes to the back of her head and Delnaz shot her a mock disapproving look; for the attitude. The songbird was the mom friend of their group.

"Of course Delnaz sees it as such, you've been playing this off for years now; be late to stuff and pretend like it was intended. They think of you as Tony Stark now," Haleh said, gesturing to the rest of her friends.

"She's twice as good looking." Pari pointed out.

Toman made a humming sound of consideration, "Not nearly as rich though."

Her friends burst into another bout of laughter and chatter at that. Toman shot her a look that was teasing and Javid shook her head. She let the banter and jokes go on for a while, simmering in the feeling of finally being in her country again, amidst some of the smartest womxns she'd ever seen and was glad to call friends.

Even Haleh seemed to relax a little as she went in a back and forth with Pari, arguing about Javid's looks. Pari was comparing her to a primaeval and Haleh insisted that Javid was just tall. Javid just watched them, laughing when either of them said something funny. She noticed that there was something between the both of them though, Pari seemed to be finding excuses to touch Haleh and the latter wasn't peeved by the invasion of her personal space.

Javid was unsure how to feel about the both of them. She'd been there and had done that with Toman and it hadn't ended well although she wasn't sure their doomed relationship was due to the fact that they were part of the same friend group. But it could make things weird between them if things didn't end well.

She and Toman had maintained a bit of awkwardness weeks after their breakup, in fact, the long distance had been helpful in helping them get over each other. It had been easier too because both of them were more mature people. Toman liked to avoid drama if she could, saying something about how her job as a private detective provided enough. Javid too had been the same way.

But Haleh and Pari were two of the most volatile people she knew; Haleh was brash and stubborn and Pari was passionate – which was a very good thing when it came to her career but as a character trait also meant that it applied to other aspects of her life including love. She fell hard and fell out of it even faster. Things could be messy if she decided to pursue a fling with Haleh.

Javid blinked, noticing that Toman was watching her; she turned her head to the side and gestured in a slight nod at a still arguing Pari and Haleh; as if to say, can you believe this?

Toman shrugged, silent, and left them.

Javid sighed, she might be acting a little too paranoid. The truth was that their mission was in its early stages and she didn't want anything jeopardising it. Deciding that she'd let her friends have some moment of normalcy, she cleared her throat. Immediately, Haleh ceased mid dig at Pari.

She turned her alert eyes on Javid, expectant.

"Has Farzaneh seen you ladies already?" She asked.

The remnants of Pari's smile slid right off at the mention of the café owner's name. Farzaneh was the reason why they were here, she wasn't much older than them and was an Afghan womxn who ran the café, many customers who visited the café had no idea that it served something other than coffee and pastries – something more priceless; information. There was a reason why Farzaneh was called the pathfinder after all.

"No, we were waiting for you. In fact, we just caved in and asked for tea a few minutes before you arrived." Delnaz said. As if by command, a womxn wearing an apron over a long, flowing dress stepped out from behind the bead curtain behind the counter carrying a large tray.

It wasn't Farzaneh but one of the two employees that worked for Farzaneh's café. The womxn set the tray on the table and set out each of their cups which was a small slim waist glass. She poured out black tea mix with cardamom and dry rose bud. Javid sent her a grateful look before asking for Farzaneh.

The womxn nodded in understanding and whisked the tray away. There was a long moment of silence between the five of them and Javid found herself lost for words for perhaps the first time in her life. She'd expected to start with some grand speech, something that would keep them motivated, especially as she searched all their faces and found traces of doubt in their eyes. There was excitement in their eyes but now, they were here in the place that would be the start of their journey and undoubtedly, they wondered if they were worthy, if they could do this. Javid had brought them together for this cause and it was her job to keep them motivated too.

She needn't have worried, as if she sensed the inner turmoil she battled, Toman said, "Where do we start from? How is this thing going to go?"

Javid inhaled a deep breath and shot her old lover a grateful look. Toman merely tilted her head to the side.

"Three years ago, I gave you ladies a brief story on this. A myth to most people even." Javid began, she wasn't sure if she was trying to remind them of the impossible scale of their mission – seeking out something most people thought didn't exist – or if she was just trying to sound grand. "The Gol-e-Zard Cave."

She paused for effect and a slow smile spread on her face when she saw that she held their rapt attention. It gave her the confidence to continue talking.

"The Gol-e-Zard cave is where the famous Gordafarid's sword is said to be hidden and it's the one thing that can save all our homes. And our mission is simple, find the sword and use it to restore balance to our countries." Javid explained. She looked at each of her friends, "Some of us have gone through things in the country that have failed to protect us, things that scared us and have made us into the womxns that we are. And each one of us at this table have sworn to make sure that we stop this never ending cycle."

There she was, giving one hell of a grand speech anyways. Maybe it shouldn't have worked, her words weren't much different from the speech that politicians gave to draw the people with their strings. They were just words after all but unlike in other instances, they came from her heart. Javid hadn't always been wealthy, her family had been born into stark poverty, her father had died in it and she might have suffered the same fate too if her mother hadn't packed his bags and taken her little daughter with her halfway across the world from the curse of their country.

Javid had sworn to return though.

Like her, she knew her friends had bore the brunt of evil in their homeland too, some of them more than others, she thought as she stared at Delnaz. It was only the ones that had crawled out of hell that could say how hot it was. That was why her words meant so much to the rest of them.

CHAPTER SEVEN
Gordafarid delayed the Turanian troops who were marching on Persia.

Javid inhaled a deep breath, meeting everyone's gazes one by one. She didn't doubt that any of them underestimated the severity of their mission but she needed them to know, their quest wouldn't be as easy as they thought it would be. She thought wryly, that the action and adventure blockbusters were to blame.

"It's not going to be like the action movies," She felt the need to clarify.

Haleh snorted at her words, "Such a shame, I thought we'd be like the Ocean's Eight characters. I even packed a stunning gown," She quipped, glancing down at her black painted nails like they were the most interesting things in the world. If one could ignore the numerous rings that adorned her fingers, they'd realise that her nails were the plainest part of this gorgeous, fierce womxn. Haleh was always dressed to metaphorically kill, even now; her cat eye liner was drawn sharp at the wing – extending longer than normal. But her nails were simple, cut short and painted the colour of asphalt. Javid wondered why.

"Sorry to disappoint, love." Javid drawled, playing her friend's game. Haleh's eyes glittered with humour and she almost smiled. Javid saw the nerves her friend was trying and failing to hide.

"Ugh, say that again but make your accent thicker," Pari cut in, wiggling her brows obnoxiously. Her quip was effective in breaking the ice and their table exploded in laughter. "I just love the English."

Delnaz rolled her eyes mildly. "Slut."

Pari took the liberty of spreading her arms out, causing Haleh to bend her head swiftly to avoid being hit in the face. "I love it when you talk dirty to me."

Javid knew that if she let things spiral, then they would never get around to talking about the Gol-e-Zard cave and subsequently Gordafarid's sword. Toman seemed to catch the warring conflict on her face and cleared her throat.

"Speaking of dirty, it's going to be dirty work trying to get Gordafarid's sword." Her mention of the sword's actual name didn't escape Javid. Up till now, their group had always referred to it as 'the sword'. Toman's use of the actual name sobered the laughter around their table and the severity of their situation sank in immediately. Javid sent Toman a silent look of thanks, she'd always been intuitive; she was a good character study. Even Javid who prided herself on being unreadable was taken aback by how Toman was at reading her. Mind and well… body.

Javid flushed thinking of it. Seemed like she wasn't the only one in danger of romance.

She shook her head and forced her mind to return to the important discussion at last. Haleh, however, immediately latched onto Toman's words. She uncrossed her legs and leaned forward.

"Yes, Javid, how exactly are we going to go about that?" She asked, her voice slightly mocking.

Javid ignored her. "This isn't the place to be getting in depth about our plans – and I assure all of you here that I've got one." She sighed, "I've planned this for years."

Delnaz, the ever peacemaker, was quick to appease. "We all trust you, Javid. I don't think any of us would be sitting here if we didn't."

Pari followed. "Yeah, you could ask us to descend down to hell with you and I'd ask you to make reservations for the finest hotel there."

Haleh rolled her eyes but she didn't attempt to banter with Pari this time. She did, however, shoot the other female a look that Javid could only interpret as interest.

"We'll talk more when we're somewhere more private." Javid said and the others glanced around the café as if they were just remembering that they were in public. Granted, the café wasn't by any means filled with people but still, Javid didn't want to risk anything getting out.

The story of Gordafarid was popular amongst Iranians. She was one of the heroines in the Shahnameh also known as "The Book of Kings" or "The Epic of Kings". It was an enormous poetic opus written by the Persian poet Hakim AbuI-Qasim Ferdowsi Tusi around 1000 AD –that was over a thousand years ago- Gordafarid was a champion who fought against Sohrab - another Shahnameh's hero who was the commander of the Turanian army - Gordafarid fought fearlessly, however, defeated by Sohrab, who only realises that his adversary belongs to the opposite sex when he succeeds in removing her helmet. He then promptly falls in love with her. Gordafarid, who does not see herself as Sohrab's equal in battle, deceives him with false promises. She takes him up to the gate of the fortress, which she enters, and the gate closes behind her. Sohrab felt like a fool, realising how easy he could have taken the fortress, instead he lost it to Gordafarid's intelligence. As It was late for the battle, Sohrab decided to wait until the next dawn to show them the meaning of defeat. But on the other side of the wall, Persian troops evacuated the fortress, travelling to somewhere safe. Gordafarid delayed the Turanian troops who were marching on Persia. Since then she came to be known as a symbol of courage and wisdom for womxns.

Javid didn't really believe in a higher being but Gordafarid came the closest to religion to her. The Catholics worship saints and Gordafarid was Javid's saint. That and Javid has strong evidence to prove that Gordafarid had been queer – making her not only a symbol of courage but the historical queer icon of Javid's dreams.

"Fortunately, nobody's going to hell. I've gathered four of you here, from different parts of the world, because you're the most important to me. Like Pari vehemently said she'd follow me to hell, I want you to know that I would do the same for all of you. I'm honoured that you chose to answer my call more than anything else in the world."

Delnaz's eyes glittered with unshed tears. "Damn you for making me this emotional."

Javid sent her a rueful smile. She shook her head, "Here comes the part we might not be too excited about, I can't guarantee that this mission will be a hundred percent safe and I don't know what kind of forces and obstacles we will face as we try to look for the sword while we are inside of the cave. If there's any one of us that feels the least bit hesitant about our chances, please, by all means – you can stand up and wash your hands off this cause. And I mean this in the kindest way possible."

For the first time, Javid felt an anxious rolling in her stomach. She'd calculated all their odds, every single step of their quest and everything that could go wrong but she'd never for once put into consideration that one of her friends might decide not to go on with their mission after all.

When she'd made her plans, she'd made plans for five; each of them having their specific role to fulfill. If one of them happened to back out now… Javid was unsure what she'd do next. Mentally, she began to make calculations, to review her plan in her mind's eye.

What if all of them leave? Her mind jeered and her heart fell to the pit of her stomach. Just when she thought she might be sick with worry, Pari spoke up.

"Don't be ridiculous." She delivered with the perfect amount of sass that only Haleh seemed to be capable of. They seemed to be rubbing off each other already and there wasn't any actual rubbing happening yet.

Haleh seemed to share the same sentiment because she smiled a little, not one of her usual arrogant smirks but a small genuine smile that almost transformed her face. It faded as quickly as it had appeared though and Javid was left wondering if she'd imagined the gesture entirely.

"Did you hear any of my spiels about following you down to hell?" Pari asked, in a more soft tone, she added. "I'm with you, Javid, all the way. There's no chance in hell I'd back out of my word."

"What is with you and hell recently?" Toman commented mildly and Pari's response was to smile cheekily.

Toman's gaze grew serious, "I don't think there's anyone here wearing rose coloured glasses. I know what I'm getting myself into and I'm with you all the way."

Javid slowly exhaled a sigh of relief. It was Delnaz and Haleh left.

In her typical womxn of little words fashion, Delnaz said, "I'm a womxn of my word, I said I would so I will."

Javid nodded. All eyes turned to Haleh who pretended not to notice, she just continued staring at her nails, turning her palm over. In the end, she looked up, ignoring all the other eyes and focusing on Javid's. "I'm in." She said simply and went back to checking her nails like it was nothing.

Javid decided she'd take whatever victories she could get. She made a mental note to have a private conversation with Haleh when she got the chance.

She realised she'd left her tea untouched throughout their conversation. She leaned forward to peer at her friends' tea glass, some of them were drained – Delnaz didn't play with afternoon tea. Pari had sipped hers; that much was obvious by the lipstick stain on the rim of her glass. Like Delnaz, Toman's tea was gone too. It was Haleh who'd left hers alone too. Whether it was a sign of nerves or something else, Javid wasn't too sure so she asked. If she let Haleh keep to herself then the tough as nails womxn would die clutching her secrets to her chest.

Haleh eyes the glass in front of her with something close to disdain, however, the action was exaggerated.

"Not a fan of tea."

A chorus of gasps went up in their little group – Javid's being one of them. All five of them were from Farsi speaking countries that spanned Afghanistan, Iran and Tajikistan, where tea is basically a national beverage. Tea is basically water.

Javid had kept the culture even as she lived thousands of miles away from her home country and she was lucky that the British also had a love for tea.

She shook her head. "How could you?"

Haleh let out an insufferable sigh. "I've broadened my tastes, darlings."

Pari snorted into her palm. "Tequila and what? Rum. Or what do the Germans drink?"

She wasn't very far from the truth, Javid had been to Germany a couple of times and they did love their alcohol. Didn't they have a whole festival dedicated to beer drinking?

"Poor thing has been drinking away her liver." Toman tried to make it funny.

"Here, have some more tea," Javid teased, sliding her tea glass closer to Haleh's.

But she was secretly relieved that Haleh seemed to be doing fine. Of all of them, she might be the most closed off. One would assume that it was Toman but the difference was that Toman was forthcoming with her emotions, she wouldn't hide when she was upset or bothered about something but she kept a tight lock on her feelings she didn't want others to see, making her hard to read. Haleh on the other hand was a fairly easy book to read, Javid could tell when she was upset or nervous but no matter how many times she called her out on it, Haleh would never admit to it. She'd present a front of boredom even though she wasn't fooling anybody.

After the group finished teasing Haleh on her beverage preference and drinking habits, Javid steered the topic back to the mission at hand.

"Now that we've gotten the motivational speeches out of the way, it's time to get down to the actual doing. I didn't just pick this café because it has a nice looking interior and decent tea—"

"—Excellent tea actually, if I do say so myself." A lilting voice cut into Javid mid speech. Javid craned her neck behind and beamed at the smiling womxn.

She stood up and pulled the other womxn into a hug.

"It's good to finally see you, Javid." The womxn said she was tall and her skin the colour of burnt caramel. She was wearing a flower patterned Kaftan and a high scarf that gave the illusion of being as tall as Javid was. She looked like royalty.

As they hugged, Javid caught a pleasant whiff of orange and sugar.

She pulled away from the hug a moment and turned to her expectant friends. Pari sat up a little faster as she usually did when she was in the presence of an attractive womxn. it was all Javid could to keep her eyes from rolling to the back of her head.

"This is Farzaneh – she owns the café." Javid introduced. Farzaneh shot her friends wide grins.

"Yeah," Haleh drawled, "I think we figured that out from the café name."

Javid ignored the sarcastic remark. "Farzaneh isn't just the owner of the café – she's who we're here to meet. She's the pathfinder."

CHAPTER EIGHT
Ferdowsi SQ, Tehran

Javid met Farzaneh more than five years ago when she'd started looking into the story of Gordafarid, her sword and the Gol-e-Zard cave. She'd begun her research as a sceptic until thorough digging had led her to Farzaneh. She'd been looking to expand her artefacts collection when stumbled upon rumours of the existence of a powerful sword that could restore balance to the world.

Thus her obsession began, she'd poured in hours into finding information, she'd bribed, threatened any additional details she'd perceived. She'd grown increasingly panicked at the object's popularity in the black market; there were plenty of other people who were after the sword's whereabouts – people wealthier and more powerful than her. It was the first time Javid had realised whatever wealth she might have paled in comparison to others.

That was when she'd come in contact with Farzaneh – the womxn was one of the few people in the world who could lead them to the sword and unlike the other few, she was the most honest. Many information brokers Javid had encountered in the past had sold information about the sword to the highest bidder; they'd been in it for the money.

Farzaneh had been different, she was the most honest, and she'd refused to tell Javid anything about the sword until she was assured of Javid's intentions about the sword. Even then, she hadn't offered too much details in fear that Javid would turn out to be like the countless other people that had sought her out. Even now, Javid still didn't have all the answers, Farzaneh wanted to meet the rest of her team, wanted to see for her eyes if they were worthy. How she would know, Javid had no idea.

But she was smiling which was a good thing. Right?

At her introduction, her friends shot up from their seats, chorusing variations of different greetings. Farzaneh received each one with a nod and a word spoken back. Javid was relieved that she'd filled her friends in earlier today about the pathfinder. They still didn't know much about their mission; save for the sword's unlimited power and the hidden route that leads to Damavand inside the cave. She knew they would have done their research too so she wasn't worried about the possibility of ignorance.

Besides, Javid remembered the feeling of awe that had encompassed her the first time she heard the true history of Gordafarid's sword. She'd felt pride in such a brave, powerful womxn that history had tried and failed to suppress and deep awe at the power that Gordafarid's sword held. Javid considered herself to be a somewhat decent orator, she didn't think she could do justice to the story, not like Farzaneh would. Her friends deserved to experience that awe. And they would, when they heard the story from Farzaneh's lips.

"So what now? What even is the timeframe for this journey?" Haleh asked, for the first time that afternoon, she didn't sound the least bit sarcastic, just genuinely curious and dedicated to their mission. It pleased Javid immensely that she couldn't help but send her friend a smile.

Pari picked off where Haleh left and Javid wasn't surprised by her own demand for answers. She might come off as playful when she was amongst friends but before that playfulness was an extremely driven womxn who liked to plan her life and choices down to a T, however would she have become the most accomplished female journalist in Kabul?

"How many days is this mission going to take? No offence, Javid, but some of us aren't as rich and would like a solid time-frame so we can plan our work excuses around them." Pari said.

Javid chuckled a little at that.

"You're the only one working a demanding job," Toman pointed out. "Delnaz and I are our own bosses."

"A week, two at most." Javid replied, she glanced at her wrist, sliding the sleeve of her coat away so she could read the watch fastened to her wrist.

"I thought we were just headed to the cave and then to the mountains." Haleh said.

Javid blew out a breath, there was so much to do and so little time. "It's not that simple but I promise that there will be an in depth discussion about this later. For now, Farzaneh has rented a car that'll take us to our next location."

They all looked at each other before agreeing on a shrug. Variations of verbal agreement were spoken aloud before Farzaneh swooped in and they were off, leaving the café across the street where Javid had parked her rented car. There was now an old jeep parked in front of Javid's car.

Their chatter quieted down as they split themselves into different vehicles. Toman wordlessly remained beside Javid and since it was a small two seat car, it was a no-brainer that the rest of her friends would be driving with Farzaneh.

The trio got into the jeep with Farzaneh, all of them piling into the passenger seat. Javid thought she caught Haleh's hand resting on Pari's waist as she climbed in last but it was already evening, the pale sun was sinking into the sky painting it a dull orange, she wasn't sure what she saw. It was only after the Jeep's door shut with a loud bang did it finally dawn on Javid that she was left alone with Toman – her ex-girlfriend.

***

Javid carefully trailed behind Farzaneh. She was still wary of driving in the snow, that worry growing increasingly as the sun began its descent to setting. She was also trying very hard to sift through her thoughts, searching for the most appropriate ones to use in a conversation with her ex-girlfriend.

She smiled internally, she might have a lot of regrets about how her romance with Toman ended but she still felt a deep fondness for her and couldn't help but reminisce about their time spent together ruefully. If she could define her romance with the other womxns, Toman would definitely be classified as the one that had gotten away. Javid had experienced several variations of love in her lifetime and she didn't think she'd had any terrible experiences that womxns her age had experienced. She remembered every one of her lovers with the right infusion of fondness so maybe it was the proximity years after their relationship had ended but Javid couldn't help but remember how she'd met Toman.

Of all the members of their group, Javid had known Toman the longest – a few months before she'd go on to meet the other ladies; she'd employed Toman's services as a detective. Javid was well off enough that she could hire the most expensive private investigative business but then, she hadn't wanted a high profile detective in charge of the case. Details about Gordafarid's sword were too sensitive to trust in the hands of some hotshot detective.

It was in the early stages of putting together a plan to find out more information about the sword; she'd decided that it was time to find out details about the last group that had sought out the sword. Javid had swiftly learnt that there were two types of people who sought the sword's power; fanatics who wanted the sword's power for themselves and people driven by pure greed, knowing that the discovery of the sword would fetch them a hefty price on the market.

These groups ranged from the wealthy to weird cult followings. Javid had wanted to know the chances of survival and what exactly their little group would be up against. Toman's contact had actually been given to her by a high profile celebrity in Iran who Toman had worked for in the past. The womxn had assured Javid of Toman's absolute discretion and Javid had made the decision to take a blind leap of faith.

She'd phoned Toman's contact the following week and they'd made an appointment to meet at her office which was next to the Grand Bazaar. Javid had been pleasantly surprised by the homey feeling of Toman's office. At first she'd been struck by how small the space was.

"You've worked with some of the wealthiest people in this country; surely you could buy yourself a bigger space to work?" Javid had asked, taken aback by the tall drawers, overflowing with files and paper documents.

Toman had fixed her with a deadpan gaze – her own version of an eye roll and said, "Appearances can be deceiving."

Javid had been baffled by the saying, she didn't understand if Toman was trying to big up her office. "I don't think there's more to this space than I already see."

Toman had leaned back in her chair, fingers locked together. "You came here instead of going to one of the fancier PI businesses, didn't you? I give off the illusion of a small, old school detective and it reels all of you in like fish to bait. The Sherlock Holmes Turquoises still works wonders."

Javid hadn't known what to say to that, but she'd known then that this womxn was perceptive, running deeper than anyone might see.

Nothing happened between them though, not at first. The both of them emailed back and forth regularly, mostly updates on the group that Javid had asked her to investigate – the last known people to journey to the Gol-e-Zard cave.

In three weeks, Toman had completed the investigation and she'd met with Javid at her hotel to deliver her findings. Javid hadn't been exactly surprised to find that getting to the Gol-e-Zard cave proved more difficult than she'd thought. The last group that had ventured to the cave had died mysteriously and so had the group before them.

Javid remembered the feeling of hopelessness crashing into her as she read through the file that Toman delivered, the womxn

watching her with that same perceptive gaze. She'd thanked Toman and had been prepared to dismiss her when she spoke suddenly.

"You're after the Gordafarid's sword?" She'd asked but it had
sounded less of a question and more of a declaration. Javid hadn't
been surprised that Toman had figured out her intentions; it was
why she'd hired her after all.

Still feeling the hopelessness, she'd jerked her head in a curt
nod, expecting Toman to declare her cause foolish – her findings
proved it anyways. Instead, Toman had said, "I know a lot more
about the sword than you realize."

"Is this the part where you tell me that it's all a myth and that
I'd be better off giving up such a foolish adventure?" Javid had replied tartly, and then regretted her words. She considered herself
mildly mannered but there was something about Toman's coolness that unnerved her. She couldn't get a read on her, couldn't tell
if Toman was setting the stage to mock her.

"This is the part where I tell you that I want to help you find it."
Toman said. Javid smiled a little to herself as she recalled how her
jaw dropped unattractively. Of all the things Toman could have
said, she hadn't expected that.

"You know what's in this file, what the report you wrote con-
cluded. All the past groups that have wandered into the cave have
disappeared mysteriously; I thought you'd be chiding me, calling
me foolish." Javid had said.

And for the first time in the three weeks of knowing her, Toman
smiled. It was a little thing, like the sun hidden in the clouds during sunset but still every bit as beautiful. It might have been how
Toman was the first person to believe in her cause or maybe it had
been her smile. But from that moment, Javid was gone.

But then they'd gone and ended. There was nothing Javid could
do to turn back the hands of the clock. All she had were memories
and broken promises.

She risked taking her eyes off the road for a brief second to glance at Toman. Her ex-lover was gazing at the road ahead of them with the same concentration Javid imagined she was wearing herself.

"You're oddly quiet," Toman broke the silence. Javid startled at the sudden sound of her voice.

It was an olive branch extended if she ever saw one. Toman wasn't exactly one to hold a grudge but Javid had been afraid of awkwardness blooming between them.

"I wasn't aware I was the loud one." Javid said with a grin. She wished she wasn't driving so she could properly engage in the conversation. Haleh might be the one known for her sarcastic remarks but Toman knew how to banter too. Javid recalled several witty conversations with her in the past, their relationship hadn't been just physical.

Javid could hear the smirk in her voice as she said, "Of the two of us, you're certainly the loudest."

It took a second too long for the implications of her words to dawn but when they did; Javid felt a flush kick up her cheeks despite the cold.

"Did you just make a sexual joke?" Javid said, choking back startled laughter.

"If I have to clarify then I reckon I wasn't very obvious." Toman said.

"You know, it was starting to feel like we would never get around to fulfilling the promise we made together," Toman added after a moment of silence.

Javid didn't answer at first, she was too busy trying to not steer them off the road and getting into an accident, the roads were too slick for her comfort.

A small truck overtook her car from behind and she honked loudly in protest. She huffed a small laugh when she noticed that it was the typical compact pickup truck with vendors on the open back, showing off the tasty fares they sold. Colourful red lights blinked sequentially from the wires that decorated the truck. Javid was very familiar to them; the trucks sold hot street food to passing vehicles and all one had to do was signal their attention by waving a hand out the window. She briefly considered flagging them down, it would surely be nice to have some Ash Reshteh in the gruelling winter of the late afternoon. Then she remembered Toman's remark.

"I think you more than anybody else understands why it's taken so long. There's so much research I've had to cover, things I only recently discovered and factors I had to put into consideration before making the decision to assemble all of you finally." Javid answered, her brows furrowed in a frown as she recalled all the delays and misinformation she'd come across in the past few years. "We weren't ready."

Toman was silent, perhaps mulling over her words. "And now?" She heard the question left unspoken; Toman knew all the risks, the lives that their mission had claimed from countless others. Heard the concern in her former lover's voice; were they going to make it alive?

If Javid was being frank, she couldn't guarantee that their goals would be achieved, that they would all come out of it unscathed and she certainly couldn't assure her friends that they'd be alive to tell stories. But she did believe in every single one of them. So that was what she told Toman.

"I believe we've got a fighting chance and I'd bet everything I have on us."

Maybe Toman heard the fervour in her voice, maybe she'd simply come to that conclusion by herself and just wanted to hear what Javid had to say, because out of the corner of Javid's eye, she caught Toman smiling, a smile so brilliant that the beauty of the setting sun almost paled in comparison.

"That's a lot of money to place a wager on. Let's make sure you don't lose, shall we?"

***

Persian techno music blared from the speakers of Farzaneh's rented jeep and Pari kept bouncing heavily to the beat which was very uncomfortable for Delnaz as the former was moving around so much that she almost ended up sitting on the latter's laps.

"Pari, please," Poor Delnaz had to shout above the beat of the music to be heard, "I'm sure Haleh is enjoying this very exotic dance you're doing and would be much happier than I am if you tried to land on her laps instead."

"I would definitely not mind at all, seeing as she's got a great looking ass." Haleh smirked.

Delnaz sighed and rubbed her forehead, feeling the onset of a headache. She should have put up a fight to sit in Javid's vehicle. But she'd sensed that there was something between Javid and Toman – some sort of unfinished business that the two of them needed to talk out, so she'd sacrificed her comfort. So much for that now. She thought she'd sit in front next to Farzaneh when they pulled over.

Some distant part of her mind was worried about the match that was Haleh and Pari in this journey. The two of them were some of the most passionate people Delnaz knew – together, they were like fire meeting gasoline, they would explode.

She supposed it was none of her business, seeing as both womxns were consenting adults. She had much more troubling matters to worry about than the sex lives of her friends.

***

"Why are we stopping?" Haleh asked.

"Frankly, I'm surprised you can stop staring at Pari's boobs long enough to notice," Delnaz murmured. The flirting had only grown in the past hour – from hushed murmurs to Pari's extremely obnoxious laugh. Delnaz wasn't having any of it, okay, maybe a part of her was jealous, not because she had any iota of feelings for any of the two womxns but because she'd been completely cut out from their conversation, forgotten like she wasn't even there.

Most people thought that Delnaz was willingly quiet when she was and although she was introverted to an extent, she still wasn't the quiet person people thought she was. She liked talking, especially with her friends and she could be loud when talking about subjects that excited her. But many people – including people she considered friends – didn't know this and tended to exclude her out of group conversations thinking that she was disinterested.

Sometimes, Delnaz thought that people didn't care much to hear her voice if she wasn't singing. She shook her head, unsure why the feelings of insecurities were welling up now of all times.

Distantly, she knew she was being unnecessarily petty and sassy but a long car ride to an unknown location could do wonders in pummeling one's good mood. She might have apologised for her tone but it didn't seem like Haleh had taken notice of her foul mood. She was sitting up, almost shoving her chest into Pari's face.

From the driver's seat, Farzaneh answered, "I'm merely following Javid's instruction."

Delnaz startled, she'd been so occupied fuming at being excluded that she hadn't noticed that Javid had overtaken them and was now leading the road ahead, though her car was slowing down in the distance.

"Why is she stopping?" Delnaz murmured distractedly, looking out the jeep window.

"And in the middle of nowhere too," Pari added but her voice was light, unconcerned by whatever reason Javid had. Delnaz thought that it was strange to think that she knew all of these womxns – not merely in the sense of the world – but really knew them, knew their personalities, their likes and dislikes, the things that made them tick.

Their group of five had been formed three years ago, different circumstances had brought all of them to Iran at the same time and they'd met each other, made an oath that same day and were together again to fulfil said promise. Since then, they'd exchanged numbers, gone on to create a WhatsApp group solely for their friendship; their friendship had bloomed online, separated by thousands of miles and at the same time by a screen.

All of their interactions thus far had been online but through it, she'd come to know these womxns, alike in few ways but differing in so many ways.

She knew that Haleh's tough exterior wasn't a façade like people would think, the womxn had been through tough stuff and it had changed her. Maybe once, she might have been soft and gooey at the centre but not now, her interior was a metal barricade, even more difficult to crack through than her external. It didn't mean that Haleh was heartless, she had just built an extra layer of protection because of her past and bracing for the future. When she let down her wall, it was just for a select few.

Toman was what people thought Delnaz was – deeply introverted, observant and sweet. Although she did have little tolerance for nonsense.

Javid was well, Javid. The unofficial leader of their little pack. She was gracious, generous and had a little bit of a hero complex, she had the desire to fix things and would kill herself trying.

Pari, however, Delnaz would say she was least close to Pari. And although she knew it was mean to think it, she was too trusting. Her comment about following Javid to the depths of hell had rubbed Delnaz the wrong way. Pari's too trusting attitude would egg Javid on even if she happened to be wrong. Not for the first time, Delnaz was glad Toman was closest to Javid, there was something blooming between the two of them and it might be exactly what Javid would need to keep her grounded and making sane decisions when it came to their mission.

"Are grey wolves common on this side because it's looking too sinister." Delnaz said as she opened the door and climbed out of the jeep. Pari and Haleh followed.

If it was possible, it was even chillier than before and she felt it through her winter weasel coat.

"Fuck," Haleh exhaled, her breath puffing a cloud of cold with the word. Pari gave her a once over look and flipped her hair over her shoulder. "Sometimes, you have to put comfort over looking fucking beautiful."

Haleh rolled her eyes, "Over my freezing ass."

Pari pretended to check out said ass, "It's too good of an ass to let freeze. Cover up sometime, Haleh."

If it was possible Haleh rolled her eyes even harder. "Ah yes, there's that dosage of conservatism I was missing from Iran. Feels just like home."

Farzaneh cracked a laugh at Haleh's quip and shook her head, no doubt appreciating Haleh's quick wit. The womxn had a razor sharp tongue which was funny when you weren't on the receiving end of it.

Delnaz moved away from the two of them just as Pari began to construct a comeback of her own. Her footsteps made crunching sounds as she walked on the snow, she reached Javid and Toman who were waiting expectantly for the rest of them.
"Why'd we stop? Are you out of petrol?"

"No, we're stopping for the night." Javid answered with a smug grin. Delnaz stared back, confused.

"Stopping where? We're in the middle of nowhere." Delnaz asked, echoing Pari's words. She stared around to check if her eyes missed something. Nope, still nothing but a scanty highway and tall trees surrounding their left and right, looking more sinister as the sun set, a stunning mix of pink and purple and Damavand Mountain looming ahead in the distance.

Javid's smile that Delnaz could only describe as cheeky grew. "Do you trust me?"

"Not when you're standing here and smirking like that." Delnaz answered. She felt a bolt of satisfaction when Toman chuckled quietly beside Javid. Haleh wasn't the only good one at comebacks, it seemed.

"Well, would you look at that, The Lion strikes back." Javid drawled, the smile on her face remained and Delnaz couldn't help but return it. The two of them continued to stare at each other for one long moment, sharing an inside joke. The Lion was a nickname Javid had given her three years ago when Delnaz told her the story of how she'd come to be a bar singer.

Delnaz remembered that night clearly, because of her rather quiet nature – really, it bordered on shyness – she hadn't meshed well with the other womxns when they first met. They'd talked above her and she'd gone unnoticed for more than half of the night, Javid had tried and failed to include her in the conversation. Delnaz had once again been prepared to fade into obscurity that night.

But Javid was nothing if not relentless, a trait Delnaz both admired and despised, she'd cut into the conversation with a determined etched in the smile on her face. "So, what's your story, Delnaz? Quiet as a mouse, it seems."

Delnaz had bristled; the last thing she'd expected was to be spending forced time with five strangers she was growing irritated with as the night grew. How dare this womxn call her a mouse? She was not afraid of standing up for herself as the nickname suggested. When she sang, her voice commanded the attention of everyone listening, a modern siren's call.

"I'm not a mouse," She'd ground out forcefully, glaring daggers at Javid.

Haleh had chortled rudely but even she'd quieted when Delnaz sent her the force of that glare. "Damn, it burns." Haleh had muttered under her breath. Once they'd become friends, Haleh had become immune to that look.

Javid had still been smiling easily though, despite being the full recipient of Delnaz glare. "I'd give mice more credit, small things, those bastards. But they're smart creatures, silently assessing and capable of causing damage."

Javid's gaze had swept her form, purely assessing. "But you're not a mouse though. I was wrong."

Haleh had snorted from the corner of the room, managing to look glamourous even leaning against the dirty car. "Is she the only one who gets a spirit animal analysis? I'm starting to feel a little bit unloved here."

Javid cast her a brief look. "You're a shark."

In true Haleh fashion, she'd lifted her hand and touched it to her chest as if she was touched, as if she hadn't been watching Delnaz too with a look that made Delnaz understand why she'd been dubbed a shark. Haleh had the tendency to pretend to be nothing but a pretty face but Delnaz knew that a much darker story lied beyond the femme fatale persona.

"Oh, do me next." Pari had chirped in, she'd gone ignored though.

"I'm not an animal." Delnaz had finally said when Javid continued to stare, gaze long and probing.

"The story, love. We've been in here for over two hours now and we've each taken turns to spill out our guts. But you, you've been silent, watching but I've been watching you – seeing your lips part as if to speak and close firmly as if you want to swallow your words and keep them to yourselves. You want to talk, the stage is yours."

It was then that Delnaz knew that Javid was more observant than given credit for. Although, casting a swift glance at Haleh told her that the other womxn had observed the same thing, she'd just chosen to be quiet about her discovery. Delnaz hadn't known whether to be mad at her for it. Every time she'd tried to speak in the past two hours, she'd noticed that it was when Haleh would cut in to announce something sarcastic and cutting. She'd thought it was mere coincidence but not again. Haleh had been challenging her silently, daring to speak.

"I'll give you a refresher on where we stopped, in case you tuned out," Haleh had cut in again, gesturing at Toman who was standing still, arms crossed over her chest. "She's just got the most tragic story, police career gone wrong."

It was the perfect opening Delnaz had needed – a link to the conversation so her input wouldn't be random.

"I thought cops didn't have hearts." Delnaz had begun, licking her lips and locking eyes with Toman, silently sending her a look of apology – she hadn't wanted to invalidate the other womxn's pain.

Pari had taken the words as a jab either way and let out a loud, "Burn!"

"You'd be surprised," Toman had said. "Want me to take off my shirt and put your hand over my chest?" Later, Delnaz would learn that Toman wasn't the biggest joker but she'd made a joke then, to let Delnaz know that she wasn't offended. Toman was easy to like and Delnaz had liked her first.

"The police were the first people I went to when my whole family was murdered. I'd been naïve, foolish even – they certainly hadn't done a single when my brother was murdered years before. Although, our side of town was crime ridden. Still, a shitty thing to tell a girl who'd just seen her family murdered before her eyes."

"What did they say?" Pari had been the one to ask, Delnaz had found her constant peppiness annoying at first. When she'd asked that question, her gaze had been sober and serious.

Delnaz gave a shrug and to others it might have looked like she was feigning casualness but the cop she'd spoken to had shrugged, while her family's bodies had been covered just a few distance from them, he'd patted her shoulder in a condescending gesture.

"Shit happens at this side of town, gang related murders are always a dead end. You're on your own, kid." She'd spoken the words in the same careless swagger. She'd shrugged again, this time feigning casualness. "I ended up in the same gang, singing for a living at their brothels to pay off the debt my family supposedly owed them and when I paid off every last debt, I left and went to make a name for myself. No sad story here." As if she hadn't told the saddest one.

Delnaz hated to be stereotypical, but she'd expected the ladies to gather around her, hug her and murmur useless words of comfort as other people did – or even worse, stare in awkward silence as their eyes swept her form, searching for visible forms of her scars.

The ladies had done none of that, Haleh continued to look disinterested. Pari swore loudly. Toman was Toman, just standing and observing. Javid however, shook her head.

"I was definitely wrong." She'd said much later when they were out of that room, walking side by side while the others were ahead and arguing very loudly. Even then, Pari had a thing for pushing Haleh's buttons and calling it flirting.

"You're not a mouse, you're a lion."

Delnaz shook her head at the memory. "I haven't heard that nickname in years."

The smile on Javid's face seemed to dim in the slightest and Delnaz was confused by it. "You still remember our conversation."

Of course, it was like Javid to be so openly sentimental. Delnaz sighed but she wasn't offended by sentiment. She actually welcomed it. She'd been the last one to arrive at Café Farzaneh and already, the other womxns had been caught up in conversation but oddly, none of them were centred on the past, about memories they'd made the last time they'd been in Tehran. They'd instead spoken randomly about anything and everything, it was a true testament to how powerful their bond was. But Delnaz was filled with nostalgia, yes, she'd known these womxns for years but most of that time had been through the phone, seeing them in person for the second time throughout the duration of their friendship caused old memories to come flooding. Yes, they were her oldest friendships but at the same time, they felt like new friends.

Only Javid seemed to get it.

"I have an excellent memory," Delnaz answered almost a beat too late. She saw something like disappointment flash through Javid's gaze but it was gone immediately she glimpsed it and left her to wonder if she'd imagined the emotion altogether. She started to say something to salvage the situation but the others – Haleh, Pari and Farzaneh – had caught up to them.

"Cap, why'd we stop?" Pari asked teasingly. Javid smiled mildly.

"We're stopping for the night, it's getting late and I can't remember the last time I drove in snow. It's too dangerous to risk." Javid answered briskly.

Haleh and Pari exchanged a quick look, no doubt wondering the same thing. Farzaneh didn't seem to be worried at all about stopping in the middle of nowhere which meant that she either trusted Javid way too much or she was in on whatever Javid had planned. Delnaz suspected the latter.

"This is no time for your cryptic sayings and there is no way I'm sleeping in the snow." Haleh sniffed and affronted.

"Yeah, me neither." Pari quickly injected.

Javid adopted a mock wounded look that quickly faded. "There's a cabin in the woods."

Delnaz glanced around her as if the said building would manifest from the thick canopy of trees and right in front of her. The chances of that happening was pretty damn impossible, they might be chasing after a powerful sword which as far as concerned was considered mythical to most people but there were still a number of things impossible in their world. Like flying houses. Javid could hack a lot of things but Delnaz considered herself in tune with world news, she would have come across information if the world's first flying house had been constructed. Why was she even thinking about this?

She chalked it up to slight exhaustion and hunger.

"Okay," Haleh drawled, "That eliminates our fear of freezing

to death but our fear of being eaten by wolves is still very valid."

"No wolves," Farzaneh spoke for the first time and Delnaz still couldn't get over how stunning her voice was – heavily accented but still spoken very gently. Coming from someone who had one hell of a voice, Delnaz found herself being impressed with Farzaneh. She gave the womxn another look, curious about her all of a sudden. According to Javid's very vague information, this womxn was some sort of pathfinder but Delnaz was unsure if she was some sort of guardian of the sword like in the movies or if she was someone else, someone far older than she appeared and perhaps mythical. She might admit to gorging her mind with fantasy novels but it wasn't too far fetched of a thought.

"And how do you know that?" Haleh said in a haughty voice. Delnaz wanted to warn her to show a little bit of respect for their pathfinder.

If Farzaneh was deterred by Haleh's snobbery, she didn't show it, in fact she was smiling and Delnaz found herself returning the action. She decided that she liked this womxn. She must have the patience of a saint if she wasn't annoyed by Haleh.

"Because it's my cabin." Farzaneh answered plainly and began to head into the woods.

All four pairs of eyes swivelled to Javid, awaiting further instruction. She sighed.

"Haleh, be nice." She warned. "Farzaneh is our pathfinder and I don't want your edginess deterring her from helping us."

Haleh tried to smile innocently, emphasis on trying because the womxn was incapable of looking innocent even at her own detriment. She did raise her hands up in surrender.

"I was just trying to get a feel of her." She said, sounding suspiciously honest.

Javid fixed her with a stern look and walked after Farzaneh. Toman followed and Delnaz scurried after, not wanting to be around Haleh and Pari. She'd had enough in the car.

Haleh let out an exaggerated sigh and proceeded to flick the ends of her silky scarf over her shoulder like one might do with hair and in typical Haleh fashion, she made the motion look effortless, not at all ridiculous. "Fine, I'll play nice."

Javid didn't break her stare down with her, looking seriously stern for the first time. It was clear that she was in no mood to jeopardise their mission and she even seemed to respect Farzaneh a great deal. "Good, thank you, Love."

Haleh huffed, turning her head away for a brief moment and Delnaz bit back her smile; did the tough cookie actually look chastised for the first time in her life? Did Javid just successfully put her in her place? Delnaz was very much interested in how dynamics would play out in their little gang, Haleh and Javid were headstrong womxns but with varying degrees of stubbornness, the latter had already claimed the position wordlessly but the former was headstrong and would be sure to challenge Javid's every decision. Or maybe she wouldn't, Haleh wasn't stubborn, she was just opinionated. Haleh was willing to follow orders but only if she was a hundred percent certain that the decision was the right one. So maybe she wouldn't challenge Javid's every decision but she sure as hell would challenge the bad ones. Delnaz thought it wasn't a bad thing, someone definitely needed to check Javid when the occasion arose.

"As much as I'm enjoying this very testosterone-esque showdown, I think we should be following Farzaneh," Pari cut in and for the first time since they'd arrived in Jajrud, Delnaz found herself nodding along in agreement.

"Sorry," Javid said with a slight smile and headed into the bush, no doubt expecting the rest of them to follow. Toman sent all of them pointed looks that basically said, be nice.

Delnaz rose up her hands in mock surrender and Pari chortled. In the end, they trailed after Toman. Delnaz gingerly walked, the ground was soft beneath her boots, sinking down easily.

The tall trees seemed to stretch on forever and Delnaz couldn't help but marvel how it was simply a different world inside this forest. The evergreen trees were showing off, surrounded by shrubbery of different kinds – some of them flowering plants. Snow rested in heaps on the ground and sprinkled over leaves like salt.

"It's beautiful here," Pari said, her voice loud and full of awe.

"Wait until you see the summer of Jajrud." Farzaneh called from ahead.

Haleh was glancing at their surroundings with suspicion, as if she expected some woodland creature to jump out and scare them. "I take it you live in the cabin all year round." She said to Farzaneh.

Delnaz too was curious, if there was indeed a cabin in these woods then she couldn't imagine that it would be comfortable making the drive from the café and then venturing through these woods at the end of each closing day.

"Of course not, dear. There's a room in the back of the café where I've made my home. I like to head up here during the weekends. There's the most stunning clear lake across the cabin and I like to fish there from time to time."

Haleh seemed pleased with Farzaneh's answer; Delnaz didn't understand why she'd been wary in the first place.

"Can't fish now though." Haleh replied, no doubt talking about the weather.
Farzaneh hummed a noncommittal response.

Just as they reached a clearing, the cabin came into sight and it looked exactly like Delnaz had imagined in her mind's eye. Small but cosy looking and there was a small greenhouse for growing herbs right in front of it. Come to think of it, Farzaneh did seem like somebody in tune with nature.

"Welcome to my humble abode," Farzaneh said, standing in front of them and in a sweeping motion, gesturing at the house.

"I suppose it would be too much to have hot water running." Pari said.

Delnaz glanced at her best friends. She recalled walking into the café early that afternoon and immediately spotting all of them – if Delnaz had to link all of them with a common similarity, it would be that all of them were impeccable dressers. Each of them had their distinct styles but they very well knew what worked for them and looked good.

Now, their layer of glamour had been peeled back in the slightest; there was snow in Javid's hair and exhaustion had settled in her face. Delnaz felt a bolt of worry for her friend, a few years ago she'd been diagnosed with cancer and although she'd since recovered it was still hard to think about that dark time in her life. Worse, it had happened way before the girls had met each other. Delnaz knew Javid enough to know that she didn't let many people get close to her and while she might appear as the typical socialite – jetting around the world and partying with all walks of wealthy people, she still didn't have many friends. She'd gone through that bout of illness alone and had fought for her life. She was okay now, past remission but Delnaz still worried.

"I can see that you're all exhausted, there's hot water running in the cabin. Go freshen up, there's plenty of time to talk through your plans – or just catch up."

They didn't need any further prompting to take Farzaneh's offer. All of them piled into the cabin and Delnaz was pleased with the rustic feel of it – the whole of it was a living room with a small kitchen at the far end of the room and an adjoining bathroom. The bedroom area had three bunk beds, two facing each other and the third adjacent to the other two.

There was a patterned mat in the centre of the cabin and there must have been a heater hidden somewhere in the cabin because there was a toasty warmth inside that made Delnaz feel better instantly. A single lantern was hung above on the ceiling, bathing the room in warm light but not too bright that Delnaz had to squint every time she gazed up at it. Like the owner of the house, everything about the cabin screamed mild and sophisticated. Delnaz didn't do too well with flashy displays anyways, she was more about muted tones, colours and ambiences.

The scent of tangerine and something woodsy hung fragrantly in the air and she couldn't help but inhale even deeper, she'd have pressed her face into one of the pillows on the bed but she didn't want to seem too weird.

"I call dibs on the bathroom." Pari announced perkily and before any of them could protest, she was already dashing into the bathroom with a speed that startled Delnaz.

The rest of her friends let out amused chuckles and Delnaz allowed a small smile to bloom on her lips. Delnaz walked to one of the bunk beds and settled down on the freshly laid bed. She didn't know why but she immediately felt at home. Maybe it was because it was Farzaneh's home and she'd come to swiftly associate the womxn with warmth or maybe it was because the cabin was obviously well lived in and loved.

"Yeah, you guys can keep fighting about the shower, I'm going to make a fire, and we can talk," Javid said. Naturally, Toman stuck to her side, muttering something about Farzaneh's guide on how she'd need help to get wood from the shed at the back of the cabin.

There was a split second of indecisiveness before Delnaz decided to stay indoors, she'd tasted warmth and she wasn't going to trade it for the harsh cold so soon. She moved around the cabin, admiring the decorations on the wall. Despite the limited space, there was an abundance of art on the walls; an antique masquerade mask and several paintings of wildlife that fascinated her. She wondered if Farzaneh had painted them.

While Haleh held a conversation on the phone, speaking in the thick drawl of what she assumed to be Dutch, Delnaz wandered to where Farzaneh was, by the small kitchen, boiling water in a kettle and bent at the waist, ransacking the little fridge.

"You've got such a lovely place here." Delnaz said softly.

Farzaneh rose to her full height to shoot Delnaz a smile. "You're kind, thank you."

Delnaz wondered if it would be rude to ask questions but the truth was that she was as fascinated with the house as she was with its owner. She didn't understand why she was drawn to Farzaneh, only that she was filled with the desire to be near this womxn, to talk to her.

"And the art, did you paint them?" She asked.

Farzaneh's lips quirked up in a brief smile, since they'd entered the cabin, she'd ditched her hat and long dark hair that reached past her shoulder spilled out unruly, making her look even softer, younger.

"I'm afraid I'm not as talented as you think I am," She said lightly.

She seemed to hesitate and Delnaz instantly clocked that the paintings were valuable to her and not in price but in sentiment. Just as she was beginning to think Farzaneh would leave her question unanswered, she said, "They're gifts from a dear friend."

"Your friend is talented." Delnaz said and she meant it. She could tell by the way Farzaneh paused mid brew of her tea to gaze up at the paintings that whoever her friend was, they were long gone. For the first time, Delnaz wondered how old this womxn was.

She might have asked if Pari didn't cut into their conversation, she was out of the bathroom and wrapped in a white towel, hair sopping wet.
"Are you cooking, Farzaneh? Haleh tells me we'll be drinking outside by the fire first. We wouldn't want to trouble you unnecessarily."

Farzaneh waved her concerns away, muttering how it was no bother. The spell between them was broken and Delnaz was left wondering when she'd get the chance to talk intimately with Farzaneh again.

By the time the crescent moon was high in the night, all six of them were sitting outside, on logs of woods that had been carried by Javid and Toman. The fire in their midst burned bright and high, at first Haleh had been concerned that the smoke would draw predators to their location but she'd been swiftly reassured by Farzaneh. Now, they exchanged stories around the fire, drinking from the bottle of whiskey being passed around.

As the night grew, Javid found herself loosening up, laughing louder than she normally did. She wasn't a lightweight and she wasn't by any means drunk but the alcohol had warmed her up, settling in her stomach and making her tongue loose. All she felt in the moment was happiness and hope. Hell, even Haleh was looking the slightest bit cheerier than before, if one could count a reduction in her usual sarcastic comments as cheeriness. Although, Javid had noticed on more than one occasion where Haleh passed the bottle to Pari on her right instead of taking a swig. She recalled that Haleh worked in the night scene, she was probably surrounded by alcohol and other kinds of substances all night long and maybe she wasn't simply interested in participating.

Still, Javid would take whatever she'd get from Haleh.

Soon, it was Javid's turn with the bottle and she shook the bottle, trying to gauge how much of the drink was left. The dark amber liquid sloshed inside of it and Javid pressed her ear close to the bottle mouth, trying to hear.

"You're wasted." Delnaz said from where she was seated, on the log of wood across Javid. But her words were light unlike the usual rebuke that they were. Javid secretly thought that Delnaz just needed to lighten up sometimes, she was always so serious. She was definitely the mom friend of their group.

Javid shook her head in response to Delnaz's words. She lifted up a finger, "I'm not wasted, I'm lightly buzzed."

Delnaz smiled, "I'll bet you can stand up on your own without swaying." For effect, she stuck out her tongue.

Javid ignored Toman's longsuffering sigh beside her. Toman had made no move to hide the fact that she was barely drinking, sure, she'd taken the bottle a few times that it had been passed to her but she'd passed most times than she'd actually taken a swig. It was no secret that Toman wasn't a big drinker, maybe it was because of the nature of her job which didn't allow her much daytime drinking – or nighttime either. Javid knew that Toman could spend even her nights tailing and tracking down details for a case.

She wished she'd loosen up though, just for this night alone.

Javid stood – or at least tried to – hell bent on carrying out Delnaz's dare but she was quickly pulled back down to the log by Toman. Her ass landed on the wood hard and she let out a loud oof, the wind successfully knocked out of her.

"Hey!" She protested.

"You looked like you were going to topple face first into the fire, wouldn't want that happening so early into our mission." Toman explained matter of factly.

"So you'd rather her topple into a fire much later into our mission?" Pari asked teasingly. Because she was lightweight, she'd opted out of drinking as excessively as they did, more content with sipping tea that Farzaneh had brewed.

Toman gave a coy shrug and all of them burst into laughter, some more maniac than the others. Javid found herself being in awe of Toman once again; one would peg Toman as being serious, one of those people who never stopped to catch a break or have fun but she was actually one of the funniest people that Javid had ever known. Sure, her jokes weren't as frequent and she tended to keep a stoic face ninety nine percent of the time but she had the driest wit and Javid loved her – she loved it.

"Toman, Toman, Toman," Haleh repeated her friend's name like it was a magic spell.

Delnaz gave a little snort and she swiftly covered her mouth as if it would reverse her action.

"I think you're actually drunker than you think, I mean, look at you smiling like you never do." Pari pointed out, her tone more teasing than accusing. Delnaz was unaware of the fact that all of her friends were tuned in to her quiet attitude, how she'd keep mum through conversations even though they very obviously interested her. She thought her opinions were being ignored but her friends wish she would just speak up for once.

"Toman," Haleh echoed again before Delnaz could answer. The latter flinched but it was almost imperceptible. Javid wouldn't have seen either if her attention wasn't solely on her.

"Yes," Toman answered wryly and the slightest bit wary.

"I'm just actually realising it now but your name is Toman." Haleh said.

Javid and Toman shared a quick glance, silently wondering if Haleh had slipped and hit her head hard when she was taking a shower. Confusion illuminated by the fire in front of them glinted in Toman's eyes, she regarded Haleh as if she was a puzzle she couldn't solve.

"How come you're named after a currency?" She asked.

The cloud of confusion cleared from Toman's face and a ghost of a smirk played on her face. "I hear that my dad named me. He was poor, wanted to jinx me to be rich."

Again, chorus laughter echoed in the night. It was only Javid that noticed how Toman clenched her fist in her lap at the mention of her father. Javid didn't know the whole story about Toman's dad and the truth was, she dreaded finding out. She'd once asked Toman about it and she'd never seen her close up like that. Her expression had become immediately shuttered, her face scarily blank before going on to warn Javid never to ask her again.

Sensing her discomfort, Javid handed her the bottle and she raised the bottle in a mock toast before tilting it up to her lips, it was because Javid was sitting beside her that she saw that Toman didn't take a single dip, her lips were pursed tightly. Javid watched as she wiped at her lips and stood up to hand an expectant Delnaz the bottle.

It was so Toman to refuse to drink even when she was hurting.

Haleh met Javid's eyes and quirked an eyebrow and Javid knew that she'd sensed Toman's unease. Javid gave a subtle shake of her head, she didn't know what Haleh was up to but she seemed like she was going to call Toman out. Haleh rolled her eyes in response but there was a slight wounded expression on her face.

Javid felt laughter bubble up in her throat, if Toman wasn't broodingly staring into the fire she might have noticed the exchange she'd had with Haleh.

"You know, I was almost named after Gordafarid," Haleh mused aloud, successfully taking the attention off Toman. Javid flushed with guilt, especially when Haleh shot her a look. She was always thinking about Haleh's caustic remarks, Haleh's I don't care aura. But she quickly forgot how Haleh was protective of the people she loved. She'd never bring up Toman's father when she knew how Toman would react to it.

Javid made a mental note to apologise to her later.

"You? No way." Pari exclaimed. She'd long finished drinking her tea out of the dainty cup Farzaneh had given her and she'd set both the cup and saucer on the ground, her leg jiggling danger-ously close to it.

Haleh smirked, "Why not? I would have lived up to the name. In fact, I bet I have a lot of things in common with her."

Javid smiled at the cockiness in Haleh's voice. Pari was chal-lenging, "Yeah, like what? Certainly not in dressing, Gordafarid was conservative."

Javid was uncertain if Pari was chastising Haleh's less than con-servative dressing, they often made jokes like that amongst them-selves; Javid liked to think that they were close enough to share dark humour with each other. But sometimes, these things were hard to tell. Especially when said jokes came from Pari who was from one of the most conservative countries in the world.

Afghanistan had been taken over by the Taliban for years, one of the first things the extremist group had done was restore the country back to the dark ages – suddenly, womxns needed escorts to walk freely in public, they were segregated in high schools and universities from their male counterparts with the thought that they'd 'corrupt' them. It became mandatory for womxns to be covered from head to toe. To put the situation in much simpler terms; womxns' rights took a nose dive six feet in a country that it had never been quite emphasised in the first place. Womxns that dared to rebel were murdered. Activists met the same fate.

But it wasn't just some story to Pari, she'd lived it and if Javid's calculations were accurate then she must have been in university when the Taliban had taken over. She imagined a much younger Pari, forced to comply with the new reign. It wasn't until a few years ago that the Taliban's reign had ended; even then things weren't going great for the country. Javid wondered if it was the reason why Pari made the decision to major in Journalism; to fight for the truth. Even with that mentality, it would be almost impossible that Pari hadn't been influenced by the conservative ideology of her country, however subtle.

If Haleh thought Pari's words were accusatory or condemning, she didn't show it, only puffed her chest up in pride. "Please, Pari, Gordafarid existed hundreds of years ago, a thousand to be exact, womxns in that era were forced to suppress their femininity, their sexuality. They were expected to grow and get married and have fucking broods of babies. Gordafarid was the exception and she was one heck of a badass exception. So yes, Pari, Gordafarid dressed like a fucking prude because she couldn't exactly strut her stuff on the streets without causing a scandal." There was passion in the way Haleh spoke, the stress of her words intense and serious in a way that Javid rarely ever heard from her. To Haleh, her fashion was a means of expressing herself, of liberating herself. Although she'd never been considered demure or conservative but in the years that Haleh had lived in Iran, she'd been less showy. Iran might be no Afghanistan but the country had also had its fair share of misogyny and sexism – Womxns died under oppression because of the country's religious foundations.

The moment Haleh had moved abroad, all that had changed; she'd been louder with her dressing and daring anyone to question her.

Javid didn't say it out loud but Haleh would have been an awesome Gordafarid if she'd been named so. Pari, however, did, "Wow, I've never heard you sound so passionate. And I concede, you would have been a fucking good Gordafarid."

"It's not too late to change your name," Delnaz said mildly. She stared with squinted eyes at Haleh. "Now that I'm looking, you actually kind of look like mother."

Javid giggled at Delnaz referring to Gordafarid as their mother.

"Damn straight I do." Haleh said. Pari leaned too close to Haleh than what was considered platonic and was very obviously ogling Haleh's lips. "Yeah, it's in the lips." And because they were tipsy on drink, the rest of them leaned forward too, staring at Haleh's lips. It might have just been the flames but Javid thought she saw a blush rush up Haleh's cheeks.

"And the hair," Pari exclaimed, reaching out to feel Haleh's silky black mane between her fingertips.

"And also the fact that Haleh is lesbian." Javid couldn't help but chirp in. It was only Toman and Farzaneh that were silent but that was typical of them. Toman wouldn't speak until she had something meaningful to say, she looked content just listening to their conversation and thankfully, the dark cloud that had been on her face before was gone, she was back to wearing a mildly amused look on her face.

"What does that have to do with it?" Haleh asked. Pari nudged her side.

"I think she's trying to say that mother was lesbian too." Pari said with a grin.

"No way, there's nothing that suggests that she was." Delnaz cut in. "Even though she is in my head." She added as an after-thought.

Javid's grin was a white slash in the dark, "I know more about Gordafarid through years upon research, I could tell you about her early childhood, how her family was like and more of that sort. Or I could tell you how Gordafarid turned down Sohrab's advances time after time."

Haleh shifted forward and Javid was happy by how interested she was in learning Gordafarid's story. "No way, wasn't Sohrab her enemy?"

Pari snorted. "Of course he was in love with her, I would have been."

"She turned down his advances several times and Sohrab was absolutely smitten to the point where he would have done whatever she asked – even calling off his troops. Gordafarid didn't only turn him down but she did so brutally that he was determined to destroy her country. There are many scholars who believe that she was lesbian and that she had a brief affair with a female soldier in her army." Javid explained.

"Wow," Haleh breathed out.

"So Gordafarid isn't only a fucking badass, she's also the queer icon of my dreams." Haleh said. There was stubborn determination mixed with awe glinting in her eyes, Javid had never seen her friend look that way and was suddenly glad that she'd shared her theory with them. Now, they were as passionate as her, connecting themselves to Gordafarid's story in a way and new ways they hadn't before.

"You've been dancing around the topic since we arrived in Iran, but how the heck is this mission going to go? I don't reckon that we'll just march to the caves and pick up the sword. What's our plan, Javid?"

Javid picked up the twig in front of her and began to draw absentmindedly on the sand. "Gol-e-Zard cave." She mimed drawing a cave-like structure on the snowy soil and looked up. "Let's start with everything about the cave that I can recall from my mind before drinking whiskey."

"Which is everything because you have a photographic memory." Pari pointed out.

Javid shook her head, breathing a small laugh. "I do not have a photographic memory, but I am pretty invested in this – years of research – so you bet that I can remember close to everything."

"Just let the womxn talk," Toman said, her tone was the slightest bit curt and as if she sensed this, she added, "Please."

All the ladies gave nods. Javid sent Toman a grateful look, one downside to being surrounded by witty people was that they always tried to insert witty quips into conversations, cutting off the main speaker as a result.

"I'm going to mansplain this with the confidence of a drunk white man, forgive me – seeing as some of us are familiar with some of the history. Gol-e-Zard Cave translates directly to Yellow Flowers so it's alternatively known as that," Javid began, she chucked the twig in the fire and rubbed her palms together to get rid of the snow. "Yellow Flowers Cave is a river cave on the southeastern slope of the 3706-metre Yellow Flowers Peak, it's a popular sight – hard to miss."

Haleh bopped her head in agreement.

"It's one of the peaks overlooking Damavand Mountain – which is where the sword will be activated but more on that later. This cave, which is located in Mazandaran province, in Polour region."

Javid raised her head and wasn't surprised to find Pari watching her with more seriousness than she'd seen in the past sixteen hours. She was after all a journalist, or at least she used to be one before she was promoted to TV Anchor at the television station she worked at. Javid got the feeling that if Pari was with a notepad and a pen, she'd be scribbling everything Javid was saying. Pari was an Afghan womxn and although the country was neighbors with Iran, it was still very unfamiliar to her. It didn't matter that Pari had visited Iran several times, she didn't have the history like Haleh or Javid did as natives.

"But the outside and its surroundings aren't as important as what's on the inside," Javid announced.

"Yeah, what we're looking for – Gordafarid's sword." Delnaz chimed in.

Toman shook her head slowly, "Yes exactly."

Delnaz didn't say anything, only arched an eyebrow in silent question.

Javid blew out a nervous part, she wasn't exactly itching to tell

her friends that their mission was more dangerous than they realised but she had no choice; she'd promised them total transpar-
ency and that included informing them about any potential life
threatening issues that they might encounter on their journey –
even if that meant it might dissuade them.

She needn't have worried. Javid was going to learn to give her
team a little more credit on the bravery front. She wasn't leading
gullible people to a quest, she was dealing with grown womxns,
womxns who choose for themselves.

She let her gaze trail over all of them, to even Toman sitting
beside her. Although the latter was privy to most of the details;
both brutal and mundane.

"The inside of the cave is covered with calcium carbonate and
there are several pools of cold water inside." She finally spoke,
dreading the looks of apprehension on their faces. She was disappointed though, she saw mild concern but nothing severe.

Javid breathed a small sigh of relief; so far, so good.

"How cold?" Pari asked.

It was Toman who answered the question in her usual deadpan,
"Cold enough to pose a slight problem but nothing too intense."

Pari nodded, seemingly appeased by the answer. "Carry on,
Love." She tried to mimic Javid's accent, drawling the words a tad
too long. Nobody laughed at her imitation. Pari didn't look offended at the lack of reception to her joke, she understood the serious
atmosphere. Pari had always been a good sport and Javid didn't
think she'd ever seen her get upset by anyone or anything. She was
just naturally one of those easy going people.

Javid continued, "The depth of some of these ponds reaches
four metres. Yellow Flowers is one of the active calcareous caves
and the birth of various calcareous formations continues in it.
Groundwater flows in this cave all year round."

"Some of us failed chemistry in school," Pari teased lightly.

"Why don't you ever ask something directly? You're always flirting, teasing." Delnaz piped up, she wasn't quite frowning but the words were clearly a jab at Pari but in typical Pari fashion, she ignored them and replied with another one of her jokes.

"Come on, every team needs comic relief. I'm volunteering my services." She quipped.

Delnaz huffed in frustration. It seemed like she was genuinely curious. But she'd picked a bad time to be curious because Javid didn't need any interruptions, if Delnaz really wanted answers on Pari's personality the both of them could chat about it later.

"Calcium Carbonate occurs in several states; limestone, chalk but, in this case, it occurs in marble."

Pari's lip wordlessly formed an 'o' sound.

"We can handle it." Javid was quick to reassure. Toman shot her a look that basically said, "Don't be ridiculous."

"Okay, fine," She hurriedly backtracked. "I'm not saying that it'll be smooth sailing for our little gang but I have a plan."

Delnaz nodded and Haleh and Pari echoed the motion.

"Okay, now on to how world peace gets achieved - Behind the waterfall, on the roof of the Gol-e-Zard cave lies two holes, when the moon is positioned directly over one of these holes, Gordafarid's sword will become visible." Javid finished, her eyes fixed on the slowly dying fire before her. The night was getting chillier and she was starting to feel it through her clothes.

"This part of the story we all know and are aware of," Pari gave a small smile. "The sword will be used to stab the Damavand's Mountain's Heart, restoring our countries to an era of peace and prosperity."

Javid nodded like a proud teacher would do to a star pupil. "Our troubles don't end with the cave though. There's an ancient prophecy Farzaneh has in an old script about the Damavand Mountain, in every known translation of the scroll, it always instructs that the sword be used to stab the mountain's heart and that part is too vague to understand."

"Mountains don't have hearts." Haleh hit the nail on the head in that usual blunt way of hers.

"What about the top of the mountain?" Delnaz asked.

A small frown marred the lines of Javid's forehead, "I'm not too sure, especially because there are several sayings about leading with the heart and not the head. The head would signify the top of the mountain but the heart has to be something else. In the past few years, I've hired teams to climb the mountain, search for anything unusual and anything that had gone unnoticed by other people that had climbed the mountain before."

"Why the worry though? I still think our most important worry here is getting the sword." Haleh was staring right at Toman and narrowed her eyes when the other womxn didn't nod in agreement. "Unless you think we've only got one shot at stabbing the heart with the sword."

Javid's silence was enough confirmation and confused murmurs rose amongst their little crowd.

"Wait, what do you mean by one shot?" Delnaz was saying, her voice shockingly louder than Haleh and Pari.

"Alright, calm down, you guys." Toman finally cut in, she shot Javid a look that clearly said, "I told you so."

Because Toman had been involved in finding out the details relating to the sword, she was more privy to information than Haleh, Pari and Delnaz who were all but clueless about what they were getting into. But Toman, she was vehemently against sharing every slight insecurity with the rest of their team, claiming that it would be a bad thing to reduce the moral of their team so early into their quest.

"They don't need to know everything, Javid. Just give them a solid plan, something to fixate their minds on. If you continue to share every tiny doubt you have about this mission then you'll poison their minds with fear and those fucking mistakes you're afraid of us making – we'll make them because of fear." She'd said during the car ride when Javid mentioned the doubts about the mountain's heart.

Javid tried and failed to ignore the stab of guilt that pierced her. She didn't plan on keeping any vital information from them; scary or not, it was going to be near impossible to keep to that promise though. If she gathered all the information she'd bought and stolen on the sword into one book in the past three years it would be thicker than an encyclopaedia so there was no way she wouldn't forget to mention something to them – no matter how small the detail was and it frightened her.

Even though it went without saying that she was the leader of their mission, she still felt the weight of responsibilities on her shoulder, weighing her down if she thought of it for too long. Everything that went wrong would be her fault, any injuries sustained, any… lives lost. She shook her head, a physical act of banishing the negative thoughts from her head. She would rather die than let those thoughts become a reality.

She exhaled a breath, the air in front of her forming a big puff of cold. The fire in front of them closer and closer to embers. She couldn't help but wonder if it was a manifestation of her own trust in her team – from a roaring fire to mere embers.

Toman was still trying to reassure Pari and Delnaz. Haleh on the other hand was staring right at her, eyes glittering with something that looked like anger, it flickered out the moment Javid returned the eye contact and she was left thinking she'd imagined it. The anger hadn't seemed directed at her though, Javid had seen Haleh wear that particular look many times. Like she was nursing an old grudge.

"Javid, you might want to say something now." Toman said through gritted teeth, she too looked and sounded angry – but clearly the anger was directed at Javid for ignoring her advice.

"Look, the mountain's heart is an important puzzle to figure out but we'll never get to it unless we focus on getting to the sword first. Banish the former puzzle to the back of your mind and focus on this one." She finally said. She barely hid her surprise when Pari and Delnaz nodded and leaned back. They seemed pacified.

For now, the voice in her head muttered wickedly. She ignored it.

"Even now, the cave isn't the first step. Pari, remember your comment about Ocean's Eight?" Javid asked, allowing a smirk to spread on her lips. She felt some of her excitement return. Now this part of the mission she was looking forward to.

"Yeah," Pari answered slowly as if she was expecting a trick.

"We do get to attend one fancy party before we go to the cave. I'm treating all of you to a girl's day out at the bougiest boutique in the city."

"Fattening us up before leading us to our deaths, heh?" Delnaz said but her voice was teasing.

Javid shrugged. "If that's what you're calling it."

"I accept your bribe." Pari said.

It was remaining Haleh who was yet to speak. For the longest time, it seemed like she might not say anything but a small sigh escaped her lips; one of surrender. "I trust you, Javid."

Javid tried not to let how much the words meant to her show. She gave a jerky nod and that was it, normal conversation resumed, more jokes were made and laughs echoed in the night, it was when the fire finally died and it got too cold to talk outside that Pari, Farzaneh and Haleh decided to retire indoors. Delnaz stayed a bit more outside, chatting with Toman – then she too stood up and walked inside the cabin. Leaving Toman and Javid alone together, for the second time that day.

For the longest time, the two of them sat side by side, not talking just staring ahead at the vast forest before them. The night was far from quiet; the buzz of insects, the distant sound of rushing water that caused Javid to marvel because she expected the lake Farzaneh spoke of to be frozen over in the sudden unforgiving winter. Somewhere deep in the woods, she heard the cry of an animal. The sound caused the hair on her arms to rise but not out of fear. It was beginning to feel as if they were lost in their own world and it was easy to forget that there were other things out there.

Javid stared at Toman from the corner of her eyes; she was wearing her usual stoic face. The one that made it hard to tell what she was thinking. Her ex-lover's ability to keep her emotions under tight leash was one of the few things that frustrated Javid. Even while they'd been together, Toman had her moments of being closed off and when they'd made the mutual decision to end their relationship she'd been as cold as stone, even while Javid had hoped she'd show one shred of emotion, offer a solution to their problems.

Instead she'd walked away.

"You don't think I should have mentioned the Damavand's heart to them." Javid said, breaking the tension filled silence between them.

Toman let out a long suffering sigh and Javid bristled. She'd known Toman long enough to tell that the emotions she refused to show on her face, she communicated through sighs and this one was long, forming a small cold cloud in front of her face.

"We already discussed this during the drive." Toman answered matter of factly. Even her voice was smooth, calm and bearing no hint of heat or anger. Her sigh spoke differently though.

"Just spit it out, Toman," Javid snapped. It was only Toman that could rile her up like this, make her feel sentimental and nostalgic and then furious in the next second. She'd thought during their drive that there was nothing but mutual respect between them, maybe even longing, she'd certainly felt it when Toman brushed a hand on her thigh briefly more than two hours ago during their drive.

"Fine, I think you're being a chicken." She finally said, her words a tad bit uncertain so she added, "Or how do the English say it?"

Javid suddenly felt the urge to laugh and shook her head, how the hell did she easily go from wanting to fight Toman to thinking that the womxn beside her was the most beautiful and adorable to ever exist. She'd never felt this way with any of her previous lovers. It was just Toman. Fucking Toman.

"Chicken as in being a coward?" Javid supplied sarcastically, fighting the smile that was threatening to bloom on her face.

Toman nodded gravely. "Yes, that. I think you're more scared than you let on and rather than admit it and face those fears. You'd rather let someone chicken out before you, hence the scare tactics with Haleh, Delnaz and Pari."

Javid bristled. "That's not true!" She exclaimed yet a part of her couldn't help but mull over Toman's words, wondering if there was some truth in it.

"You need to have faith in this mission, Javid, have faith in us. We assure you that this mission won't make it very far before it collapses on its pillars."

Javid was silent, this time no longer defensive, just considerate.

"I'm fucking terrified, Toman." She admitted. "But it isn't exactly for the reasons you think."

"Then why?" Toman's words were harsh and challenging but her voice was uncharacteristically soft.

"I'm not terrified of dying." She let out a huff of a laugh that was more of a sigh than anything else. She felt Toman inching closer, closing the small distance between them until Javid could feel her, close and warm. "I've come fucking close to dying in the past and there was a time where I even thought I'd die and I wasn't afraid then – just filled with a sense I'd lived life without leaving any impact. Now, that was fucking terrifying."

Toman's hand reached for hers and gave a squeeze. Javid blinked back tears, recalling the darkest moment in her life. The moment she'd received the cancer diagnosis, she'd felt crippling fear. Suddenly time was ticking faster than it had ever. She'd thought she would die and then came the realisation that she hadn't done much throughout her life.

More than twenty years ago, Javid and her mother had immigrated from Iran to England; seeking a better life from all the chaos and suffering in their country. Javid had always been grateful for her mother's sacrifice and it was only when she was older than she realised how moving away had cost her family. Her mother had died barely ten years after leaving Iran and till this day, Javid thought that her mother had been killed by a broken heart, leaving her culture, her extended family and her home for greener pastures. Maybe a part of her had felt burdening guilt, thinking of her leaving as a betrayal to her country.

Javid could understand that, she'd grown up trying to hold on tight to her culture. She'd grown up feeling like a fraud; in England and far away from Iran. She'd tried to remedy that as an adult; giving away her wealth to Iranian charities, not one, not two but as many as she knew. Still, it hadn't been enough. So when she'd been diagnosed with breast cancer and the cloud of death hanging over her, she'd felt like a failure.

Javid didn't think of herself as particularly religious, she did believe in the paranormal but not in the way that most people believed. She'd always despised organised religion. But while she'd been sick, she'd prayed to every deity there was, swearing to finally do something about her country's less than stable state if she got better. And when she did get better, she'd thrown herself into finding how she could make her country better.

It was in the middle of discovering Gordafarid's sword that she'd met Toman and eventually, Haleh, Delnaz and Pari. So maybe she was terrified after all but not in the way that Toman was. Yes, she was afraid of getting this far and failing so she was waiting, telling her friends the most uncertain parts of their mission and wanting them to call her out on how ridiculous her whole plan was. She was afraid of leading them to their deaths for nothing.

She told this to Toman, blinking back tears.

"Javid," Toman's voice was filled with exasperated fondness. "I hate to stress this again but we all know what we're getting ourselves into. I swear there isn't any of us wearing rose coloured glasses. It's going to be dangerous and I hate to say this even more but we might get hurt."

Toman turned, jabbing a finger at Javid's chest, the closest to outwardly passionate one would get from her. "And it's not on you. We're grown womxns and we made the choice."

"You can't bear the whole weight of the body on your shoulders, Javid."

"Easier said than done, love." Javid tried to say lightly.

Toman shook her head, "I just know we'll be having this talk again, let me save all my wisdom for some other time." The words had their intended effect and Javid choked out a watery laugh. She noticed that Toman's hand was gripping hers tightly and contrary to what she thought, she did feel calmer at Toman's reassurance.

Javid was once again taken back by how Toman always managed to be level headed in the most anxious situations. She'd never seen her appear anything other than rational. She wanted to ask how but she kept her thoughts to herself, selfish as it was she rather liked Toman being unreadable, maybe even aloof sometimes. She liked Toman being the reassuring rock to lean on, she needed somebody like that on this journey.

Haleh was stubbornly pessimistic and she was usually the last person to offer reassurance of any kind. Delnaz was a milder version of Toman but she too usually needed reassurance. And Pari, well, Pari was optimistic, too optimistic than realistic.

Ignoring the voice in her head that warned her not to start anything she wasn't ready for, she turned to face Toman. She used one hand to lift Toman's chin so she was facing her too. Although it was far too dark to make out of all Toman's features, Javid could have sworn that Toman's eyes were heated, daring and Javid couldn't resist, she pressed her lips to hers.

For one long second, they remained like that, their lips just touching. Then Toman deepened the kiss, her hand leaving Javid's and moving to the back of her head. Javid didn't know how long they continued to kiss – tongues tangled in a heated dance -- exploring each other with the certainty of old lovers who were very much familiar with each others' bodies.

Eventually, Toman pulled away and shot up to her seat as if she couldn't bear to be closer to Javid anymore. Javid tried and failed to ignore the sting of hurt she felt.

"It's getting cold." Toman said pathetically, as if it hadn't been cold prior to the kiss they'd shared.

Javid considered saying something, calling her out but in the end, the ire she felt deflated like a balloon. She didn't exactly blame Toman. It took two to tango and their relationship hadn't ended on the best terms and Javid suspected that Toman had been hurt the most. She wouldn't be keen on a rehash of it either if she was Toman.

It was a bad idea to resume their relationship from where it had crashed and all they were dealing with was just leftover feelings. Javid mentally patted herself on the back for her analysis. She didn't come to Iran after years of being away to rekindle romance, she was here for a much higher purpose.

Still didn't stop her from remembering the feel of Toman's lips on hers.

Toman's sigh broke her from her thoughts. "I hate the winter."

"Yeah, me too." Javid said distractedly.

Toman continued to look down at her. "You still haven't drafted an official itinerary for us. Where are we going from here?"

Javid from an hour ago wouldn't have hesitated, she would have told Toman everything, asked her input for reassurance but now, Javid was frightened at how easily they could return back to what they'd been. It would be best to distance herself from Toman.

So she hesitated and said, "You'll find out tomorrow."

Toman nearly flinched but quickly recovered, she gave a stiff jerk of her head. She wasn't stupid, far from it. She was the smartest person Javid knew and understood cues faster than most people. "Alright. Good night."

Javid inhaled a deep breath, she didn't let herself feel any regret. She sat in front of the dead fire and the pile of burnt wood for a long time, freezing her ass off.

CHAPTER NINE
You're Worthy!

Javid didn't feel any better in the morning when she woke up. Part of it was because she was used to living in the best comfort that money could buy that she wasn't quite comfortable sleeping in Farzaneh's plain sheets. But the bigger cause was that she couldn't stop thinking about Toman; their kiss and how she'd hurt her with her curtness. She didn't think she'd ever shut Toman out, ever.

She knew that she should apologise and tell Toman that she was merely afraid, afraid of rekindling their flame – the flame that was no by means extinguished, judging by the fierce passion in their kiss. Javid couldn't erase the memory of the kiss from her mind; couldn't stop replaying in her head until it was a never ending loop. She'd thought things were done and dusted with Toman, that they could just be friends and mission partners now. Obviously, she'd been bloody wrong. Javid didn't think she could do casual with Toman; they couldn't just be friends. But they had to be something because the last thing she wanted was Toman resenting her for the hot and cold game she was playing.

Javid made up her mind to have a frank discussion with Toman, she owed her that much; and besides, it was the straights that had weird conflicts and arguments much like this one.

With that resolve in mind, Javid took the rest of her shower. She was in much lighter spirits when she was out of the cubicle sized bathroom. She was up earlier than the rest of her friends. On one of the bunks, Delnaz and Toman slept; Delnaz snored at the top without any inhibitions at all, finding freedom in speech in her sleep. A small smirk tugged at the corner of Javid's lips and she shook her head, droplets of water flying around. Haleh and Pari shared the other bunk, surprisingly; they had not 'accidentally' found themselves together in one bed. Pari might play the long game but once Haleh wanted something, she went straight for it, no pretence.

She briefly considered that Pari and Haleh were only teasing each other and that their sudden interest in each other wasn't serious. Javid made a mental note not to let whatever their relationship was to bother her. One; because it might be nothing and two - and - most importantly, it was none of her fucking business.

They were heading into the city today; it was time to put their plans into motion. She chose a beige double collared coat on black high waist slacks. She wore a pair of converse shoes.

She checked her phone for the time and saw it was a few minutes past five am and glanced back at her friends' sleeping forms. On a closer squint in the dimness of the cabin she saw that Toman was gone and that she'd arranged the sheets and pillows to look like a sleeping form.

Javid shook her head to herself, huffing a quiet laugh. Did she really think she'd get up earlier than Toman? She made no move to find her though, Toman was naturally an early riser and Javid didn't think that Toman would want to talk to her after what transpired between them a day ago. She did deserve to be left to her own thoughts and Javid would apologise to her when it was proper.

She did wake Farzaneh up though and the two of them set out into the cold wet morning where the pale sun hung in the clouds sleepily. Javid thought she could close her eyes and imagine herself back in England again, not because of the blistering winter but because of the pale sun.

She didn't quite detest this weather though, having developed an indifference towards the cold. Gone were the days when she let the weather reflect and ruin her mood. But winters in Iran – especially at this time of the year was the slightest bit unusual.

As if she could read her thoughts, Farzaneh tilted her head up and inhaled deeply. "The winter is a surprise to you, isn't it?"

The fact that they were discussing something so banal made Javid smile a little, Javid liked to think that she and Farzaneh had something of a friendly relationship.

"Yeah, it is a bit surprising." Javid answered, her words breaking off at the end as she jumped over a fallen tree trunk. She didn't know where they were going this early as this trip was all Farzaneh's idea but Javid trusted her enough to know that whatever Farzaneh wanted to show her probably had something to do with their mission.

Farzaneh was dressed in jeans, tall boots that were meant for hiking and a thick black coat that swallowed her form, Javid couldn't stop glancing at her.

"The scientists will tell you about climate change." Farzaneh began, halting in her sentence when Javid cast an amused look at her.

"And what do you say?" Javid asked. She was beginning to think of Farzaneh as the witchy aunt even though the other womxn was barely older than her.

Farzaneh flashed her a mysterious smile.

"It's not what I think, Javid, it's what has been happening. It's like the earth has sensed that certain parts of it will experience change in the next few weeks and it's bracing for it. Hence the unusual weather."

"Hmm," Javid mused aloud. Although she was aware of higher forces, powerful ones behind the scenes of life. To have it put so bluntly by Farzaneh was a bit startling.

"And if you have been observant, you'd notice that the world around you seems to have changed; perhaps a little livelier than you remember it." Farzaneh continued, gingerly removing the obstacles of branches in their path.

Javid was thinking of the snack truck that had run past them while she'd been driving yesterday; the truck and its bright string lights. Everything had seemed heightened during the drive.

"You're thinking of it, aren't you? Going over every sight you've experienced in the past forty eight hours since you arrived in Iran," Farzaneh commented.

Javid shook her head absentmindedly, not in the negative but because she was lost in her mind, contemplative. "Yeah, I can think of a few instances. I don't know but some things have become sharper in focus, the sights a little brighter and the people a little rowdier."

"It's almost like the whole city – damn, the whole country is buzzing with anticipation of something even though they aren't sure exactly what it is. If I had to place my finger on it, I'd say that magic is in the air." Javid added.

Farzaneh paused mid stride and gave a single nod, like one a teacher would give an attentive student. "You've been noticing these things, just shoving them to the back of your mind because you don't understand them."

Javid didn't know what to make of that, briefly she wondered if all the weird things she'd ever witnessed throughout her life chalked up to some magical explanation. She wondered how many more powerful relics existed out there, silently influencing their locations and waiting to be found. She was suddenly glad that Farzaneh had chosen to share this little insight with her seeing as she would have never put it all together on her own. Not even Toman would have, Javid had to admit to herself. Her ex-lover was a believer in factual things, not to say that she wouldn't believe in the supernatural if she was confronted with it but she didn't quite understand these things. Not like Farzaneh did apparently.

Not for the first time, Javid wondered if Farzaneh was a pathfinder to other things; other historical relics.

"How do you know all these things?" Javid found herself voicing her thoughts aloud, her voice a slight yell as they arrived in front of a clearing in the woods.

Farzaneh turned around to stare at Javid. "I'm the pathfinder of the sword, Javid, you know this already."

Javid hesitated for a second, unsure how to form her thoughts in words.

"Yes," She stressed the single word, still looking for the right words with which to ask her question. "But I always thought that it was a self acclaimed nickname."

The look of confusion on Farzaneh's face lingered and Javid sighed.

"Okay, I'm going to try and frame this in a different manner – an example if you will. Do you watch sports, Farzaneh?" She asked.

The other womxn blinked slowly and for a brief second, Javid thought she might be offended and was quick to clarify, "I didn't mean to be rude but you don't strike me as someone who keeps in touch with modern pop culture and that includes sports. And your café – the decoration gives off this rustic feel, I think it reflects your tastes." She was babbling, she realised but was too far gone to stop.

Farzaneh did stop her though, cutting into her spiel smoothly.

"Your observations are astute, Javid, I'm not obsessed with western pop culture or its shenanigans. And I think sports are rather dull." She didn't sound offended too, just deeply amused. Javid exhaled a small puff of air, drawing her coat with both hands.

"In wrestling, many wrestlers have these weird names they call themselves, usually really terrifying nicknames that are meant to scare opponents and appear tough to the fans. One might choose a name like The Scorpion."

Javid watched the moment that realisation dawned on Farzaneh. The other womxn exhaled a small laugh.

"You think that the pathfinder is like one of those nicknames; solely for show and to sound like something I am not." Farzaneh said with a small shake of her head.

Javid jerked her head in a nod. "Yeah, kind of like that. Not that I think you're a fraud of course, I just… I already know how you go by that name seeing as you're pretty much the only reason this mission exists. You know more than anyone else about Gordafarid's sword and apparently a lot about how the world is already affected by the mere probability that we will find it."

"You want to know how I know these things, right?" Farzaneh asked.

Javid nodded again. As if she found the whole situation hilarious, Farzaneh laughed, this time the sound was nothing like the delicate sound she'd emitted just minutes ago, it was deep and loud that it started the birds perched on the trees around them that they took flight into the sky, Javid watched in awe thinking there must have been at least fifty birds. And she hadn't even noticed them. For the first time, she took in her surroundings, they had reached a clearing and in the middle of it was a large tree stump, wide enough that about twenty people could sit comfortably on it. But it wasn't the abnormal size that baffled Javid, it was the familiarity of it. She felt like she'd seen something like this tree stump before, in fact, she was too busy staring intently at it that she didn't notice that Farzaneh was calling her name. it was only when the womxn shook her lightly that she snapped out of whatever trance she'd been in.

"Are you alright?" She asked, the corners of her face crinkling in concern.

Javid shook her head, to clear the last bits of weirdness away from her mind.

"Right, I'm sorry, I got a bit distracted by that," She nodded ahead at the tree stump in front of them. Farzaneh followed her gaze and a wide grin spread on her face.

"Of course, I forgot about the map's luring effect on strangers. Believe it or not, there are things in this little forest that would shred you to pieces if you weren't found worthy of the map's knowledge." She explained.

Javid reeled back in surprise. "What in the bloody hell?" She raised up a hand when Farzaneh tried to speak, a part of her mind tried to warn her that she was crossing the line from polite to rude. She knew more than anybody else not to cut off a womxn when she was speaking – or worse, when she tried to. It was just that Farzaneh's words had left her more than a little baffled. First, she'd called the huge tree stump a map and second, the mention of creepy creatures ready to devour her if she was found unworthy didn't sit very well with her. And again, map?

"Did you just call that tree stump a map?" Javid asked incredulously.

Once again, Javid was grateful for Farzaneh's easy disposition because she didn't look angry that she'd been cut off. Maybe she was used to the reaction of others when she showed them the tree stump. That begged the question of how many people had been to this very clearing and how many of them had been found unworthy?

Pleasant thoughts, Javid chided her mind. She was not going to think about being found unworthy. Unlike many other people Javid had encountered in her search for Gordafarid's sword, she had pure intentions about the sword's power and she intended to use it for the original purpose. If this tree stump turned map wanted to search her freaking heart for pureness, it would find nothing but good intentions. She inhaled a deep breath, feeling a little reassured by her thoughts.

"The stump is a map and you asked how I know the things that I do. I'm afraid to disappoint your imaginations about me being a witch of some sort."

"That is a real bummer." Javid deadpanned. Farzaneh thankfully got the joke and smiled.

"But the truth is that everything I know about the sword; its origin, its power and how to find it was learnt from this map." Farzaneh said, her voice catching a little in awe. Javid found that awe a little contagious, granted she didn't see anything too special about the stump yet other than the size but she liked how Farzaneh had probably been aware of its existence a long time yet her voice held the awe that one would expect from a first time seer.

"You see, if we walk a little deeper into these forests, you'll find an old house left in ruins from a fire that happened over fifty decades ago, my mother's side of the family used to be guardians of the map of the sword. It was our duty to protect the truth and make sure that it didn't fall into the wrong hands. For almost a century, my family has been doing that, until one of my ancestors was tricked by a man seeking the sword." Farzaneh paused and for the first time since Javid had known her, her voice was tight with barely restrained fury. Javid was grateful that she wasn't on the receiving end of it and was very sorry for whoever would be stupid to cross this womxn.

"The man was seeking the power of the sword for himself and once the secret of the map was revealed to him by my ancestor, he burned out house to the ground, killing almost every womxn in that place." Now Farzaneh's voice was low with grief.

"Since then, the secret of the map has been guided even tighter than it was before."

"What," Javid cleared her throat, almost dreading the answer to the question she wanted to ask. "What happened to the man?" Nothing good, she hoped. Still, she couldn't help but be slightly terrified of the map and consequently, the sword. Now it made sense why all the groups that had ventured out to get the sword before them had all met deaths or strange disappearances that had become urban tales. She couldn't let her friends meet the same fate.

Farzaneh did smile this time and it was a brutal and deadly thing. "He died in this very spot we stand on."

Javid was grateful to be spared the gory details, yet she couldn't help but glance down, as if she'd find some hint that something terrible had happened on the ground she stood on.

"Why did you bring me here?" Javid asked softly. "Or rather, was that story the reason why you've brought me here?"

Every emotion was wiped clean from Farzaneh's face. "Many people have found my contact before you. Many have tried to convince me to help them with their cause. Some made no attempt to hide their greed, offering generous bribes and everything you can think of."

Javid wasn't sure whether to feel proud on that aspect, she wasn't so innocent after all; she'd bribed whoever was necessary to get information about the sword and its power. The only thing she hadn't done was maim or kill anyone to get what she wanted and she wasn't sure if it made her better than anyone else.

She didn't regret any of it but unlike others, she'd done all that bad with good intentions. Did that still make her worthy? Or was she tainted? There was only one way to find out.

"You're the first person to actually come to me with the intention of saving our worlds." Farzaneh shook her head. "I believe in you, in your cause but the map is the ultimate decision maker."

"No hard feelings," Javid said and meant it. She understood that Farzaneh was carrying out her noble duty. Besides, there was not a single part of Javid that had expected any of this to come easy. Proving herself worthy to this tree stump wasn't even the hardest part, she would have to prove herself over and over again; to her friends and to her country.

Farzaneh gave her a tight squeeze on her shoulder and together, they walked towards the tree and Javid realised that the low thrumming sound she'd heard in the air wasn't coming from any insect buzz, it was coming from the tree stump. And it was bigger, even closer than it had been from a distance. It was still too early in the morning to see clearly but Javid found her breath being taken away at the intricate design on the tree stump and saw that Farzaneh had been right. The smooth surface of the stump was carved carefully, painting a clear story and not just any story; the story of Gordafarid.

But it was far too foggy to see much and Javid felt a strange frustration well up in her — she had to see more. At the thought of it, the surface of the stump was aglow with stunning blue light, illuminating the story. An awed gasp escaped her lips and she found herself taking a step forward, breaking free from Farzaneh's hold on her wrist.

The blue light traced the whole story, starting from the birth of Gordafarid; a child born with greatness written in the stars for her, the story moved on to the great war, the one that Gordafarid had fought in and won by sheer strength and wisdom. Her sword had been blessed by the higher power, which filled it with immense power. The story continued with Gordafarid giving up the sword, hiding it for a special day that her people might need its power again.

Then the story ended, in a flash of brilliant light which faded to a dull glow, revealing what Javid now knew to be a map, leading right up to the Damavand mountains, to the heart of it where the sword would be put. Sudden clarification filled Javid and she knew what the heart was, knew what to do with it.

It wasn't until Farzaneh muttered the words, slightly awed that it dawned on Javid, causing a shiver to run down her spine.

"It's never lit up like this before, not for anyone and it did for you. Javid... You're worthy."

By the time Javid and Farzaneh returned back to the cabin all of her friends were awake and dressed – even Toman was back and brooding from the looks of things. Delnaz stood in the little kitchen space, cooking it seemed. All eyes turned to the front door the moment it creaked open and a chorus of voices exploded at once. Her friends were some of the smartest people that Javid knew but they had their moments of childishness that caused her to shake her head fondly.

"Ladies, please, I can't answer all your questions at once." Javid shouted above the noise.

Haleh beat Pari to the chase. "Where did you go? Pari already had theories about Farzaneh kidnapping you and murdering us. Oh, and that we were next." As if she was just noticing Farzaneh's presence by Javid's side, she gave a slow blink. "No offence, Far."

The new nickname was drawled and dripping in saccharine.

"None taken." Farzaneh said, waving a hand meant to demonstrate waving away Haleh's words. Haleh narrowed her eyes as if she suspected Farzaneh was mocking her. Of course she could dish it out and not take it in return. Javid rolled her eyes at the ridiculousness of Haleh in this situation. Haleh was used to people letting her get away with everything, to challenge Haleh was to draw her attention to you.

"Please don't listen to Haleh. I didn't think you kidnapped Javid, I was worried for the both of you. It's freezing out there and I thought the both of you might have been eaten by deer or some other wild creature in that forest." Pari rambled, she looked to Haleh, Delnaz and Toman for help. "We were all worried about you two."

Toman who'd been silent up until now looked up from frowning at her phone and said, "Speak for yourself, I saw the two of them leave."

Javid pinned Toman with an accusing look. "And where did you go to? I certainly didn't see you when Farzaneh and I left." She winced when her voice sounded sharp and not lightly teasing like she'd meant for it to sound.

Blissfully, Toman didn't seem to take notice, she was back to glaring at her phone which Javid assumed was dead and for a long, uncomfortable beat, Javid thought she would ignore her. "I'm sorry, I didn't mean to make you worry," And she sounded that way too. "I was behind the cabin searching for cellular reception." Toman held up her phone. "I was returning from the back when I saw you two walk deeper into the woods."

Javid didn't know why she'd been worried in the first place, Toman wasn't the kind of person to hold petty grudges. It didn't mean she hadn't been hurt by Javid shutting her out and Javid still owed her one hell of an apology.

"Are you trying to get in touch with your family?" Pari asked.

Javid moved to her side of the room and shrugged off her coat, casting it on the lower bed; she wanted to change her pants too. The ends of her slacks were wet from the snow but she'd probably have to wait, it was already seven in the morning and if they wanted to stick to the schedule that she'd meticulously planned out, they'd need to leave soon.

Javid registered Toman's snort of derision absentmindedly. "I could go years without talking to anyone from my family."

"Is family trauma a requirement to be a part of this group?" Delnaz said sarcastically from the kitchen area; Javid could see that she was brewing a kettle of tea.

"I have no family trauma." Javid chirped in. She half considered stepping into the bathroom to use the mirror but she didn't want to miss any of the conversation, no matter how trivial it was. Besides, she didn't need the mirror to know that her cheeks were flushed and not just from the cold – and her eyes were brighter, alive than they'd ever been. Javid had not just been handed hope, she'd been given purpose. Not that she'd ever doubted the authenticity of her mission but what she'd witnessed an hour ago had changed things, changed her and introduced her to a whole new world that she'd never thought existed beyond her wildest dreams. And she couldn't wait to tell her friends about it.

"Neither do I," Haleh added, a little grudgingly as if admitting that she had a normal family meant losing her street credit.

Delnaz reeled back on the balls of her heels in surprise. "You? No way, I'd have bet enough money on mummy issues."

"Haha, very funny." Haleh said, but there was no heat in her tone.

"You were probably dropped as a child then, because something has to explain why you're so…" Delnaz trailed off, looking to Pari for help.

"Finish that sentence, I dare you, Delnaz."

It was a strange thing to watch Delnaz banter so freely with Haleh.

"Cold." Delnaz finished, a cheeky smile on her face. Haleh just leaned back, sitting on the floor with one shapely leg crossed over the other.

Haleh casually flexed her wrist or rather, the glinting diamond tennis bracelet on her wrist. "It must be the diamonds. You know how those western rappers call gems ice."

"Real smooth, Haleh." Delnaz gave a snort and turned off the stove. She poured tea into a cup and began to stir.

Javid moved away from them to where Toman was pacing, phone raised in the air in search for cellular connection. "Hey, are you alright? You seem really desperate for the connection."

Toman halted mid pace. She shook her head, her ponytail whipping back and forth. She was wearing the same cap from yesterday but this time she hadn't bothered with tucking her entire hair into it. "Some of us work remotely, you know." She said although there was no real malice in her voice, there was still a sarcastic undertone that caused Javid to bristle. "I'm trying to get a connection to contact a client awaiting updates on his case."

"I'm sorry, I didn't know you would be working while with us — on this mission." Javid regretted the words the moment she spoke them. She winced at her lack of tact knowing that her statement all but questioned Toman's loyalty and priorities. "I'm sorry, I didn't mean for it to come out like that." She gave a sigh, wondering how it was barely two days and she was already screwing up whatever friendship she'd been trying to build between the two of them.

Toman kept her face carefully blank, she nodded her head — the only outward sign that she took no offence. "Apology accepted. And I'm not working, at least not exactly. I was in the middle of a case before I got your message."

"Is it anything interesting?" Javid asked but she knew the answer already. Toman had retired from the police force for her own peace of mind, so while she might sigh and grumble about the predictability of her clients, she craved that same predictability. It was safe and it was hard to make terrible mistakes that would cost innocent lives. After all, the kind of jobs she took were cheating scandals or missing pet cases. Both are likely to end without any-one getting too hurt. Divorce is a trendy thing straights have got going on, by the way, Toman was fond of saying.

"Just the usual, husband wants me to find proof that the wife is cheating. He's extra paranoid too." Toman added. Javid gave a sympathetic wince on her behalf. "Hence the calls at random times even though I've told him several times that the process isn't like a swipe of his credit card and boom, house bought."

"He's desperate though, " Javid said, unsure why she was de-fending Toman's pesky clients. The truth was, she was just grateful that Toman wasn't the type to hold a grudge and was still talking to her.

Toman seemed to mull over Javid's input and gave a shrug. "I don't doubt that." She said, and that was that, she didn't offer any more information. Javid wondered if the slight sting in her chest was the same thing Toman had felt when she'd been shut out.

"You're not asking me where I went with Farzaneh," Javid said softly, too soft that it was a wonder that Toman heard it above the cacophony of conversation happening around them.

"I trust that you're going to tell us when you get the chance to." Toman answered dismissively like there was nothing to worry about but Javid noticed, she noticed how she had blatantly lumped herself with the others. Not that there was anything with including herself as part of the team but she was so clearly throwing Javid's words back in her face. Reminding Javid of how she'd shut her down moments after they had shared their kiss. And the worst part of it all was that Toman meant no pettiness, she was just saying out loud what Javid had been afraid of saying. She'd definitely received the memo loud and clear.

"Toman, I'm sorry for what I implied last night. it's just--" Javid trailed off, she didn't exactly fancy herself an orator but she was a solid talker, it was the usual Toman effect to make her sound like a bumbling teenager.

"Look, it's fine, Javid. You were protecting yourself and you've always been especially glad at doing that

The words, though perfectly ordinary, caused Javid to flinch and cause a well of indignation to rise up in her. Did Toman just seriously imply that Javid was naturally close off?

Javid inhaled a deep breath, trying to chase away the hurt she'd felt bubbling up in her, she told herself that Toman was allowed to be hurt and petty if she wanted. Then again, this was Toman and petty wasn't her style; if she gave a scathing assessment of character then it was sure to be a hundred percent true and the reminder didn't settle well with Javid. Still, she'd tried to apologise and she'd been shut down but no grudges were being held. They could move past this and go back to being friends.

"Right, I'm naturally protective and not just of myself. Of all of you, I would do anything for you all." She said, wanting to add more specifically; especially you, Toman. She didn't, only flashed a brief smile at Toman. "Well, I'm sorry there's no cell reception. I'd offer my phone but I'm pretty sure it's the same thing."

"No worries, we'll be in the city soon and I'll be able to send messages to my heart's content." Her words were dry, Toman humour that for the first time, Javid was unable to understand.

CHAPTER TEN
Jajrud to Abali

They were back on the road but this time, Delnaz was sitting shotgun in Javid's two seat car. Javid was a picture perfect poster child for concentration, her gaze strictly ahead and unwavering, her hands firmly on the steering wheel. On the sides of the road were trucks clearing out snow to make way on the highway but blissfully it didn't seem to be snowing anymore, in fact the sun was out in full force, working too to melt residue snow on surfaces.

"I feel blessed seeing the beauty of Jajrud for the first time." She said aloud.

Javid's gaze didn't waver but she did admit, "It's the same for me, I haven't been in this city for far too long, it didn't feel like I deserved to come here and have some fancy vacation by the river; stay in a fancy cottage and pretend like my people aren't suffering."

Javid did have a bit of a hero complex, Delnaz thought but not unkindly. It wasn't a terrible thing to care for and love ones country. Heck, Delnaz loved Tajikistan and cared about her people but she didn't bear their burden on her neck and beat herself up about it. She'd been offered the chance to save Farsi-speaking countries and had gladly taken it but she wasn't sure it was quite the same thing for Javid. Immigrant kids often felt a splitting guilt for leaving their countries; seeking better lives and finding it as if there was some pre-written prerequisite in the universe that said they had no right to be happy about having better opportunities if their country continued to suffer. Delnaz didn't think that was a healthy thought to carry and she didn't want to mention this train of thought to Javid who would no doubt become instantly defensive.

She chose to change the topic to what she thought was a lighter one, "Does it snow like this often?"

She expected Javid's stern face to soften and get lost in memories of a wintery Tehran but instead, the skin of her forehead dipped slightly in a frown and Delnaz wondered what she'd said wrong.

"Oh, about that, Farzaneh says it's an unnatural winter, it doesn't usually snow in Tehran or its suburbs, and at least not during this time or with this intensity." Javid said.

Delnaz nodded as if she understood and she did, a little. Her flight to Tehran had almost gotten canceled because of the weather; it wasn't a pretty winter – the kind that seemed flowery and magical. No, this one was all blizzard and storm, taking the parts of the city's power with it. She wasn't surprised that it wasn't natural.

She waited for Javid to offer more information about it but she was back to wearing her stern expression. Delnaz gave a tired sigh; she suspected Javid and Toman weren't on good terms. She'd thought that the way they stuck together for the drive to the cabin meant that there would be rekindling of their romantic flame. They'd even seemed so in tune with each other in a way that gave Delnaz hope. She wasn't in the habit of pairing her friends together – the thought of Haleh and Pari together still felt uneasy for her – but she'd always thought that Toman had a soft spot for Javid and that Javid had reciprocated those feelings. Now it was barely day two into their mission and they were avoiding each other's company.

When they'd left the cabin, trudging through the thick of the forest to return to the side of the road where Javid and Farzaneh had left their cars, Delnaz had loudly claimed shotgun with Javid. The ride sandwiched between Haleh and Pari had been nothing short of nauseating and the last thing she wanted was a repeat of it. She'd expected to be lightly rebuked by Toman but the said womxn had her eyes on her phone, raising it in the air at odd angles that deeply amused the rest of them.

Javid too had remained silent, talking with Farzaneh in hushed whispers that made Delnaz curious. Even when they'd burst out of the forest and into the highway again, she'd made a beeline straight for Javid's car – expecting Toman to race her to it. It hadn't happened. Toman had silently gone with Haleh, Pari and Farzaneh. And Delnaz had ended up with Javid. A decision she was slowly coming to regret. Normally, she enjoyed Javid's company but not now when she was frowning broodingly.

"So you're just going to dangle that important piece of information over my head like bait and not actually tell me the whole detail?" Delnaz asked sarcastically. This was what she'd been trying to avoid, her friends getting into relationships with each other. It was all fine and dandy when they were in the honeymoon stage but when the fights came, it became awkward for everybody.

Javid took her eyes off the wheel for a brief second to meet Delnaz's gaze, confusion swimming in their depths. "Pardon me, love, did I say something wrong?" She did sound genuinely confused and Delnaz realised that Javid was unaware that she was brooding visibly and worse, she was clearly lost in her thoughts. That couldn't be a good thing for driving.

"You were talking about how Farzaneh told you that the weather was unnatural." Delnaz prompted.

"Oh, yeah," Javid echoed as if she'd forgotten words that had been said less than two minutes ago. "She said that this happens every time some group goes looking for the sword. I don't know how to explain it or if it makes much sense but the sword is connected not only to Iran but also to other Farsi speaking countries."

"Like Tajikistan and Afghanistan, sharing the same language,"

Javid gave a nod, "Yeah. The sword's power is connected to these three countries – stronger in Iran because that's where it is located. It's so powerful that even the slightest hint of it being discovered can change our worlds. The snowstorm in Iran and the power being out as a consequence. Farzaneh told me that the sign manifests in strange ways and for some reason, all it does is give me a lot of hope about this, about our mission. If it hasn't been found yet and it has the power to change the world around us, you can only imagine how it would change us for the better when we find it."

Silence settled over them for a long second. Delnaz was filled with awe and a little fear; they were dealing with something much stronger than they'd thought they were. She shook her head, trying to stick to the optimistic side of it. They were going to make history in a matter of days and they were going to save their countries.

"So, did you?"

Javid's sudden question snapped Delnaz out of her thoughts. She blinked, returning back to the world of melted snow, away from the image of grandeur that had formed in her mind. "Did I what?"

"Notice anything out of the ordinary when you were in Tajikistan? Especially when you were leaving."

Delnaz hummed a noncommittal tune; it was only when the garbled melody burst from her lips that she realised she hadn't sung once since she arrived in Iran. She'd never gone a day without singing, when she wasn't singing at work; she was singing at home, warming up and testing her pitch. Singing had once been something that she enjoyed doing until she'd had to use that talent to survive then it hadn't been special for her ever since. Now as she hummed as she thought, she knew that it was the first time in years that singing hadn't been a chore for her. She thought of Javid's question, about noticing anything out of the ordinary when she was leaving her home country. Truthfully, she'd been too excited about leaving that she hadn't paid much attention to anything.

She closed her eyes, inhaling as she tried to remember being back in the back seat of the cab that drove her to the airport.

She remembered that it had smelt cloying sweet in the cab as if the driver had left fruit to rot. She remembered that the radio had been on, the bass set high and loud, celebratory music pulsed through the vehicle, thinking about it now, she ought to have been annoyed by the raunchiness of the music but she hadn't been. Despite the smell, she'd bobbed her head along to the music, she had looked out the window and saw that the streets had been transformed; somehow the colour of the night had been brighter too. Everywhere around her, people had been dancing, drinking on the side of the streets, celebrating something she wasn't a part of.

The moment had seemed Technicolour and Delnaz wasn't sure how to explain it to Javid, at least not in a way that wouldn't sound silly; 'there was dancing and drinking everywhere so yeah, there's your sign'

She shook her head at last, clearing the vision in her head. "Not really. I mean, the mood on the streets had seemed more celebratory than anything else. It wasn't close to the blizzard in Iran."

Javid didn't look at her as if she was stupid; she just shook her head, smiling genuinely. "Iran is the home of Gordafarid's sword; I think a blizzard makes sense. But I believe you; I'll take celebratory over fire falling from the sky in Tajikistan."

Delnaz let out a small chuckle at that.

"It's a good sign, Del," Javid added almost reverently.

The last thing Delnaz wanted was to be accused of being a sceptic so she kept her thoughts to herself, peacefully nodding along. She had a feeling though that even though she'd told Javid that nothing had happened in Tajikistan, Javid would have found a way to relate it to the sword. She wasn't a skeptic, she believed in the sword's existence and definitely in its power but Javid was starting to remind her of a fanatic and she wasn't sure how to feel about that.

***

"You are quiet." Toman said, half hesitant in the drawl of her words as if she was afraid she'd set the two of them off and they would go wild in the car.

Haleh rolled her eyes, leg crossed over the other and spine straight as if she was seated front row at a fashion show and not in the back of a jeep that kept jostling with the bumpy road. "Let me guess, Delnaz told you how we couldn't keep our hands off each other."

Pari looked up from the book she was studiously reading; Toman had glimpsed the cover earlier and knew that it was written in Farsi. "I think we scared her." She said seriously.

Haleh shook her head, a slow smirk spreading on her face. "No, we broke her."

Toman shook her head from side to side, she didn't understand what Haleh gained from the little games she liked to play with people.

"Delnaz didn't have to tell me anything, the two of you have been flirting since yesterday at Farzaneh's café." Toman pointed out, she gave a tired sigh. She normally didn't mind silence but she needed out of her head briefly and the two people she'd been counting on to hold conversation had chosen to be strategically silent.

She didn't bother trying to talk to them, she leaned back in the seat and closed her eyes, try as much as she could but she was still hurt by Javid's actions the previous night. She'd thought they were friends before anything else and because the romance side of their relationship was dead and buried didn't mean that they were nothing. But Javid had treated it just like that, as if she couldn't be just friends with her.

"Is there a reason why you're brooding?" Pari asked, cutting through Toman's thoughts.

She could feel their eyes on her, curious. Toman was the last person they'd ever expect to talk about her feelings and maybe they thought she'd make an exception now. She didn't though, not because she was in the habit of being closed off but because

Javid probably wouldn't want that. They weren't like Haleh and Pari with the habit of making their private business public. If Javid wanted to pretend like all was fine and dandy between them then Toman would oblige her wish.

"I haven't been able to get a hold of my niece." She opened her eyes and finally admitted the other thing that was bothering her. Her friends' reactions were comical.

"You have a niece?" Pari.

"You have family?" Haleh.

A huff of laughter escaped Toman's lips. "Cutting, Haleh." She deadpanned.

"What's wrong with your niece?" Pari asked, already closing her book on her lap in concern, ready to give all her attention to Toman.

Their concern unnerved Toman in the slightest because she wasn't used to having so many people show concern for her so obviously. Toman didn't have much people she could call friends – scratch that – outside of Haleh, Pari, Delnaz and Javid, she didn't really have friends. Sure, there were people she could hang out with if she wanted, she'd once been in the police force and she still had a lot of contacts in the force. She wasn't exactly starving of phone numbers on her phone. But she preferred to keep most people at arm's length, not for a fear that they'd hurt her but because she'd grown so weary of social interactions and obligations that she'd rather keep them to the bare minimum.

She didn't need anyone to do anything for her. Pari's concern was welcome though, strange to Toman but very welcome.

"She didn't come from the stork, you know. Of course she has family," Pari rebuked Haleh lightly. "What's wrong with your niece?"

"Nothing's wrong with her. I'm her legal guardian since her parents died a few years ago. Anyways, she's at university now and I try to call her almost every day but I haven't been able to because of shitty network connection because of the snowstorm."

"And you're worried about her," Pari finished. "I'm sure she's fine, Toman. Stuck in her dorm yeah but she'll be okay."

Toman knew that a part of her was being irrational – she'd always been good at calling herself out on her own bullshit like a totally independent womxn. Helia would be fine but Toman still hated being cut off from her for almost two days. Javid's message had come at a particularly inconvenient time but Toman had stuck to it because she'd promised. She'd sent Helia a detailed email on her whereabouts just in case and even though Toman had mostly good feelings about their mission it didn't stop her from preparing for an alternative ending. She didn't plan on dying any time soon but a part of her was still feeling sentimental, wanting to hear her niece's voice; make sure she was fine too because the snowstorm had come without warning.

"I know that." Was all she said in response to Pari's reassurance.

"Doesn't hurt to hear it still," Pari said softly. "Keep trying to get in touch with her though."

Toman gave a curt nod and for the first time that day, shoved her phone into the deep pocket of her coat. Pari was right after all, it was nice to hear vain assurances sometimes.

"You mentioned something about the blizzard coming with no warning, is it something that happens often here?"

It was Farzaneh that answered, "No, it's not. In fact, this is an abnormality."

"And you know why." Toman said, her words weren't a question, just a confident statement. It wasn't too farfetched to say that Farzaneh knew everything that was concerned with Gordafarid's sword and everything else in relation. It wasn't difficult to deduce that the weather change was all thanks to the sword, although she didn't know how but she was sure Farzaneh would explain.

"Seriously?" Pari's voice was coloured with surprise. Haleh sat forward a little, a calculating look entering her eyes.

Haleh's eyes met Farzaneh's eyes from the dashboard mirror, she averted her eyes and stared out the window, watching the scenery pass by swiftly, the sun was out now and unlike yesterday – it came back in full glory. The snow was almost vanished from the road. She turned back to the conversation to see Farzaneh nodding in that sage way of hers. "Tehran is reacting to the possibility of Gordafarid's sword being discovered at last."

"By creating an unforgiving blizzard?" Haleh sounded incredulous and Toman didn't grudge her for it.

"If we had any sense of self preservation, we'd be giving up on finding the sword instead of moving in its direction." Haleh added but her voice was refreshingly jocular, carrying a hint of excitement in it as if the realisation that they were gambling with their lives was hilarious, no, as if it was a challenge. There was nothing else in the world that Haleh loved more than a challenge; pretty girl supposed to be off limits, long lost sword with the ability to destroy them – all were the same to Haleh. She never saw the difference.

"Do you know how many years Gordafarid's sword has waited to be found?" Farzaneh asked, her voice a soft, deadly thing that made the hair on Toman's arm stand up. There was intensity in her voice that she had never heard before. Toman liked to think that she was a good judge of character and her first impression of Farzaneh had been that she was softly spoken and soothing, with the type of voice that was reminiscent of a good storyteller. It seemed that Farzaneh could be terrifying too. Not that Toman had underestimated her in the first place. She had to be terrifying or at least powerful enough to earn the title of pathfinder. There was definitely more to the eye than Farzaneh seemed.

"I don't know, years?" Haleh answered uncertainly, even unsure her answer was sharply directed like an accusation.

"Hals, if you track the history of the sword's existence, it's not just years – it's fucking centuries." Pari cut in.

Farzaneh nodded her head from the driver's seat. "Pari is right. The sword has been hidden away for more than centuries. After Gordafarid basically won the war she led against Sohrab and the

Turanian army, there were plenty of rumours how her sword was enchanted and how she'd triumphed over her enemies because of its power. No matter if those rumours were true or not. Gordafarid never picked it up again, she chose to hide the sword for two reasons – to keep the power away from unscrupulous people and in the case that the sword would once again rise to the occasion and save our people again."

"Wow, you talk like an historian. How do you know so much about the sword?" Pari asked, she sounded deeply impressed.

"Pari, she's the pathfinder." Toman said dryly.

"What does that have to do with the weather?" Haleh asked, trying to steer the conversation back to the original question.

"Iran is the home of Gordafarid's sword and every time the sword has come close to being rediscovered, the signs begin to manifest physically; in this case, as a snowstorm." Farzaneh explained.

Toman glanced at Haleh, saw that her curiosity wasn't the slightest bit abated, it seemed that Farzaneh's answer had only stoked her curiosity like a flame. It was understandable. Haleh wasn't exactly a sceptic but she wasn't the type of the person to believe when it was said that the sky was blue. Haleh would be determined to understand how and if it was the truth. Toman didn't think Haleh would find the answers to her question satisfactory – she'd just want to answer more questions.

"Whoopee doo – I'm sorry, Farzaneh, I'm in no way saying that you're a liar but I'm a big believer in concrete evidence backing a supposed truth." Haleh argued.

"No offence taken." Came Farzaneh's good-natured reply.

"But how does the sword know that it is close to being discovered?" Pari finished Haleh's question, she too looked like she wanted to know. Pari had a master degree in investigative journalism and although she spent her days at work co-anchoring a popular show, she still knew how to do the former.

And although Toman didn't show it, she too was curious. She didn't doubt the extent of Gordafarid's sword but there was still much she didn't know.

Pari caught the quirk of Farzaneh's lips in the rearview mirror as if she thought their questions and doubts were amusing. Maybe it was to her; after all, she was unarguably the one of all of them with the most information on the sword.

"In all these hundreds of years of the sword's existence, only two groups have gotten close to getting to the sword. Alas, Gordafarid knew what she was doing when she hid the sword – choosing to keep it in a place that pretty much guaranteed that it would never be found and if it was, only by the most resilient, worthy team."

"Let's go ahead and ignore that she just pretty much said our chances of discovering the sword are close to zero." Haleh muttered under her breath, but loud enough for Toman and Pari to hear it.

Toman's jaw dropped when Pari rolled her eyes at Haleh's behaviour. It seemed like Pari was equally sick of her attitude. Haleh needed to understand that there was no reason to be so challenging all the time; questioning motives, hurling quick jabs at the slightest provocation even when she was with friends. Toman wondered what had happened to Haleh to make her so defensive.

"Did you choose to ignore the part where she said the sword can sense when it's about to be found and consequently parts of Tehran is trapped in an unforgiving winter?" Pari snapped, or at least this was the closest to chiding as she'd ever been.

Pari was incapable of sounding stern with her friends. She just cared too much to do that. But this time, there was no misunderstanding that Haleh's doubt had displeased her very much. It was probably this realisation that caused Haleh to give a long sigh, the closest to defeat one would get from her.

"I'm sorry, Farzaneh," She echoed, her voice stripped of its usual sarcasm and sincerity shining through. "You'll hear no more interruptions from me as you finish your explanation."

Toman didn't get to see Farzaneh's reaction; she was staring outside the jeep window and noticed the moment Javid's two seat rental overtook Farzaneh's jeep. Farzaneh's pathfinding skills would be put to good use later but at the moment, Javid was running the show again. And for the first time ever, Toman didn't know what the plan was. She was so used to Javid disclosing close to everything to her that being shut out last night hard hurt. It wasn't even that the rejection was romantic; Toman could understand Javid not wanting to rekindle their romance because if she was being honest with herself, while she had a lot of unresolved feelings for Javid too, she didn't think a rehash of their whirlwind romance was the best thing, especially not at this time.

Still, she wished Javid would see her as more than an ex-lover, or start to see her as a close friend – which they'd been even before all the fucking and fighting.

"How does the sword know when it's going to be found?" Farzaneh echoed Haleh's question. "I can't tell you that." Maybe she was afraid that Haleh's promise was going to be broken so she swiftly added, "Not because I don't want to but because even I don't have all the answers. The title of pathfinder has been in my family for almost as long as the sword's existence. We're tasked with the responsibility of guardian and it's our duty to make sure the sword never falls into the wrong hands. There's something I showed Javid early this morning, a magical map – if you will – that tracks the sword's location. The grooves in it light up and trace the points, paths leading to the map, usually when this happens, I know that it means the sword is being hunted."

"Why didn't you show it to us?" Toman asked. She wondered if anyone else was offended that Javid had automatically become their leader. It wasn't that Toman wanted to be in charge anyways, she was perfectly content with following Javid's plan. Heck, she trusted Javid. But being relegated to the position of followership and being shut out of most of the important information didn't sit well with her.

"The map has been in my family for centuries. My ancestors died because they trusted the secret of the map with someone who had malevolent intentions." Farzaneh said matter of factly, not at all sorry that she'd kept the secret of the map from the rest of them. Toman could respect that conviction, could even respect her perfectly logical reasons but it didn't mean she wasn't still put off by the secrecy.

All her friends liked to think of Toman as the reasonable one, the steady rock when it was needed. The truth was that she'd learnt to keep her emotions under wrap for as long as she could remember; perks of growing up in an abusive household. It was a tough habit to break even now. The people in her life had already come to know her as a reliable friend which made it even harder for her to express herself. Sometimes, Toman wanted to rage but most times she was left gobbling down any feelings that rose up in her. She'd wanted to shout last night too. Instead, she'd let Javid's cutting words slide.

She let Farzaneh's words slide now.

"I guess that's understandable," Haleh said.

Silence bloomed in the small confine of the jeep until Toman was filled with the overwhelming urge to break it, to say something.

"You said there have only been two groups that have gotten close to acquiring the sword and its power, what happened to them? I feel like we need to sync our information since I've done some research too – what went wrong with the groups before us and how can we make sure we don't make the same mistakes that they did." Toman said, her voice fervent in a way that it rarely ever was.

Farzaneh was silent for a minute. She just stared ahead at the road before her; the countryside was fading, the fields of frozen sunflowers drifting behind them until several, fairly modern buildings began to pop up on both sides of the road, scanty at first but as Farzaneh drove past a sign that read; welcome to Abali city. The Damavand Mountain loomed in the far distance like an ominous shadow of the road. In less than two weeks, if all went well, they would be headed to the mountain, to make history, no, to rewrite history. For the first time, Toman had the wind knocked metaphorically out of her, she was still thinking of the grandness of it all when Farzaneh spoke.

"The first group perished in the Yellow Flowers Cave, in fact, the story made local news when it happened over fifty some years ago." Farzaneh said, her voice unnaturally cold as she spoke. She sounded detached as if she was reading from a piece of paper. "My mother told me the story of how it happened. They were so close to the sword, but in the end their group had been divided – priorities different. Some of them had pure intentions with the sword and others, not so much."

Toman shared a glance with Pari and Haleh and knew they were wondering the same thing; were their intentions pure.

"Javid knows this but the rest of you do not, so I'll say it again; the sword will never fall into the wrong hands – it can never happen or it would spell doom for the whole world. Gordafarid knew that and she went through extreme means to make sure the sword was protected." Farzaneh continued. "But the recent group – two womxns who I met ten years ago, were the last group to attempt to find the sword and save our countries."

A shiver ran down Toman's spine, the way Farzaneh talked about this new group, with pain in her voice. Those womxns must have meant so much to her, she must have cared for them.

"Were they not worthy?" Haleh asked hesitantly, her voice a soft whisper.

Farzaneh ignored her question even as her fists tightened around the steering wheel. "Shirin Shah and Nazanin Hesami."

The former name rang a bell of recognition in Toman's mind; Shirin Shah was a renowned and reclusive sculptor. She'd become even more reclusive in recent years and hadn't carved a sculpture in a decade. Shirin had simply stopped existing, she'd stopped making art, stopped making the rare appearances at important functions as she used to. The art world had been sent into shock, their beloved artist had just seemed to cease existing. Toman only knew that much about her because the news had taken the whole world by storm; art lover or not.

Pari and Haleh didn't seem to register the names, their faces blissfully blank. But Toman's was racing, Shirin Shah had attempted to find Gordafarid's sword and she'd obviously failed. And Nazanin Hesami could be the reason why.

"I'll tell you the story of Shirin Shah and Nazanin Hesami; they were like you, looking to rewrite history. I'll tell you how they met. You'll hear the story of how they fell from Shirin's mouth soon."

Realisation dawned on all three of them but it was Pari who breathed the words to life, "That's why we're going to a party. Shirin Shah will be there."

Farzaneh nodded. "Nazanin Hesami was an arts journalist and Shirin Shah was a womxn on a mission to save her country…"

CHAPTER ELEVEN
Tehran, October 2021

The mall is surprisingly crowded at this time of the night. Nazanin pauses in her steps as she realises that the quick run to grab wine for dinner at her parents' house in an hour's time might not be as quick as she thought.

She hesitates, eyes sweeping the small crowd gathered at the Morvarid food court to her right. There is the distinct smell of grease and warm dough in the air. She ignores the growl her stomach gives.

She only has split seconds to make a decision; arrive at her parents' house without a gift or brave the night crowd. She shakes your head — the thought of settling on the former choice causing her grip on her handbag to tighten. Her mother would make passive aggressive comments about her being a struggling journalist and her father would shake his head and remind her that a medical degree would have been the better choice. Already, she could hear their voices in her head and she takes a subconscious step forward — brave the crowd it is.

She quickens her steps, skillfully weaving through the crowd before her like a footballer would dribble past a line of defenders. Hurried apologies leave her lips the few times she bumps into people. She doesn't wait for the sarcastic comments that will no doubt follow.

Beside, she has other things to worry about, her parents are also unforgiving. She steps into the grocery store and lets out a small sigh of relief as it's not as crowded as the main entrance of the mall. There are a few people around though, a womxn dressed in a suit darting around with a shopping basket placed at her hip like one would carry a baby.

Nazanin's eyes follow the womxn for a brief second and she allows herself the luxury of making up a story for the womxn. Maybe she's a working mother or a wife who still has to make grocery runs even though she leaves her office late. The womxn probably gets a lot of shit from people about being too career oriented and how her family is going to suffer for it.

She shakes her head, drawing herself away from the fantasy that is growing in her head. Nazanin used to want to be a writer, it was a whole phase when she was about seventeen until her father told her that writers starved to death on their dreams.

She never went past the occasional romance short story but some days, she finds herself wanting to pick up a pen again, reimagine the stories of ordinary people. Another dream crushed by the parents, her mind mockingly reminds her.

She takes brisk steps towards the aisle, walking past tall shelves of baby formula. This mall is just a ten minute drive away from Turquoise's building but she's rarely ever here to shop. She favours a small grocery shop across the street where she lives. As she continues to weave through aisles, eyes squinted suspiciously at each shelf, she realises that she has no idea where the wine aisle is.

She pauses, looking around for an employee. She hears low conversation and makes a sharp left turn, skidding to an abrupt stop to prevent what would have been an embarrassing slip on the tiled floor.

Nazanin places one hand over her chest in relief and looks up. There's a male employee in a red shirt gazing at her with deep amusement, he definitely saw her almost fall.

She plasters a bright smile on her face that is every bit as false as it looks.

"Good evening, sorry to bother you." She starts, wincing a little at her own words. She's often been told that she needs to be a little more assertive. She's within every right to ask this employee for help, that is his job after all. "Can I be directed to the wine aisle?"

The employee smirks deeply, his eyes roaming her form in a way that made her uncomfortable. Her eyes dart to his name tag — Phillip. Knowing his name makes her feel a tad better, a name means information to report if he continues to make her feel uncomfortable.

Thankfully, he wordlessly gestures to the shelf behind him and Nazanin bites her lip.

She mutters a low thank you and moves to stand in front of the tall shelf, browsing the options of wine. She knows nothing about wine, it's usually her elder brother's duty to bring the wine for family dinners but he's been in the United Kingdom now, doing his PhD in Law.

She texted him earlier for the name of their parents' favourite wine and now, she's realising the mistake she made. She never asked him how much it was.

Nader prior to leaving for the UK was already well to do as a lawyer in the firm he worked in. He made four times her salary, he could easily afford to buy his parents expensive wine.

Nazanin could not, at least not without breaking through her savings. She hesitates, the stubborn urge to prove to her parents that she's doing well as an art writer battles against logic. She doesn't make enough being a junior writer for Turquoise magazine. Writing about art might have seemed like the perfect picture on paper — something that would pacify her parents, she'd gone to journalism school after her bachelor's in art — but it's far from how she imagined her life. It's not as glamourous as Pinterest boards, she spends her days churning out uninteresting articles. There's far too less field work for her as a junior writer.

In the end, she settles for a cheaper bottle of red wine and hopes to hell that her parents don't notice the difference. Satisfied with the completion of her task, she wanders around for a few more minutes, grabbing potato chips and splurging on a new lipstick.

In less than twenty minutes, she's paid for what she bought and is walking back to her car. The euphoria from a few minutes ago has faded, she doesn't remember where she parked her car.

She stands between a van and a red sports car, glances around and flinches when a car door slams in the distance. A street lamp buzzes and flickers off. She shakes her head, silently reminding herself that she is a perfectly reasonable womxn. There isn't some monster blending in with the darkness, watching her. She just needs to find her car and not be late for dinner.

Nazanin resumes her search and as she weaves between rows of parked cars her fear gives way to mild irritation, the sole of her pumps clicking in quick, curt steps. It is only when she pauses for a moment that she realises that somebody's been following her.

She heard their footsteps, a lot more subtle than her own but she was too angry to pay any attention to it. It's only when she stops now that the person screeches to a too late stop. She drops the plastic bag she'd been holding on her other hand, the wine shatters inside but Nazanin doesn't register that either. Her other hand is digging furiously into her handbag, rummaging for the can of pepper spray she keeps. Her knuckles brush the cool can but before she can pull it out a sudden force slams into her skull.

Bright light explodes in her vision and she stumbles back, tripping and falling to the floor. Nazanin bites down on her tongue and warm blood fills her mouth, she spits it out, blinks heavily to clear her vision.

A man stands over her, the street lamp behind him is too dim but she catches a glimpse on his face, notes his red shirt. Although she cannot see it, she's sure he's smirking.

The employee from the wine aisle.

She scrambles to sit, he reaches for her arm and drags her to her feet like she's a rag doll.

"I saw the way you were looking me inside." He mutters into her ear.

A ragged sob breaks from her lips. Her mind is racing at a thousand miles, somehow it feels like she's dreaming. Because this can't be real, she cannot be getting attacked by a man she only noticed because of how uneasy she felt in his presence. She barely spoke one word to him.

He presses his lips into her neck and bile rises in her throat.

"Please." She screams the word and regrets it when a heavy hand clamps over her mouth, pinching her nostrils close. She kicks him in the shin and the monster has the audacity to laugh. His hold momentarily slackens and she tries to jerk away again.

She receives another blow to the side of her head and falls to her knees.

"Help, somebody help!" She screams.

He pulls her up to her feet again and slaps her heavily. "Is this how you want to play it? I saw you looking at me!" He yells, as if it's outrageous she's fighting back.

Nazanin mutters something else, a plea, her lips move but he strikes her again and again. She's pretty sure that if her attacker wasn't holding her up, she'd be on the cold ground. Dark spots dance in her vision, she tries and fails to fight it, dreading what will happen if she passes out.

He's tugging at her skirt now. She weakly tries to hold on to the memory of his name — Phillip — a name means that this happened, that he exists, that...

Her attacker is suddenly thrown off her and she collapses on the ground, bruising her arm as she tries to break her fall.

A female shout breaks the night, she hears the sound of bone crunching over and over again. She blinks several times, crawls to her knees and finds her attacker knocked out cold and a womxn dealing blows to his face.

"Is he dead?"

The words don't leave her lips but she must have made a sound because her rescuer looks up, fist hovering mid air.

The womxn straightens and gives Philip a final kick. She reaches for Nazanin and offers her a hand. For the longest second, Nazanin just stares at the womxn, it's like a scene out of a superheroine movie; the heroine — cape fluttering in the wind reaching out a hand to the person they just saved.

Except, this womxn isn't wearing a cape, just jean overalls and tall combat boots. She also has the longest dreadlocks Nazanin has ever seen on anyone in real life. The night breeze is not strong enough to cause them to sway and something tells her that very little can shake this womxn.

It's only when the womxn slowly lets her outstretched hand fall that Nazanin realises that she has been staring for too long. Shame burns through her body as she casts a look at her attacker. Somehow she feels ridiculous.

"Are you hurt?" The womxn says.

Nazanin is silent. She contemplates playing off the whole situation. "Only my pride."

"That man hit you." Her rescuer says darkly. "More than once." The womxn's eyes flicker away briefly. "Is he your boyfriend?" The womxn sounds so appalled that Nazanin manages a tiny smile, a movement that hurts. In fact, everywhere hurts, especially her face.

"No, he works in the mall. He... He followed me out." Her

voice is smaller than she wants it to be.

"Do you want me to come with you while you make a report?" The womxn says.

Nazanin shakes her head quickly. She's still shivering and it's not because of the cold. She doesn't want to report this man, what if he finds her again?

What if he hurt some other womxn? Both parts of her mind continue to war against each other.

"Please, I just want to go home." She says in a hurry.

"At least let me take you to the hospital. You're hurt."

"Where did you learn to fight like that?" Nazanin asked, ignoring the offer.

The womxn cracks a smile. "I used to be a warrior."

Nazanin blinks, unsure if she's supposed to laugh. She just stands there, shaking in the cold.

It's her mysterious rescuer that takes a look around and picks her bag up. "I believe this is yours."

Nazanin takes it quietly, reaching into it immediately and pulling out her pepper spray, holding it out between both of them. The womxn's stance doesn't waver, she doesn't seem hurt.

"I'll walk you to your car." She only says.

Nazanin is embarrassed by how relieved she feels.

True to her word, the womxn walks a few distance from her and she doesn't try to initiate conversation or pressure Nazanin to report the incident to the mall security.

After what seems like forever, Nazanin finds her car, tucked between two vans. She unlocks her car, feeling numb now. She gets into her car, casting one final look at her rescuer before shutting the door and pressing on the lock.

Nazanin sits there for a long time, waiting for tears, for hysterics or any emotional outbursts. She was certain she would die tonight, she'd come close to something worse. She glances down at her hands, mentally tracing the lines in her palm. She takes out her phone and texts her mom.

Won't be able to make tonight's dinner. I'll come by the house on Sunday.

It's the first time she's cancelled on her family's usual dinner. Earlier tonight, she'd been obsessed with impressing her parents with her wine choice. Less than two hours later, she just wants to go home and shower away all evidence of tonight. Priorities change faster than one can predict.

***

Two months later...

The air conditioner is broken and Darius is unashamedly chewing on his egg and fish salad. Nazanin can't stand the smell of fish and for all Darius's less than casual bragging that he's a mechanical engineering graduate, he's made no attempt to look at the air-conditioning.

Not for the first time, she can't help but wish she didn't share an office space with four other junior writers for Turquoise media outlet. Her coworkers are nice enough, but they have opposing habits that drive her crazy. Pooneh for example is the youngest of all of them — 22 years old and fresh out of the university — in the office and is obsessed with blasting trap music from her computer, claiming she's unable to work without music.

Nazanin is the opposite, she likes to maintain a fairly quiet work environment. Maybe if she was a little more assertive, she'd work a compromise with Pooneh. Or Maybe Pooneh is just too stubborn. Either way, all her coworkers drive her close to insanity each day.

She massages her temple with two fingers as Darius begins to hum as he chews. Her fingers hover above the keyboard of her laptop and her eyes drift to the little right corner at the bottom of the screen, noting the time — 9:30pm. Her article is due by 10pm. She knows she won't get any writing done.

Her brows dip in a furrow as she imagines the look on her editor's face as she asks for a time extension. Bijan — like he asks all the writers to call him — will remind her that she isn't exactly writing groundbreaking journalism.

"Hesami, you can't even write an article about the benefits of charcoal drawing in two days. What will you do when the big articles come?" He'll say, massaging his wrinkled temple and looking out of his depth. Bijan is in his late fifties and is the editor-in-chief of Turquoise. He's a man desperate to hold on to any wisps of youth and deluded to think that Turquoise will ever partake in any form of groundbreaking journalism.

Maybe once. The reason Nazanin joined Turquoise is because they used to be the it magazine when it came to art reporting. Those glory days are long gone — ended when the magazine was bought out by a former fashion model looking to turn the magazine into the Iranian Vogue. He failed and thrust the shambles into the hands of the first editor-in-chief he could hire.

Now the magazine's spread is full of sloppy written articles and spreads of art stationary; Here's the watercolour you should try out as a budding artist!

Only poor, wannabe artists actually read Turquoise for all Bijan's talk about groundbreaking journalism.

Nazanin gives a loud snort at the thought.

"What are you laughing about?" Darius asks, cutting through her thoughts. She blinks, she had forgotten his presence for a second.

"Nothing." She mutters, because she'd like to keep her job. Everybody knows how much Darius is a blabbermouth. He isn't such a bad coworker and he's one of the few good writers on Turquoise, Nazanin enjoys debating art with him. The both of them share a similar disdain for the unusual rise of people calling themselves artists. Except, in a small crowd of terrible Turquoise writers, Darius has gotten it into his head that he's the best thing since Sourdough sliced bread. Or rather, the best writer since Reza Ghassemi and he wears his pride high on his shoulders.

Nazanin won't deny that he's good but she hates how he so blatantly hates on the other writers to kiss up to Bijan.

"Are you ever going to finish that article?" He asks, coming to her desk to peer into her laptop.

She pauses and looks up — big mistake when he breathes out a laugh and she catches a strong whiff of the fish on his breath. She hates the way he stands too close to her and fights the urge to rudely tell him off.

"Bijan is too generous with all of you." He straightens, adjusts the belt on his waist and smirks. Nazanin gives him a look.

"Maybe Bijan should stop asking to write stupid articles that nobody wants to read. If he lets me write the topics I pitch at team meetings, maybe I'd write faster."

Darius rolls his eyes. Nazanin watches as he returns to his desk to tidy it up. He tosses the takeout pack into the bin and grabs the suit jacket he'd slung over his chair hours ago when the heat became a little too much. She didn't understand why he dressed like he was a corporate worker. To impress Bijan, probably.

"That's not how you do things." He argues. There's spinach between his teeth. Nazanin bites back a smile.

"Hmph." She mutters noncommittally.

"Bijan has a vision. You and the others will realise that soon when you get sidelined when the big news arrives." Darius continues.

Her eyebrows raise at that. Darius for all his talk was the first one to know when the decision to lay off the entire printing department was made.

"Big news?" Nazanin tries to sound nonchalant.

His smile grows even more smug, any more and he'd tear his face into two halves. She rolls her eyes.

"I'll be writing a feature soon, Nazanin Hesami . Watch out." He says, slinging his laptop over his shoulder. He walks to the door and waves a hand over his shoulder.

"Goodnight, Darius." She says lazily. She breathes a sigh of relief when he's gone. His words stay with her though. Turquoise hasn't written a feature in over a year. Features involve a high rising or celebrity artist — ranging from poets to sculptors to painters. There's usually a photoshoot and a launch party. Nazanin has been writing for the magazine for a few years now. But she's never written a feature and she might never, at least until under Bijan.

It's easily the most frustrating thing about her job, how she gets sidelined, her potential wasted on articles that don't interest her. At least Pooneh writes for the children section. She just writes filler articles, the ones that are skimmed impatiently before being flipped to the next page.

She recalls the first article she wrote, she was so proud of her name in the byline that she sent copies of that issue to her parents. It hadn't even mattered that the article she'd written was about introductory tips for new painters — no difference from thousands of articles on the internet. She'd been proud of it nonetheless. The next weekend at her parents', she'd asked what they thought about her article, she'd seen the blank look on her dad's face. He hadn't read her article. She'd never sent them any of her issues after that. So now, she tries to pretend that she isn't bothered that Darius is going to be the lead writer on whatever feature is coming.

He deserves it, she tells herself. She plasters a forceful smile on her face as she types a brief email to Bijan asking for an extension. At 10pm, she shuts down her laptop and stretches, her ruffled blouse rising with the movement. She grabs her bag and tucks her laptop under the same armpit, pepper spray can in the other. She rarely ever works this late at night and she isn't taking any chances this time.

As she walks out of the office, thoughts of that night fills her mind. It's the first time she's let herself think of it since it happened. Nazanin is wary of strangers, of dark alleys. She hasn't been to the mall since that night and sometimes, she thinks she's being followed.

But tonight, she isn't thinking of her attacker. She's thinking of the womxn that rescued her.

A small smile tilts her lips. She walks past Bijan's office down the hall. She's surprised when she finds the lights on and when she looks through the glass doors, she sees that he's talking to a womxn.

She tries to walk by quietly but his eyes catch hers and he stands from behind his desk. He mouths her name and beckons her.

He's going to chew into her, she can just tell. She pushes the door and enters, each time she's taken aback by how sterile his office is, the minimalist interior looks like something out of an interior decor magazine; white sofas for visitors, white wallpaper, tall potted plants in both left and right corners. There's no art anywhere in the office. Hell, even the junior writers' office has a couple of paintings on the walls — one of them a gift from a former featured artist.

Bijan is dressed similarly to Darius; grey suit and turtleneck shirt. At least his air-conditioning works.

"Hesami, I haven't received your article submission." Bijan is saying but Nazanin's eyes are on his guest. Her dreadlocks are packed up in a high bun but it's her. The womxn who rescued her.

The womxn swivels in her seat and catches Nazanin's eyes as she enters. There's a moment of blankness and then recognition.

"Hesami." Bijan shouts, slamming a fist on his table. She flinches at the sound of her name, Bijan is usually all bark and no bite but he's never taken things this far. For a brief moment, she thinks he'll fire her.

"Bijan, aren't you going to introduce us?" The womxn says,

her voice is a careless lilt but there's a smile playing on her black painted lips. Nazanin finds her eyes drawn to the womxn's mouth. She's never seen anyone wear black that bold, her eyes narrow infinitesimally, it isn't black — just a deep maroon.

Bijan seems to remember his guest and her jaw drops when he laughs abashedly and hurriedly apologises, all signs of the furious boss gone. Nobody, not even Darius can get Bijan to stop during his screaming fits.

"This is Nazanin Hesami, she's a junior writer for us." He says, gesturing a hand at Nazanin. "I don't think I need to introduce you if Nazanin knows her onions." It's a slight jab at her skill as a writer.

The womxn tilts her face up, even though Nazanin stands taller, she still manages to be intimidating. A sudden vision of her pummeling her attacker flashes.

"She might know my name but she doesn't know my face." The womxn drawls, in one smooth movement, she rises to her feet and holds out a hand. "Shirin Shah."

Nazanin gapes at the hand, the womxn's — no — Shirin's twinkle in delight.

"Are you going to leave my hand hanging again?" She asks.

"Again?" Bijan asks, looking from one womxn to the other in confusion.

Shirin lets her hand fall and Nazanin continues to stare. The womxn who saved her life isn't only the most badass womxn she's ever seen, but she's also the sculptor taking the world by storm with her creations. Nazanin has a few favourite art pieces; Michelangelo's David, Da Vinci's Starry Night and Shirin Shah's Artemis.

Shirin Shah is half Greek and half Iranian. She came into the art limelight when she sold her Artemis sculpture for a billion more than seven years ago. The famed sculpture was later auctioned off to a British Museum, launching her name into the international spotlight. The womxn through it has managed to keep her face out of the media coverage, choosing anonymity. There are a few grainy pictures of her on the internet but nothing detailed, she rarely granted interviews or requests for photoshoots. She is dubbed the modern Michaelangelo of sculpture because of her controversial work, she created full sculptures, many of them sexual, many of them depicting gory violence.

Those hands that punched the hell out of a predator are also the same hands she carves perfection with. Suddenly coming back to her senses, she reaches for Shirin's limp hand and shakes it profusely.

"Thank you, thank you." She mutters over and over. A soft smile appears on the sculptor's face. Only the both of them understand.

Bijan clears his throat harshly, breaking the moment. "I wouldn't want to keep you, Mrs Tavana." It's a clear dismissal of Nazanin.

"Ms." Shirin corrects but her smile is less genuine and more warning. Nazanin supposes she should be embarrassed by how much she knows about Shirin Shah's life — that is everything there is to know.

"Right, it was nice to meet you, Ms Tavana." Nazanin says, it's a gross understatement. Her whole life has been made.

"Call me Shirin."

Bijan's face says that Nazanin should do anything but that. She pretends not to see.

"Sure, Shirin." She amuses the sculptor as if she'll see her again. She wonders if Shirin is the feature Darius spoke of, and jealousy burns in the pit of her stomach.

She spins on her heels and leaves Bijan's office. She's going to go home and get intoxicated.

The next morning, Darius and Pooneh beat her to the office. The last writer, Effat is on maternity leave, she's at least seven years older than Darius who is a year older than her, Effat is usually the buffer between the three of them, Darius and Pooneh often team up to be unbearable but Effat's age card puts them in their place every time.

Nazanin walks to her desk after muttering a good morning greeting to the both of them. Already Pooneh is blasting some underground SoundCloud rapper and Darius is talking about how watercolour art isn't real art. Pooneh is agreeing.

"Could you turn down the music?" Nazanin cuts into their conversation.

"I can't work without music." Comes Pooneh's robotic answer. Nevermind that she's perched on the edge of her desk and sipping coffee mid words. "You're not working and I have an article due." Nazanin points out.

"Are you on your period?" Darius asks. He laughs at his own joke and pats down his tie.

Pooneh smacks his arm but she's giggling too.

Like she always does, she lets their comments slide and sits at her desk and gets to work. Maybe when she receives her paycheck at the end of the month, she'll invest in noise canceling head-phones. Sometime after 10am, she types the last sentence of her 1000s word article and submits it through email. Lunch comes and goes and she returns from eating at the fusion restaurant across the street and meets chaos in the office.

Bijan is re-knotting his tie and Pooneh is fixing her hair, spritz-ing almond oil on it and combing. It's the same frenetic energy she glimpsed in the photography department one floor below when she walked past.

"Is there a meeting?" She asks.

"Shirin Shah is coming in," Pooneh glances down at her watch. "— less than twenty minutes." She shrieks.

"She's our new feature." She adds.

Darius wordlessly reaches for Pooneh's mirror, Nazanin catches the slight tremor in his hold. He's nervous. "Bijan could have given us a warning." He moans.

Speaking of the devil, the said man walks past their office, poking his head through the door. "Town Hall, now."

All twenty five employees of Turquoise gather into the conference room. The excitement in the air is almost contagious, Turquoise's first feature in a while also happens to a world famous celebrity, it's the most interesting thing to happen to the magazine since its inception. A part of Nazanin is excited, Shirin Shah is a fascinating womxn. The bigger part of her is bitter, she's going to watch Darius get what she wants. He's not a better writer than she is, he just happens to be the most likeable.

She sits in the back with Arezoo, the closest person to a friend she has at the magazine. Arezoo is only passing time at Turquoise, the girl is the daughter of a popular Tehran politician and got the job as a photographer assistant because her father wants her to get a 'real' job. She doesn't care about art, or taking pictures of art and Turquoise's measly paycheck doesn't do anything for her.

Arezoo's dream is to be a photographer at Vogue. She's already built a huge followership on Instagram and is an influencer of sorts. So she spends her days at work talking crap about everybody.

"Interviewing Shirin Shah is a dream of art writers. Look at Darius, he looks like he might wet his pants." Arezoo says. She wiggles her eyebrows suggestively and Nazanin bites back her laugh.

It's true, Darius has wormed his way to the front and is trying to appear cool but the way he jiggles one foot every few seconds gives him away.

Somebody put him out of his misery, she thinks. Bijan steps into the room and Shirin Shah follows. The room erupts into shouts, it doesn't matter that they didn't know how this womxn look like. She dresses in a way that causes heads to turn twice — once and again to do a double take. Fierce makeup, check, head held high, check.

Arash, the lead photographer, is at the front of the conference room, taking pictures of the moment.

"I have an announcement to make." Bijan begins, he looks pleased, cheeks stretched wide in a big smile. For once, he's not just all talk. "Turquoise is doing a feature on the magnificent Shirin Shah."

The room erupts into deafening applause, Arash's camera clicks away and Shirin smiles indulgently. Nazanin's heart thuds in her chest, she watches Darius's face.

Unfortunately, Bijan drags out his speech, he talks about how he's proud of his staff, of the magazine, of how Turquoise has stayed true to its mission. Everyone in the room hangs onto his every word though, not because he says much sense but because he's building up the anticipation, reeling them in slowly. Everyone in the magazine wants to know which writer is covering the feature; who gets to unravel the mystery that Shirin Shah is? Who gets to bring glory to Turquoise?

"The photography team will cover the launch party and Ms Shah has granted her permission for a photoshoot at her studio in Abali city."

Polite applause follows this time too, but less vigorous. Get on with it, Bijan, damnit.

Bijan wipes his nose with his hand, a few distance from him, Darius straightens his tie. "The writer to cover Shirin Shah's feature is... Nazanin Hesami."

What. The. Fuck?

The room erupts into chaos again. Darius shoots up from his seat, his eyes search the room wildly, looking for her. Nazanin shrinks back in her seat even as Arezoo shakes her to stand up. In front, Shirin Shah is grinning broadly, something tells Nazanin that she's gotten exactly what she wanted. Bijan definitely didn't make this decision.

She should be thrilled that Shirin wants her. But she's unsure why. Eventually, she rises to her feet, she meets her saviour's eyes from across the room; challenge accepted.

Bijan doesn't take long to inform her about the truth the morning after. "If it was up to me, Darius would have been in charge of writing this feature but Shirin Shah specifically asked for you." His eyebrows are scrunched up together as he looks at her, the way one would look at a ten thousand piece puzzle — with misunderstanding.

His eyes sweep her form and Nazanin is sure that he's not appraising her ensemble; white faux fur coat over palazzo pants and baby blue pumps. He's searching for the special something, what Shirin Shah must have seen that he's missing. Nazanin hates to disappoint him, she isn't sure why Shirin chose her either. She is a damn good writer and she is better than Darius but Shirin Shah doesn't know that. Heck, she is sure that Shirin Shah didn't know her name up until yesterday.

"Either way, you're not a terrible writer." The closest to a compliment she will ever get from him. Bijan glances down at the open file on his desk, he wordlessly scribbles on a piece of paper and hands it to her. "Shirin Shah wants to get into this swiftly. You're to have dinner with her at this restaurant to discuss details." She glances down at the paper and mouths the words written silently. The restaurant is a familiar one, she's been there once with her family to celebrate her brother getting into his Ph.D program last year.

For the rest of the day, excitement bubbles in the pit of her stomach because, finally, she's going to get some answers. She was mulling over reasons why a womxn she only met once under unfortunate circumstances would pick her to do the most important job. The only reason Nazanin can think of is pity and the thought of it makes her stomach roil. It's terrible enough that she was almost beaten to death, but that someone else witnessed it. After logging off her computer for the day, she slings her coat over her shoulder and grabs her things. Not surprisingly, Darius disappeared, she glances at his desk and feels a twinge of guilt — a feeling she shakes off immediately, reminding herself that she isn't any less deserving.

Pooneh left about an hour ago, the younger womxn had been predictably cold to Nazanin throughout the day, obviously picking Darius's side. Nazanin finds that she isn't quite bothered by her coworker's coolness. She's never been friends with them anyways. It might make for a tense work environment but it's nothing that she cannot handle. She banishes all thoughts of her coworker from her mind and makes her way out of Turquoise's building. It's lightly drizzling outside and she skitters the small distance to her car.

A few minutes later, she's singing loudly to the car stereo as she navigates the highway. Nazanin finds the city is ever rowdy in the nighttime; Turquoise is located in the more swanky area of the province filled with new buildings — a popular Shomali restaurant, headquarters of leading banks, nightclubs and one thirty storey skyscraper belonging to a conglomerate.

The restaurant; Romance is among them. She once read a piece on a food blog and it was ranked as Abali's second most expensive restaurant, it's why her mother chose the place to celebrate Nader's scholarship, her mother enjoys spending money. Romance is certainly a place where a world famous artist would like.

Despite the light traffic on the drive, Nazanin gets there a few minutes before eight pm. She heaves a sigh of relief as she finds that the parking lot is scanty. It is a Thursday night after all.

Even though she's been here before, she finds herself surprised by the warm ambience of the interior of the restaurant. The decor is charmingly reminiscent of a grand ballroom, high ceiling with ancient Roman motifs painted on it, dark yellow light glows from the chandeliers suspended. The seats are tall chairs with velvet red plush that remind Nazanin of thrones. The waiters milling about the room were dressed formally, fitting suits and bow ties.

A maître approaches her with a smile, smoothing down an already smooth skirt in an absentminded gesture.

"Welcome to Romance."

Unusually flustered, Nazanin blinks several times. She's suddenly nervous. "I.. sorry, I have a reservation, under the name Shirin Shah."

The waiter checks her tablet and a smile stretches even wider in a manner that takes her aback. She doesn't remember the staff being this smiley.

"Of course, your friend is waiting." Before Nazanin can say a word in answer, the womxn is already leading, expecting her to follow, weaving expertly through the dining area.

Nazanin thought she was early and it turns out that Shirin Shah has been waiting for who knows how long.

A stuttered apology leaves her lips the moment she's at Shirin Shah's table even though the maître is right behind her.

"I'm so sorry to have kept you waiting."

The said womxn sitting down blinks in confusion. "Darling, you're early. Please sit."

She feels her cheeks heat up in a blush but she hurriedly takes the seat facing Shirin and bangs her knee on the side of the table rattling the glassware on it. She swallows a silent curse and looks up to find that Shirin Shah is fighting a smile. The warmth of it takes her aback, the smile is almost familiar but before she can think on it, the sensation leaves her.

"You're a clumsy one." Shirin says.

"Only when I'm nervous." Nazanin says lightly.

Shirin Shah arches an eyebrow but she doesn't say anything. The maître clears her throat, reminding both womxns of her presence.

"I'll send a waiter to come take your orders in a few minutes." She beams.

Nazanin looks down at the table for the first time, a bottle of wine with two tall glasses was waiting for them.

"I'll have to turn down wine." Nazanin says.

Shirin pauses in the action. "You don't drink?"

She isn't a big drinker and it's easier to go with that excuse so she nods.

"Liar." Shirin echoes softly. "You bought a bottle of wine that night."

So they're finally bringing that up. Nazanin stiffens in her seat, it's a topic she'd like to avoid but it's also one that might give her answers.

"Is that why I'm here? Selected because you pity me?" The words leave her lips in a bitter scoff. She can hear Bijan's groan of disapproval in her ear. "Ms Tavana." She adds hurriedly to soften her words.

"Call me Shirin. And yes, and no."

"That doesn't make any sense."

For the first time, Nazanin sees something like impatience flash through the other womxn's eyes. She's crossing a line here, the womxn is world famous and chose to grant her little art magazine the chance to interview her. She could easily change her mind. Nazanin knew this but still, she didn't back down.

Shirin seems to sense this and releases a sigh. "You're persistent." She says but it sounds like a compliment. She leans forward in her seat, all traces of her previous smile gone. "I have seen many womxns in your situation."

Nazanin barely holds in her flinch.

"I've been there a time or two too." She admits gruffly. "So I feel a kinship with you. But that's not why you were selected to be in charge of this interview. When we saw each other again at the office, I was surprised so I asked Bijan about you. I read a few of your old articles and I liked them so I asked for you instead."

She leans back. "In the end, Turquoise needs this feature and I got what I wanted, you."

There's something about the way her eyes appraise Nazanin. It's not like the familiar feeling she got a few minutes ago, this one feels almost intrusive. Is Shirin Shah checking her out?

Oh, is that what this is about?

Nazanin purses her lips, oddly flattered. Of course it's strange that this womxn might be into her but nonetheless, it's Shirin Shah.

"Oh." Is all she can say.

Shirin tilts her head to the side, just as it seems like she's going to say something, their waiter arrives. A tall man with a bright smile on his face that seems to rival the maître. Are all the staff this smiley?

Nazanin is buzzing with impatience, she's a tad curt with stating her order and cuts off the waiter when he begins to go into deep detail about tonight's chef special. Finally, he leaves, with a snap of the electronic notepad in his hand.

"You wanted me." Nazanin says, desperate to pick up from where they stopped. "I'm flattered that you consider me that way."

Shirin pauses mid sip of her drink.

"What?" She sounds genuinely taken aback. "What are you talking about?"

Too late, Nazanin realises she's misinterpreted her words. She shakes her head, torn between laughter and embarrassment. Wouldn't it have been something though to find out that the reason she'd been chosen was because Shirin fancied her?

"I... Nothing."

Shirin looks suspicious but she lets it go, "Nazanin Hesami, I must admit, the reason I chose you to write my article is because I read one of yours. You wrote an article on a sculpture by a fast rising Iranian artist in the diaspora. Her sculpture was of Gordafarid."

Nazanin remembers the article and nods, she won't go as far as saying that her article went viral but it did bring in a lot of views on Turquoise's website. Gordafarid was an important historical — albeit fictional — figure for Iranian womxns, she'd single-handedly taken Sohrab — and delayed his troops who were marching in on Persia.

"Your article gave me hope. You did your research on Gordafarid and I was impressed by how much you knew, or better to say how much you care…." Shirin says, her eyes glittering in the deliberate dimness of the restaurant.

Nazanin gives a nod.

Shirin leans forward, her lips curving up in a smile as if she senses Nazanin's confusion. "Nazanin, what if I told you that Gordafarid was real — is real. What if I told you that she left behind a powerful relic that could save our country?"

Her confusion grows, she wants to tell this womxn that she's crazy but she's never seen a more serious expression in her life. There's a little desperation in Shirin's face that Nazanin cannot ignore. Beside, the story of Gordafarid is one that has always fascinated her; the story of a womxn sick of bullshit and deciding to take matters in her own hands. Nazanin can relate to that, so maybe it's why she leans forward, so close that she's almost touching foreheads with Shirin.

"Alright, so tell me."

CHAPTER TWELVE
Affluence Hotel, Abali

Javid tried to catch Toman's eye the moment they walked through the revolving glass doors and into the vast lobby space of the hotel in Abali. Delnaz let out a small gasp of shock at the stunning interior space; grand, golden chandeliers were suspended from the high ceiling and glinting golden light that bathed the whole lobby in a stunning hue of green light. Regal looking sofas were arranged orderly in the waiting area which faced the reception area. Staff wearing golden green agate and black uniforms milled around, some of them wheeling away luggage.

Javid had stayed in some of the best hotels around the world, so much that she'd become muted to the opulence of the interior designs. It was the case now, sure, she thought the hotel looked nice, it was top five in the country and she'd chosen it with the comfort of her friends foremost in her mind. She'd wanted them to have one day to be pampered before they faced the harsh reality of their mission. She'd expected them to be taken by awe but they were strangely quiet. Even Delnaz's gasp was demure. Haleh was surveying the sights before her with a disinterested look, Pari was doing the same. And Toman, as usual it was difficult to tell what she was thinking but for some reason, Javid thought she could sense anger radiating off her in waves.

The moment their eyes met, Toman looked away, jaw clenched.

"Is this place not living up to your expensive taste, Haleh?" Javid teased, trying to break the tensioned silence in their little group. Haleh was used to fancy things, Pari did well enough for herself too.

The distracted haze on Haleh's face seemed to clear a little, she shook her head. "Oh, it's alright." But there was none of her usual haughtiness present in her words.

"Very posh," Farzaneh answered, probably to pacify Javid. She too sounded distracted and Javid couldn't help but wonder what had happened during the drive. With the exception of Delnaz, the rest of them were acting suspiciously weird.

Rehashing it out in the middle of the lobby didn't seem wise so Javid murmured her thanks to Farzaneh. "I'm going to speak with the receptionist about our booking." She didn't wait for their distracted answers and walked off to the receptionist; a womxn around Javid's age wearing a black and green uniform that the hotel staff wore. She looked up from her computer with a practised smile on her face when Javid's shadow fell on the counter.

"Welcome to Affluence, how may I be of service to you today?" She asked, Javid's eyes fell to the name tag on her chest; Meg, it read.

Javid cleared her throat and wore a smile of her own, "I booked the penthouse space a few days ago."

Meg's eyebrows rose up before she could control the motion, no doubt having assessed Javid by appearance. Affluence was aptly named, rooms were booked weeks in advance by the country's wealthiest and here was Javid, dressed casually like she was headed to a corner shop. She didn't look like she was Affluence's usual clientele. Javid was used to the judging gazes she got when people discovered that she was wealthy and besides, her mind was too occupied to think that a receptionist was judging her. She was thinking of her friends' unusual behaviour.

"What name is the penthouse booked under?" Meg asked, cutting through Javid's wandering mind.

"Javid Aref." Javid answered curtly.

"Please give me a few minutes to confirm," Meg said cheerily but there was an undertone of suspicion in her voice. Javid supposed it was because she hadn't requested for the VIP treatment. She also knew the owner of the hotel and had called in a favour. The hotel usually provided a VIP treatment for anyone renting the penthouse, which included a lot of fanfare on arrival. Javid hadn't been interested in making a show of their arrivals.

"Sure," Javid said with a wave of her hand, she ran the same hand through her hair and tossed it over the other side as she waited. The slight ruckus going on in the lobby made it hard but once Javid strained to hear, she caught classical music playing from hidden speakers. She thought she might recognize the piece so she tilted her head to the side; she was almost lost in the music when a low voice called her name.

Javid jumped a little, startled, whirling around to face a stern faced Toman.

Toman was looking a bit concerned, "Are you alright?"

Javid thought that she ought to be answering that question but she pursed her lips together and jerked her head in a nod. "Peachy, you?"

Toman ignored her question, looking fierce wearing a khaki jacket and leather trousers, it seemed she'd borrowed a page from Haleh's fashion, nothing as flashy but nonetheless daring in a way that was so obviously Haleh. Javid couldn't help but smile a little.

"You looked a little lost there," Toman said, her voice was soft but she didn't sound angry like Javid had sensed a few minutes ago. Javid hesitated, wondering if it would be a good idea to poke the bear. Toman wasn't a believer in talking about feelings at all and if Javid pushed, Toman would only clamp up harder.

Javid felt a rush of affection for this stubborn, beautiful womxn standing beside her. She wanted to hold her, to kiss her.

"I was just listening to music." Javid finally answered. Toman looked adorably confused.

"Is that British code for something else?" Toman asked and Javid realised that she couldn't hear the music. So she leaned closer to Toman, touched a finger to her lips. For a moment, the world around faded away and it was just the two of them. Toman's gaze fell to Javid's finger and Javid was filled with the urge to part those lips with her finger and then with her own lips.

Suddenly, someone cleared their throat and time seemed to resume again. Toman flinched away from her. Javid turned around; it was Meg who'd cleared her throat. Thankfully, she looked blissfully oblivious. Although same-sex relationships and marriage had been legalised in Iran three years ago, it still didn't mean that all the people are used to seeing queer relationships in public. It was one of the reasons Javid had steered clear from her birth country all these years, feeling like an outsider and torn between a country that accepted her sexuality (England) and her birth country (Iran) is new to the notion of her sexuality.

Toman was well aware of this and as a womxn, who'd grown up in a conservative country, she'd learnt to bury her true self, she'd learnt to hide and old habits die hard.

"Ms Aref, the penthouse is ready for you and your friends." Meg was beaming – genuinely this time that she'd confirmed that Javid had in fact booked the penthouse – and very oblivious as to what she'd interrupted. "I'll ring the valet to help to bring up your things."

Javid gave a distracted nod but she was looking at Toman whose face had gone painfully blank. She gave her a pleading look, let's talk about this, her eyes said. Toman gave no indication that she'd seen the silent message. She kept her impassive mask steady up until a uniformed valet arrived and Javid handed him the keys to her car and Farzaneh's.

Meg introduced them to one of the hotel managers who bowed deeply to the waist to greet them. Javid saw the curious looks he sent their group of six. It was a bit uncommon for six womxns to arrive at a hotel together, much less book the most expensive suite in the hotel. They were dressed casually too and not like business womxns. Javid didn't offer any explanation – she didn't owe him any – and in the end, he swallowed his curiosity and offered all of them complimentary glasses of champagne which they downed in one go. Javid saw the looks on all their faces and knew they wished the drink was something stronger.

All of them were then led to the penthouse, they took the VIP elevator up to the fifty floor where the penthouse was.

This time, all of her friends gave awe filled gasps the moment they stepped out of the elevator and into the hallway. Ten minutes ago, Javid would have given anything to hear that sound but now she was distracted by what had transpired between her and To-man but not too distracted that she didn't appreciate the interior décor of the penthouse. As they walked down the short hallway, she took in the polished hardwood floor that was a rich brown. They were a shade darker than the walls.

The end of the hallway gave way to a vast living space with floor to ceiling windows – offering a panoramic view of the city and the ski resort – showcasing the same muted colours, brown floors, white sofas that sat on a Kashan rug.

The manager bowed again and shook Javid's hand intensely. "Your bags will be brought up soon. Feel free to ring up the staff – we provide a twenty four hour service and I shall do everything in my power to make all of you feel at home here." He said vehemently, as if he was making an oath. Javid was deeply amused by the whole display. She gave him a too wide smile and dismissed him. When he was gone, conversation broke out.

"Wow, Javid, I knew you were going to treat us but this is… I mean… wow!" Pari teased.

Javid smiled a brittle smile. "I guess," She answered modestly as she usually did and secretly, she felt a little uncomfortable by the attention she was getting. So she feigned a casual nod, "You guys feel free to explore the place." That was the only cue her friends needed, Pari set the book she'd been holding down on the coffee table and strolled into the adjoining rooms, Delnaz was behind her and the two of them had struck a conversation about the penthouse décor.

Farzaneh and Toman exchanged a look and followed after, leaving Javid and Haleh alone.

Javid watched warily as Haleh's gaze sharpened, some of that stubbornness returning to her eyes. There was a steely determination in there too that told Javid that Haleh was itching for an argument. She ransacked her brain, trying and failing to think of a valid reason why Haleh might be angry. She came up with none and sighed.

She thought Haleh might start with a bruising jab or some insult but she was surprised by Haleh's words – or rather words. "When?"

Javid blinked slowly as if she suspected a trick. "When what?"

"When were you going to tell us about Shirin Shah?" Haleh asked, this time her voice was devoid of any malice, she just sounded tired. Javid's heart skipped a fearful bit.

The truth was, she'd never planned to hide Shirin Shah from them, she would have filled them in before the party and sending them in blindly wouldn't have helped anything. Not once had Javid thought of Shirin Shah as a secret she was going to keep from them. She didn't understand why Farzaneh had told them and was even more surprised that she had.

Farzaneh knew Shirin Shah, she cared for her and she was devastated by what happened with Shirin's partner; Nazanin.

Javid considered playing cool, she could see the defensive set of Haleh's shoulder, her arms crossed over her chest. No, Haleh wouldn't take a casual answer.

'I never planned on keeping Shirin Shah a secret." Javid answered warily. "You would have found out about her tonight – you all would have."

"It's her party we're going to, isn't it?" Haleh asked.

Javid wasn't surprised that Haleh had put the pieces together. She shook her head, "Technically, you're right and if all goes according to plan we will see Shirin Shah at the party. But it isn't her party, it's a charity function organised to raise money for climate change and my sources told me that Shirin will be making an appearance tonight – there'll be little press surrounding the event so Shirin will remain out of the public eye like she's been for the past years."

Shirin Shah was a recluse and that was putting it mildly. She'd erased herself off the earth since what happened years ago. In fact, if Javid's sources were correct then it would be Shirin's first appearance at a public function this year and the timing couldn't be more perfect for Javid. The only reason Shirin was showing up in person was because the charity cause was apparently very dear to her. The climate change was a recent concern of Shirin Shah, it was as if it must have something to do with the Yellow Flowers Cave or rather what happened in it.

Javid had every intention of finding out what had happened and now to stop it from happening to her friends. Farzaneh didn't know the full story either.

"How do you know that she'll talk to us?" Haleh asked, when Javid parted her lips to speak, Haleh raised a hand to cut her off. "Never mind. That's why Farzaneh is with us." She narrowed her eyes, she walked to the sofa and perched down on one arm. "That's awfully convenient for you."

"For us," Javid pointed out. "I'm not doing this for me, Haleh and this isn't my mission. It's our mission." Before Haleh could quip in, Javid continued, "And yes, Farzaneh being here at the party will help."

Haleh crossed one lap over the other. "Might?' She asked, one eyebrow arched up.

"Might, because Shirin Shah never told Farzaneh what happened. What makes you think that she'll tell her now?"

"So you're saying seeking out Madam Shah is unreasonable?" Haleh asked.

Javid met Haleh's gaze. "I'm saying I'm going to do everything I can to get Shirin Shah to tell us what happened to her partner. I'm telling you that I'm not manipulating Farzaneh to be here and I'm not manipulating anyone else here. Bloody hell, Haleh, give me some credit. You've known me for years."

Haleh was too cool to show guilt, she just raised her chin up and looked away for a brief second. Javid broke eye contact and saw that the rest of her friends were standing by the mouth of the hallway, watching them.

"I'm betting you all heard that." Javid said wryly.

"Pretty much everything." Pari said. Delnaz nodded in agreement.

"And we trust you," It was Toman that spoke, her words carrying steely conviction.

"So, what's the plan? How do we get Shirin Shah to tell us everything?"

Javid turned to face her friends, she shook her head lightly, feeling exhausted all of a sudden even though she'd gotten plenty of rest last night and it was mid afternoon. While she was glad that they'd gotten the conversation out of the way, she was tired of the back and forth in the past forty eight hours and some.

"There isn't any plan." She finally said, she tensed, expecting one of them to challenge her again. She was half tempted to tell the next person to challenge her to take the metaphorical steering wheel and lead them instead.

"I say we go on our knees and beg Shirin Shah to help us." Pari said, her tone only half joking.

"Shirin Shah doesn't hate us, I'm pretty sure she'd help us if she could." Toman interjected. "The matter of her helping us isn't the problem, is it?" She looked to Farzaneh for help. The other womxn nodded.

"Shirin is one of the warmest people I've met in my life. As I've told Javid in the past, this isn't about Shirin helping us. To her, it's about reliving one of the worst moments in her life. I've never seen anyone shut down the way Shirin did when Nazanin didn't return with her. She blames herself and worse, she hates herself." Farzaneh said, her voice dulled with pain like Javid had never heard before.

Javid knew that Farzaneh believed there was someone out there who would one day find the sword and save the Farsi speaking countries. Maybe at one point, Farzaneh had believed that that someone could be Shirin Shah. Shirin had been the other person the map had found worthy and Farzaneh had held hope for Shirin, she'd even helped her too. But something had gone wrong.

"We still have to try to talk to her." Delnaz said.

Farzaneh closed her eyes as if she was in physical pain. She opened them a second later and Javid thought she saw tears swimming in their depths. "That is necessary."

What then had gone wrong with Shirin and Nazanin in the cave?

Javid knew that she shouldn't think such thoughts. She should be optimistic, it was too early in their plan to think so wrongly. Besides, she was the leader of their little group and there was nothing more infectious than fear. So she put up a smile, not too bright that her friends saw through the shit and not too small that it didn't inspire bravery.

"Let's worry about Shirin Shah helping us later. If we want to get into that party, there's a fancy dress code so we need to go shopping." Javid took out her credit card from the inner pocket of her coat. She held it up with two fingers and wiggled her brows. "This card has no limit."

At first, she thought none of them would bite the bait but Pari cheered obnoxiously, nudging Delnaz who sent her a false glower.

"We can have our Ocean's Eight moment, ladies." Pari said.

Delnaz gave a snort. "I've never seen that movie."

Pari let out a mock outrageous gasp, "A traversity, travesty, we'll remedy someday. But I'll give you a quick summary. Lesbian womxns do badass things while wearing stunning gowns."

Haleh who couldn't pass up an opportunity to prove somebody wrong chirped in, "They were not lesbian."

"Everything is lesbian if you look hard enough." Pari affirmed. And that was all it took for Haleh and Pari to start bickering like children. As they did, Pari sent Javid a knowing wink.

Javid smiled.

CHAPTER THIRTEEN
Tehran, June 2029

THREE YEARS AGO.

Javid is surprised by how much things have changed in her birth country. She left Iran when she was barely a tween merely months after her father died in a car accident. Her mother had been worried that somehow her beloved daughter was next, her eyes were suddenly opened to the terrible state of her country. Her dear husband might have lived if the country's healthcare wasn't in shambles, if he'd gotten the medical care that he needed urgently. Mrs. Aref made the decision to make a better life for what was left of her family. So she made the proper preparations and months after her husband was laid to rest in the soil of his country, she left with her daughter to England.

Javid has found herself torn between two identities throughout her life. She'd been an anomaly, growing up in a foreign country and beating the odds enough to become wealthy as early as in her middle age. She certainly had the means to return home to her country all these years, yes, she's kept abreast with all the news in Iran, she constantly donates to Iranian charity — over dozen of them all. Javid has no use for all her money, she's made enough to be comfortable for the rest of her life so she just gives it away slowly. Iran has always been the centre of her philanthropism.

Even then, she's mostly steered clear of her country, taking vacations in other parts of the world, avoiding Iran like the plague and not because she was ashamed of her country — far from it, she's always been proud to tell people when they ask where she's from that she's Iranian.

As she grew up though, she found herself being torn between two identities; English and Iranian. She's even come to be more accepted in England; all parts of her; race and sexuality. In Iran, it would be a different story. For the longest time, Javid found herself distancing herself from Iranian society, feeling a little resentful of her people; the bigotry, the homophobia and the misogyny. So she never visited.

Gordafarid's sword, a long lost relic that was rumoured to have enough power to restore Iran to a new age. Javid has never fancied herself to be a believer in anything, except maybe in herself but in recent times, she's starting to believe in the existence of things that she once considered fanciful.

Perhaps it's the near death experience that has changed her perspective of things. Made her want to cause a bigger change in her country.

For now, she's been emailing the private detective back and forth, digesting all she's gathered about the sword. There's still so much to discover, many missing pieces in the story but Javid knows enough to make her want to believe.

Even though she left Iran at a very young age, she grew up hearing bedtime stories about her. She recalls her favourite part of the story, where Gordafarid charges into battle set to save her people;

But one of those within the fortress was a womxn, daughter of the warrior Gazhdaham, named Gordafarid. When she learned that their leader had allowed himself to be taken, she found his behaviour so shameful that her rosy cheeks became as black as pitch with rage. With not a moment's delay she dressed herself in a knight's armor, gathered her hair beneath a Rumi helmet, and rode out from the fortress, a lion eager for battle. She roared at the enemy ranks, "Where are your heroes, your warriors, your tried and tested chieftains?"

All of the stories have spoken of Gordafarid's bravery and it is only recently that Javid has discovered that Gordafarid's sword is a thing. Apparently, Gordafarid's weapon was blessed with power and after the battle she'd won, she hid the sword.

And from what Javid has gleaned so far about the sword, it's that it has the power to restore all Farsi speaking countries to a powerful and problem free era.

It sounds so simple, so easy to Javid but she is swiftly getting the feeling that it isn't so.

In her last email exchanged with the private detective, she found out that plenty of groups had attempted to find the sword and use it for their own gain. Most of them had perished, their bodies discovered years after.

The thought of death would have been enough to scare most people but not Javid, she's brushed lips with death recently and lived to tell the story. In fact, almost dying had caused her to realise that she wants to do more and she thinks Gordafarid's sword is the key.

Even through all this, she's been distant from her country, all her correspondence with the private detective have been via email and phone calls. She knows how the detective looks like from a picture on her website and Javid has heard the cool calm of her voice, steady like moving water. She knows this much about the detective but she has never met her in person.

Well, she's about to remedy that in an hour's time. But the beautiful detective isn't Javid's only reason for visiting her country for the first time in years. Just a few months ago, Iran finally legalised same-sex marriages and relationships. For the first time, Javid thinks that she can breathe easy, she can raise her shoulder up in pride in her country. It's about time, maybe even a development that has come a little later than most countries of the world but she's still happy about it. She isn't naïve to think that it'll be smooth sailing for all queer people in Iran but it's the start that she's been waiting for.

What better time to visit than during Pride Month?

Javid has an itinerary of things to do while she's in the country; there's so much to catch up on that she's basically bouncing on the balls of her feet. But she'll start with meeting with Toman first. For some reason, Javid finds herself a little nervous, so much that she's analysing every item of clothing she's got on; her white silk turtleneck top and black jean trousers, black leather coat, and matching leather wraparound boots. She wants to make an impression on Toman.

Although they have only exchanged emails, their relationship had taken a casual turn in recent times. And it all started a few weeks ago when Javid had asked how Toman was at the end of her email. The action had been an absentminded one, she hadn't expected Toman to answer it but she had. Then they'd started talking about things other than Gordafarid's sword. Javid doesn't want to put a name to what they have going on but it's quite close to friendship.

About forty minutes later, Javid finds herself in the cafe across the street from the Firouz Palace she's staying at. Toman is already there, sipping tea from a dainty cup and glancing at the watch on her wrist – of course she is part of the rare percentage of people who still wear wristwatches. She and Toman have discussed fashion a little and she knows that Toman has a bit of an expensive taste, she likes to splurge on her looks and it's clear now. She's wearing a white ruffle collar cardigan and a black tiered pattern skirt with boots.

Javid doesn't know why but she smiles. For a while, she stands in the entrance of the café, just watching Toman, the way her eyebrows furrow when she glances at her watch, the little show of impatience in the tightening of her red painted lips.

She raises her head and her eyes meet Javid's from across the room. Javid feels a flush creep up her cheeks and hope that Toman cannot tell that she's been standing there for minutes like some kind of creep. She's in her late thirties for hell's sake, she's not some bumbling teen stalking a crush. She walks to Toman.

Toman is not quite smiling but there's a small curve to her lips that Javid notices.

"You're late." Toman says and Javid thinks that her voice is even more soothing when heard in person. "I don't like tardiness," Toman says matter of factly as if Javid isn't technically her boss. But there's no bite in her words, only a playfulness that would be hard to detect for someone who doesn't know Toman. Javid doesn't think she can ever understand this mysterious womxn but she's getting close to learning her mannerisms.

"Nice to see you too, Toman," Javid says. The both of them sit at the same time and soon a waitress arrives to take Javid's order, she distractedly points at the first name on the menu and the waitress scurries off, cheerfully announcing that she would be back soon. Javid hopes not, she wants Toman to herself. Javid doesn't have a lot of friends and she's never made friends with someone this quickly, nor felt a connection like she does with Toman. She's just easy to talk to.

For the longest second, the two of them just stare at each other as if one cannot quite believe that the other is here. Javid shakes her head and breaks their stare down.

"Let me refresh your memory, Javid. You're looking a little lost." Toman says dryly. "You asked me to look into recent groups that journeyed to the Yellow Flowers Cave in search of the sword."

In the past few weeks, Javid and Toman have discussed almost every topic on earth; humxn rights, womxns' rights, Iranian culture and cuisine, each other's jobs but they have never talked about the sword on a personal level. Of course Toman provides the information on whatever she's discovered but they have never actually talked about if Toman believes in the existence of the sword, in its power. She wonders if Toman thinks of her as fanciful, a bored rich womxn looking for some excitement.

Javid finds that she cannot keep her curiosity under wraps anymore, she has to ask. She waves a hand, brushing Toman's light teasing. She leans forward and voices her question aloud, "Do you actually believe in Gordafarid's sword?"

The skin between Toman's forehead dips in the slightest, the only sign of surprise. She smiles. "I assume you're going to tell me why you believe and I'm going to listen to you. I've discovered some of the strangest information in the course of this past few weeks. There's something going on, isn't there?"

It is the only push Javid needs, she nods.

Toman's smile widens, "Alright, convince me."

CHAPTER FOURTEEN
Who knew that shopping could do a 360 on their moods?

Of course, Javid didn't think that she could only attribute the light atmosphere amongst her friends to taking them out for dress shopping at one of the designer boutiques in the city. They'd finally cleared the air; all grievances had been aired and all questions sufficiently answered. The trust amongst them had been further solidified and all she'd had to tell them was that their mission was well and truly doomed. A slight exaggeration but still the gist of things.

"Such a shame that Farzaneh chose not to join us," Delnaz said for what felt like the tenth time, she was obviously disappointed that the pathfinder had passed on shopping. Javid noticed Haleh's eyes narrow in Delnaz's direction, looking like she wasn't the only one wondering if something else was going on between Farzaneh and Delnaz. Of all of them, Delnaz had the shortest dating history, she was demisexual. She liked to form a connection with people first. Javid had noticed her getting close to Farzaneh and she had chalked it up to pure fascination. The way Javid too had felt about Farzaneh when they first met.

"You've taken a liking to her," Haleh remarked in that her usual astute way.

Delnaz flushed guiltily, "Why would you say that? I'm just concerned about her."

Haleh gestured to herself, "So am I, so is everybody but we don't sigh dolefully and repeat it every few minutes."

Predictably, Delnaz bristled. "Some of us wear our hearts on our sleeves, and we can't all be deadpan like you."

Haleh had been called worse and she didn't react to what was an accurate description of her character. She shrugged a shoulder and twisted one of the many rings on her fingers. "I'm just saying. You talking about it doesn't change that Farzaneh isn't here. If you're concerned about her, just go back to the hotel."

It was a challenge, one that caused Haleh's coffee-brown eyes to glitter knowingly. She knew Delnaz wouldn't rise to the bait.

Javid watched their interaction keenly, waiting for if it got too tense so she could step in. Truthfully, Javid didn't understand why Haleh liked to bait Delnaz. It was as if she wanted to test her limits, wanted to push her until she snapped and if Javid didn't know better, she might have thought that Haleh fancied Delnaz.

Delnaz on the other hand was becoming something of an expert of dancing at the edge of the cliff before pulling away right as she was about to fall. She didn't react this time either, turning away from Haleh to inspect a dress. Javid found herself impressed by her self control.

Haleh narrowed her eyes but she didn't attempt to bait Delnaz even further and she didn't look impressed, something like frustration caused the corners of her lips to pinch. It confirmed Javid's suspicion that Haleh just wanted Delnaz to unravel like spools of thread. *Why?*

"*Hmm*, I wonder if choosing long gowns is practical," Pari mused aloud, fingering the ends of a silky backless red dress with an expression of lust on her face. Again, she cut through the tension like a pro. This time unwittingly.

There was a glint of excitement in her eyes that caused Javid to smile; her friend had already been bought by the promise of shopping but she'd been more impressed when they got to the high end boutique and realised that Javid had reserved the whole store for them throughout the afternoon.

"Why ever won't they?" Delnaz asked. She was running a hand down the hem of a little black dress with a critical look in her eye. Javid thought it was adorable.

Pari gestured vaguely, "We might bunch the hems, you know as we attempt to escape the party."

Haleh gave a derisive snort, "It's not a fucking robbery. We're just going to talk to Shirin Shah."

Pari smirked, "Well, you never know. We might need to reclaim some artefact or the other."

Toman shot Javid a look, a Toman equivalent of rolling her eyes. Predictably, Haleh was less subtle. She rolled her eyes effusively, always the last one to hide how she was feeling about someone.

"Javid, you're the leader – do something to curb this Ocean's Eight fantasy she's got." Haleh said, pointing an accusing finger at Pari. But she was only half teasing in her accusation, she'd come to really enjoy teasing Pari, not only because it filled her with a warm feeling but also because Pari enjoyed bantering like nothing else. Other people might take Haleh's sarcastic comments to heart but not Pari.

Pari tried and failed to tamp down on her grin, it stretched to the corner of her lips. "You'll be eating your own words when you have to run down a flight of stairs wearing a long fitted gown."

"I'm sure," Haleh said in a voice drier than the Sahara Desert. She looked away from Pari to glance around the racks and racks of dresses, something like distaste flashing through her eyes. Ah, of course, none of these dresses looked like something Haleh would don much less be caught dead in. They were noticeably more conservative, not at all like any of the bold, risking fashion that Haleh preferred. There was the occasional cleavage baring dress but Javid tried to see the clothes from Haleh's eyes – they were boring to put it bluntly.

"Besides, I wouldn't be caught dead wearing any of these gowns." Haleh drawled, her voice tinged with slight mockery and echoing Javid's previous thoughts. Javid hid her smile at how good she was at predicting her friends.

Pari let out a mock gasp of outrage, going the extra mile by miming clutching invisible pearls. "How could you say that? The dresses are gorgeous." She shot Javid a tiny smile, "Thank heavens you're paying, I can't decide on a single choice."

"You're welcome," Javid said dryly, half distracted. She walked closer to inspect a dress; it was a starry midnight blue fabric; the pale afternoon sun streaming in from the floor to ceiling windows in the boutique and catching the dress in the light. The dress had thin straps, a thigh high slit and a deep v neckline that plunged very low, a little too much than Javid was normally comfortable with. But she could visualise herself wearing this dress and she felt a dart of excitement for tonight. Pari wasn't the only one harbouring Ocean's Eight fantasies. Yes, she was the leader of their mission and she should have been above action movie fantasies. But if she let herself think of the impossibility of the mission ahead, if she allowed the dread bubbling in the pit of her stomach to settle, then she'd be bowing out in early stages. Besides, a little fantasy never hurt anyone. She let herself think of wearing this stunning dress, strutting into that fundraiser and confronting Shirin Shah; she even let her imagination run wild – visualising some kind of espionage; most of all she imagined Toman's reaction to seeing her in this dress and she decided that this was it – this was her dress.

Too late, Javid realised the conversation around her had come to a quiet halt, she raised her head, and she'd been engrossed in the mental image playing in her mind and had been quietly touching one tiny strap of the dress. She felt her cheeks go hot with embarrassment when she saw that all her friends had stopped talking and were looking at her.

"You're looking at that dress like Haleh's been looking at Pari's boobs," Delnaz said lightly. Haleh snorted a laugh but she didn't disagree.

"It is a gorgeous dress," Pari said, turning an assessing eye on the dress. She walked to where Javid was standing and took out the dress from the rack. Her eyes returned to Javid, sweeping her form up and down and thrusting the gown in front of Javid's body. Pari lit up, "It looks like it was made for you."

Even Haleh chirped in, "Yeah and it doesn't look as boring as the other dresses here."

Javid's lips quirked up in a smile. "Thanks, Hals." She said in a deadpan tone.

"It's gorgeous." Delnaz agreed, her frown was gone. "How are you going to do your hair? I think you should pin it up.

Haleh and Pari immediately got into a debate about suitable hairstyles. But Javid only had eyes for Toman who was staring her with a scarily blank expression. Javid offered her a tiny smile, trying to hide the hurt she felt at her silence. Just when Javid thought she might say something to break the ice – maybe one of her rare jokes, Haleh cut in and the moment was broken. Toman moved away to look at the jewellery on display in the vitrine.

"Right, Javid?" Haleh was asking.

"Sure." Javid heard herself echo.

Javid thought it might be best to leave Toman alone for now.

***

"You do know that sticking the two of us together is a fucking explosion waiting to happen." Pari pointed out, Javid huffed a laugh but she didn't realise that Pari wasn't trying to be funny – she was speaking pure facts.

The look of exhausted disgust on Javid's face every time she was reminded that two of her friends had paired themselves together romantically would never get old to Pari. Javid wasn't stupid, she'd come to terms with the fact that something was going on between Pari and Haleh and that there was nothing she could do to stop it but it didn't mean that she wasn't disgusted by every flirting display they put up.

Secretly, unbeknownst to the rest of their friends, Haleh and Pari had struck up a deal to be as nauseating as possible in front of their friends; their deal included excessive displays of attention and no attempt to hide the growing sexual tension between the two of them. The truth was though, that despite their grand displays, nothing had happened between the two of them. Yet. Pari was still mulling over whether she wanted that platonic relationship to be more.

Although, Pari mused, she didn't think that Haleh would be making any move anytime soon – if it was up to her. Pari was a lot more astute than most people knew; at least the people that knew her. Her bubbly persona tended to confuse people – they couldn't reconcile the fun loving, bubbly womxn with the shrewd journalist turned TV anchor. She'd never been able to understand why she'd been boxed into one personality; as if she couldn't be both. Still, she did enjoy it sometimes when she was underestimated, made shocking the hell out of people a good time. And she could observe people and they wouldn't even know about it.

Javid might be one of the few people who saw past Pari's mask. And then there was Haleh too, who was slowly figuring it out.

Still, she enjoyed Haleh's friendship, she liked teaming up with her to piss off everyone else. And well, there was no denying the sexual attraction between them. For some reason though, outside of the usual flirting and suggestive remarks, Haleh gave no indication that she wanted to make good on them.

Pari was the slightest bit wary of her, it was hard to tell what she was thinking most times. It was hilarious that her usual perceptiveness was useless with Haleh. It was like trying to read a blank page. Even now, it was hard to tell if she was pleased by Javid pairing the two of them together. It also hadn't escaped Pari's notice that Haleh was considerably the least enthusiastic one of them when it came to talking about their mission, sure she'd shown some enthusiasm when talking about Gordafarid but Pari had mostly sensed wariness and fear whenever the topic of their mission was brought up.

Naturally, she was curious. Haleh had more bravado and swagger than anybody Pari had ever known. What was she so afraid of?

"You're asking the wrong questions, Pari darling." Haleh cut in, there was something like fury in the slight trembling in her voice. She was pinning Javid with a stare so sharp that it could cut glass. "Why Pari and I? Why not Delnaz and somebody else? Or maybe even Toman?"

Toman looked up from the magazine she'd been reading at the mention of her name – pretending rather, she wasn't fooling anyone – but there was no visible reaction on her face.

The tension in the room grew; the rest of their friends; scattered around the seats in the room looked uncomfortable. It was Pari's cue to try and break through it. She sorted through her head trying to think of something very witty to say.

"Speak for yourself, Haleh, I'm very much capable of being sent downtown to retrieve a package." Which was exactly what Javid had asked them to do – go downtown to get a package from someone who was waiting. Of course, it was a little surprising that the delivery couldn't be made directly to the hotel they were staying at but maybe Javid didn't want eyes on them. That seemed like a reasonable enough reason.

It was typical Haleh to be suspicious of everything. Not for the first time, Pari wondered what she'd gone through to make her so wary and closed off.

"Would you stop trying to play peacemaker for once?" Haleh asked, turning to face Pari with a glower. She flinched, more than a little hurt that Haleh had shut her down like that. Haleh, however, was not done with her jabs. "Allow confrontations to happen, you don't need to meddle as if you're part of an anti-bomb squad."

Pari opened her mouth and then closed it again, affronted. She had no clever joke to say in return. Worse, she felt tears sting her eyes. She blinked severally and turned her face away from Haleh.

"Haleh, stop." Javid said, her voice like steel. It wasn't enough to cause Haleh to back down.

"No, Javid." Haleh pressed, it seemed like she might say more, explode even and reveal the reason why she was being uptight about being sent on what looked like a straightforward errand. "Why not somebody else?" There was a desperate plea that Pari caught, almost buried in the tight cord of anger.

Javid crossed an arm over her chest and shook her head, "You're Iranian, Haleh and you're familiar with this district. I need you."

Because Pari was watching Haleh closely, she caught her slight flinch at the mention of her nationality. Pari frowned; she would have never guessed that Haleh felt some kind of way about her country. After all, they were all here to make their countries better places.

Of the five of them, Haleh and Javid lived in foreign countries. Pari knew that Javid had left Iran when she was a child, but Haleh had grown up in Tehran, she'd moved to Berlin in her adult years.

Haleh's scoff was a gunshot in the tensed silence, "Bullshit, Javid and you know it. Toman is Iranian and Farzaneh is a citizen too." Haleh pointed a sharp finger at Farzaneh who had been frowning at the exchange. "She's lived in Tehran for years."

Haleh jabbed a finger at Javid's chest. "Don't do this."

Toman and Delnaz exchanged a look, it was clear that they were baffled by Haleh's explosive outburst.

"Haleh, what's wrong?" Delnaz asked tentatively.

Haleh didn't answer, she ran a hand through the dark mane of her hair and blew out a breath. It looked like she was trying to gather every bit of her composure. "Fine, fine." And she brushed past Javid and into the adjoining room.

It was a little easier to breathe in her absence and Pari sensed that they were all dying to ask why Haleh had reacted the way she had. All of them wore similar looks of confusion; furrowed brows, eyes darting to the room where Haleh had escaped into as if they expected to hear an explosion or some sign that Haleh was taking out her fury on the furniture. The only person who didn't look baffled was Javid, confirming Pari's suspicion that Javid had deliberately picked the two of them or specifically, Haleh for the errand.

What could be downtown?

"Okay," Delnaz drawled, stretching the last letter. "Since everyone is trying to respect Haleh's privacy, I'm going to say it. What was that about?"

Javid shook her head, "That's Haleh's story to tell you if she wishes." She jerked her head in Haleh's direction. "She's in there, you can ask her by yourself." There was some amusement in Javid's tone as if she thought it might be funny to witness Haleh tear one of them to shreds.

Delnaz looked like she might hurl herself from the edge of a cliff than do exactly that so she wisely kept her mouth shut.

"Pari, come with me please." Javid said, beckoning Pari with a hand. Pari didn't ask where they were headed to, only followed Javid out the door and down the hallway to the elevator.

"Please don't take Haleh's words to heart." Javid said as she punched in the button for the lobby.

Pari leaned against the cool metal of the elevator walls, she tucked her hands into the pocket of her coat – the perfect picture of calm. Inside, she was anything but, she couldn't deny that Haleh's words had stung but she tried not to take to heart.

"I'm sure she didn't mean it." Javid added half heartedly.

Pari cast her a wry look, she didn't believe Javid believed that at all. "My grandmother used to say that the words of a drunken person are the truest she'll ever say. I added my own sentence to that little proverb; a furious person always speaks the truth – sure, that truth is usually laced with malice but the truth is the truth."

Javid looked contemplative. "You think her little comment about your ice breakers being born out of some inane desire to prevent confrontations is true?"

She watched the number icon above the elevator doors change. "I grew up in a fucking volatile environment, my parents used to have screaming matches every time. I think it's definitely influenced my chirping in with jokes to prevent fights from happening."

"But it's not a bad thing. Maybe a part of you does it as a defence mechanism but your quips, Pari, they're helpful. In conflict resolution, it's called diffusion. You should be a diplomat." Javid said matter of factly.

Pari smiled. "But Haleh's also right. Confrontations should be allowed to happen sometimes or people just bottle up their feelings until it explodes it everybody's faces."

"That wasn't a confrontation though," Javid said just as the elevator doors slid open with a low whirl. The two of them stepped into the busy lobby. Classical music played from speakers while hotel staff milled about, some of them wheeling luggage.

Javid headed for the receptionist. "Haleh's complicated."

Pari laughed a hollow laugh, "Tell me something I don't know, Javid."

Javid tried to catch the receptionist's eye, but the young womxn was otherwise occupied by several customers. She sighed, suddenly, Pari saw through Javid's usual confidence and glimpsed exhaustion marring the lines of her face. It suddenly dawned on Pari how much planning Javid had put into their trip, into their mission. She was the brains behind everything, tirelessly working to make sure that everything happened according to the plan. She didn't even understand why Javid had assembled all of them together, the womxn was single-handedly running the metaphorical show – she could have saved herself all the stress and drama and hired a crew to help her find Gordafarid's sword. She felt the ridiculous urge to hug her friend but she ignored it. She'd help Javid by be useful and if that meant working with a cold and secretive Haleh then so be it.

"Haleh is complicated," Javid repeated, placing a firm emphasis on the last word as if it was paramount that Pari understood this. "And I don't mean difficult. Haleh is actually one of the easiest going people to work with and be with – you probably already know it." Javid added, obviously alluding to the romance she and the rest of their friends thought was blooming between Haleh and Pari.

Pari found it hard to set her straight, it was a little amusing to be fooling their friends so easily but now she couldn't let Javid know that she actually know much about Haleh – that Haleh was as closed off as ever, sure she knew how to set Pari's pulse racing with a single heated look but that was as much emotion that Pari glimpsed from Haleh; desire and the occasional exasperated fondness.

"Haleh reacting the way she did is very much valid. You know that she left for Germany when she was twenty six – after being dismissed from the force." Javid was saying.

Pari recoiled. "Haleh was in the force? Like the police force?"

Javid sounded even more surprised, "You didn't know?" Something like suspicion entered her voice, "Then what the hell do you two even talk about?"

Pari bristled at the accusing tone of Javid's voice, "We don't do a lot of talking, that's the point, Javid." She retorted, watching as Javid's face crumpled in disgust. She would have laughed if she wasn't peeved by Javid's earlier assumption of her relationship with Haleh. Although it brought her some sense of amusement when she rubbed in the nonexistent physical aspect of her relationship with Haleh, she didn't like it that her friends had come to see that relationship as strictly physical and nothing else. As if Haleh was only in it for a dumb fuck.

"That's not cool," Javid muttered.

Pari shrugged. "It is what it is." She said in a terrible English accent to mock Javid.

"Are you mimicking me?" Javid asked with a gasp of outrage and Pari couldn't help it, she giggled.

"If it helps, your accent is really contagious." Pari said.

If it was possible, Javid looked even more affronted. "Like cholera." She echoed incredulously. She shook her head, her expression becoming serious again. "Haleh didn't tell you she used to be a cop?"

"Like I said, we don't do much talking," Pari repeated her earlier words, only this time, there was no amusement in her words. Internally, Pari was combing through every interaction she'd had with Haleh in the past few days. It wasn't true that they didn't talk much – they hadn't even kissed yet – all their conversation was Pari filling in the silence by talking about herself and Haleh responded with sarcastic quips. Once, Pari had asked her how it was like to live in Berlin and be part of its wild nightlife, Haleh had obliged her in short, curt words. Yes, it was every bit as dangerous. Yes, there were drugs. No. it wasn't as wild as Ibiza.

She didn't offer any details whether she liked her job or not and Pari had been all too happy to keep talking about herself.

"She told you that?" Pari asked, trying and failing to keep the jealousy out of her tone.

Amusement twinkled in the depths of Javid's pale grey eyes, "Do you really think that Haleh would willingly volunteer vulnerable information about herself?" Javid asked.

Slightly, put off by the question, Pari shook her head. "Then how do you know?" She asked, more than a little afraid of the answer that Javid would give – judging by the grim and slightly guilty look on her face.

"I had her looked up," Javid finally answered. Pari blinked, baffled by the choice of words.

"By looked up, you mean?" She asked.

The look of guilt intensified, Javid shoved her hands behind her back and looked away for a second. "Investigated."

"What?" Pari shouted. Plenty eyes turned to her and she realised she'd raised her voice. She felt her cheeks flush and reduced her voice to a murmur. "You had Haleh investigated, for what reason? She isn't a fucking criminal."

"I know that," Javid snapped. She rubbed her forehead, "I had all of you investigated."

A cold shiver that had little to do with the cool interior of the hotel lobby. She could think of a few things in her past that she was ashamed of, things she never wanted another soul to find out, except – Javid probably knew these things now. Shame caused her cheeks to burn and she glared hard at Javid.

"Do you not understand the concept of privacy? Why the fuck would you do that?" Pari fired off the questions harshly, clicking each one off her fingers. "You don't have any fucking right to do that, Javid."

To her credit, Javid did look sorry. She raised her chin in defiance though. "I'm sorry there was no other way but I'm not sorry that I did it."

Pari took a step backward from her friend, no, Javid. She'd trusted her and maybe she'd overestimated how much Javid trusted them. Obviously, she didn't trust them at all.

"You could have asked." Pari snarled.

Javid gave a derisive scoff. "Right, and Haleh's so graciously narrated the story of her life because you asked nicely." The fight seemed to deflate from her and she shook her head, "Look, I didn't do it out of some perverse desire. I met all of you three years ago, bonded with you and let you into an important secret. Forgive me if I wanted to know everything about the womxns I was going to be working with. I didn't do it for me, Pari, I did it to make sure the secret of Gordafarid's sword was safe."

Even though she wanted to, Pari couldn't deny the logic of that thought. It didn't mean she felt any less violated, any less betrayed that Javid had done that. She wondered if it was possible for the both of them to be justified.

Her wavering expression must have been visible because Javid pressed on, "I wish there had been another way."

Pari sighed, "But if you could go back in time, you would still do it all over again."

It was a rhetorical question and Javid didn't answer.

"I'm guessing you didn't find anything that makes us unworthy

of being part of your team." She tried to make the words sound like a joke and winced when they sounded accusing and unforgiving. Javid didn't waver though, she must have expected Pari's furious reaction.

Something occurred to Pari and she couldn't help but voice her concern aloud, "Wait a second, Toman's a private detective. Did she?" She trailed off, finding it unable to finish her question. It was damned obvious that Javid was close to Toman in a way that none of them were and Pari even had a suspicion that something had happened between them in the past but unlike her friends, she didn't really care, seeing as both womxns were grown and consenting adults.

She couldn't stomach the thought that Toman too had been involved in this scheme, that she'd been the one to poke into their lives, searching for dirty laundry to report back to Javid.

Javid shook her head, "No, Pari. I hired several investigators but Toman wasn't one of them."

Relief coursed through her like a cool breeze in the summer. "Oh, good."

"She would have never agreed to it." Javid added, deadpan, she saw Pari's questioning look and jerked her head in a nod. "Yes, Pari. Toman isn't aware that I had everybody investigated."

"Including her." Pari had to clarify. Javid didn't answer though, she looked away and it seemed as if she might try to get the receptionist's attention again as she glanced at the counter. But she turned her head away and sighed.

"That's how you know about Haleh's past." Pari remembered Haleh's outburst, the fear she'd tried so hard to mask. "She pleaded with you, whatever you're asking us to do it must be difficult for Haleh. And that's not the only thing – she knew that you knew."

"Yes, she did. Because I told her years ago when I had all of you investigated."

Pari flinched. She was suddenly angry too, was she the last person to know?

Again, Javid accurately read the question on her face, she hunched her shoulders together and nodded. "Yes, Pari you're the last one to know."

"Why?" Pari asked, she braced herself, waiting for Javid to drop the bomb and tell her that she wasn't trusted. Although for whatever reason, she couldn't imagine.

"Because I never thought I needed to. Of all of them I thought that you would understand the most – you used to be an investigative journalist. You're used to doing research, going undercover when it was necessary." explained Javid.

"That's the fucking point, I do get it. That doesn't mean it doesn't make my skin crawl!"

Javid nodded, "Fair."

"I'm surprised Haleh didn't beat you up for this." Pari added grumpily.

Javid smiled a little, "Me too. But in my defence, I told her years ago and like I said, Haleh is a lot more practical than you think. She understood and she made me swear not to tell any of you anything about her file."

Pari deflated a little. "So you didn't bring me down here to tell me why Haleh reacted the way she did earlier?"

Javid raised an eyebrow. "What happened to respecting one's privacy?"

Pari flushed and looked away. "Then why? Haleh is afraid of confronting something or someone downtown but where do I factor into this errand?"

Javid looked at her for the longest time, her eyes assessing until Pari felt uncomfortable, she didn't know what Javid was searching for and was afraid of falling short. Finally, Javid spoke.

"Honestly, there's no special reason. You're accompanying Haleh because I see the way she is around you, you ground her." Javid remarked, she sounded sure too.

Pari laughed a little hysterically at Javid's assumption. She remembered being offered the job of co anchor a year ago, she'd been doubtful of her charm – everyone knew that TV stars had to be a little fake on the job wearing smiles and sunshine even when they might feel otherwise. Turned out she wasn't so bad at faking things.

Maybe she and Haleh were better actresses than they'd thought, fooling all their friends into thinking they were something more than was true. She didn't have the heart to confess to Javid now, despite the shock a few minutes ago, she still didn't want to disappoint Javid.

"I don't think I have that much pull over Haleh," She couldn't resist saying, she expected Javid to look disappointed but a slow smile spread on her lips instead.

"Have some faith, Pari."

"In you or in Haleh?"

"Both of us."

Pari only had one question left. "Javid, why are you doing this? Forcing Haleh to confront something she moved half way to the other side of the world from." She could think of a few fears in her own past that she didn't want to be faced with. She would hate it to be forced to confront them. She felt a little pang in her chest for Haleh, her outburst suddenly made all the sense in the world and even a little understated. She'd confronted Javid in her usual quiet fury, a little desperation lacing through the anger. Pari tried to imagine herself in that situation, she would have done more than jab a finger at Javid, that was for sure.

"She can't run forever. And that's why she'll show up, she'll go downtown even if it kills her. Because Haleh is practical like that. And there's no ultimatum attached to this errand, you do realise that, Pari?" When Pari was silent, Javid added, "I'm not making her do anything, she could say no and I'd head downtown to get it myself. Haleh can say no, but she won't."

It was another glaring difference between them; Pari would have definitely said no. or she might have gone through with it, hesitant to disappoint Javid. Maybe Haleh was just like her after all.

She didn't say anything in answer to that. Javid waited for a few awkward beats to see if Pari would ask any other questions and when she didn't, she finally approached the receptionist.

"Has my package arrived yet?" Javid asked.

The receptionist beamed, nodded her head vigorously – an action that amused Pari greatly. Earlier, she'd regarded their group with some suspicion, judged them even but now that she was aware that they'd booked the penthouse suite, she'd done a 360 and was kissing their asses.

"Yes, ma'am." She bent slightly to retrieve a brown envelope and handed it to Javid.

Javid muttered her thanks and stepped away from the counter, letting the person behind her walk up to the receptionist next.

"What's in there?" Pari asked. She thought Javid mightn't answer. The damn womxn was secretive like that and Pari got the sinking feeling that Javid was not done revealing all the tricks she had up her sleeve. Pari supposed she should be grateful and relaxed; they couldn't have chosen a better leader for their mission seeing as Javid had all the resources, thought forty steps ahead of anybody and seemed fearless. Another time she might have appreciated Javid's shrewdness but not now.

Javid hadn't said anything yet about Pari's file, but she must know that Pari had a secret of her own, one she never wanted to be found out. Javid mightn't tell the others but Pari wondered if one day, she too would have her secret dangled over her head, forced to do something she didn't want to. She wanted to trust that Javid would never do that but she wasn't so sure anymore.

Pari bit down on her lip hard, enough to stain her teeth with lipstick and draw blood. Javid didn't seem to notice her apprehension as she stared down at the envelope, eventually she looked up and smiled.

"It's nothing you need to worry yourself about – just the location where you'll be meeting our delivery person." Javid answered.

"I thought we were meeting them downtown." Pari said stupidly.

Javid eyed her with something like pity, "It's got to be more specific."

"And what is this package we're supposed to be getting?"

Javid's grin was a sharp slash, causing her high cheekbones to be more prominent. "Information, love, the package is information."

CHAPTER FIFTEEN
We failed Masoumeh(s)

Back in the penthouse, Haleh looked pretty much back to normal. Pari saw that she'd changed her clothes too – she was now wearing a short patterned overlap skirt, few inches from her knee and a black sweater that was surprisingly modest, her thigh high boots were a polished black that glistened, Pari swore she could see her reflection if she bent to check.

Haleh let her hair cascade down her back and there was not a stitch of makeup on her face. She looked younger but not any less fierce, especially with the fierce scowl on her face, Pari was grateful when she turned the heat of it on Javid. The two of them seemed to communicate wordlessly before Javid was forced to break the stare – whatever she'd been trying to tell Haleh was falling on deaf ears it seemed.

"Took you two long enough." Haleh said, her voice colder than ice. There was not a hint of her usual sarcasm in it. Pari was almost afraid of her.

Javid seemed to shrug off the vicious stare Haleh was shooting her, "Here, this is for you." She held out the brown envelope. For the longest, tensioned filled moment, Haleh just stared at it. Pari could see the cogs in her head wheeling, her mind crunching over several possibilities. She was well aware that Javid was giving her a choice, a chance to back out if she wanted to. For a second too, there was hesitation in her coffee brown eyes and briefly, just *briefly*, Pari thought Haleh wouldn't take the paper; that she'd tell Javid to go to hell. But it seemed that Javid was right, Haleh never backed down from logic.

Finally, she snatched the envelope from Javid's hold nearly ripping the tip. She seemed to inhale deeply before addressing Pari.

"Do you want to grab a coat before we head out?" She asked.

Pari startled, was it her imagination that the ice in Haleh's voice thawed a little as she spoke to her?

Too late, she realised she'd been gaping at Haleh. She heard Haleh's sharp sigh of impatience and blinked.

"Uh, right, I'll just grab my coat." She said hurriedly before Haleh decided to stomp out into the hall and leave her behind. She definitely looked like she might.

"Don't bring a purse," Haleh murmured distractedly as she unsealed the envelope and flicked through whatever was written on the note inside it. "Where we're going isn't exactly safe."

Pari's jaw dropped, her eyes darted to Javid and then to Haleh's, waiting for an explanation. There was none forthcoming. She forced herself to stay calm, when she'd been an investigative journalist, she'd gone to shady places in chase of information for a story. This was no different, except the fate of their worlds was at stake. No pressure.

Except, she was very much feeling the pressure, she shrugged on her coat and wordlessly, she and Haleh left the penthouse. Every now and then, Pari would cast her a quick look, trying to see through her impassive face, wanting to glimpse any sign of life or emotion at all. She'd never felt so awkward around Haleh and she didn't like it.

They walked down the street together; Haleh's steps surprisingly unhurried, as if she didn't have a single care in the world but the tightness of her jaw gave her away. Pari shoved her hands deeper into her coat, grateful she was wearing it. The snow was practically nonexistent in the city but the air was cold, the sun a pale, almost invisible ball in the sky. The less than welcoming weather didn't take away the city's life, almost everywhere Pari looked there was something going on – sounds of traffic and music, the smell of street food and something dirty hung in the air, causing Pari to wrinkle her nose in distaste when she inhaled.

She was thinking of something to say, the perfect icebreaker that would snap Haleh out of her dark thoughts. She found herself coming empty and briefly considering if staying silent was the best course of action anyways, Haleh's barb from earlier still stung and she'd rather that not happen again. She wasn't good at dealing with humiliation, especially from a womxn she liked.

How, she found herself thinking, did she always find herself in these situations? Falling first and becoming unbelievably attached. Pari considered herself unlucky in love, she was already the citizen of a country who still murdered people like her – for daring to love openly. Love had never been on her side. In her lifetime, she'd loved many womxns, becoming attached to the point of clinging. None of those affairs had ended well.

There was the one time when she'd been involved with a married womxn, that hadn't been fun.

"What are you smiling about?" Haleh's gruff voice cut through her thoughts and the present rushed into her. She was slightly disoriented by the sound of Haleh's voice that she almost rammed right into a street light pole. Haleh's arms came around her and steered her to safety. Pari's cheeks burned with embarrassment.

"I was smiling?" She stuttered. She made brief eye contact with Haleh.

Haleh rolled her eyes but the action was lacking any malice, she seemed like regular Haleh. Pari treaded carefully, not wanting to set her off again.

"Yes, you were smiling. Why?"

Pari looked down, at Haleh's hands bunched into fists. How her steps seemed to slow even more than before, wherever they were going, they were close and Haleh was obviously dreading it. Pari looked across the street, seeing that there was a park. Now, how to get Haleh in there without being too obvious?

"Well," Pari said, she swiped her tongue over her bottom lip, stalling for time. "I was thinking of that time I was involved with a married womxn."

Pari could see that she'd taken Haleh aback with her words and a wide grin spread on her face; it wasn't every day that one caught Haleh off guard. She was going to enjoy this very much, thank you. Haleh gaped for a second and shook her head, trying to reassemble her mask of indifference but that was humour so obviously shining in her eyes. The two of them had stopped walking now, hogging the narrow sidewalk. "Of all the things I thought you'd say, that wasn't one of them."

Pari gave a modest shrug, trying to contain her smile. Was that respect echoing in Haleh's voice? "Why not? I'm capable of fiendish things too."

Haleh shook her head, "Believe me, I know that. I've never thought of you as some innocent flower. And frankly, it's like some unspoken rite of passage of being a lesbian – have a torrid affair with a married womxn." the way Haleh said it, with some bashfulness that It was obvious she too had been in the same situation before.

Pari's eyes narrowed, it was not surprising that Haleh would have had many lovers in the past. Maybe she was even polyamorous. But that didn't mean she wanted to hear all about Haleh's sexual conquests. "I assume you've been in the same quagmire before?"

Haleh smirked, "Several times. Let me be honest, the first time was probably like your situation," She waved a dismissive hand, "You fancied yourself in love and you believed she was going to leave her husband you. But she didn't."

Even thought Haleh's assessment was pretty much accurate, Pari still bristled, it was one thing to be reminded of one's foolishness and it was another to be pitied for it. Which was why it gave Pari deep satisfaction to say her next words, "Actually, she got pregnant."

Haleh wasn't blown away but she did huff a laugh of surprise. "That's new."

"I broke things off. But you? Why would you get into relationships with married womxns more than once?"

Mischief glinted in Haleh's eyes, she took a step close to Pari to allow a disgruntled womxn and her toddlers pass. But she was standing so close to Pari, so close that Pari could smell her flowery perfume, so close that their chests were merely a hairsbreadth from each other. She'd always thought that she was a little taller than Haleh but they were evenly matched now; thanks to Haleh's boots. That little height difference, the fact that it gave off an illusion of Haleh being more dominant, it caused Pari to flush with heat.

"The thrill of getting caught, Pari darling." Haleh whispered, she tugged at the ends of Pari's hair almost playfully. Pari told herself it was relief she felt when Haleh finally stepped away.

"Those were fun times," Haleh added, almost cheerfully. Then she was walking again, leaving Pari more than confused and a little turned on.

But as they resumed their walk, Pari felt all Haleh's good mood from a few minutes ago drain out of her. The dark cloud of apprehension hung over her once more and it was close to being contagious. If there was something that existed on this not so green earth that Haleh – the most fearless person Pari knew -- was afraid of, then shouldn't they all be afraid too?

The words were on the tip of her tongue; just ask, Pari, she chided herself. Just when she thought she might, Haleh gave her no warning, clamping down on her wrist out of nowhere and dragging her across the street.

"What the fuck?" Pari stumbled over a crack in the road. Cars honked angrily at them and Pari waved a frantic hand in apology. When they were safe, Pari whipped around to glare at Haleh.

"You could have gotten us killed!" She shouted.

She barely registered that Haleh was as still as a statue but the only telltale sign of her anxiety was in her shaking hands. All the anger left Pari's voice, leaving concern.

"I was going to leave you to all your secrecy, Haleh. I wasn't going to say a word but I have never seen you like this, look at you, you're white with fear." Pari took a step forward, a hand outstretched. Haleh flinched away. "I'm--"

Pari cut in stubbornly, "Don't feed me that shit, you don't look fine. Your hands are shaking."

Haleh glanced down at her own hands as if she hadn't been aware. She glared as if her own body was betraying her. "You don't have to know, it's nothing you have worry yourself with."

"Well, I'm worried anyways. If anything, we're friends." Pari said firmly. "And I'm a part of this, you can't just leave me in the dark."

Haleh threw her head back and laughed, but there was no humour in the sound. "You'll find out soon enough."

Pari had to try again, she could feel Haleh retreating into her shell, hiding her emotions as if it would stop the turmoil she was feeling inside. "Why didn't you just say no to Javid?"

Haleh shook her head, "Because she's right." Was all she said.

Pari let out a growl of frustration but she marched right after her. Haleh walked into the narrow alley between a bakery and a bank. The narrow path stank of rotten food and urine, nothing could have prepared Pari for the stench. She gagged and slapped one hand over her nose.

"Are you setting us up to get mugged?" Pari said through her muffled palm, at first she didn't think Haleh heard her and she was about to repeat herself very loudly when she was cut off.

"No, but we will be if you insist on being a chatter box."

"Well, I wouldn't be a chatter box if I knew where we were

going and who we were meeting." Pari retorted but she kept her voice low.

She thought she heard Haleh sigh but she didn't slow down. Pari's thoughts began to wander, she could only imagine how this alley would be in the nighttime. She shivered violently, although she knew practically nothing about country's crime rate, it still wasn't a farfetched assumption to think that places like this would be crawling with all types of criminals when it was nighttime.

Finally, the alley gave way to a new street and suddenly, Pari understood why Haleh had asked her to leave her purse back at the hotel. So far, all she'd seen of Iran was busy airports, glamourous hotels and high end boutiques. She was seeing the less glamourous side now; broken down houses lined this street and half finished constructed roads.

Pari felt a pang in her chest, it was like being transported back to her own childhood. She'd grown up in a place like this, amongst people who suffered like her family did and still daring to hope for a much better future and existence. Even to a young Pari, studying had been a means to an end, she'd been best in her class not because she was a true academic but because she'd believed that studying, getting those good grades meant an out of the horrible dregs she lived in. Then the Taliban had taken over Kabul and those dreams had been halted and at one point, almost impossible to achieve.

She shook her head, trying to clear the thoughts from her head. She saw that Haleh was looking at her and realised that she'd been standing rooted to the same spot for a long minute. For a moment, she thought Haleh might see her, might even understand but then that spell was broken.

"No need to look so disgusted, I promise the filth doesn't seep into your expensive coat." Haleh said scathingly. Pari didn't deign her with an answer, she could see that her friend was resorting to cutting comments as a defence mechanism.

"Is this where we're meeting our informant?" Pari asked instead.

Haleh gave a jerk of her head and they continued on. People

lived in this street and the more they walked, the more people they came about. Little children running around, a few local businesses and street stalls.

Haleh seemed to shrink into herself as she walked, keeping her head down as if she was afraid of being recognized. They stopped in front of a grocery store and Haleh pushed open the two doors. It was the only building that looked decent, the exterior was painted a fresh white that caused it to stand out from the other structures around it.

Although the interior wasn't much to look at; several aisle of products but on a closer look, many of the shelves were empty. The air smelt a little sterile, like bleach.

Haleh walked up to the cashier behind the counter; a plump middle aged womxn with dark brown skin. She wore no name tag on her T-shirt. They exchanged greetings in Farsi and Haleh murmured something about wanting to see a man in the back.

The womxn gestured at the door on her right and Haleh muttered her thanks.

Pari was almost afraid to see what or *who* was behind the door especially with the whole shroud of mystery Haleh had been wearing since the moment they left the hotel. She blinked in surprise when the door led outside the store – or more accurately, behind it. They were now standing in front of a similar building but shabbier.

There was a signboard on the right side that read 'police station'. Pari remembered Javid's words, that Haleh used to be a police officer. Was this where she'd worked then? Pari found it hard to imagine Haleh working in such a place, she stuck out like a sore thumb, and she was beautiful, too beautiful for this place. Pari realised how shallow she was being and felt her cheeks heat up.

A man opened stepped through the entrance of the station and walked up to them, he was dressed casually; in jeans and a polo T-shirt. Was he an officer too?

"Haleh *Hanifnejad*, how many years has it been?" The man asked, he cast Pari a curious look but he didn't say anything to her.

"I thought you swore that you would never step foot here again, I reckon those were your last words." The man threw back his head and laughed mockingly.

Pari waited for Haleh's outburst, she wanted her to put this man in his place. But when she looked at Haleh's face, all she saw was shame. This wasn't the tough, confident womxn that Pari knew and liked. She wanted to shake Haleh, to snap her out of whatever hell she'd trapped herself in.

"Bijan," Haleh said flatly.

The man – Bijan -- continued to chuckle and Pari had never wanted to pummelled somebody to the ground so bad. He shook his head, "You remember my name, seem to recall something you said about wanting to forget every single thing about this place." The humour leaked gradually out of his voice until he sounded cold and Pari found herself a little afraid of him. She edged closer to Haleh, not sure if she did it for her own comfort or for Haleh's.

"Yeah, well, that sentiment still stands." Haleh said and Pari wanted to whoop in joy; there was the Haleh she knew. It was ironic that Pari preferred a very cold and sarcastic Haleh than a cowering, docile one.

Be cruel to the whole fucking world, Pari thought, *just fight back – I don't care if you're fighting me too.*

Bijan looked taken aback by the sudden vigour in Haleh's tone and she didn't stop there, she took a step forward.

"You sure as fucking hell know that I would burn this place to rubble if I could. Picture this, Bijan – a young womxn, who'd gone through shit herself, studying hard, taking all the necessary exams just so she could join the police force and making a fucking difference in this fucking world." Haleh wasn't shouting but her words had the same effect as if she was shouting, her voice was quiet, only a little audible above the distant sound of childish laughter and play. Each word was spat out like a gunshot and Pari was very thankful to not be on the receiving end of it.

Dimly, she registered that in all of Haleh's tough exterior, she'd never been like this with her friends. Sure there were moments when her quips crossed the line from deep sarcasm to cutting re-marks but she'd never been outright cruel.

"This young womxn finally gets into the force, she's desperate to help people but she finds that the force is more corrupted than it is good. She watches as the so called good guys, stationed in one of the shittiest parts of the city to fight a gang problem, mind you, end up being the ones causing all the havoc. Charging money in return for protection, taking whatever they wanted, whenever they wanted it. Crossing the line and raping a twelve year old!" Haleh's last sentence was a fucking whip cracking the air and land-ing in impact; tearing through skin. Pari gasped, her head reeling from impact. She was looking at Bijan in a new light, one that was painted in disgust.

There was one thing all the Farsi speaking countries had in common; an extremist religious government that preached right-eousness and would take an axe to anyone falling short – and the only people who ever did were womxns, young girls and children. The Taliban taking over Afghanistan had been the exact same case; an extremist group who'd declared the intent to restore the country back to what it had been; where everybody obeyed the demands of religion. Once upon a time, Pari had been resentful of that religion, she'd even agreed with the Islamophobic assessments of the western media; that the religion the Taliban claimed to fol-low was not one of peace but one of strife and violence and hate.

Until Pari had done a little searching for herself and discovered that the religion itself was not the problem, it was the government using it as a guise to carry out their cruel injustice. Pari was not at all surprised that Haleh had witnessed that injustice first hand.

Haleh's scathing laughter drew Pari back to the present, "the young womxn was naïve, thinking it was her chance to right a wrong – she didn't know the evil came from within the force that swore to protect and serve. We all failed Masoumeh, me most of all because if she hadn't come to me – I wouldn't have tried to poke and poke and she would still be alive."

"So, fuck you, Bijan. I didn't come back here for you to gloat." Haleh's eyes swept the man's form, her eyes barely disguising the deep disdain and disgust in them. "And I see you're still into your old tricks, selling high class information to the highest bidder like the fucking traitor you are."

Bijan flinched and growled low in his throat. He looked like he might do something drastic like try to hit Haleh. But he must have taken in her stance, the way her shoulders were held high and stiffened and her hands bunched into fists. She was bracing for a physical fight and best believe she was ready.

Plus it was two on one. This pathetic man didn't stand a chance.

In the end, Bijan just handed her the bright yellow file he'd been holding. He tried to look as if he was unaffected and uncaring about Haleh's jabs – which were no doubt true – but it was obvious in the clenching and unclenching of his jaw.

"Looks like you're being the messenger for illicit information, look at you thinking you're any better than I am." Bijan spat. Haleh's only answer was a look of genuine pity, she snatched the file from Bijan's grip and spun on her heels, her back to him.

"Oh and one last thing, Bijan," She said in a deceptively jovial tone.

"What?" He asked, trying and failing to hide how wary he felt.

"I am done with you and I'm done with this fucking place. The next time I'm here, it'll be to raze this shithole to the fucking ground." And with that, Haleh was opening the backdoor that led into the grocery store and walking into it without a backward glance. Pari didn't bother to deign him with a final look either. She scurried after Haleh.

Several minutes later, they were back leaving the alley, this time with no words exchanged between the two of them. Pari was a little lost in her thoughts to remember to complain about the stench, she was thinking that Haleh had grossly overestimated the dangerousness of their errand. Sure, they'd been in one of the shadiest looking parts of town but the dangerous element hadn't been the people who lived in it, struggling to make lives for themselves. It was the cops, the ones set up in that part of town to protect the people.

Pari was beginning to think that there might not be much of

a difference between Afghanistan and Iran; both countries were ridden with the same type of corruption, the only difference was that one was a lot more deceiving than the other. It reminded Pari of what was at stake, why they needed Gordafarid's sword, it was the only thing that could save their worlds and usher them into an era of peace and prosperity.

She was also thinking that Javid was wrong, Haleh hadn't needed her for anything, and she was as strong as ever – capable of fighting her own battles. Pari tried to shrug off the pang of hurt that the realisation made her feel, she was very happy that Haleh had finally confronted what she'd been running from for years and while it might not bring her much peace, it was definitely the closure that she needed, the motivation to put her all in for this mission. It was still a little embarrassing that Javid had bigged up Pari's usefulness only for Pari to realise herself that she wasn't needed.

"You're quiet," Haleh said. Pari looked at her and shook her head. They'd emerged from the alley and back into the more beautiful streets, they looked nothing more than silly camouflage to Pari now; constructed to hide the deeper ugly of the city.

"You complain about me being a chatterbox, I adhere to your advice and now you're chastising me for it." Pari meant for the words to come out airy and uncaring but she sounded irritated instead.

"I didn't ask you to shut up, I just said to find a middle ground between chatty and mute." Haleh murmured sarcastically.

"There she is!" Pari exclaimed, throwing up her hands mockingly, she almost hit a passerby in the face.

"Be *very* careful what you say, Pari." Haleh said softly, her voice full of danger.

"I don't get why you wouldn't just tell me. I felt like a fly on the wall, intruding." Pari said and winced, she didn't mean to sound self centred and make it all about her. She shook her head, that wasn't what she'd meant. "I would have supported you."

Haleh was quiet for a few seconds before speaking, "I know."

She admitted. "And you were not a fly on the wall. If I didn't want you with me, I wouldn't have budged to Javid."

Pari blinked, unsure she'd heard wrong. Did Haleh just admit to being wrong for once?

"And wipe that look off your face, I can admit when I'm wrong when it happens. Although there are very rare circumstances in which I am." Haleh's voice was lightly teasing.

"Will you tell me what happened?" Pari asked in a small voice, she held her breath, waiting to be shut down again.

Haleh nodded curtly. "But it's kind of a long and heavy story." She gave Pari a look that was almost shy, "There's a park just over there, we can sit down and talk."

Pari laced her hand through Haleh's, the latter jerked in surprise but she didn't pull away. At least not at first, she gave Pari's hand a small squeeze before letting go

"Okay, let's talk."

Of all the mental images Pari had conjured when she'd received that message from Javid about their mission, she certainly hadn't factored this one into any of her numerous fantasies – she'd imagined threading through dangerous paths, fighting masked villains -- which was strange seeing as they had no competition from any other group seeking the sword, at this point everyone with enough knowledge about the sword knew that seeking it was a death mission – even though it was a vain fantasy. She'd certainly not imagined sitting on a swing with Haleh, kicking her legs up in the air like a child.

It was nice though, the weather was still too cold, causing the park to be almost empty people – a few walked their pets, but there were no children in sight. Pari found that she rather liked the privacy, she couldn't remember the last time she'd been in a public park; she was too busy with work to finally get the dog she'd been wanting to and she didn't have any friends with children or many friends at all. But this was nice.

She sent Haleh a fleeting look, wondering what she was thinking; she saw that Haleh was already looking at her with the same watching eyes. Despite the cold, Pari felt her cheeks heat up in a blush. She cleared her throat, trying to regain some semblance of control.

"What was going on back there?" She began hesitantly, although Haleh had made it clear that she would answer any questions Pari had and although Pari had pieced together most of the stories – she was a journalist after all –she was still afraid to ask Haleh the deep cutting questions, partly because she didn't want her to relieve what was no doubt a traumatic experience for her and partly because she was afraid Haleh would shut her down again, her promise be damned.

"Javid told me that you used to be a police officer." Pari added. She was still watching Haleh carefully.

Haleh cracked a small smile, "You don't have to look at me like I'm going to start flipping tables at the slightest trigger."

This was where Pari's humour came in handy. "There are no table around for you to flip." She said with a smile.

Haleh rolled her eyes.

"There are park benches," Pari offered with a look of mock innocence. A small laugh escaped Haleh's lips and Pari tried to ignore the warmth that filled her chest. Sure she liked making people laugh, she liked breaking tensioned filled silence but she thought that she might like making Haleh laugh best.

Dangerous territories, her mind warned, *this isn't the time to get attached*. So she buried the feeling deep in her chest and forced herself to concentrate on the conversation at hand.

"I get the metaphorical mention of tables. And no, I don't expect you to start flipping tables and getting furious." Pari answered. Still, the question remained in Haleh's eyes.

"Haleh, you're closed off, you don't talk about your feelings. You look at everybody with suspicion and I'm the last person who's going to blame you for that. It just feels like, you offering now, feels too good to be true."

Haleh looked contemplative for a second or two. "Have you ever known me to go back on my word though?" Haleh asked, then she seemed to realise something. "It's a little ironic that we've known each other for three years, most of our friendship has been communicating from thousands of miles away from each other. So, of course you don't know me."

Pari flinched, unable to help herself. *Told you*, her mind mocked.

She inhaled deeply and glanced down at her glove covered hands, as if she was reading something from them. Pari wouldn't go as far to say that Haleh looked vulnerable in this moment, that she'd put down her guard. There was still that stubborn blankness in her eyes but her voice was softer somehow, cushioning every blow her words carried.

"I never go back on my word, Pari." Haleh said firmly. "I said I was going to answer any questions you had and I'm going to."

She looked up from her hands, and squinted ahead, staring at nothing and everything. "Yeah, I used to be a police officer. I'd always wanted to be a cop since I was a kid. You must have pieced together some stuff from that bastard's ramblings." She added darkly. Pari nodded as if receiving a correction, they were not going to address Bijan by his name, got it.

"I grew up in a fairly middle class family, safe but not safe enough that we didn't see all kinds of horrible shit happening around us. We weren't blind to that. My father was an attorney, working for a mid level law firm, he was into property law but my first perception of law was cool people in suits bringing the bad guys to jail. I wanted to be just like him." There was a fondness in Haleh's tone that Pari had never heard before. It was clear that this tough as nails womxn loved her father. Briefly, Pari wondered if he was still alive.

"At first I wanted to be a lawyer but then I went through a tomboy phase in secondary school." Haleh continued, her cheeks pinkened as she spoke.

Pari couldn't help but express her surprise, "You used to be a tomboy?" She asked with a surprised laugh. She tried to imagine this very feminine Haleh wearing boy clothes and keeping her hair short and wearing a forced swagger in her steps.

Haleh laughed, looking more carefree than Pari had ever seen her. "I like to call it my first lesbian awakening."

"Wait, there's more?" Pari deadpanned. Haleh gave her a smug look.

"It takes several stages of metamorphosis to become this awesome." Haleh shot back. She shook her head, "Well, I excelled at sports in school, I was captain of the basketball team, and I also ran cross country."

Pari was not at all surprised by any of these achievements. Haleh was one of those rare people who'd been awesome and sexy from when they were old enough to be.

"I was also good very good at the academic sides of school too. My family were so proud that I was going to follow in my father's footsteps. Then he was murdered."

Pari gasped, "Oh, my, Haleh, I'm so sorry."

Haleh shrugged. "That was a long time ago."

"Doesn't mean it still doesn't hurt." Pari said wryly, thinking of her own self.

"Anyways, it was a collision with a drunken driver. The man was never caught, left my father and fucking ran. It was torture, it was then that I realised that I didn't want to be a lawyer; I didn't want to drag the criminals to court after he'd been caught. I wanted to be doing the catching." Haleh said. "I studied hard too, wrote all necessary exams. Trained hard."

"I got in. There are more than forty police stations in Tehran and its suburbs, maybe about ten in this province. All of them reporting back to the district. I was stationed in here, the station was new too – put in place to combat gang trouble in the area. The people living there live under terrible conditions – you saw that for yourself. A few of them tended to fall into the wrong parts. We were put in place to stop that. But the superintendent in charge was a fucking corrupt man, he let the shit go on under his nose for a cut of the money."

"Suddenly, my dream of catching the bad guys was foolish – I'd joined them instead. Still, I was determined to be the good one out of all of them. I thought I could make the difference alone. I was wrong. A young girl came into the station one day, I can never forget that day." Haleh's voice wavered, her eyes a little distant as if she was lost in a memory. "She was wearing the most tattered dress, muddy, her hijab had been partly ripped from her head and parts of her hair spilled out. There was a dark red stain on the front of her dress."

A shiver ran down Pari's spine.

"She was with her older sister. They'd come to report a rape. I was the only officer at the station that day, the rest of them had gone out to watch some football game."

Indignation rose up in her chest and Pari clenched her fists. It didn't matter how many times she heard the stories of shitty cops, she would always be furious for their victims.

"The girl was crying, she could barely get any words out. I was trying to get her to tell me if she'd seen the face of her attacker. A few of the cops return to the station, they were arguing some pointless thing. The girl looks up and then she's pointing at one of the fucking cops. My colleague."

Pari had figured out most of the story herself but her heart still dropped to her stomach at Haleh uttering the words aloud.

"Long story short: I tried to get justice for her, wrote to the fucking district. Nothing happened and Masoumeh killed herself." Haleh said, until that moment, her voice had been flat but something seemed to shatter in her, her voice caving in on the strength it had been forced to carry. Pari reached out, covering her hand with her own. She breathed out a little sigh of relief when Haleh didn't pull away.

"I quit the force after that. My dad left his life savings to me and I left the country. I became a different person, if you know all the kinds of illegal shit I've been up to in Berlin." Haleh laughed but there was no humour in the sound. "The truth is, I didn't leave out of anger, it was shame, Pari, shame that caused me to run away. I failed Masoumeh." She said matter of factly, no self loathing in her words, just the solid certainty of a womxn who'd said the words so many times that she'd come to believe then.

Pari didn't bother trying to disprove her even though for once, Haleh and all her pigheadedness were wrong. Haleh didn't need that, she'd come here today because there was a chance to save a million other *Masoumeh(s)*.

"We're going to find the sword," Pari said instead.

Haleh nodded, "We have to." She said with urgency.

"So," Pari said, trying to lighten the mood. "What's in that file? Did Javid tell you anything?"

Haleh glanced down at the paper in her lap and frowned. "Yeah, as a matter of fact, she did."

Pari rolled her eyes. "How surprising that she didn't spring it up on you this time." She really needed to talk to Javid about her leadership style. Maybe Toman found all of that secretiveness and bossiness sexy but Pari wasn't digging it anymore; Ocean's Eight be damned.

"What's in the file?" She asked.

"It's relating to Shirin Shah." Haleh said. "Shirin and Nazanin made it to the cave, they were so close to getting their hands on the sword, but Nazanin got trapped and Shirin had to leave her to go get help. The local police were involved and sent out an alert to other stations in the area."

"Including the one you used to be a cop at," Pari finished.

"Yes, there was a whole report and everything. I know that we've been using the term disappear when talking about Nazanin Hesami but that's not what happened. She was killed and this file contains all the details."

CHAPTER SIXTEEN
Knitting and Manicure work wonders as meditation

Delnaz breathed a sigh of relief when Haleh and Pari opened the door and stepped into the room together. She stood up from where she'd been sitting and ran over to them. There was something in both their gazes that stopped her cold, she had a feeling that they wouldn't welcome a hug. That and the long, brown file that Haleh held in front of her like a shield.

"You two are okay!" She exclaimed.

A light of amusement entered Haleh's eyes, it was a mere flicker but Delnaz caught it before it was gone. "I didn't know you were expecting us to return injured or maybe even dead."

Pari nudged Haleh's side. "Be nice to her, she looks so happy to see us." And because Pari was smiling, Delnaz didn't hesitate again, she drew her into a quick hug. She broke away from the hug a second later and turned around to glower at Javid who was sitting down on the single seat sofa, her legs spread out before her like a king. Her eyes were twinkling with amusement.

Delnaz pointed an accusing finger at their leader, "If it wasn't for Javid who refused to tell us nothing about where the two of you were going."

"I thought I'd get rid of our least favourite members before our mission started," Javid drawled.

"Haha, you've got jokes, Aref." Haleh deadpanned.

"Glad to see you two in one piece." Javid teased, casting a glance at Delnaz who flushed. They were making fun of her being worried. Well the next time, Delnaz would simply not worry.

"I told you not to bother," Toman said without looking up from her knitting. Yes, Toman was knitting. Delnaz had been surprised when her friend whipped out yarn and needles and started twisting them, her hands fast and familiar with the motion. "I've got to have something else to do when I'm not brooding." Toman had quipped dryly when Delnaz had gaped at her.

"Are you going to tell us where they went to and what Haleh is doing with that mysterious looking file, Javid?" Delnaz asked with false sweetness as she returned to her seat beside Farzaneh.

Javid gathered her legs together and sat upright, her posture going from relaxed to serious in one blink. "Thank you, Haleh." Some unspoken exchange seemed to pass between the two of them as Haleh handed her the file.

For several minutes nobody spoke as Javid combed through the file, mouthing the words a few times, with each minute, her expression seemed to grow grimmer. Whatever she was reading, it wasn't good at all. Delnaz tried to look the perfect picture of calm, she'd always been good at looking serene when she wasn't – part of the perks of being a performer. She looked and saw that even Toman had stopped knitting and she realised she'd been knitting a beanie. She wondered who she was knitting for, she didn't think she'd ever seen Toman wear wool.

"I asked Haleh and Pari to retrieve the police report on the incident that occurred years ago at the Yellow Flowers Cave. With Shirin Shah and Nazanin Hesami."

It was impossible to miss how quickly Farzaneh sat up, her eyes blazing with anger. Delnaz thought that she looked like some sort of otherworldly goddess, her dark hair cascading down her back and her regal colour patterned kaftan. "What have you done?"

Javid raised her chin up, "I'm looking out for the safety of my friends. For all of our safety and I'll go above and beyond to do that. This quest for the truth also concerns you, Farzaneh."

Farzaneh shook her head, dark hair swishing from side to side at the motion. "I don't like this, Javid. This poking and prodding. Shirin is no doubt traumatised by whatever happened that night, she's withdrawn from society because of that night – I was already against seeing her, disturbing her again. Now, you're doing more digging, far more than I'm comfortable with."

Delnaz thought Farzaneh was being a tad melodramatic, there was no sin in what Javid had done, it also didn't mean that Shirin Shah wasn't allowed to be afraid of whatever had happened to her friend. Two people could be right and valid at the same time.

Javid stood up, "With all due respect, Farzaneh, I think that anyone would be honoured to be your friend. To have you be so protective over them. Because that is exactly what you're doing now, you're being Shirin's friend." Javid spoke softly but her tone was firm at the same time. "But this mission is bigger than that."

Delnaz was surprised when she caught Haleh jerk her head in a nod of agreement. Of all the people she expected to be on Javid's side, Haleh would have come in last and none of them had forgotten the tantrum she'd thrown just hours ago right in this very room.

But she went ahead, she listened to Javid, didn't she? Delnaz's mind chided. That was correct, for all her protests and pleading, Haleh had gone ahead to do what Javid had asked her to do.

The whole room was silent, waiting for Farzaneh to protest. She didn't. There was nothing unreasonable about Javid's actions.

"I just wish you would let us know these things before you do them. Springing random surprises on us, it's starting to get old and angering." Haleh said.

To everybody's surprise, Javid nodded. "I agree. It's just, I'm used to be the womxn behind the scenes an awful lot that I can't stop. I requested for this report months ago, before I even had the thought of finally assembling all of you here for this mission. I promise, there aren't any more unpleasant surprises on the way."

"But there are going to be surprises?" Delnaz asked wryly.

Javid's grin spread slowly. "Only the ones that ends up saving your asses."

All of them seemed to mull over that and gave simultaneous shrugs. Delnaz found that she wouldn't mind a Hail Mary type of surprise in the future, of course, she hoped it would be smooth sailing for their little gang, however unlikely that wish was.

'Alright, now that that's out of the way, this file," Javid raised it up. "Details how far Shirin and Nazanin made it to the sword. They were struggling through the cave, at that time of the year the water levels were higher than they'd predicted and I think Shirin had sustained a few injuries, none threatening but enough to slow her down."

"They were so close," Farzaneh said in a broken whisper of a voice.

"Farzaneh, forgive me for asking you this and I don't mean to be rude at all. But why didn't you guide them, like you're doing with us? You're the pathfinder, they needed you." Pari said.

A look of deep pain flashed through Farzaneh's eyes and it was Pari's turn to be nudged not so gently.

"No, no. You're not being rude." Farzaneh was quick to reassure Pari with a strained smile.

Farzaneh inhaled a deep breath, "The truth is that Shirin didn't want my help."

There was sudden silence, this time, everyone in the room exchanged confused looks. Delnaz could tell that they were all thinking the same thing, in probably varying degrees of niceness.

Haleh was probably thinking something along the lines of, "Is

Shirin Shah fucking stupid?"

Delnaz was thinking the same thing but without the profanity. Although none of them — excluding Javid — had ever seen Farzaneh's power in action, none of them seemed to doubt her. It was as simple as Javid trusting her and they trusted Javid's intuition.

"Why not?" It was Toman who asked, her voice was carefully neutral and Delnaz was thankful for her natural tact. The rest of them were a lot more passionate and wouldn't be able to hide the fact that they thought Shirin Shah had questionable judgement.

"Shirin is a lot like you, Javid." Farzaneh began, jerking a nod in Javid's direction.

"In what way?" Javid asked.

Farzaneh smiled a little, "The both of you are careful planners. Javid I'm yet to discover the extent of yours, but let me ask you one question. For the past three years, you've carefully mapped out the location of Gordafarid's sword, you've done your research, spoken to all the right people. Created a tight knit plan with your crew." She let her eyes roam around the room, meeting each of their gazes briefly.

"What would you do if you met someone, someone who wanted to be part of that carefully put together crew?" She asked.

Javid didn't hesitate with her answer, "I don't think there would be space for them." Realising what she'd said and the reason for Farzaneh asking that question, she flushed. But to her credit, she didn't try to take back the words. Because they were true and pretending otherwise would be cruel to Farzaneh.

Farzaneh didn't look glad that she was right. She just gave a shrug that said, do you see what I mean now?

"Shirin was exactly like that. She'd spent years researching the sword too. Like you had, she met me much later on and by then it was too late to alter all her plans around me. All she wanted to know was if she was worthy of finding the sword and what her — their chances were. You see, Shirin had crafted the most genius plan, she'd found out that previous groups that had sought out the sword had been in groups of five, six and even more sometimes. They'd never made it back alive."

Delnaz almost missed the quick look that transpired between Javid and Toman. It wasn't quite a look of fear, but there was something else there. Javid must have known all these statistics, she probably knew the numerical odds and chances of their survival and they were still going through with this. She had a plan and Delnaz was choosing to trust the plan.

Still, Farzaneh's words didn't do much for morale.

"Shirin thought she had the perfect solution to that. So she created a crew of two — herself and Nazanin Hesami. A crew of two people in sync with each other was easier to manage, less people to worry about while in the cave. Less resources wasted. To include me in that plan would have scattered the whole thing, so she didn't."

This was the part where Haleh would have quipped in with a sarcastic comment against Shirin Shah but it seemed like she'd gained a conscience in the past hour that she'd been gone. That or Haleh wasn't as heartless as Delnaz thought. Or she wasn't even heartless at all. Was she? It was an almost impossible feat to figure out who Haleh was beneath all that sass and sarcasm.

"So what killed Nazanin Hesami? How did she die?" Toman asked, steering them gently to the initial topic of conversation.

"Even this file can't say and that's why attending tonight's fundraiser is still very much in our itinerary." Javid said. "At this point, only Shirin Shah can tell us what happened that night."

"What if she doesn't? What if it's too painful for her to talk about?" It was Pari that asked.

Haleh grimaced, already knowing the answer. They would be heading in blind then, at risk of whatever had murdered Nazanin Hesami. That didn't sound like a very good option to Delnaz.

Javid hesitated before answering. "There might be another way."

All eyes snapped to her.

"A way to know what happened that night?" Delnaz asked hopefully.

Javid shook her head. "No. A way to know if our journey will be smooth sailing."

"Are you going to tell us more about this way?" Haleh's deadpan tone was back.

"I will, we'll talk about it while we get manicures." Javid said with a wave.

"Let me guess, this mysterious way also happens to be at the fundraiser?" Toman asked. "And it wouldn't happen to be..." She trailed off. "Never mind. Let's go get manicures."

CHAPTER SEVENTEEN
The crown of the night!

"Javid, you look stunning. You have a great eye for fashion." Pari said, meeting Javid's eye in the vanity mirror. She stepped back a little, admiring her style.

Javid gave a modest shrug, it felt like months that she'd found the midnight blue dress on the hanger even though in reality, it had only been hours ago, not even up to a day, heck not even up to twelve hours. Then, she'd had a whimsical fantasy, she'd imagined wowing Toman wearing this dress.

It seemed so far away now, a desire so silly. Because they had much more serious things to worry about; find Shirin Shah and acquire the priestess' eye. The latter sounded so incredulous that Haleh had laughed hard when Javid mentioned it. She'd seen even the doubt on Toman's face.

Information on what was the priestess' eye was an artefact Javid stumbled upon early days into her research on Gordafarid's sword years ago. She hadn't only been banking on the existence of one powerful relic, she'd hoped to find many. And the deeper she went into her research, the less likely she discovered the possibilities of more than one artefact existing. She'd discovered that many relics that were now displayed in Iranian museums used to be conduits for great magical power and over the hundreds of years of their existence, they'd become weak and whatever magic had existed in them had drained out slowly until it was nonexistent.

Javid had heard of a powerful mirror that was once rumoured to grant the holder the power to find anyone they wished to, just by imagining their face. She'd tracked the mirror down for a while and had even found it – she'd bought it in an art auction – only to discover that it had none of its rumoured powers. It was around the same time she'd discovered the existence of the priestess' eye, by then she'd known Toman and had asked her to track down the object.

The priestess' eye was an emerald that had once belonged to a powerful Persian priestess who allegedly had the power to glimpse the future. She'd worn the jewel on her forehead, between her eyes and through the jewel, she'd been able to foretell certain events. She'd served a few queens in her lifetime. More than thirty years ago, a group of archeologists had discovered her remains, with a certain jewel still between her eyes.

Javid had had Toman track down the jewel; it had gone from being in a museum to being auctioned to the highest bidder for tens of millions. And was going to be auctioned off again tonight at the fundraiser for climate change; the same fundraiser Shirin Shah was going to be at tonight. It was a perfect kill two birds with one stone situation – except, her friends didn't have much faith in the priestess' eye.

"You're still thinking about what Toman said, aren't you?" Pari cut into Javid's thought.

Javid smiled a little. "Toman and I have researched many relics. She doesn't quite trust in the existence of this one – no, scratch that – she doesn't think it's reasonable to trust in the emerald. We've stumbled upon other relics, tracked them down even. I even bought a fucking stupid mirror for a hundred thousand quid and it turned out to be devoid of any magic." Javid didn't blame Toman for shutting down the idea immediately.

"Not worth risking, Shirin Shah is more paranoid than ever and there will be very important dignitaries at the fundraisers, even local celebrities too. Which means there will be maximum security. And what? You're going to have the most inexperienced team trying to steal one of the items being auctioned? That's dumb, Javid and you know it." Toman had said, her eyes blazing with fury in a way that Javid had never seen before.

Javid couldn't deny that she wasn't right. Toman was fucking right.

'I know, love," She'd countered back in the calmest and most collected voice. All their friends had been watching them, more than a little surprised at the showdown. Javid and Toman had always been a united front. They'd never clashed on opinions before, at least never so publicly. "And I'm not proposing that we steal it."

Javid had swept her gaze over all of them, feeling more than a little like she was pitching the most dangerous job to them. She was fine with never getting her hands on the emerald but if they could look into the future, then they could see what was coming before it arrived, they mightn't even need Shirin Shah's help anymore. Javid already felt guilt that their questions would no doubt uproot the womxn's existence and throw her back into the nightmare that she'd lived years ago.

"The priestess' eye is the crown of the night, the last thing to be auctioned. I've been at these events a lot in the past to know that such an expensive object would be saved for last, a duplicate put in a showcase and the real thing kept safe. Only the lucky bidder would be having the real thing at the end of the fundraiser. We just need to find where it'll be put, get me close enough to it so I can use it once. That's all. The jewel isn't leaving with us."

She'd seen that she was convincing them; oh, not Toman, the determination in her face was unwavering but the rest of them, the seed had been planted and they were beginning to think that not-stealing the emerald wouldn't be so impossible after all.

A bitter smile had spread on Toman's face, "There would still be the matter of security. Like you said, the emerald is the crown jewel of the night. There is no way it would be left alone for just a second. And there's the cameras."

"Are you kidding me, love? For one, this event isn't going to be televised, there will be minimal press. Two, only the most important of the most important will have received an invite, no nonentity will be there. Or so they reckon, aye?" Javid had let her confident grin spread, it was a little false but not entirely. She'd won over her friends; they were glancing at each other and nodding.

"Besides, we aren't stealing it." Haleh had pointed out with a smirk of her own. Javid had been reminded of the moment she'd discovered Haleh's past, that she used to be a cop like Toman. It had been difficult to believe, surely one didn't go from a life of protecting people to breaking more than ten laws oversees and pretty much running the most illegal nightlife organisations.

Toman had thrown her hands up in a rare display of exasperation, "I can't believe you would agree to this, Haleh. What's next? Delnaz throws common sense into the air?"

Delnaz had shot Toman a withering look that almost rivalled Haleh's. "Let's not act like Javid is suggesting this to gain some twisted rush of adrenaline. This is about guaranteeing our own safety."

"And Farzaneh? Care to chirp in and say something?" Toman had snapped, Farzaneh had looked slightly taken aback, surprised at being included in the conversation. Javid made a mental note then to talk to her later, she'd noticed how Farzaneh tended to sit out of group discussions, as if she didn't quite feel among them. "You're the pathfinder, have you heard of this emerald and its supposed power."

To her credit, she'd swiftly recovered and smiled, "Yes, Toman, I have heard of the priestess' eye."

Toman had looked the slightest bit chastened. She sighed then and settled back in her seat, "I have never doubted Javid's good intentions. But the road to hell is paved with them. Some things are just too dangerous to risk." Try as much as she did, Javid still let out a tiny sigh of relief. Toman restating her belief in her was reassuring. She regretted fracturing the easy camaraderie between them, Toman had been her right hand; a person to bounce off ideas to and with. Now she was as good as unapproachable.

"We're not going to get caught." Javid said firmly.

"And if the emerald turns out to be useless?"

'We're not going to get caught." She'd repeated. And in the end, Toman had stopped arguing.

Javid didn't doubt herself now, even though Toman had opposed the plan, she was still going to help them. And the truth was that Javid wasn't worried about getting caught. She was worried about the emerald being as good as useless, and then she was thinking of Gordafarid's sword. What were the chances that the sword would suffer the same fate, let's say in the next fifty or so years to come? Or perhaps even shorter. What if the power of the sword wasn't as it had been in the past and what if it wasn't enough to save their world?

Time was definitely not a luxury they had on their side.

"You okay in there?" Pari said.

Javid blinked, "I'm alright, love." It was only a half lie anyways.

She recognized Pari's expectant look and grinned, "And how could I forget, you look absolutely stunning, Pari." She whistled dramatically. As expected, Pari preened under the attention and although Javid was playfully laying things a little thick, she couldn't deny that Pari did look stunning. Her hair hung in bouncy waves over her shoulder and she wore a plum coloured sleeveless cocktail dress that stopped just a little above her knees. She was wearing black kitten heels, completing her look. Javid was swiftly discovering that Pari's fashion wasn't exactly flashy, she favoured more muted tones, darker colours than brighter ones. She was arguably the most modest of all of them in dressing, possibly an ingrained fashion that was hard to break.

Still, she looked beautiful.

A knock sounded on the door and a second later, Toman was stepping into the room, her eyes alert, only pausing when she looked at Javid. Her gaze only stayed for a brief second before flicking away. She cleared her throat and glanced down at it even though she wasn't wearing a watch – she usually did though.

"It's been seventeen minutes since Haleh, Delnaz and Farzaneh left. Isn't it safe for us to hit the road too?" She asked. Javid was a little slow to answer the question, she was too busy staring at Toman's dress, struck with the realisation that it was the first time she'd seen her so dressed up. Toman didn't like flashy either, she was wearing a navy button-up sheath dress that reached past her knees. It was fairly modest, the little buttons working up her chest and stopping a little, exposing a bit of cleavage. Javid tried not to ogle.

It had been her idea that they arrived in separate groups, each of them assigned different missions. Haleh's team would find Shirin and Javid's team would go after the priestess' eye. It was a good plan, in case Javid's group was caught, so the others would be able to leave without being involved. Still, she was confident that they wouldn't get caught.

It was time for the first phase of their plan; arrive at the party.

Javid had obtained a blueprint of the hotel floor the fundraiser was being held in. The emerald would arrive about an hour after the event started, in a bulletproof vehicle. She'd tracked down the security company in charge of the event too, they were only sending in a few men; no doubt thinking that tonight would be an easy job for them.

The emerald wouldn't be staying in the vehicle throughout the night, it would eventually be moved to a suite and left mostly unattended to. The problem was causing a distraction big enough to divert the guard's attention from the emerald but not too big a diversion that it caused them to call for backup help.

Javid blew out a breath, it was time to get this party started.

CHAPTER EIGHTEEN
Shirin Shah is standing tall.

Shirin Shah's beauty was obvious from the photo Javid had shown them earlier. But not in a way that was conventional; when Haleh had first heard of the womxn, she'd imagined an impossibly beautiful womxn with defined cheekbones and all sharp angles. But the womxn was quite the opposite; she was a little on the tall side but with generous curves and a round face that made her look innocent – a girl next door kind of appearance.

Haleh was curious to find out how that face had changed in the last few years since she'd been spotted in public, how that face had fared through guilt, grief and loss. So far though, she was no show.

It had been more than an hour since Haleh, Delnaz and Farzaneh arrived at the party, although they didn't quite stick out like a sore thumb; blending in well amongst the expensive scents of perfume and beautiful gowns. Haleh had still noticed more than a few lingering, curious looks sent their way. It was probably because the guests milled about the room, stopping to socialise with familiar faces and well, Haleh didn't know anybody at this party. Swanky parties weren't her usual scene; she was used to dark underground places with techno music blaring from speakers so loud that she couldn't hear herself think.

She closed her eyes for a brief moment, transporting herself to that place where the smell of sweat, lust and cheap perfume hung in the air, bodies slickly gyrating against each other. Although she didn't exactly miss it, but she couldn't deny that she was well in her element there than here with its fancy brightly lit chandeliers suspended low, a live band playing classical music, wealthy people socialising quietly. There was the pleasant hum of conversation in the air, totally unlike the noise that Haleh was used to.

It had been years since Haleh had felt so out of place, so un-comfortable. She wishes Javid would have put her on the 'steal the emerald' team. The only thing she could do to take the edge off was drinking and she was already on her third glass of champagne and the waiter was shooting her judging looks.

Haleh sighed, she supposed she should make some attempt at admiring the art hung on the walls like the other guests were doing – she'd even spotted Delnaz doing the same. She searched for her in the small crowd now and found her chatting with an older gentleman. Haleh had been surprised, to say the least to see Delnaz fit in here snugly like a glove. Even though Haleh was the leader of this team, Delnaz had taken charge, since she'd walked into the party, she'd swiftly blended in, chatting and gazing at art.

Even Farzaneh had adapted quick, not as sociable as Delnaz was being but at least she wasn't rooted to one spot like Haleh was doing.

You really ought to move, her mind reminded her. So she did, her legs carrying her to one of the paintings, one that a few people had been admiring earlier. She saw that it was an oil painting of a womxn with an elegant hairdo – her dark hair swept up, letting her high cheekbones shine. Her eyes were a deep, dark brown that looked a little familiar to Haleh. The womxn looked regal, chin raised and eyes narrowed in the slightest as if she was daring the observer.

Haleh found herself staring at it a long while; she'd never really been into art, never understood what other people meant when they called a piece of art mesmerising or when they claimed it made them feel things. Even now, she wasn't sure that she understood, sure the womxn in the painting was stunning and by default the painting was stunning too. But what was she supposed to feel looking at it?

She shook her head, her hands itching for another drink. Except that she couldn't. She wasn't a lightweight by any means but she'd rather have her full wits with her tonight. There was no telling what Shirin Shah would be like when they found her.

"Did you ever date an artist?" A familiar voice came from behind Haleh.

Haleh barely held in her flinch. Damn it, she'd been lost in her thoughts. She didn't turn around to face Delnaz, she just shrugged, feeling her friend coming to stand beside her.

"Have I ever what?" Haleh asked, she'd heard Delnaz's question just fine but it had taken her aback. Haleh had the strangest relationship with Delnaz. It wasn't that they didn't like each other – they did. It was that they liked to openly criticise each other's weak points; Haleh usually took shots at Delnaz's timidity and Delnaz would criticise Haleh's sarcasm. In Haleh's defence, sarcasm was hardly a weak point though, timidity on the other hand…

Anyways, their bickering usually made Haleh wary when Delnaz spoke to her directly.

Delnaz's response to Haleh was an eye roll but she did repeat the question again, with exaggerated patience. And they said Haleh was the sarcastic one.

Haleh who never shied from talking about her dating history, answered, "A few. Never a sculptor though, I've always wanted to date one of those. The things they're rumoured to do with their hands." Haleh added just to annoy Delnaz. When she didn't fall for the bait, she asked, "Why though?"

"Because the womxn in this painting kind of looks like you." Delnaz answered.

Haleh's first instinct was to deny it but she saw the slight resemblance, so vague that she couldn't point a finger to exactly what physical feature she shared in common with the womxn in the painting.

"So you think one of my old lovers painted this?" Haleh asked sarcastically, finally connecting the dots with Delnaz's earlier question.

"It's called a joke, Haleh," Delnaz shot back.

Haleh grinned, she liked sparring with Delnaz almost as much as she enjoyed teasing Pari. It was fun because Delnaz was otherwise mild mannered, carefully spoken but she was capable of being witty. It was a side she didn't show often, a side she allowed to wither because she was too shy. Too bad for her that Haleh was hell bent on drawing her out of that shell or die trying. As far as Haleh was concerned, witty people were a dying breed – even more than courageous people.

The both of them turned away from the painting, silently searching the crowd… and nope, Shirin Shah was still nowhere to be found.

"Do you think she will show up?" Delnaz asked, voicing what Haleh was thinking.

"Javid said so." Haleh said but she didn't sound convincing. If the rumours were true, then Shirin Shah was the most paranoid womxn on the planet, choosing to become a recluse. She'd stopped making her world famed sculptures, stopped being spotted in public. She'd basically stopped existing. Tonight was the first social invitation she'd accepted in years; nobody but them knowing that the cause was a dear on to her – climate change. The fluctuating levels of the waters in the Yellow Flowers cave had contributed to the difficulties in getting the sword and probably influenced Nazanin Hesami's death. Although the police file hadn't mentioned how Nazanin had died, only that she had.

Maybe Shirin had chickened out, it was her first public appearance in years and even though this event was having minimal press coverage, it would still be revealed to the world that Shirin Shah had been here tonight. There would be speculations; how she'd looked like at the fundraiser, what she'd been wearing, why she'd gone into hiding. Haleh wouldn't blame the womxn if she decided not to show up after all.

"She'll show up," Haleh repeated, this time her words were infused with confidence.

"There's only so much sipping champagne I can do," Delnaz said a bit cheekily.

"And chatting with stuffy people." Haleh added. Delnaz laughed softly.

Haleh realised that this might be the first time that the two of them were chatting so freely, without taking jabs at each other. It was nice.

"I hope Javid and the others are having much better luck than we are." Delnaz said after a moment of silence between them.

"I don't think that anything has gone wrong. Yet." Haleh said.

Delnaz rolled her eyes. "Typical Haleh pessimism."

"There is a difference between pessimism and realism. I'm not at all saying they'll get caught but there is a chance that they will. Best to prepare for both outcomes."

"It's a wonder that you and Pari get along, much less date each other."

Of course, Haleh and Pari had all their friends fooled by the nonexistent romantic relationship between them. But there was something wry in Delnaz tone that made Haleh think that she wasn't as fooled.

"Pari is actually a lot like me than you realize." It was true, everyone saw Pari and thought she was ditzy because she liked to make jokes and rarely took anyone serious. But Pari was a lot rational than they knew.

"It's not the same and you know it." Was Delnaz's answer. She was right; Delnaz was rarely ever wrong in her assessment of character – she was astute and Haleh couldn't deny it.

There was a sudden commotion, murmurs rose to a high and the two of them turned around, searching for the source. A beautiful womxn had walked into the party, she was wearing a simple black dress with a sweetheart neckline; standing out in a small sea of flashy dresses. But it wasn't the reason why many were staring and whispering behind their palms. Haleh recognized her at once.

The womxn was Shirin Shah.

CHAPTER NINETEEN
Fucking home wrecker!

Javid stumbled drunkenly down the brightly lit hallway, giggling to herself and clutching a half empty bottle of champagne. While she kept up the act of stumbling, her eyes darted around, searching for cameras up and hidden. Naturally, hotel suites didn't come with cameras but this was a different night and an important event. She didn't find any and wondered if the hostess was simply confident or just stupid. Possibly the former; the fundraiser was a small event and only a few people had been invited, and only the wealthy. There were however, two hefty men standing guard outside the door at the end of the hallway. Javid's eyes narrowed in the slightest; she was sure that that was where the priestess' eye would be – behind that door.

She carried on her drunken act, giggling to herself occasionally until she reached the end of the hallway and came to a halt before the guards. They gazed at each other then at her with no suspicion but plenty of wariness; they'd taken in her stunning dress which no doubt was expensive, the teardrop diamonds of her drooping earrings and they'd written her off as a drunk socialite.

"I'm looking for the bathroom," Javid drawled, making her accent more prominent. The two guards exchanged another look, this time more amused as if to say; *can you believe all these rich people?*

One of the guards gestured at a door, Javid nodded like he'd said the gravest thing in the world. Then she began to stumble in the direction that she'd been given. She opened the door and found that she was in a bedroom.

There was a canopy queen sized bed with pale pink bed sheets. The room reminded her of a young girl's with the soft pink design. She headed straight for the door leading to the bathroom, in there she removed her phone from her clutch and dialled a number.

Toman answered on the second ring, "All in place?" Her voice was distant and slightly crackly. She and Pari were waiting in a nondescript rented car down the street, waiting for the signal to come up to the hotel.

Javid nodded, then she realised that Toman couldn't see her. "Not quite yet. I was right. There are no cameras in sight, only a couple of guards. Two guarding the elevators that lead up to the penthouse suite and two guarding the door where I assume the emerald will be. The auction is yet to begin and Shirin is nowhere in sight." Javid relayed.

She heard Toman's deep sigh and felt a small stab of irritation, it was clear that Toman was against this plan – clearer than day and night – but it didn't mean that she had to be so obvious about it, so immature. Javid tried to wave away the thought as soon as it came but it didn't mean that that wasn't how she felt. Anyways, the last thing she needed to think about was Toman's behaviour. She tried to focus on the task at hand.

"You think she won't show up?" Toman asked, sounding slightly worried.

"I'm not sure, she should show up – she accepted the invitation and everything."

"She might have changed her mind." Pari's voice came.

Javid clenched her free fist, it was too early in the night for things to go wrong with their plan. "Let's just get on with our part of the night."

Toman cleared her throat, "Alright, let's do this." To her credit, she sounded more confident than she had all night. Javid couldn't tell if it was one of Toman's carefully put up front and she didn't really care if it was fake. As long as Toman was cooperative.

"We need to cause a huge distraction, something that will draw the guards away from the door long enough that we can get in and get out before they return. Any ideas?" She asked. they'd been brainstorming this part throughout the whole night. Haleh had suggested – with too much enthusiasm -- that she start a brawl. And right now, it was the only option in sight but then it might lead to Haleh getting arrested and Javid's influence in the city didn't run that far. She'd been gone for far too long.

"I think we might have no option but to start a fight." Toman's voice came, distracting Javid from her thoughts.

"Haleh can't do it though." Javid said. It was almost funny how the both of them pretended they hadn't shot down the idea of a brawl earlier. Oh how the tables turned.

"I will." Toman offered.

Javid was silent for a few seconds, the words slowly sinking into her mind. She laughed, a little too loudly and winced when the sound echoed in the spacious bathroom. She stared at herself in the mirror, she'd mused up her hair in the slightest to sell the drunk look; her eyes were bright, looking more than a little crazed. She shook her head at her reflection.

"Javid? Are you there?" Toman's voice came again and Javid realised that she'd been silent for too long.

"Yeah, just trying to imagine you picking a random fight." Javid said with a small smile on her face.

Toman gave a snort, "Believe it or not, I was a troubled teen and got into plenty of fights when I was younger. It was only in my adult years that I realised I could channel my anger into some-thing more productive."

Javid thought she could hear Toman smiling and she watched in the mirror as her own smile grew. It was almost pathetic how much she enjoyed talking to Toman, even better hearing Toman speak so freely about her earlier life. Of all of them, Javid had made the decision not to look into Toman's past. Not because she was afraid of finding something very shady, it was just that she knew all there was to know about Toman and she trusted her, back then she'd trusted her more than she'd trusted the rest of their friends. She knew that Toman had grown up in an abusive background, left that abusive background and become a cop, quit that job because of guilt and an injury and then become a private investigator. Toman wasn't like Haleh who hoarded secrets to herself. Toman would tell you if you asked but she'd never mention it again and she would never talk about her past if she could help it.

As a result, Javid treasured the occasions when she would talk about it with her because it meant that she meant something to Toman. These days, she'd been feeling less and less that Toman cared. "Alright, do it." Javid said with a resigned sigh.

"It'll be fine. I know you're worried about me getting arrested but at most, I get escorted out of the party. I won't be breaking any body's heads. Just a small blow."

"And I promise not to assault some important figure – like let's say, the president." Toman joked.

Despite herself, Javid gave a little giggle, it was hysterical, in an 'I can't believe we're doing this' kind of way.

"Try not to, love." Javid said with a small sniffle.

Toman murmured something, to Pari, she guessed. And then she spoke again, "I'm going to put you on speaker, Pari is a bit miffed that we've cut her out of the conversation."

"Right, go ahead." Javid said.

"So, what's the plan?" Pari asked, her voice businesslike in a way that wasn't usually Pari but at the same time was her. Javid imagined it was the kind of voice she used at work.

"Alright, listen very carefully." Javid began. "Toman is going to come up here and start a fight, remember, don't hurt anyone too hard."

"Your faith in me is astounding." Toman said dryly.

"You do look like you've been bottling up a bit of rage over the years." Pari quipped, a hint of her usual playfulness shining through.

"If I were, I'd be in jail by now." Toman shot back. "Back to the plan."

"Toman's going to go in there and start a brawl, make it believable, accuse some random man of sleeping with your girlfriend. I'll go and get the guards. Pari, you're going to be right behind Toman and then I'll come get you. I need someone by my side."

"Roger that," Pari said.

"Got it," Toman said.

"I'll send you a text in the next few minutes and then you can come." She didn't wait for a reply from any of them, she hung up and dialled Haleh's phone.

Haleh picked up on the third ring. "Is it urgent? Shirin Shah just walked in."

Of all the things Javid had expected her to say, she almost dropped her phone in surprise. The truth was that Javid had begun to lose all hope that Shirin Shah would show up tonight. Until now, she felt a surge of hope in her chest. Finally, all systems were back up and running. They might be able to pull this off after all.

"That's good. Once she spots Farzaneh, you won't even have to lure her to you. Just convince her to give us a chance to talk to us. The phase two--"

"You mean the steal the powerful foreshadowing emerald phase?" Haleh asked, her voice almost drowned by the cacophony of noise in the room.

Javid rolled her eyes. Unlike Toman, Haleh sounded impressed by the plan, she thought that stealing the emerald would be cool, not because it was an instrument that could save their asses but because she thought it was badass. She could only wonder the kinds of trouble and illegal shit Haleh got herself up to in Berlin.

"Yes, that phase. It's underway now. Just do your part and everything will be fine."

"We've got this." Haleh said in a cool and confident voice, firm as if she'd sensed the inner turmoil that Javid was feeling and wanted to reassure her. Haleh wasn't exactly the reassuring kind, she liked to say things as they were which meant that her words weren't an attempt to comfort Javid, she must genuinely believe that their goals were attainable. Javid found herself being strengthened by that certainty.

"Alright. Text me when you three have got Shirin Shah cornered and willing to help us." She added.

The both of them didn't bother with a goodbye greeting, hanging up almost at the same time. Javid inhaled a deep breath, she set her clutch down on the skin and patted her hair down, combing through the thick mane with her fingers.

She was trying to look presentable since she would be the one to raise the alarm to the guards. A few minutes later, she walked outside the bedroom and returned to the party. She saw that the auction had begun. Javid tamped down on the urge to bite her nails; shit, they were supposed to have gotten to the emerald before the auction started. She assumed that the emerald would be the star of the night but she wasn't so sure anymore.

A tall, bearded man in a suit was rambling on about an antique teapot set that had apparently once belonged to Iranian royalty almost seven centuries ago. Javid spotted Haleh and Delnaz right away, they lingered behind the excited party, their backs turned to her. Farzaneh and Shirin Shah were nowhere in sight.

For a second, Javid hesitated before scurrying after them. She tapped Haleh on the shoulder.

"Jeez, it's just you." Haleh turned, her fist half raised as if to strike a blow. Javid batted her hand away, her eyes were still searching around the room looking for Farzaneh.

"Where's Farzaneh?" She asked when she didn't find her in the crowd.

"Shirin Shah spotted her and ran out the door as quickly as she arrived. I swear I've never seen anybody so scared." Haleh said grimly. "She's definitely got a secret or more to hide."

"What?" Javid exclaimed, her voice loud enough that a few eyes turned to her. "Why didn't you go after her?"

"Farzaneh. She immediately went after Shirin."

"And she asked us not to follow." Delnaz added. Javid felt some of her hysterics drain out of her, she trusted Farzaneh and if there was any of them Shirin Shah would hear out, then it was Farzaneh.

"Farzaneh will text us when it's okay for us to meet her." Haleh was saying. At the same time, Toman stepped through the doors, followed closely by Pari.

Javid tensed, knowing what was coming. She wondered how Toman was going to go about it, she watched as Toman approached them and for a second, her heart dropped to the pit of her stomach thinking that Toman had come to tell her that she was chickening out. But Toman brushed past them as if she didn't know who they were. She continued to weave through the crowd where the auctioneer was calling the starting price of an ugly looking painting, people were already starting to bid. Toman pushed through the crowd, bumping past a few people rudely. She didn't stop until she was in front of a young womxn – no younger than she was and wearing a simple sheath dress. Without any warning at all, Toman pushed the womxn, causing her to stumble several steps back and into a few people who pushed back in surprise.

The man recovered with surprised rage, "What is? Who are--" He was cut off when Toman slapped him across the face.

"You fucking home wrecker!" Toman cried out in a voice so melodramatic that Javid almost believed the throbbing emotion in her voice.

CHAPTER TWENTY
Self-inflicted Scars

Hell broke loose soon after. Javid was caught between feelings of horror and being impressed; Toman didn't stop at a slap, she pulled the poor, innocent, screaming man by the shirt. A few people tried to get between them, tried to get a hold of a hysterical Toman but her grip was strong. More than a few people watched with open mouthed expressions of horror and intrigue, like watching a train wreck happening. The auctioneer was one of the people trying to hold Toman back but he swiftly got an elbow to the cheek and stumbled several steps back.

"Oh my God." Delnaz exclaimed.

"Oh my God," Haleh echoed the same sentiment but she sounded more impressed than appalled. Of course she'd sound appalled.

Toman's eye caught Javid's and she gave an imperceptible nod of her head. It was Javid's cue.

She spun on her heels and ran back into the hallway, holding on the hem on her dress as she ran. The guards tensed the moment she reached them, her own urgency infectious.

"A fight's broken out!" Javid cried out in Farsi. She gesticulated wildly, she deliberately made her voice sound breathless; it wasn't so hard to sound frenzied; her heart thud a wild beat in her chest. She bent down, pretending to catch her breath, "They're going to kill each other. Do something!"

Her words were like a gunshot in the air and the two burly guards were off, brushing past her and down the hallway, she waited until they were out of sight. She took out her phone and texted Pari.

Come meet me.

Pari arrived a minute later, throwing glances over her shoulder as if she'd expected to be followed. She did seem out of breath.

"You should see Toman out there, she's got a strength of steel." Pari said once she was no longer panting. She gave Javid a meaningful look, "You're one lucky lady, Javid. To have those hands on me…" Pari pretended to shudder.

Javid shot her a look but deep down she'd been thinking the same thing. She checked her bare wrist before she remembered that she wasn't wearing a wristwatch.

"How many minutes do we have before the guards break it up and get back here?" Javid asked, ignoring Pari's lewd remark.

Pari was silent for a few seconds, "Not much. Toman's got all attention on her, hurling accusations and playing the part of a jealous girlfriend. She's got everyone hanging on to her stories and the guards look torn, they want to 'escort' her out but she's resisting."

Javid jerked her head in a nod. "We'll make it enough time." She said and twisted the knob of the door. it was cool to the touch. She heaved a sigh of relief when it twisted under her grip. She knew how to pick a lock and had come prepared in the case that the door was locked but that would have been time wasting.

She stepped into the room and was surprised to find that it was a study. The study was brightly lit. An office chair behind a vast oak table, bookshelves manning the left and right sides of the room.

Javid's eyes didn't linger on the minimalist décor for long; it wasn't really her style anyways. Instead, her eyes found the safe, tucked in the right corner of the room. She swore very loudly and ran a hand through her hair.

"What?" Pari asked, for a moment, Javid had forgotten that she was in the room with her and almost startled at the sound of her voice.

Javid wore a fierce scowl on her face and pointed, "That, that's the fucking problem."

"Oh fuck." Pari echoed but with less of the intensity Javid had sworn with. She looked to Javid keenly and she realised that Pari was expecting Javid to do something. Because that was her job as leader, she loved and loathed the duties that same with it, now the feeling angled towards intense loathing and confusion. Their time was ticking, there was only so much time that Toman could buy them with the dramatics she was displaying. The guards would be back soon and they'd be found in here.

Breathe, she told herself, breathe and think.

"You're looking at me like I'm renowned for having expertise in cracking open safes." Javid said when Pari continued to stare.

"Don't you have an expertise in safe cracking and a million other random skills?" Pari asked innocently.

Javid shrugged, "I hate to disappoint you, but I don't."

"Duly noted, so you think the emerald is in that safe?" Pari asked. She pointed and Javid followed her outstretched arm, "And not here." She was pointing at the bookshelf on their left, the second row of it to be precise, where a small glass box was wedged in between books, showing off an oval shaped emerald nestled in red velvet plush. Pari clapped Javid on the shoulder, "You should win an Olympic medal for how high you can jump into conclusions."

"It's a shame that game doesn't exist." Javid shot back clumsily as she padded toward the shelf, her step a little hesitant as if she was waiting for something incredibly freakish to happen now that they'd seen the emerald. But there was no tense atmosphere – just their own impatience mixed in the air. And there was no power pulsing in the room. It looked like an ordinary emerald in any equally ordinary study.

"Are you sure this isn't a copy? I read somewhere that they make replicas of art to display in museums and that the real thing is often kept away, safe." Pari said.

Javid jerked her head in a distracted nod, realising that she'd unwittingly agreed to Pari's statement. "Well, not exactly, love. It happens sometimes." She reached for the glass showcase, surprised to find the box deeply warm to the touch that she almost flinched. The little action did not go unnoticed by Pari.

"What's wrong?" She asked.

"The box is warm."

Pari reached out by herself to touch it, her expression grew curious as she ran her palm over the surface of it. "It's close to fucking freezing in here. How?" She asked, trailing off.

Javid hadn't even noticed the chill in the room until Pari mentioned it. She shivered, searching the room discretely for air conditioning, wanting to make sure that the chill wasn't some supernatural effect the emerald was having on the room. She touched the box again, searching for a latch. "I'm not sure." She answered vaguely. She found a small notch and flicked it open. The both of them paused, waiting for some grand effect to occur.

"I think we've watched too many action flicks." Javid said with some amusement. The emerald was barely bigger than a finger and not quite as long, it was smaller than she'd expected. She turned it over, staring down puzzledly at it. it was still warm to the touch but not uncomfortably so.

"What now?" Pari asked and for the first time, Javid didn't have an answer to her question.

"Javid, we're running out of time here." Pari said a bit more urgently, her eyes straying to the door once.

"I just need to think, Pari," Javid hissed, her voice almost a cruel snap. She started to pace now, her fists clenched. She glanced down at it again, it was oddly shaped too, jaggedly so, as if it had been cut roughly. This wasn't the powerful emerald she'd seen in grainy photos.

"Fook," Javid breathed out.

"Oh, no, I don't like that word." Pari murmured. Javid halted mid pace to stare at her in amusement.

"Why not? You swear a lot." Javid chuckled.

"It's that look in your eye, Javid, you look like you want us to take this little jewel with you. Please, tell me I'm wrong." Pari ranted, flailing her arms up, "Because in case you little British ass has forgotten, that's called stealing here."

Javid shook her head, her mind already made. This wasn't supposed to happen, yes. She definitely hadn't planned to steal this powerful jewel, it was supposed to be a tool to use and then leave behind but nothing was as it seemed. This tiny thing in the palm of her hand couldn't be the same jewel she'd read about with the capacity to grant a user the ability to see into the future.

But Javid's gut was telling her to take the emerald with her and her gut feelings were rarely ever off or unreasonable. So she made up her mind, jerked her head in a nod at the door.

"Let's go." She told Pari.

Pari groaned aloud, "I came to this party as a law-abiding citizen. And here I am, aiding and abetting a crime. Does it ever drive you crazy just how fast the night changes?"

"You're driving me crazy," Javid said under her breath. She snapped the open box shut and headed for the door, knowing that Pari would follow.

They returned to the party, Javid was surprised to find that Toman was being led out in that moment. She was still playing the role of the angry girlfriend. Javid searched the room and found that the poor man who had been accused of wrecking Toman's nonexistent relationship was nowhere in sight.

As Toman was led away, Javid caught her eye and gave a single nod.

"Oh, we are so going to get caught." Pari was muttering over and over again.

"We are if you keep wearing that look of guilt on your face," Javid reprimanded her. It genuinely looked as if Pari would have a meltdown. Javid quickly scanned the room for the rest of their friends. She didn't find Haleh or Delnaz or Farzaneh.

She sent a text to Haleh telling her that she was leaving the party. It was best that they didn't leave with each other.

"Alright, we're leaving."

The look of relief on Pari's face was so obvious that Javid nearly laughed.

***

The night ended with Haleh sitting in Shirin Shah's limo. Not that Haleh was complaining, she was used to the finer things of life, finer tastes, expensive alcohol, designer fashion and plenty more. She'd been in a limo several times so she wasn't complaining this time, she might have even enjoyed herself if this was a vacation. But it wasn't, they were on a mission.

She'd been tuning out most of Shirin and Farzaneh's emotional reunion. When Shirin had stepped into the party more than half an hour ago, she'd spotted Farzaneh almost right away and had turned a fascinating shade of alabaster and looked like she would swoon.

Haleh had made the move to approach her but Farzaneh had begged her not to. Because Shirin Shah was like a bird in the sense that she was elusive and would fly away when she was startled. And she happened to be running away from an unspoken past. So they'd agreed to let Farzaneh talk to her while Haleh and Delnaz stayed behind at the party in case Javid needed them.

Then Toman had arrived with a performance worthy of an Oscar – Haleh had been extremely entertained – and Farzaneh had whisked Shirin somewhere. Less than thirty minutes later, Farzaneh had texted them to meet her outside the hotel.

Now her phone was ringing and it was Javid, Haleh allowed herself to breathe a little easier. She would never admit it but she'd been worried about Pari and Javid. She'd been worried that they would get caught, Javid had presented the plan as a quick get in and out but every minute longer they'd spent away, the chances of their getting caught increased. Toman had needed to stretch out her performance for even longer, weaving a sob story of how she was an abandoned, scorned socialite figure and how a 'wicked' man had come to ruin her love-life.

"Hello," Haleh said into her phone, careful to keep her voice barely above a murmur. There was something about the intense conversation Farzaneh and Shirin carried, they spoke in Farsi, sharp and pointed, Haleh understood Farsi just fine and she even spoke the language well but she hadn't spoken the language in years – refused to. It was impossible to forget her first language

Farzaneh was speaking too fast for Haleh to follow correctly. They were arguing about why Shirin had all but erased herself from existence. Shirin called Farzaneh a coward in a tone so venomous that Delnaz flinched. Ah so she was also following the conversation despite pretending to be pointedly admiring her nails.

"Please tell me that you and Delnaz made it out of the party safe and that you're now with Shirin Shah and Farzaneh." Javid was saying.

"We're fine," Haleh said, she glanced at a very pissed off Farzaneh – although she'd barely known the other womxn for three days, she still didn't think she was capable of fury, only her usual hippy dippy calm that had secretly frustrated Haleh. At least now Farzaneh was more humxn than Haleh had ever seen her.

Or maybe you just want everyone around you to be bitter and jaded like you are, her mind taunted. Haleh ignored her thoughts.

She kind of liked Farzaneh angry.

"We're fine." Haleh repeated. "We made it out okay. Are you and Pari out?"

Haleh didn't doubt Javid's intuition very often but she'd been worried when Javid had chosen Pari to be by her side. Pari was the picture perfect model of a law-abiding citizen and despite all her yapping on and on about Ocean's Eight, she'd be the first person to chicken out of actually committing any crime. Haleh would have been the wise choice, but Javid had chosen Pari instead, for reasons she didn't still understand. Sometimes, Javid felt too much like a puzzle with new missing pieces popping out of nowhere. Haleh didn't understand her anymore.

Haleh had been worried about Pari would be caught in the crossfire of Javid's plans.

"Yeah," came Javid's answer but there was something else in her voice, something she wasn't saying. It caused Haleh to sit up a little straighter.

"Did something go wrong?" Haleh asked.

There was a pause, and then, "Not exactly. Let's meet back at the hotel − with Shirin Shah." Javid answered, all traces of un- certainty was gone from her voice. She was back to sounding like cool, confident and slightly infuriating Javid. It grated on Haleh's nerves, she was sure that Javid wasn't telling her everything.

"Well, Shirin Shah doesn't look like she wants to help us." Haleh drawled. That she was sure of, she had expected to see a womxn physically hunched over by grief, maybe more than a little bit teary eyed too. But Shirin Shah just looked pissed off, as if she'd rather be answer but in their presence. She'd stopped bicker- ing with Farzaneh − the latter looking equally furious.

A grief stricken womxn's heartstrings would be easier to play, easier to manipulate into helping them. A furious womxn, howev- er, that was a different story.

"Damn." Javid expelled.

"Yeah, shit is right." Haleh muttered distractedly. Shirin Shah was looking right at her, a calculating look on her face.

"Where are you? We can come meet you there instead." Javid asked, the urgency back in her tone.

"One second," Haleh said into the phone and removed it from her ear. She sent Shirin a cold look, one that usually sent people flinching away from her. Shirin wasn't quite immune to it, her shoulder rose in indignation but Haleh saw a flicker of worry in that hazel gaze. "Mind telling me where this limo is headed. We have friends waiting."

When Shirin didn't waver, Haleh reluctantly added, "Please."

A flicker of a ghost smile appeared on Shirin's face before fading immediately. "Farzaneh has convinced me to see your leader."

Haleh narrowed her eyes, she put her phone back to her ear. "Never mind, we're headed back to the hotel. Farzaneh was right about *her*." She added because she knew Shirin was listening and Haleh hadn't met anyone she didn't want to piss off.

Javid said something in reply but Haleh was only half listening, Shirin held the other half of her attention. Haleh hung up and Shirin pounced on the bait just as Haleh had anticipated.

"What did Farzaneh say about me?" Shirin snarled the words between her tightly clenched jaw.

Delnaz immediately looked weary and she shot Haleh a warning glare that was ignored. Haleh so wanted to unravel this stubborn womxn in front of her.

"She's right beside you, why don't you ask her?" Haleh shot back but there was barely any venom in her voice, she didn't dislike Shirin at all. She was rather indifferent but she'd found out that the best way to discover a person's true self was by knowing who they were when they were furious.

Farzaneh was quiet, looking ahead at Delnaz, she seemed to be pointedly ignoring Shirin. Haleh's grin spread wide.

Shirin laughed, the sound was as beautiful as it was cold.

"You're all day-dreamers. Farzaneh has fed you with disillusioned tales of grandeur. She's told you that you're the chosen ones and you believe her." Shirin shook her head.

Delnaz cut in before Haleh could reply. "I'd be very careful with what you say next, Ms Shah."

Shirin was taken aback by the sound of Delnaz's voice. Haleh had always thought it most unusual that Delnaz had the most beautiful singing voice but her speaking voice was much rougher, deeper even. Coupled with her softer features, a round face, a kind smile. One would certainly never expect her to sound like the spark of two rocks struck against each other.

Shirin had definitely been startled, she blinked several times and looked from Delnaz to Haleh as if she was seeing them in a new light. Haleh wasn't going to give her the privilege of a fresh start.

"You were calling us foolish." Haleh reminded her coldly.

"And you insulted Farzaneh's insight." Delnaz added, when all eyes turned to her, she flushed under the lights in the limo. Haleh swallowed her smirk, she had been suspecting that Delnaz had a thing for Farzaneh.

Farzaneh raised her head, something like surprise glinting in the depths of her eyes at Delnaz's defence of her character. She flashed a small smile at Delnaz, looking a little like herself.

Shirin Shah sighed, leaning back in her seat. All the fight seemed to leave her body in that moment and in its place, tiredness settled in. She looked more like the grief stricken womxn Haleh had expected to see, worse, her shoulders were slumped as if she was bearing the weight of the world on her shoulders.

"I'm sorry, Farzaneh," She finally said, her voice barely above a whisper. If Farzaneh was surprised by Shirin's change in mood and apology, she didn't show it. She just nodded her head. "I understand your feelings, Shirin. Don't think that I haven't questioned myself, my abilities since then."

Shirin shook her head, "The thing is, none of this is your fault.

I've thought about everything I could have changed, gone back to the past a million times trying to find the place where I fucked up."

"You're talking about your friend, Nazanin Hesami." Delnaz cut in, her voice made deliberately soft.

Shirin gave a hollow laugh. "Nazanin *isn't* – wasn't just my friend."

"You were in love with her," Haleh said aloud in realisation. She shared a startled look with Delnaz. She was starting to find more than one similarity with Shirin Shah's mission years ago and theirs now. It was almost starting to feel like fate was repeating itself over and over again. And none of fate's games had ever ended well.

Shirin didn't answer for the longest time and Haleh didn't expect that she would; her expression had shuttered, her face was carefully blank but her eyes shined with stubborn tears and pain. She sighed, "Farzaneh has briefed me on everything. Your Javid reminds me a lot of myself, hopeful and with plenty of faith that I could change the fate of the world." Shirin banged her head softly against the headrest of the seat. "I was wrong and so naïve. Too confident to the point of stupidity."

"But the sword was meant to be found." Delnaz cut in, a little impatiently as if she couldn't stand Shirin feeling sorry for herself.

Shirin barked a harsh laugh, "I used to think the same thing too. You want to know what I think, Gordafarid's getting a kick out of this in the afterlife or wherever it is spirits go. The sword was never meant to be found, only to punish those thinking that they're pure enough, with good enough intentions to possess its power. We're all greedy as fuck, wanting something that should never be in the hands of humxns."

Haleh didn't bat an eyelid, "Well, thanks for the advice, but it's not exactly the one we need."

In an instant, Shirin's gaze became wary. "Of course. Farzaneh's told me everything about your group."

Haleh had expected a violent refusal, not this contemplating look Shirin was wearing. She assessed the other womxn. Shirin Shah had mastered the art of brooding, reaching the highest level of looking good while looking as if she'd discovered the worst extents to how the world could be shitty.

"You're not saying no." Delnaz said, she was unable to keep the surprise from showing in her voice.

That ghost of a smile flickered again on Shirin's lips. "You want me to tell you about the single most traumatic thing that has ever happened to me."

Shirin sighed, fear swimming in the depths of her eyes. "I knew this day would come."

Haleh swallowed a witty retort. Best not to piss her off when they were just getting on her good side.

"Yes, you're right. I'd rather not talk about it and if you ask me, I'd tell you to abandon this mission before its too late to do so. You might not even be alive to warn the next group of stupid people — they call me the lucky one and that's not saying much." Shirin said, rolling up the sleeves of her dress, at first Haleh thought they were tattoos, until she leaned closer, a shiver running down her spine she realised that they were scars. Thin, spindle marks ran from her wrist upwards and disappearing into the rest of her sleeves. Haleh racked her head, trying and failing to think of a situation where a person would end up with such gruesome scars.

Haleh hesitated then shrugged, what was the point of deciding to spare Shirin's feelings when they were going to end up stomping on them again?

"And those scars, did you get them from the..." Haleh trailed off, failing to find the right words to describe what had happened to Shirin and Nazanin. Event seemed too casual, suggesting a happy ending where there was none. Accident seemed like too much of an assumption, if there was anything Haleh was sure of, it was that whatever had happened to Shirin and Nazanin was far from being an accident.

That left her with no other words. In a very rare display, Haleh squirmed in the slightest, finding herself in a tight corner she couldn't back out of.

Shirin's eyes glittered dangerously as if she genuinely enjoyed seeing Haleh squirm. Haleh didn't back down from that gaze though and after a few seconds, Shirin's gaze became soft.

"Yeah well, I still can't find a single word to describe the shit we went through." Shirin's gaze clouded with something like sadness. Her hazel eyes were haunted when they weren't glaring. She noticed Haleh staring at her and her gaze hardened, Haleh wasn't sure what she'd glimpsed in her gaze but something told her that Shirin Shah didn't want to be pitied.

"And no, my scars aren't from that." She added matter of factly, firmly. Case closed, her tone said. She wouldn't be entertaining any more questions.

Haleh narrowed her eyes, she visualised the scars again, the thinness of them. She felt a sudden chill that had nothing to do with the cold of the limo. Were those scars self-inflicted?

She didn't dare ask, not only because it would be rude but also because it would be cruel. Haleh knew a few things about self-inflicted scars, mostly the emotional kind but it didn't mean that she couldn't be sympathetic with the other kind. She swallowed her curiosity with ease.

"I assume it was your friend who called," Shirin said. "Where are we meeting her?"

Haleh muttered the name of the hotel. There was no other conversation between the four of them and although the silence was almost suffocating with tension, Haleh didn't mind it so much.

She was itching for them to get the impending conversation over with. The past hour in the elusive Shirin Shah's presence had done nothing but send her curiosity skyrocketing to higher peaks than Haleh had thought possible.

It was time for the womxn to talk and let their little gang know what they were in for.

CHAPTER TWENTY ONE
Just like their Togetherness

Although the living room space in the penthouse was spacious enough to host thirty people for a party. It was feeling a little crowded with their party of seven.

Pari and Delnaz had brewed coffee and ordered room service. There was a cart containing different sugary snacks in the middle of the room, it had been mostly left untouched except for Haleh nibbling on a few pieces — who knew the bitter sarcastic womxn had a sweet tooth.

Javid had however indulged herself in the brewed coffee, the night had been plenty of eventful, there was currently a potential powerful emerald sitting pretty in her purse to show for it — a detail she was yet to share with the rest of her friends — and who knew that racing to save the world could leave one so exhausted. She felt tiredness settle in the crevices of her shoulders like a clingy lover so she hadn't turned down coffee. She was beginning to feel the effects of the stimulant creep into her brain, she sat up a little straighter.

For the past ten minutes, her friends had busied themselves with changing out of their itchy fancy clothes into more comfortable ones — only Haleh remained in her evening dress, she was perched stiffly on the arm of the seat and watching Shirin with a keen eye as she nibbled on a snack. Haleh wasn't looking at her distrustfully but more like the other womxn was a puzzle that she couldn't crack and Haleh didn't enjoy puzzles.

Shirin was seated with her spine ramrod straight. She'd turned down the snacks but she was sipping a dainty cup, drinking tea that Farzaneh had brewed. Javid couldn't help but stare at her, feeling a little Starstruck.

Javid was an avid art collector, she had her own personal collection of art worth millions of pounds. In recent years, she'd got into other mediums of art, including oil paintings and sculptures. Then she'd come to know of Shirin Shah, famed in the artwork for her realistic marble sculptures and her elusiveness. Shirin Shah rarely ever attended her own gallery openings, rarely ever attended award shows to receive honours bestowed on her, rarely ever made public appearances. She'd become something of an enigma in the art industry and that mysteriousness only fueled her popularity and subsequently her art.

Javid owned a few of her pieces too. She'd always wondered about Shirin Shah but she was far from the erratic and dedicated fan. She did, however, feel a little Starstruck sitting in her presence. She had to remind herself that this wasn't a fan meeting a favourite celebrity. Shirin Shah possibly held their lives in her hands, she must know it.

Javid cleared her throat, unsurprised when all eyes met hers. For the past few minutes, she'd played the perfect hostess, asking if her guest liked her tea and if she wanted some scones with it. It was time to get down to business.

Shirin looked a bit wary but at least she wasn't sitting at the edge of her seat, skittish like a bird preparing to fly away. And Javid wasn't going to treat her like one.

"Thank you for coming with us, Ms. Shah" Javid began. Shirin swiftly cut in.

"I think we're pretty much on a first name basis, Javid. I mean, you and your gang did intrude on my party and all but coerced me into coming here tonight. Please, call me Shirin." There was a little bit of humour in her words, a hint of the womxn she'd probably been before all the trauma. She reminded Javid of herself a little.

Javid bobbed her head in acknowledgement. "Alright, Shirin. Thank you for helping us."

Javid noticed how Haleh's brows quirked up at that. But Javid isn't like Haleh with her brash words and scathingly honest truths. Javid likes to play the part of diplomat, not every battle is won by sharp exchange of jabs. Some of them are slower, subtler than Haleh would like.

Shirin huffs what should be a laugh but the sound comes out like an amused sigh. "I haven't agreed to help you yet."

Javid didn't miss the deliberate addition of the last word, it meant that she was willing to be persuaded. The truth is that Javid isn't afraid of Shirin not helping them. She is more than a hundred percent sure that this womxn will, there's not a single malicious bone in her body and though a different womxn might baulk at talking about her most scarring experience, Javid is sure that Shirin isn't that way at all.

"But you will help us." Javid said confidently. There was a beat of silence and for a moment, her confidence wavered. She thought that she might be coming on too strong by the warning look that Farzaneh shot her.

But then Shirin's lips spread in a half smile and all the metaphorical clouds cleared up again.

"I like your confidence, Javid. It reminds me of myself." Shirin said, deftly skipping the question she wanted to ask. If there was one thing that Javid has learned about Shirin Shah's public elusiveness, it is that the womxn sitting before her might be the most cunning to ever exist. Everything she did was calculating, her image was carefully controlled.

"You want to know how I know you'll help us?" Javid continued, ignoring Shirin's words.

Shirin froze, for the first time looking like the metaphorical bird poised to take flight at the slightest sign of danger.

"Because you still hold hope in your heart about the sword getting found. You may deny it, you may not even admit it to your own self but you still very much want this country to be safe and you think we might be the ones to achieve that." Javid said, Shirin parted her lips, ready to get a word in, but Javid didn't let her — she wasn't done talking yet. "Please, Shirin, don't lie to yourself. You said it yourself: you and I are more alike, that means I know when you're calling your bluff. And you're spewing a lot of bullshit right now."

Haleh whistled, whether in support of Javid's statement or something else. Javid wasn't entirely sure, as usual it was difficult to get a read on Haleh. But this time, she wasn't bothered that she couldn't tell what her friend was thinking. This moment wasn't at all about Haleh.

She met Toman's gaze and she gave a subtle nod of encouragement. In that moment, Javid realised that all was forgiven; she and Toman were okay again. She let out a tiny sigh of relief, she hadn't even known how bothered she was about not being on speaking terms with Toman made her. Not until now. Toman's encouragement caused Javid to steel her spine even harder, to press on and say the words that would cause Shirin to unravel.

"So, help us, Shirin. Help us save our worlds." Javid said, this time more softly than firmly.

Like a spool of thread, Shirin unravelled. She didn't burst into tears or do something equally melodramatic. She just relaxed her shoulders, slouching a little in a manner that made her look younger than she was.

"You're right, Javid." Shirin said, she glanced into her cup as if there was something interesting inside it then she set it down on the table before her. She sat a little straighter but this time instead of looking guarded, she just appeared more serious. "It's always our hope in this country that pushes us to our deaths. I can't say how many lives, how many people have surrendered their whole bodies and souls in the hopes that their sacrifice is a stepping stone towards making this country a better place. Hope killed Nazanin."

Farzaneh bowed her head, in some gesture of respect for the dead or to hide her tears, Javid wasn't entirely sure.

"But we were made to hope. It's the only thing keeping me alive. To the public eye, I disappeared mysteriously, wiped myself off the face of the earth even. Not everybody knows why, except for a few people." Shirin's eyes flickered to Farzaneh with something akin to sorrow. "I assume that all of you think that I was hiding in the shadows, licking my wounds and grieving both the loss of my best friend and the disappointment that my mission to save the world became."

"No offence, I was thinking that." Haleh said. Nobody faulted Haleh for her honesty, something told Javid that the last thing that Shirin Shah wanted them to do was coddle her like she was a new born calf. The womxn was much more cunning than she was given credit for.

"None taken," Shirin said lightly. "I was doing all of those things but I was also making sure that someone found the sword someday. After me, there was another group that tried to go after the sword. I did reach out, I tried to help them in whatever way I could. It didn't stop them from meeting their deaths. They were ambitious, more than a little selfish, wanting the sword to bring glory back to Iran if only they could share some of it for themselves."

"I heard about you Javid. Although I didn't know that you were assembling your own group; and from several countries too. I don't believe in good luck but I'm pretty sure that this means something, that all of you believe in the story of Gordafarid and the sword's power."

Shirin inhaled a deep breath, "you want to know what happened to Nazazin Hesami."

Javid didn't bother denying it. She jerked her head in a single nod. "Yes, we do."

Shirin's eyes took on a distant gaze as if she was reliving something unpleasant. "You've done your research, Javid. You know how the water levels in the cave rises because of climate change."

Javid nodded again, there was anticipation in the air amongst them. They were finally going to know what happened to Nazanin Hesami and not out of some perverted curiosity but because knowing could save their own lives.

"Well, the water levels were high that evening. We'd been trudging through the cave from afternoon, dressed in the proper gear for cave walking." Shirin said, her voice taking on a flat edge. Javid knew that it was her way of detaching herself from the situation, from feeling so that telling would hurt her so much. It was a tactic that Javid was familiar with. She could confirm that suppressing didn't help at all but she didn't mention that out loud, it wasn't as if she could prefer a much more suitable alternative for dealing with pain.

"The cave seems to go on forever and the walls were jagged with limestone, the water levels rising higher and higher as we went in deeper. Nazanin wasn't worried, she was braver than I am. I was getting a bit worried, I hadn't expected the water levels. You see, weeks before our expedition, we took rock climbing lessons, we hiked almost daily, we took first aid lessons."

Javid began to feel a little inadequate. She hadn't made any such arrangements for their group. Should she have? It was a little too late for that now, seeing as they were leaving for Gol-e-Zard Cave in two days time. Maybe they should take a first aid course. But a voice of occurred to her, if all the lessons in the world hadn't saved Nazanin Hesami and spared Shirin Shah of a horrible trauma, then what even was the use of those lessons?

Not for the first time, Javid began to wonder if there was some otherworldly power preventing the sword from being found. If it was that easy, then the sword would be in someone's possession in all the hundreds of years that it had been put in the cave. Javid didn't really believe in the existence of spirits or ghosts, she might have been exposed to a world of powerful swords and magical relics but they didn't work in the typical way. Surely there wasn't some ancient, vengeful spirit hunting down wanderers.

Javid shook her head and forced herself to focus on Shirin's story.

"But neither of us were particularly excellent swimmers. We'd accounted for every possible scenario but water." Shirin was saying.

A shiver ran down Javid's spine. Would they also have to face the same difficulty or would some version of their hell be created in that cave?

"I suggested we go back, that we tried another day but Nazanin was stubborn." Shirin said with resignation and barely disguised awe. She wasn't at all placing any of the blame on Nazanin. She'd very obviously admired the other womxn and still very much did.

"Anyways, we did go on. We made sure to hold on tightly to the bits of limestone jutting from the rough cave walls." Shirin said, she was fighting harder and harder to keep the detachment in her voice and she was failing terribly. Her voice grew rougher, harsher and fell to a ragged whisper. Javid might have been afraid that she might cry if her eyes weren't as dry as ever, glittering with grief and fury but dry.

Javid wouldn't even fault her for crying. Pari was openly crying, teardrops slithering down her cheeks, she wiped then away angrily. Javid caught the look of pain on Haleh's face, how she clenched her fists tightly. Toman's jaw was clenched, she wouldn't allow herself show any more weakness than that. Farzaneh looked downright devastated. Javid could only imagine how much she loathed herself, maybe even blamed herself for what had happened to Nazanin even though it wasn't by any means her fault. That was the saddest part about Nazanin dying, that there was nothing that could have been done about it.

Shirin exhaled sharply and sat up straighter. "The water began to ripple."

There was a furrow in-between Javid's brows. She didn't understand even though her heart thud a too fast beat in her chest.

"Like there was something beneath it."

A shiver ran down Javid's spine.

"I'm sorry but what the fuck." Haleh expelled loudly.

Shirin attempted to laugh, but she failed pathetically. "I think that was my first thought when I noticed it. But there was something underneath the water, what it was, I can't say till this day. I've spent years turning over that fucking evening in my head, playing it over and over like it is my favourite movie and not my biggest fucking nightmare. There was something under the water; it wasn't a shark or any fish or anything I could see.

"It took her right from under and the water turned red. I think I pissed my pants, eyes darting wildly, waiting to suffer the same fate. But there was so much blood, it had to be Nazanin's. I never saw what got her and I never saw her body come up. It was like she disappeared. I would have thought it too if it wasn't for the red everywhere."

Not a single person dared to breathe, hanging on to Shirin's every breath, every pause, every word.

"I still don't know how I made it out of the cave. I called the local police when I was out, shaking like a fucking leaf and cold, so cold. They were furious when they arrived — locals often got lost in the cave, children even. It was a popular tourist spot but it was dangerous to venture too far out alone."

"But they did search, they saw the red water but no Nazanin. No body was found and there was nothing in the fucking water."

Shirin cracked her knuckles, the sudden pop sound startling all of them. "You think that you can be the chosen one, that you can find the sword and change the world. Be my fucking guest. Yes, I would like it if the sword was found but I can't lie to you about the shit I saw."

Javid was rendered speechless, for the first time she was wondering if it was best to put a halt on their plans, to rethink every fucking thing she knew about the sword. She'd expected Shirin's story to be gory, but she hadn't expected that their greatest threat would be some unknown creature slithering in the waters, waiting for blood. How did one fight something they didn't even know?

Shirin's eyes roamed the room, settling on each of them.

"You're all scared, good. Because this isn't going to be easy. You mightn't all come back alive, you may not even get to the sword."

"Congratulations, you managed to scare us properly. Want a medal for that?" Haleh snapped. Javid couldn't tell if Haleh was scared exactly. She'd seem Haleh scared before, when she'd made her confront her past. This wasn't like that time. Javid felt a surge of pride for her friend; Haleh had been the hardest to convince to join their group. She'd told Javid several times that she didn't have a single heroic bone in her body.

But that had been a lie, Haleh had run thousands of miles away from home to prove that lie; she'd once tried to be a heroine and to her, she'd failed at her chance. She didn't think that she was worthy of one anymore. Javid had always believed in her anyways and she couldn't be prouder that Haleh was sticking up for their cause. Before Shirin could recover and say another word that would strike fear into their hearts, Toman snorted, once and again before chuckling loudly.

"Wait, is that what Shirin thinks she's done to us? Scared us out of this mission?" Toman said, she shook her head from side to side. "With all due respect, Shirin, I don't think there's any of us here that has a preconceived notion of being a hero. We are not in this for the glory; you said it yourself that you have seen plenty of people, heard their stories of how they laid their lives down in hopes of making our world a better place. That is exactly what we're doing; it isn't foolish to hope or to be scared. Fear keeps us in check." Toman's voice didn't waver for once.

"I am truly sorry for your loss and words cannot express how truly terrible it was to witness something like that. Javid has never kept the truth from us though; we all know now that we might not come back from this alive, heck, we may all die." Toman continued, she caught Pari's look of horror and quickly added, "And we may not. But we're willing to take the risk knowing both endings."

"And I think that is fucking inspiring, fucking brave of us." Toman added firmly.

Javid couldn't remember the last time she'd cried but she felt herself blink back tears; not of sadness and not of joy but she was just so fucking proud of her friends; of all of them.

"I've come pretty close to dying, Ms Shah. I'm not afraid of going toe to toe with death again." Delnaz said in her usual quiet voice.

Pari smiled, she didn't look so scared anymore and her fears didn't make her any less braver than Haleh who wasn't scared. *Fear keeps us in check,* Javid thought.

Shirin Shah didn't look offended or taken aback by any of their vehement declarations, in fact, she was smiling, broadly with her teeth exposed. She shook her head, "Javid, you did pick the right people." *So her words had been a test after all?* She didn't like that; if Shirin Shah had founded them any less 'brave', would she have scorned them? Think them weak?

Maybe that was the mistake that Shirin had made, maybe she'd been too optimistic.

"I never doubted that for a fucking second." Javid answered firmly.

"You seem to have covered every angle of this. When are you planning on getting to the cave?" Shirin asked.

"Soon enough." Javid said but she wasn't entirely sure anymore. She didn't doubt her team at all and even at all their declarations of bravery she wasn't keen on losing any of them, to strange flesh eating serpentine creatures or anything else that the cave might throw at them.

Shirin nodded. "I still have every bit of research that I made on the cave, I discovered a path underneath the cave that leads directly to the Damavand Mountain amongst other things."

Javid was already aware of the path but it had all been shaky knowledge and she didn't exactly have a concrete map. This was exactly why they had needed Shirin Shah on their side.

"I'll be expecting them." Javid said.

There was a long moment of silence and Javid realised that everything that needed to be said had already been said. Shirin seemed to come to the same realisation.

"It has been nice meeting all of you." Shirin said, rising to her feet.

"Liar," Haleh shot back softly.

Shirin grinned and shrugged. "I might have disappeared from society but I still have my manners. Let's never do this again – this soul baring talk, it was long overdue and everything but there's a reason I kept it all buried inside of me for years. Find the sword and save Iran, my beloved country." She added, more seriously.

"We plan to." Toman said.

"I'm going to return to the auction, it was quite the ruckus that you lot caused. I hope it's still ongoing." Shirin said, there was a tiny frown on her face. it seemed that the cause did really appeal to her.

"I'll walk you to your limo." Javid said.

"I'll come with you." Toman added, standing up the same time that Javid did.

Javid shot her a warm smile. Toman didn't quite smile back, certainly not as broadly as Javid had but she was smiling. Shirin said her goodbyes, hugging each of them one after the other. She saved Farzaneh for last, giving her the longest hug, she whispered something that Javid didn't catch but the words must have been sentimental as Farzaneh's eyes glistened with tears.

Shirin pulled away, held her friend by the shoulders and said in Farsi, "Live, womxn, live."

Maybe it was the timing of the words but Javid felt those words resonate deep in her, as if they were meant for her. She'd been close to death before, nearly tasted the last kiss but she'd lived. She wanted to say that she would gladly give her life to get the sword and she did mean it, but saying that she had nothing to live for? That was the ugliest lie of all time. She wanted to live, at least for this womxn by her side.

***

The ride down the elevator had been quiet, now all three of

them walked out into the open air of the night. It should have been past midnight by now, Javid wasn't even the least bit exhausted, she was still running on adrenaline high from earlier.

Shirin's limo was one of the few vehicles in the hotel's parking space and it stuck out like a sore thumb amidst other vehicles. Javid, Toman and Shirin strode towards it silently.

Javid was mentally checking if there was anything she'd forgotten to ask Shirin, she couldn't think of anything right now.

Shirin walked up to the driver's window and knocked on it; the dark window slid down, revealing a middle aged womxn wearing a disapproving frown. Shirin said something to her and the other womxn sighed and shook her head. Javid had a sinking suspicion that their relationship wasn't just employer and employee; they were together or at least there was something between them. Javid was comforted by it, although she still didn't know the exact specifics of Shirin and Nazanin's relationship, she was glad that Shirin had somebody by her side; it wouldn't take her pain away – only death could do that, not even time – but it never hurt to have somebody by your side, to stay with you in the bad days and in the good ones, holding a hand out whenever it was needed.

Shirin turned to Javid, "This is where we part." She produced a glossy black business card and handed it to Javid. "This card contains my personal information, including my phone number and email address, you can reach me through it and I will forward all the research information to you."

Javid took it, flipping it over and her fingers tracing the embossed letters.

"Thank you for everything, Shirin." Javid said, meaning the words too.

Shirin cracked a smile at that, "It was the right thing to do. Do you know that Farzaneh once tried to find the sword on her own?" She asked.

Javid recoiled and she could tell that Toman felt the same shock standing beside her. Farzaneh hadn't ever mentioned it.

Shirin hummed a laugh, "I didn't believe it either when she first told me. But she did try and she failed. She didn't even make it far into the cave – although she never told me why."

Javid was still reeling from the sudden discovery. Why would Farzaneh keep something like that from them? She wanted to give her the benefit of the doubt but she was a little angry at that omission. If Farzaneh tried to reach the sword and she didn't make it there, so they shouldn't fully rely on her practical ability.

But Shirin did, her minds reminded her. So whatever entity guarded the sword – that was what Javid was referring to it as from now – didn't always kill. There had to be a pattern there, a reason why. That reason could potentially save all of them. But Javid didn't have a head for mystery, that was Toman and Haleh's thing; it was why they'd been cops before and why Toman now made a living solving mysteries.

"The point is, Farzaneh failed once on her own and decided to continue being a part of a team. Maybe the ones that make it back – like me too – have to do the same; warn, provide information and all that." Shirin said. "It's the right thing to do." She repeated firmly.

"Well, thanks anyways." Javid said.

Shirin snapped her fingers suddenly, "I forgot, before I go, there's something I need to give you, Toman."

Not many things surprised Toman but this time she was very much surprised. "Me?"

Shirin laughed, "Yes, you. You really inspired me with your speech."

Toman's lips flattened in a line and Javid knew that she was offended by Shirin's choice of words, the word speech implied that Toman had been calculating in her declaration, rehearsed in her words. Javid half expected Toman to voice her displeasure out loud but she didn't.

"I don't think that warrants a gift." Toman said flatly.

Shirin gave a nonchalant shrug, "Perhaps it doesn't. But my instincts tell me that I'm supposed to give this to you and I rarely ever not listen to my instinct."

"Wise words," Toman said mildly.

Shirin's hands went behind her neck, released her necklace, and dangled it before Toman. It was a silky black cord with a crescent black sword pendant that was all sharp edges.

Javid tilted her head to the side; there was something familiar about the pendant but she couldn't place why.

For a brief moment, Toman seemed to hesitate before reaching for it. The necklace was unusual but no doubt stunning.

"And what is this supposed to do?" Javid asked.

Shirin's answer was a cheeky grin. "You'll find out soon enough."

"You could just tell us." Toman suggested dryly. "And we could do away with all the fucking mysteries."

"I'd believe that if you didn't have a fucking sparkle in your eyes, Toman. You love mysteries and you're going to thank me for this." Shirin said, she bade them final goodbyes and a few minutes later, her limo was pulling out of the parking lot and driving away.

When she was gone, Javid shook her head, "That lady is strange as hell."

Toman smiled. "That is the understatement of the year." She was still gripping the necklace as if she'd been handed a live snake instead. Shirin Shah had been a little wrong about Toman; she didn't quite enjoy mysteries, sure, she was good at solving them but she'd been doing so for so many years that she'd come to grow bored of them.

She holds out the necklace in front of Javid. "You might want to take this." She said.

Javid shook her head, "No, there's a reason Shirin gave it to you. It's yours."

Toman smiled and Javid could tell that she was pleased. This was the most interaction that they'd had in days and Javid felt like she'd finally found cool water in the middle of a sweltering desert. She and Toman were alright again, all was well with the world.

"I do like how it looks like." Toman said, glancing down at the necklace. "it isn't anything flashy, and its light like feather." It wasn't that the necklace wasn't striking in its own right but it wasn't a beauty that was noticed immediately, it was one that was only acknowledged when one was up close to it.

"Aren't you sure you don't want to at least have a look at it? It might be something interesting." Toman said with some concern.

Javid obliged her request, taking a step closer until there was barely any space between their bodies. She notices the flush of Toman's cheeks and hid her smile. She was relieved that Toman still wanted this, still wanted her and was affected by Javid's nearness.

Although it was a little difficult to focus on anything other than the rising and falling of Toman's chest, Javid tried. It was the pendant that drew her attention, there was something familiar about the outline of the G shape.

"I think this might be a relic." Javid said aloud.

Toman was familiar with a few relics, she'd been the one to investigate the existence of a few of them after Javid discovered that Gordafarid's sword wasn't the only object of power out there in the world. The two of them had been able to track down a few of them but they'd all been stripped of their magical powers.

They'd learnt that the magic in certain relics had a shelf life and would often leak out of the objects over the years until they became useless. The sword was an instrument of great power and probably still had about fifty decades or so before it began to lose its power; even then it would be a slow, gradual process. It was one of the reasons why Javid was in a hurry to get the sword. The magic shelf life of the sword was a rough estimate, there was no telling if it would still hold the same power in the next couple of days. And there weren't plenty of individuals out there that studied magic.

"May I?" Javid asked Toman.

"Go ahead," Toman said. Javid reached for the pendant, finding it cool to the touch, she turned it over and realisation hit her hard like a knock to the head.

Javid laughed, loud and free. Toman stared at her as if she'd gone mad. Javid couldn't help it, couldn't help but melt at the adorable look of confusion on Toman's face, she grabbed her face and kissed her. Hard. It was nothing like the kiss they'd shared days ago, this one was more heated; the both of them throwing all sense of reasoning into the air. Javid kissed her hard; their tongues duelling and dancing with each other. Javid drew Toman by the waist flush against her, their soft bodies melting together and burning up in desire.

Javid wasn't sure how long they kissed, only felt deep regret when she had to pull away to breathe again.

"What was that for?" Toman asked, her lips looking thoroughly ravished.

Javid's hand reached out to touch Toman's cheek, "I've been an idiot, waiting this long to do that. I feel like I've wasted too much time; pretending like you're not the yin to my yang. We're complete opposites but balancing each other in the most perfect way. I've known that for a long time, maybe I was a little scared of it. Because choosing you would mean choosing this country and I haven't been ready to confront all my fears in a while."

There was a shinning intensity in Toman's eyes, she blinked and shook her head. "You're an idiot." She said teasingly. Not one for grand declarations of love. But Javid knew she felt it anyways.

Toman had grown up with a terrible father who chose a bottle of alcohol over and over again; she'd sworn never to be anyone's second choice. She'd willingly ended things with Javid years ago because she'd been unwilling to become a second choice. She'd distanced herself from Javid days ago too, unwilling to be used and cast aside again but now, she was taking Javid back because she was smarter than even Javid knew. And she knew that this time, she was first. Not an afterthought.

"I know, love." Javid said.

Toman smiled. Javid mimicked the action. The both of them continued to stare at each other like goofy teenagers.

"Stop it." Toman warned but she was still smiling. "Back to this relic."

Javid nodded. "I know what it is." She huffed a laugh. "This entire night has been strange to say the least. Everything seems to be falling into place for us."

"Don't jinx it." Toman said mildly. Javid rolled her eyes because she knew that Toman didn't really believe in jinxes.

"What is this anyways?" She asked.

Javid nodded, "Come with me, I'm going to show it to you."

✻✻✻

The priestess' eye didn't fit into the pendant as if it was meant to stand out and alone; just like their togetherness.

"This is too much good luck in one night," Pari was being sarcastic, shaking her head even though she was smiling big. Delnaz repeated the same thing Toman had said about jinxing luck.

"What's it going to do anyways?" Haleh asked, arms crossed on her chest, ever the skeptic. She was asking the important questions though. Haleh could be a pessimist but she was also rational.

Toman wore the necklace around her neck, her finger tracing the edged of the pendant. Javid would have liked to say that the emerald had glowed when it had been fixed unto the pendant but it hadn't; nothing magical had happened. None.

"Technically, we don't even know if it still has any magic in it." Farzaneh said matter of factly.

Javid had explained to them how relics worked. The amount of interest Haleh had shown almost concerned Javid; she feared that Haleh might take up hunting down magical relics after their mission. And if there was anyone who could track down all those elusive relics, then it was Haleh.

"So it's useless." Haleh deadpanned, not looking really impressed by the emerald or the necklace. She thought it was pretty but that was where the compliments ended. Without power equals useless to Haleh.

"That isn't a hundred percent certain." Javid corrected. "I don't think Shirin would have given it to Toman if it was otherwise."

Haleh snorted. "Shirin might just have a crush on Toman."

Even though Javid knew that it wasn't the truth, she still stiffened. Haleh was grinning and too late, Javid realised that she'd fallen into her trap. She glowered in Haleh's direction.

"That could be true, she kept sending these appreciative looks in Toman's direction when she was talking." Pari said, ever Haleh's partner in crime, they did fit well together.

"I assure you that that isn't true." Toman dryly, but she looked a little relieved that they had all stopped staring at her neck, Toman didn't like being the centre of attention for too long.

Javid cleared her throat. There was still something important that they needed to talk about. She had half a mind to push the discussion for tomorrow under the guise of her friends needing to rest but it would be taking the cowardly way out. She'd never felt so close to her friends, all the secrets between them had been aired out, they knew what they were in for and even though the thought made her heart squeeze painfully in her chest, they knew that not all of them might make it alive.

"There is something we still need to talk about." Javid said suddenly. The budding conversation came to a halt.

"I don't know about you guys but I'm tired of all the talking we've done tonight. I want to crash and sleep, after all, we make it to the cave in two days." Delnaz said.

"That is exactly what I want us to talk to us." Four pair of startled eyes fixed on Javid as if she'd just told them that Gordafarid's sword was nothing more than a story.

"What else is there to talk about? Please, don't tell me that you were actually influenced by what Shirin Shah said." Haleh sounded incredulous.

Javid shrugged. "Let's not pretend like she didn't raise very valid points."

"Like what?" Haleh asked stubbornly. "Like telling us to be afraid and that we are already going to die. No offence, Farzaneh." She added as an afterthought.

Farzaneh sighed tiredly. "None taken, Haleh, please. Even though Shirin is my friend, it doesn't mean that she is right about everything or that you should be afraid of criticising her. You aren't insulting her or me; there is a difference between saying Shirin is wrong about something and calling her a stupid bitch."

Javid was a little surprised; she didn't know that Farzaneh was even capable of swearing. Apparently, nobody was above swearing when the situation called for it.

"Afraid of Shirin Shah?" Haleh gave an obnoxious snort. There was something in the careless way that Haleh spoke, she was obviously exhausted and it was causing her to be even less polite. "I'm more afraid of turtles. And I do want to call her a stupid bitch but now isn't the time. I need Javid to remove her head from her ass. Jeez, I thought you were a womxn, why are you being such a dick?" Nobody could even take her seriously, not when she punctuated her scathing words with an adorable yawn.

Okay, Javid needed to get this over quickly so that Haleh could catch some well needed sleep.

"Pull my head out of my ass?" Javid echoed. "Shirin was reasonable and you know it. Have you ever been mountain climbing? Do you know how to disinfect a cut?"

Haleh sent Javid a glower. "I used to be a police officer, you forget that. I know how to plenty things."

"Oh, such a bad girl." Pari quipped. Haleh gave her a light shove.

"I can't do anything that would endanger any of you." Javid snapped. "I see the self loathing Shirin feels and fuck it, I don't want to be like her; going over what I could have done right."

"Javid, Shirin Shah did everything right. She chose one other person to be on her team because it was safer – being responsible for two lives. She and Nazanin took every freaking course on the planet and still, shit happened. And I hate to break it to you but we're already going to do dangerous stuff and we know this. We're prepared for anything that might happen." Toman said calmly.

"I'm afraid that we aren't ready." Javid said, her voice smaller than she wanted it to be.

"When will we be ready?" Delnaz asked softly. Javid didn't have an answer to that.

"Listen, Javid, do you remember how we met?" Toman asked. "How this group came to be?"

Javid raised her brows, she was a little unsure why Toman was taking her down memory lane. But she nodded.

Toman said disappointedly, "I don't think that you really do. Don't worry, I'll remind you."

CHAPTER TWENTY TWO
Tehran, June 2029

Pride day in London was thousands of people marching through the streets, waving colourful flags and singing songs. Javid can very well remember her first pride parade, she'd just come out to her mother – she'd been one of the rare immigrants who had blended seamlessly into their new country, adopting the new, liberal ways of living but still managing to hold on tight to the culture of their birth countries. Javid had grown up in a very Iranian household, eating Iranian food but also adopting the English lifestyle.

For years as a teen and eventually, young adult, she'd been more than a little afraid of coming out to her mum, despite the fact that she was a hundred times less strict than the traditional Iranian parent. But surprisingly, when she'd confessed to liking girls, she'd shrugged and told her that she'd suspected since she was sixteen and having zero crushes on boys. She'd always been studious choosing books and her education above every other thing, she'd acknowledged but it had been natural for girls her age to still be overtaken by hormones.

"It was that or asexuality." Her mum had added, "And both of them are fine by me; it's your life, Javid."

She'd even attended her first pride parade with her – she hadn't been the flag bearing or waving type but she'd come. Javid recalls the memory with a lot of fondness for her mother; a single mother who'd lost her husband and had played the role of both parents for her teenage daughter. She's especially grateful for her mother's acceptance. Javid doesn't remember much of her early tween years in Iran but she'd already known since as young as six that she wasn't like her friends; she'd always known that she liked girls but she'd never been able to say it out loud because young as she was, she knew that she would have never been accepted.

Javid's coming out to her mother was a bless, she was relieved to have been accepted but slightly guilty because her birth country would have never been accepting of her. She has pointedly ignored visiting her country since then; she still cares about the welfare of her people and donates to more than a dozen charities – one of them including a charity that secretly caters to young LGBTQ+ youths in Iran. She has been determined to continue ignoring Iran until a year ago when the very first bill to legitimize same-sex marriage and relationship was passed. She remembers waiting with bated breath, for the first time, daring to hope that things might be headed in the right step for her country.

Now a year later, that hope has finally become a reality and maybe she has let herself become carried away. She expected more pomp and cheer in the streets of Tehran but there's nothing. She's been in the city for three days, arriving just in time to participate in what she thought would be a huge cheerful occasion.

She's sorely disappointed that even though people like her are now declared free to love as they will, there are still plenty of people that hate to see that happen and will gladly go out of their way to bully and intimidate others that want to celebrate. Bully and intimidate are much milder words than what the hateful people can do. Javid doesn't blame the hush-hush affair; she rather understands it. Even in a liberal society like in England, she still faced a lot of homophobia as a queer womxn; it's definitely going to be a hundred times worse in Iran – an otherwise conservative and religious country.

She tries to look on the bright side as she sips coffee in a shop just a few minutes walk from the hotel she's staying at.

There's a pride banner hung above the counter in the coffee shop, in fact, it was why she stepped into the shop – the coffee is not half bad, definitely bland compared to the rich, expensive kind that she's used to but she definitely didn't step into here for the coffee. She glimpsed the banner from outside and decided to step in and support a business that supports queer people so loudly. She bets that they get a lot of shit about it, maybe even a few threats.

Try as much as she can, she doesn't think Tehran looks any different than it did when she left almost two decades ago, she was starting to feel a little foolish, as if she'd dreamt up the whole monumental event. The pride flag is proof that she did not.

She sips her coffee, tries not to grimace and glances around at the shop, there are a few young people hanging around, a man on headphones works on his laptop, coffee already forgotten. Javid picks up her phone from the table and glances down at it as if expecting a text to pop up on the screen. She already knows that her private detective; Toman isn't the texting type – she doesn't even fancy technology, only choosing to use them because of the easy communication. Javid knows that if there was a way for Toman to drop all types of technology and communicate with clients telepathically, then she easily would – that was how averse she was.

Javid shakes her head, smiling a little at her own inside joke. She did not expect to become friends with her private detective. The one she'd hired to track down a mythical relic of power. Most times, Javid finds it hard to tell what Toman is thinking but she is pretty sure that Toman had thought of her as foolish when they first met. Foolish, impulsive and rich. She could tell that Toman got a lot of clients like that; often wealthy and with too much time on their hands.

Javid likes to think that she's convinced Toman though and somehow, along the way they have become close friends. She checks her phone again, this time her smile dipping down into a frown. It isn't like Toman to be tardy.

She takes another measured sip of coffee and glances around

the room again, this time catching the eye of one of the customers. She looks about Javid's age, maybe a year or two younger. She sits by herself at a table, eyes fixed ahead at the entrance of the shop. She's wearing the most stunning coat; a cream coloured thing with a large bow on the waist. If this was London, Javid would have no problem walking up to her and asking for the brand name. Javid doesn't consider herself shy by any means, but there's just something about this city that makes her the slightest bit hesitant.

Still, she tips her head in a small nod at the womxn and goes back to her coffee; she frowns when she tips her coffee up to her lips and finds it empty. She sighs, just when she thinks she might order another cup for herself, she looks up to see the womxn she was staring at slide into the chair before her.

Javid blinks, surprised.

"Sorry to bother you." Javid is surprised when the huskiest voice comes out of this sweet looking womxn's parted lips. She smiles brilliantly, recovering quickly.

"You're not bothering me," Javid says, she pauses, wondering which of her thoughts to share. "I was actually going to come over and say hi." A half lie but still, she was sincere.

She points at the womxn's coat. "Your coat is stunning." She says.

It's the womxn's turn to look surprised; she glances down at herself as if she'd forgotten what she's wearing. "Oh, thank you." Her eyes flit up to meet Javid's. "Do you want it?"

Javid recoils, "Right here?"

The womxn smiles and gives a careless shrug of her shoulders, "Why not?"

A couple of reasons runs through Javid's mind. She isn't yet sure what to make of this womxn before her, she is bolder than most people that Javid have met but there is something on her face, a nervousness that she cannot quite hide well. Javid cannot help but wonder if this womxn was like her; back in her home country after years of being away and waiting for a beautiful womxn in a café.

"I barely know you and you barely know me." Javid says after carefully considering her words.

The womxn raises two bushy eyebrows up, she is kind of hairy and there are the faint traces of stubble above her lip. She looks beautiful still, in a way that Javid finds it difficult to look away. "I'm offering you my coat with no ulterior motives in mind. I'm not really attached to it, I promise. And look," She shoves her hands into the big pockets by the side of the coat and turns them inside out for Javid to see. "There's no bomb in my pockets or secret cameras."

She leans closer and Javid catches the faintest whiff of whiskey on her breath. Ah, that explains it, she's been drinking.

"What did you have in your cup of coffee?" Javid asks, feigning politeness. She crosses her arms under her chest expectantly. She spied the womxn drinking out of a mug a few minutes ago. Javid finds herself suddenly concerned by this coffee shop. Did they serve alcohol in their beverages?

The womxn before her flushes deeply, turning a satisfying shade of red. "Alright, you've got me." She raises mocking arms up in surrender. She lifts up one end of her coat, revealing a small flask wedged between her jeans. Javid can't help it, she laughs, throws back her head and lets out the loudest chortle known to mankind. She's drawn quite a few curious eyes to them but none linger – maybe the rate of crazy womxns in Iran has tripled since she was last in the country.

"In my defence, I'm a little nervous." She whispered the second sentence hurriedly. Javid found her curiosity increasing, she was no doubt fascinated by this womxn. Maybe it was the alcohol making her so brazen.

"Why ever, Love?" Javid asked, leaning forward in the same way, to outsiders, it looked like they were close friends sharing a secret. Javid was very amused by their interaction. If she was being honest too, she was a little nervous being back in her birth country for the first time in years, being let down by the lack of cheer and pride on the streets of Tehran.

The womxn narrowed her eyes, "Your accent, it's a bit strange."

Now that Javid knew that the womxn had been drinking, she could hear the slight drawl in her voice. She gave Javid a once over, "You look like you're from here but your accent."

"I'm British," Javid said with some amusement. It didn't matter what age or time it was, the British accent was still one that drew plenty of fascination and made plenty of impressions. Javid's new friend didn't seem impressed though, the skin between her forehead was wrinkled in the slightest as if she found Javid's accent strange rather than interesting.

"Oh." She said and shrugged. "I was drinking because I was nervous. I'm in Iran for a show."

It took Javid a few seconds for the words to sink into her head, "Oh, you're a performer?"

The womxn smiled a little, her smile wasn't anything grand but it was clear that she was very proud of what she did, "Yes, I sing."

"I hope your show goes well." Javid says politely. After that, there's a moment of awkward silence between the two of them; the silence that occurs between two strangers.

"It's not just my show tonight, I don't mean to boast but I've been slowly touring Tajikistan where I'm from. It's nothing big, just a few fancy bars. I've been sought out to play in Iran for months now but I've always turned down offers."

Javid gets the sense that this womxn doesn't have too many friends and has been wanting to get this off her chest. Many people would be uneasy to have a stranger unload on them like this – and rightfully so – but Javid doesn't see the harm in listening, after this night she doesn't have to see or talk to this womxn ever again.

"Why?" Javid asks and means it. She isn't just listening out of the goodness of her heart, she's curious too. Maybe a little too much. But it was rare that Javid finds somebody this interesting.

"I don't like this country." She says matter of factly, without any consideration to spare Javid's feeling.

If Javid is supposed to feel any indignation on behalf of her country, it's a little slow coming. If anything, her amusement grows. "Why?" She echoes her former question.

"It's too much like where I am and if I had enough money, I'd pack my bags and move far away, maybe to the west." She's shredding the paper napkins on the table to pieces, her fingers shaking not from the effects of the alcohol but from her own anger.

"I feel the exact same way." Javid hears herself say. Isn't that why, despite all her love for her country that she still steers clear, running away from visiting? Isn't that why she feels more English than Iranian?

Javid's new friend smiles a little. "You're the first person to agree with me. Everyone expects patriotism for a country that's done nothing but fail us countless of times. I thought Iran was like that too, until same-sex marriage was legalised a few months ago. I was looking forward to attending the first Pride march today." Her words are a bit hesitant now, her gaze fixed on Javid as if she expects her to freak out. Instead, the most genuine smile spreads on Javid's face. She suddenly understands now, nobody travels all the way to another country to celebrate Pride month if they aren't a member of the community. Javid finds herself being filled with huge relief.

"You feel disappointed, you came all the way expecting a huge fucking festival, not this hesitant quietness." Javid says, because it is exactly how she feels.

Surprise glitters in the womxn's eyes. "Yes. How did you know that?" She asks.

There's no reason for Javid to be untruthful so she says it, "Because I feel the same bloody way." She says darkly. "I almost thought I'd imagined the whole announcement on the news months ago."

The womxn gives a giggle, or rather, what sounds like a mix of a half sob and a giggle. "You got that right. I felt the same way, I've been in town for two days now and I've been very confused. It was only spying the pride flag hanging up above the counter from outside this shop that was the only sign that I did not imagine the whole thing."

"Me too." Javid says with a hint of a smile. She won't lie and say that this whole conversation she's had has done a 360 on her mood. She still feels a little angry, cheated out of something. But it's nice to know that she isn't alone in her feelings of righteous indignation. "I'm Delnaz." The womxn finally offers her name. this time, Javid does smile warmly.

"And I'm Javid. It is nice to meet you, Delnaz."

Without asking, Delnaz leans forward and grabs Javid's hand to shake very enthusiastically.

"I'm sorry that Iran has been so disappointing to you on your first visit." Javid says jokingly.

"At least the cuisine is good." Delnaz says with the same humour. She sighs and leans back in her chair. "I was really looking forward to celebrating today." There is a wistfulness in her voice that makes Javid feel a pang of hurt. She was also looking forward to celebrating today, today was supposed to usher Iran into a new era, one of positivity, of peace and acceptance.

The reasonable part of her expected this, she knew that in a country so conservative, there is no way that this new change would be received so positively. Javid even feared for the safety of members of the LGBTQ+ community in Iran, despite their newly acquired justice, it still isn't exactly safe for them to be out in public and celebrating so loudly. Still, she had hoped. And that hope had died a slow death like a flower wilting away.

Not for the first time, Javid feels hopelessness when she thinks about her country, it seems that Iran can only be saved by divine and supernatural forces. And Gordafarid's sword is Javid's last hope.

She discovered the existence of the sword not up to a year ago, and she, who had never been good at believing in the existence of higher deities and forces had slowly become to believe. She plans to find the sword and use it for the good of her country and its neighbours.

Gordafarid is one of the heroines in the Shahnameh "The Book of Kings" or "The Epic of Kings", an enormous poetic opus written by a popular Per-

sian poet around 1000 AD. She was a champion who fought against Sohrab (another Iranian hero who was the commander of the Turanian army). She delayed the Turanian troops who were marching on Persia. She is a symbol for courage and wisdom for Iranian womxns and even womxns from Farsi-speaking countries like Tajikistan and Afghanistan. It is rumoured that Gordafarid went into battle with a sword that was blessed by gods, a sword that she went ahead to hide in the Yellow Flowers Cave.

Javid believes that Gordafarid did so for when Iran would be in great need for the sword's power. In the past year, it's been a little pet project of hers; researching information to find the sword. It's how she knows Toman – because she hired her to find information on the past groups that have tried to find the sword. She hasn't learned much about them – none of the groups have been successful and even fewer of them have made it back alive to tell the story but she has learned a few things; that nobody has ever ventured into the Yellow Flowers Cave alone. Nobody was foolish enough too, the journey alone is rough and dangerous enough.

Javid has slowly come to realise that it's a journey she cannot go on alone but still, it's something she'll have to worry about when the time was right. For now, she still needs to do her research.

Delnaz clearing her throat snaps Javid back to the present. Her new friend looks the slightest bit apologetic, "I have to head back to my hotel."

"To rehearse?" Javid asks, trying to clear her thoughts of Gordafarid's sword and its complexities. She keeps telling herself that is a bridge that will be crossed when the time is right. But she isn't so sure that there will be a right time waiting to happen with the way her country was headed. If she wants to save her country, then she has to start acting like it and putting plans into motion instead of hiding behind ideas. A ludicrous idea occurs to her, so sudden and so crazy that Javid almost laughs out loud at it.

"Rehearse?" Delnaz asks with an adorable crinkle of her nose as if the concept of rehearsing as a singer is so unheard of. Javid almost feels really foolish for suggesting it in the first place. "I don't rehearse." Delnaz adds with sass to rival a diva, or maybe she is one. Javid cannot imagine her as one, she looks at Delnaz and the first word that comes to mind is adorable.

"Why not?" Javid asks, bracing herself for another hilarious anecdote.

Delnaz lifts her chin up in true diva fashion. "I have never rehearsed for a single moment in my entire lifetime."

Javid blinks back in surprise, she expects to see a hint of a smile on Delnaz's face, something to show that she's joking but there is nothing but seriousness on that baby face.

"Okay, it looks like you're actually being serious." Javid mutters under her breath, Delnaz catches the words anyways and smiles wider, cheekier. Javid shakes her head from side to side. "You have to be joking, even the best of the best rehearse before a show. What makes you so special?"

Delnaz scoffs, "I can't fault you for your disbelief, you've never heard me sing before."

Javid smiles at her confidence. "You have my curiosity piqued." Damn straight, that curiosity chart has skyrocketed since Delnaz slid from across the room into the chair in front of Delnaz.

Delnaz smiles again but this time there is something shy in it that immediately endears Javid towards her. There is something about Delnaz that reminds Javid of a bird, maybe a songbird now that she knows that Delnaz sings. Yes, a songbird. "You should come watch me tonight." She says.

Javid was expecting the invitation, but she still smiles. "I'd love to." It's not like she is doing anything special while she is in Iran. In fact, she was only going to stay for a couple of days in the country, celebrate queer people and eat authentic Iranian food. There's already been a damper on the first plan but that doesn't mean that she can't stick around to attend Delnaz's gig. It would be nice in fact.

"Prepare to be blown away tonight. After you hear me, you'll know why I don't ever need to rehearse." Delnaz is saying but Javid is only half listening, already excited for tonight. She's almost forgotten that she's supposed to be meeting Toman here, she wonders if Toman will go with her to watch Delnaz tonight. She can't hide the thrill she feels at the possibility of spending a night out with Toman. Nothing has happened between the two of them yet and Javid isn't entirely sure what she wants from her. She only knows that there's sizzling attraction between the two of them and that she wants to act on it, wants to do more than accidentally on purposely brush Toman's hand with her own.

"Do you have a pen with you?" Delnaz asks, when Javid shakes her head, she stands up and walks toward the counter to talk to the person standing behind it. A few seconds later, she returns with a pen and scribbles down on a paper napkin. She slides it over to Javid. "I'm performing here tonight. you can bring friends or a girlfriend, if you like." She shrugs. "The more the merrier."

It seems as if Delnaz had made the same conclusion that Javid did. Javid realises that her new friend is as astute as she is adorable.

"It was nice to meet you, Delnaz." Javid says, meaning it. "And I will see you tonight. Me and my friend."

Delnaz seems to deflate, "No girlfriend?" She pouts. She laughs at Javid's look of confusion. "Sorry, I've been watching you for a long time. You looked like you were waiting for somebody – you kept glancing at the entrance."

"She's not my girlfriend." Javid says, she doesn't know what possess her to add a confident "Yet."

But it's almost worth it seeing the cheeky grin that spreads on Delnaz's face. "That's the spirit. Happy Pride Day and month, Javid. I will see you tonight."

Javid stands up at the same time that Delnaz does and hugs her for a brief second. "You too, Delnaz."

Less than three minutes later, Delnaz is gone after returning the pen. Javid is thinking of calling Toman again when she looks up and sees as she steps through the entrance of the café. She's dressed in muted colours as she usually prefers, black jeans that and a cream coloured high necked shirt. She wears a hat over her head with most of her hair tucked into it. Javid has come to learn that Toman has a penchant for wearing hats and caps. The way she's so casually dressed tells Javid that she's probably been undercover. Toman prefers the term private detective and she usually takes on the cases of wealthy people, some of them wishing to catch a spouse in the act of cheating, learn the secrets of their enemies and find some long lost relative. To Javid, that all sounds very boring, especially when she discovered that Toman used to be a police detective. Toman opened up via email that she particularly enjoys the boring, mundane routine of being a private detective and that she left the police force to live a boring and unexciting life. She told Javid that a traumatic incidence drove her out of the force but she didn't say what.

Javid didn't ask the details to be polite. She watches as Toman scans the café with that wary gaze of hers; the one where she looks as if she constantly expects a knife wielding assailant to spring out of the daylight shadows and attack her. Javid supposes that it is a habit from her police detective days that she hasn't been rid of. Toman finds her in the corner and settles down in the seat.

"Hello, Javid." She says in her usual, formal, polite manner of speaking. Sometimes, Javid wonders how she likes Toman. She's been with different kinds of womxns in her adult life and she's always had a thing for the carefree, spontaneous womxns. The kinds she went on vacation with; the ones who knew how to have a good time inside and outside the sheets. Toman isn't uptight by any means, she isn't above the occasional dirty joke or even flirting. It's that Toman is measured in every aspect of the word; carefully choosing her words, her friends, her clothing, and even ordering her tea. She's nothing like Javid who often thrives on spontaneity. Javid has heard in the past about how opposites attract but she's never really believed it, never really encountered it until now.

She's utterly fascinated by this enigma of a womxn before her and she doesn't even like puzzles. Toman waited until the server had taken her order before speaking. "I apologise for my tardiness. I suddenly got a lead on a case I'm working on and had to dash over. Did you get my text?"

"No." Javid says with surprise. She picks up her phone and scrolls through it, finding that she silenced all notifications from coming through. She removes the setting and finds one text from Toman. She smiles sheepishly. "I didn't check well." She mutters, not liking how she behaves like a bumbling schoolgirl in front of Toman. She wants to imitate the cool front that always keeps.

Toman waves a hand, "That's alright. I hope you weren't too bored." Her eyes glitter with humour and Javid's lips cure up in a smile. It's an inside joke between the two of them. Toman admitted a while ago that she pegged Javid as a bored socialite when they first spoke on the phone. "Who the hell spends their money and time investigating fictional objects?" Toman had said with laughter in her voice. "I've gotten a lot of strange jobs since I became a private detective but believe me, I have never been asked to track down information on a mythical object of power."

Since then, it had become a joke between them.

"I was entertained actually. I met a girl." Javid begins, carefully watching Toman's face for any flashes of disappointment. It seems like working Toman into a jealous rage to get her to confess feelings that Javid is sure are there isn't such a solid plan after all. Toman's face looks as blank as ever.

"Hmm." She says with some interest. She leans back in her seat. "Tell me all about this girl."

And Javid does. Toman sips tea in between each sentence, she soon begins to relax, even doling out a smile or two when Javid mentions something funny. Javid feels satisfied at the end of the story about Delnaz. Delnaz isn't the only one who reminds Javid of a bird. Toman does too, in the sense that she might take flight if Javid says one wrong word.

"She wants us to watch her sing tonight." Javid adds.

Toman looks a little taken aback. "Us?"

Javid smirks, "I told her about us, love."

Toman almost spits out a mouthful of tea. "Us?" She echoes again.

"Yes, I told her about my friend, *you*." Is it Javid's imagination or did she just see something like disappointment flash in Toman's eyes?

"Hmm." Toman says.

"You're coming with me tonight." Javid declares, leaving no

room for disagreement. Defiance flashes through Toman's eyes and Javid feels overcome with the desire to close the distance between them and kiss her.

"I--"

"Please, *love*. Even cheating husbands take a night off from cheating. I'm paying for the hours, add it to my bill but instead of working, I'm asking you to take the night off and go dancing with me."

Toman's lips curve in the slyest smile. "I thought we were going to watch your friend sing."

Javid doesn't miss a beat, she is done playing subtle and she's never really been shy to go after what she wants anyways. Attractive intelligent womxn and Gordafarid's sword. "Where there is music, there will be love." She says.

"You're not even asking me what the latest I've found about the sword." Toman asks, returning to her serious disposition for a moment. Javid pushes all worries and concerns about the sword away from the front of her mind. It can wait, the sword isn't going to get miraculously discovered in the next couple of hours. Javid is beginning to realise that finding Gordafarid's sword will be something that takes months, if not years of planning. So, yes, the sword can wait. But Javid is tired of bidding her time and waiting for Toman to make the move. So, yes, they are going dancing tonight.

"Tell me everything when you're looking into my eyes on the dance floor."

***

"You really know how to pick the great date night spots, Javid." Toman says sarcastically when the car pulls up to the curb. Javid ignores her and hands a wad of cash to the driver, muttering at him to keep the change.

"Sarcasm is beneath you, Toman." Javid shoots back, a little teasingly. But she is a little worried, it's been years since she was last in the city so she isn't at all familiar with all the entertainment hotspots. When Delnaz mentioned that she was a singer and that she was performing tonight, Javid visualised a swanky bar, one of the expensive ones where a live band plays jazz and its patrons drink expensive alcohol. What she didn't expect is this rundown place; the building shady looking and half hidden in the dark of the night, the street light right next to it buzzes and flickers off every few seconds. A few people hang outside in front of the bar and smoke.

Javid spots a womxn in a tight dress hurl the contents of her stomach near the streetlight. For the longest moment, she just stands there and gapes at the sight.

Toman gives a sudden snort besides her, "I've never seen you look so horrified." She laughs again and even though it's at Javid's expense, she still finds herself smiling a little. Toman doesn't laugh very often and Javid has already managed to make her laugh twice tonight, yes, the bar might be shady looking but as far as Javid is concerned, the night is going pretty well.

"This doesn't look like any of your fancy spots, I reckon." Toman is saying. Javid shakes her head but she's still smiling at the absurdity of it all. Her time in Iran isn't going at all like she expected it would be. "For one, there's no valet for your car and no complimentary champagne the moment you step foot into the building." Toman says, sounding like she's having way too much fun.

"Yeah, yeah. I'm bougie and I accept it." Javid drawls. One thing she never does is pretend to be somebody she is not. So she doesn't take Toman's taunts to heart – they're just that, playful teasing.

Toman glances at her, "You seem oddly fine with this."

Javid shrugs. "Did you expect me to have a diva fit?" She asks.

Toman is quiet for a second. "Honestly, no. You may be rich but you're not like the rest of your folks. I figured that out the day you snorted a laugh when we spoke on the phone that one time."

Javid echoes the same sound now. Toman's approval warms her more than she cares to admit, screw it, she isn't at all ashamed to admit that she cares what this tenacious womxn thinks of her.

"I'm just a little bummed out that I promised you a night full of swanky dancing and end up bringing you to the shadiest looking place in the city. What even are our chances of getting mugged?" Javid asks and she's only half joking.

Toman shoots her a baffled look, "How the hell am I supposed to know that?"

"You used to be a police detective." Javid points out a little carefully, Toman doesn't really like to talk about her past in the police force. Javid is aware that there is a lot of unresolved guilt that makes the topic a very delicate one. Honestly, Javid doesn't care either that Toman has made a lot of mistakes. If only it was that easy anyways.

"Yes, a police detective not a walking crime rate statistics book." Toman replies in her usual wry humour. Javid breathes a little easier that Toman took the joke well. Maybe their night will go well after all.

"Listen, I'm sorry I brought you here. We could leave if you want to, we could go back to my hotel and drink some whiskey." Javid says.

She nearly flinches when Toman takes her hand, she looks up to find Toman smiling at her confidently, none of that anxiety that Javid is feeling, wondering if she's ruined all chances with Toman even before their night out begins.

"And what happens to your new friend?" Toman asks.

Javid feels a pang of guilt in her chest. Delnaz is new to the city and from their conversation at the café, it doesn't sound like she has a lot of people cheering for her tonight. Javid wants to impress Toman tonight but she also came here for her new friend. "You're right."

Toman shrugs and smiles easily, "I often am."

Javid rolls her eyes, "And humble too."

"One more compliment from you and I might start to think that you're in love with me." Toman quips.

Although her words are said jokingly, but Javid can't help but wonder if they contain an iota of truth in them. Maybe Javid isn't quite in love with Toman but she is pretty sure that she likes this womxn way more than a silly crush or some teenage infatuation.

"If we get mugged, I might leave you for dead and run." Javid says.

"You're the one dressed swanky and in turn, you made me dress swanky. Look at us, we look ridiculous and even worse, we look rich. We're definitely getting mugged." Toman says. Javid silently accepts the blame, she was the one who told Toman to wear a nice dress. And she does look nice, more than nice. For once, Toman let her hair cascade down her back and she wears a knee length dress with thin straps and kitten pumps. She looks like she's headed to dinner at a fancy restaurant not some shady club that looks like it has seen too many drug deals.

Javid nudges her slightly. Toman winks.

"But don't worry, I've still got my ass kicking skills with me. Just stick close to me." She adds, her voice dropping to a husky whisper. Javid smiles and runs her hand up Toman's face, she says in the most serious voice, "My heroine."

The two of them continue to stare at each other for the longest second until they hear a sudden crash and jump away from each other.

"Alright, let's do this,"

***

It's been a long time since Delnaz has felt any pre performance anxiety. She's been singing for almost as long as she could talk.

Everyone always talked about how she was destined to be some famed singer. The fame bit has become a dream she doesn't want but performing is like air to her. It's not surprising that she ended up making a living out of her voice. But it is the first time that she's singing far away from her home country.

In Tajikistan, Delnaz sings at a fairly popular bar in the busy heart of the city she lives in. She makes decent cash, enough to live and be comfortable. She's had plenty of music agents, famous producers and record label owners walk through the doors of the bar she sings in, hear her sing and try to snatch her up, they always tell her stories of how they have never heard a voice like hers, how she is destined to become the next big superstar. No matter how starry and beautiful their dreams for her sound, Delnaz has always said no. She was perfectly content singing in a bar and making money.

Until a few months ago when she performed at the wedding of her boss' brother as a favour to her boss, as usual, she had wowed everybody. She'd even been approached by some music executive who also tried to woo her. But unlike the others, he started small, asking to set her up on a small tour around the country.

"See if you like it, it is only a taste of the superstar that you can become."

She almost turned him down but she couldn't deny the appeal travelling around the country, all expenses paid and doing nothing but singing had. So she had taken up his offer and months later, she can admit that she has enjoyed the tour, she likes singing – that has never changed – but she finds that she still has no passion for all the promises of greatness that has been whispered into her ear since she was young. Delnaz craves a simple life; singing when she can, saving up money that she might never use and donating the excesses to charity, wanting to help her country any way that she can.

It's why she's nervous tonight. Tonight isn't only her first show abroad, it's her last for the tour and despite all the fun she has had, all the different kinds of people she's met, all the places she's performed, she is still firm with the realisation that this isn't what she wants to do for the rest of her life. She's going to have to shoot a gift horse in the mouth or however the famous proverb goes.

Plus through it all, there' s a part of Delnaz that can't help but be disappointed by her tour; she's been to a lot of places; both beautiful and shabby in their own rights but she still cannot say that she's formed any meaningful connections with any of the people she's met. She hasn't made any friends, nor any plans with anyone to keep in touch when she returned to Tajikistan. That was one of the reasons she'd wanted to go on tour in the first place.

She smiles a little at herself in the mirror, thinking of Javid. It may be a little too early to tell but Delnaz already likes Javid and she did accept her invitation to come tonight. Delnaz didn't have a normal childhood by any means but she still can't help but feeling a little apprehensive. She imagines this would be how the rejected girl in high school feels like trying to fit in, trying to impress the more popular girls.

Granted, this is the real world and not high school. Besides, Javid will be there tonight, to cheer her on. For some reason, this soothes Delnaz's nerves. She blows out a breath and combs her hair to the side. She normally doesn't dress fancy to perform but tonight she's made an exception; brushed out her curls and straightened them, she's wearing a stunning backless red dress with long sleeves, her dress matches the bold colour of her lipstick and when Delnaz stretches her lips into a smile, she looks sensual, otherworldly even. She finds that she likes looking like this.

She stands up and walks to the door, it's show time.

***

Haleh is very bored, or rather, more accurately, the boredom is a front for the uneasiness roiling in her stomach, she hates being back in Iran, especially after taking the coward's way out a few years ago with her tail between her legs. She swore to never return, that nothing would make her come back to this cursed country, all of its corruptions and failures. But the anger is a front for some-thing much darker; Haleh loathes herself.

So many people have come before her, determined that they would be one of the good ones in a sea of bad people, that they would be the one to change their world. She was like that too, believing with wide eyed foolishness. And when she'd failed, it had been devastating, so she'd run away and convinced herself that she hated her country.

She didn't think that she would return too but despite her resolve to stay away all these years, she'd still kept in touch with the news. And when she saw on the news months ago that same-sex marriage was finally legalised in Iran, she'd felt hope for the first time in years. That same hope had caused her to take a flight.

And end up in same city she'd been running from. All of that hope she'd felt earlier had bled into nothing, Iran taking and taking from her until there was nothing left to give. She'd come to the city to partake in the first pride parade but just at the airport, she'd watched two teenagers wearing pride flags take a beating from a police officer. The old Haleh would have walked up to them, demanded to know what was going on. The new Haleh just watched with clenched fists, not because she was afraid but because she knew that the police officer wasn't the only problem; there were thousands of others just like him and she couldn't fight all of them. She had tried once and it hadn't ended well.

She'd left the airport moody, feeling her hope and excitement drain out of her a little, she'd held on tighter with a clenched fist, determined that there had to be something good about the day.

But walking the streets of Tehran, she soon realised that there wasn't going to be a huge pride parade – there would be no grand celebration of queer love and queer people. No, queer people might have become 'justified' by the law but for years, they had suffered beatings, cold blooded murders and hate. It wasn't going to stop just because a piece of paper said so.

Haleh should have left, she should have booked the next ticket out of the country and left, like she had years ago. But for some reason, she is still sticking around, brooding and gnashing her teeth through it all but at least she's still here.

Reasonably, she hadn't wanted to be on her own. So defiantly, she had scoured social media in her hotel room, searching for smaller pride events happening around the city. She hadn't needed to dig too hard, she'd found an event at a bar a few minute walk away from her hotel. The bar was apparently owned by a gay man; and the event was nothing fancy, just offering free drinks to every queer person that showed up. And there was some singer performing too.

Haleh hadn't hesitated, she was only staying two more days in Iran and her flight was booked already. Might as well spend her last days in the country wasted and in the midst of people like her. because even though Haleh may deny it when she's asked, she does feel lonely and she has never been the one to pass up the opportunity for free drinks.

An hour spent in the bar though and she realises that being surrounded by tacky pride decorations doesn't take any of the edge away, all she does feel is her anger growing. She doesn't like how queer people aren't allowed to celebrate pride freely, instead they hide in secret bunkers and toast fearfully to their new acceptance. Plus the music she was promised isn't here yet. Raunchy pop music plays from speakers and the crammed bar stinks of sweat at people gyrate to the beat of the music. She briefly considers leaving but the thought of being back in her empty hotel room doesn't hold much appeal.

Haleh looks up at the entrance, watching as a striking couple enter the space looking too glamourous for a shoddy place like this bar. Haleh isn't sure why she automatically assumes that they're a couple; they might be friends – but the taller womxn's hand hovers behind her companion's back in a protective gesture. They are dressed to the nines; wearing stunning gowns and looking fit. She sits up a little straighter, a small smirk blooming on her lips; she kind of enjoys how the taller womxn looks a little apprehensive, eyes darting around the room as if she expects someone to jump out of thin air and attack her and her date. It appears like a case of being at the wrong place.

The womxns walk up to the bar and remain there for a few minutes, just when Haleh is getting bored of them, they walk towards the back corner of the bar where Haleh is seated; bottles of beer in their grip. They settle down near Haleh.

"It's thankfully better looking in here." The taller one says in a British accent, sounding very much relieved. The other womxn gives a snort. "So London has made you soft," she says in a raspy voice.

The two of them continue to make small talk and Haleh finds herself zoning out.

There's a makeshift stage in the middle of the room and a band fine tuning their instruments. A womxn in a shimmery red dress is in the middle of it all, chatting away with the pianist. Haleh cocks her head to the side and wonders if this womxn is tonight's singer. Another ten minutes pass,

Haleh orders another beer and guzzles down the watered down drink, it takes more than a few drinks of alcohol to get her drunk or even lightly buzzed – years of being used to the hard stuff tends to do that to one. Haleh finds herself reminiscing about her first year in Berlin and finding herself working in the underground club scene; she had started out as a lowly waitress, a foreigner learning the ropes in a country full of people who looked so different than her. Her nights were lonely and she took to drinking.

Haleh shakes her head, trying to clear the dark thoughts from it. She's getting a little impatient when she hears the first hum of music. Her head snaps up, the womxn in the shimmery dress is singing, her voice the most melodic thing Haleh has ever heard in her life. Most singers would introduce themselves first before delving first into the song, but this womxn doesn't, she just carries on to her song. All around in the bar, Haleh can see that the noise and ruckus of conversation is dying down. The singer's voice has completely captured the attention of everybody in the bar.

For the first thirty seconds of the song, Haleh doesn't pay attention to the lyrics – the womxn might be singing in Spanish or Dutch or even alien language, Haleh doesn't give a shit about that, she's focused on the voice; of how this womxn sounds like a thousand angels, like the most beautiful thing that Haleh has ever heard.

Earlier, Haleh didn't get a good look at the singer's face; she does that, glaze over faces when she sees people. The truth is that Haleh has been with the most diverse people, men and womxns. She's become more or less uncaring of how people look like. Now, she's more than a little curious to get another look at this womxn's face, she expects to see the most remarkable looking womxn, surely someone who possesses a voice this good has to be beautiful.

Haleh finds herself a little disappointed. The singer isn't ugly by any standards; her hair is a dull shade of brown that has been combed through and left to fall limply behind her shoulders, she's wearing makeup but not much of it. Her face is round and she isn't smiling as she sings. Haleh is more than a little vain but even this womxn's ordinary looks don't cause her to lose interest.

Haleh finally pays attention to the words; she's singing in Farsi, a song about loss and freedom. The song is hauntingly beautiful, her voice rising higher in an almost scary pitch as it reaches its climax. And then it ends, abruptly. There is silence for a short beat before the whole bar erupts into thunderous applause, cheers and foot stomping.

The couple next to Haleh are whooping harder than everyone else, the taller one mostly; beaming and everything.

"Delnaz, you sound amazing!" she is saying, clapping as if her cheering words aren't enough. Haleh wonders if she's friends with the singer – *Delnaz*.

Delnaz soaks up the applause with a stoic face but there's no mistaking the glint of pride in her eyes. Something tells Haleh that Delnaz is used to this kind of reception. She must have been told so many times how beautiful her voice is, how haunting and how touching,

Maybe she is a little tired of it too – Haleh knows that she would be, although being beautiful cannot compare to having a great voice, Haleh has been on the receiving end of compliments because of how alluring she is, she's had her eyes compared to stars, had her poet lovers writing about the shape of her lips. Somehow along the line, all the compliments have blurred into one meaningless thing. She's stopped smiling at the awed comments, stopped feeling anything less than mild annoyance. *Yes, I'm beautiful, yes, I've been told that I have hips like Cleopatra.*

She imagines that is how Delnaz feels and even though the only thing Haleh knows about her is that she's a great singer, she immediately takes a liking to her.

Along with every other patron in the bar, Haleh settles back into her chair as Delnaz launches into another number; this time a little more upbeat. Haleh finds herself bopping her head along to the music, feeling something akin to joy spread in her chest.

And so it went on, Delnaz switching from lighthearted songs to devastating one. Soon enough, the whole bar is clapping along and cheering too. Even Haleh hums a little, tapping a beat on the table a few times. Delnaz's closes the set with a cover of a popular Iranian pop song that causes the crowd to cheer raunchily. At the end of it, Haleh is clapping and smiling more than she has in one night than she has in the past few days that she's been in the city – hell, she's smiling more than she has in years.

Delnaz leaves the makeshift stage and weaves through the crowd, accepting words of praises with smiles and waves. She kindly turns down offers to buy her drinks, heading solely for her friends – the striking, cheering couple.

Haleh finds herself eavesdropping again while pretending to scroll through her phone.

"Javid! You came." Haleh hears Delnaz voice says and she flinches back a little. Delnaz's talking voice is hoarse, like smooth gravel instead of the light lilt of her singing voice. She doesn't sound bad talking, just different than what Haleh expected.

The taller womxn, Javid rises from her seat to hug Delnaz. Haleh looks up in that moment and catches the sheepish smile on Javid's face.

She gestures at her girlfriend or wife. "I brought a friend too." Okay, so they're not couples. Haleh tells herself that she's only disappointed because it means her assessment was wrong and not because it is a shame that these two good looking womxns aren't together.

Haleh is engrossed in her thoughts that she almost misses Javid's next words.

"… is Toman." She gestures to the womxn beside her.

Toman's smile is smaller than Javid's but not because of insincerity, there's as much warmth in her smile as there is in Javid's.

Damn it, why is she impressed with these random strangers? Haleh has had the opportunity to meet all kinds of people – the good, the bad, the in between, the beautiful and the ugly. She's had wealthy lovers, she's met important people and only a few have impressed her. Yet she spends just one hour in this seedy looking bar and finds herself wishing she was friends with three strangers. Maybe it's because Haleh has been pursued all her life – people have always wanted to be *with* her, to *be* her. it has never been the other way around and it's slightly unsettling to feel differently for what may be the first time in her life.

Or maybe you're too shy to make friends, her mind taunts. Haleh frowns at the thought. She listens to the three of them make small talk. A few drinks are brought over to their table and Javid and Toman toasts to Delnaz. Through it all, Haleh grows increasingly miserable. She shoots up from her seat suddenly; the chair makes a loud screeching sound and almost topples back on the floor. The music playing dulls the sound of it but even though there was no music playing, she doesn't think anyone would notice. Everywhere she looks, people are talking with friends, several couples have taken to dancing. Everybody is with somebody – everybody except her. Haleh hasn't cried in years and she isn't about to start now but she cannot ignore the hollow in her chest at the feeling of loneliness, sure the music took the edge away briefly but the clawing feeling of emptiness is back.

"I need a smoke." Haleh says aloud and to no one, she snatches her purse off the table and walks past Delnaz and her friends and towards the entrance of the bar. A few seconds later, she bursts into the open air and nearly gags at the smell. There's the rancid smell of garbage and vomit in the air, smoke too. Earlier when she arrived at the bar, she saw a few people loitering outside, smoking and making out but she's the only person out here in the night now. Like a fucking loser. The streetlight head buzzes for a second, the light flickering before stabilizing again.

She fiddles with her purse and opens it, pulls out a pack of cigarette and lighter. She tucks her purse underneath her arm, shoves a cigarette stick between her lips and lights it. She puffs out air through swollen cheeks and watches as the smoke swirls in a random fashion before dissipating. She takes another drag and another.

"You're feeling the magic, right?" a voice comes.

Haleh nearly chokes. She coughs and coughs, slapping her chest hard. She turns at the moment the womxn steps out of the shadows, she was standing near the streetlamp and Haleh didn't even notice her. She blinks, trying to adjust her eyes to the darkness, she narrows her eyes when the womxn marches up the short steps to come and stand besides Haleh.

"Are you insane?" Haleh hisses.

Her new companion laughs and shakes her head, her fancy bob swishing side to side. She looks like she stepped out of a company brochure; wearing a black suit and pants with her lips are painted a bright red. Her hands are tucked into the pockets of her pants and for the first time, Haleh notices how cold it is outside, she is so used to dressing skimpily; short, shiny leather skirt and a leopard print top – if it can even be called that; it's more of a tightly fitted bralette, the material flimsy and thin, clinging to her chest sensually. Haleh is past feeling self conscious about how she looks and dresses but she stands out so starkly compared to this strange womxn.

"Maybe a little." The stranger says, smiling widely. Haleh shifts away from her in a less than subtle action. She wants this womxn to know that she isn't comfortable with her nearness.

Thankfully, she doesn't attempt to close the distance that Haleh has created. Haleh would hate to punch her in the face; she just got her nails done and well, this womxn has a pretty face. Yes, Haleh isn't much moved by pretty faces anymore but that doesn't mean that she cannot acknowledge one and appreciate one.

"You didn't answer my question," the cute womxn says.

Haleh groans aloud and rolls her eyes. "I don't want to talk to you." Lie, she isn't really bothered by another presence out here in the dark, she almost welcomes it. The thing is that, the tugging feeling of loneliness in her stomach isn't a new one, she's bore the brunt of it for years, surrounding herself with lovers – sometimes more than one at the same time – and booze and some of the most morally grey people, so grey that they were downright despicable. She was used to picking fights and making enemies, anything to drown out that roaring loud silence in her chest.

She's back in Iran and there's nothing to shield her from the gravity of her loneliness. The beer sucks, for one. So maybe being around this annoying, pesky womxn isn't too much of a punishment.

"You could go back inside or tell me to get lost." The womxn says, she waits for several beats, waiting for Haleh to turn her away. Haleh hesitates, somehow she thinks that this womxn needs the company more than she does.

"I'm Pari." The womxn says, smiling a little. Haleh gives a task of acknowledgement but she doesn't offer her own name.

"I see that you're playing hard to get," Pari says, "Don't worry, I love a challenge."

"Are you always this assuming? It's annoying." Haleh drawls.

"The annoying part is kind of a gift."Pari quips.

Haleh tamps down on her smile before it can show.

Rarely does Haleh meet somebody that matches her quip for quip – the truth is that most people afraid to talk to her, not that she blames them,; she wears the most emotionless mask when she's with other people and this gives off the aura of unfriendliness.

"To put it simply, you look like you want to kill people." One of Haleh's old lovers once told her.

"So, friendly stranger, I was talking about the magic of the bar – the one that sent you out here." Pari is saying. The cheerful lilt in her voice is ever present but there is something fake about it.

"I have no idea what you're talking about," Haleh answers flatly. She almost wants to push Pari with sarcastic and cutting remarks, she wants to push her to the limit and cause her to snap; to get rid of the false cheerfulness that she's wearing like one would wear like an armor.

Pari said firmly, "Pay attention, sweetheart."

Haleh raises her brow at the term of endearment, she's been called worse but somehow this one doesn't really grate on her nerves. Does she really crave attention and friendship this much that she would lap up the bare minimum like a needy animal?

She realises that she's been too quiet for a long while so she takes another drag of her cigarette and rolls her eyes. "Don't call me sweetheart." She realises that she's fallen into a trap when Pari smirks wide. Haleh shakes her head, feeling oddly turned on by the possibility that Pari tricked her. She does have the strangest kinks.

"Then you can just tell me your name." Pari says, winking to punctuate her words.

Haleh doesn't miss a beat, "Not a chance in hell, sweetheart."

"It's so lonely in there. You look around and get slapped in the face with people and their *people*. Celebrating with each other and all that shit." Pari sounds a bit forceful and Haleh's brows quirk up in surprise and pleasure. Finally, she's letting go of all that happy nonsense. "I'm jealous of it, of them." Her voice is lower now, something like sadness in the timbre of it.

Isn't it too early to start pouring your sob story on a stranger? Haleh wants to say, she bites down on her lip though, the words are too cruel for even her to say. It would feel a lot like kicking a puppy while the poor thing is down.

"Don't you have friends that you could have come with?" Haleh hears herself ask. She nearly laughs at the irony of it all. Well, in her defence, she could have come with somebody, call up any of her sex partners to accompany her to Iran. But somehow she doesn't think that they would appreciate this place, even she'd looked at it with scorn when she first arrived. Besides, Iran is still very much the devil she has been running from and letting people who mean very little to her have a glimpse into her vulnerabilities made her shudder.

"I'm not from here." Pari says, Haleh pretends not to notice how she dodges the question. "I'm actually an Afghan."

"Oh," Haleh echoes. Pari's loneliness is a little different from hers. Afghanistan is still very much a third world country, womxns' right are still a constantly debated topic and it was only in recent years that the country was freed from the reign of the Taliban; a terrorist group that took over the country for years. Queer rights still take the backseat in the discussion of humxn right issues, talk less of being accepted. If Haleh is right in her assumption and Pari is queer, then she must acknowledge Iran's new legalisation of queer marriage with something akin to jealousy. It's the most innocent form of it that Haleh cannot bring it in herself to be mad about it.

"None of my family knows – granted I don't have too many of those anymore." Pari gives a sad laugh and shakes her head. "There happened to be a work conference happening in Tehran today and after it I snuck out of dinner with my coworkers to be here."

Haleh just lets her continue speaking, Pari needs to get this off her chest. It has been a long time since Haleh talked to her heart's content; about the things bothering her. she can only imagine how therapeutic it feels for Pari – who no doubt has been bottling up her feelings for a long time.

"Hence the suit," Pari says, giving a small whirl as if she is wearing a ball gown instead. Haleh smiles this time.

The two of them are silent for a few minutes, and even though Haleh might not admit it out loud, she does feel the tinny bit relieved that she isn't alone.

***

Javid isn't surprised that she's having a good time, although she was a little worried that Toman wouldn't get along with Delnaz and vice versa. But all three of them were getting along, Javid was a little bit tipsy on beer, a warm, pleasant buzz filled her and she has been laughing harder in the past two hours than she has in a while. Delnaz is funny, in the sense that she blurts out every thought she thinks of and Toman reciprocates with her usual wry humour.

This wasn't how she imagined tonight but she's glad she came here anyways. The bar hasn't miraculously lost any of its shoddiness, the beer wasn't really good and terrible Iranian rap now played from the speakers. Still, it didn't reduce any of the calm she felt. And the cheery on top is Javid holding Toman's hand underneath the table. It might seem like a mundane achievement but it was Toman who reached out to grip her hand first. And besides, Javid doesn't mind if Toman wants to take things slow.

Javid is thinking of how she might make a move on Toman, maybe try to kiss her tonight when she hears sudden commotion. Tables toppling over and screams renting through the music. Toman shoots up from her seat at once, eyes scanning and looking for the source of trouble. Through the noise, someone shouts, "Police!"

It is then that Javid hears the sirens, louder now and then that she understands what is going on. Fear slithers down her spine as she locks eyes with Toman.

"We need to leave!" Toman shouts, already gripping Javid's arm. Even though the moment seems a little inappropriate, Javid cannot help but wonder if this was how Toman had been like when she was a cop.

Not for the first time that night, Javid swears under her breath, regretting wearing a gown and heels. Sure, she looks pretty but try running through fucking chaos in a fitted dress and heels. She clamps on Delnaz arm and the three of them try to waddle to the front of the bar.

Someone slams into Javid from behind and sends her toppling face first into a table. Toman catches her by the waist and draws her up. By then, it is too late to try and make an escape from the bar; they are already surrounded by policemen who raise their guns in the air, several of them are kicking and dragging out people.

If Javid thought that the bar was rough looking before, it looks even worse now – looking as if an earthquake happened.

Soon enough, the three of them have handcuffs slapped on them. Toman and Javid are cuffed together and if the situation isn't so frightening, Javid might think of it as romantic. But for the first time, the feel of Toman's skin so near hers doesn't send her heart into overdrive, she's boiling with fury here, already having a good guess as to why they're being apprehended.

Someone must have discovered their celebration and called the cops, maybe even made an official noise complaint against the bar. Although queer people might be free to love, the law didn't cure hate in the hearts of despicable people.

***

And that's how Haleh finds herself sharing a cell with Pari, couple from earlier and the singer. Fate has a wicked sense of humour, she acknowledges.

An hour ago, Haleh saw the sirens of the police cruisers, she should have taken off into the night, she had been about to when Pari spun on her heels and shouted that they had to warn everybody inside the bar. Haleh isn't a heroine, she does things for her own interest only, she had been fully prepared to take off into the night and never return. But Pari had insisted and Haleh had hesitated, that few seconds of being stuck between doing the good thing and doing the selfish thing caused her to be thrown in jail tonight.

Many people that know Haleh may peg her as a bad girl -- she certainly fits into the persona of bad guy – they would expect several piercing (to which they are correct, she has seven of them), tattoos even (she only has one) , badass dressing (also correct) a string of broken hears trailing her steps (accurate) and several stints in jail. The funny part is that she ticks every box in the bad girl to do list but she's never been to jail. It's even more hilarious because she used to be a cop.

But it seems as if there is a first time for everything. Haleh gives a snort at that, breaking the silence between them.

Oddly, the small, musty smelling cell has been quiet since the five of them were shoved into it and locked. Haleh expects Javid and Toman to be discussing a way out of this, maybe Delnaz to even sing a song or too – yes, she's still bitter that she isn't friends with any of them – but they've all been quiet.

Pari is sitting on the lone bench in the room, a rickety thing that looks like it might cave under Pari's weight any moment. Her head bent between her laps, if Haleh doesn't know better, she might think that she is asleep.

At Haleh's snort, all eyes turn to her. She blinks innocently at all of them, looking anything but that. When they don't say anything, she does the fifty fifth sweep of their little space; white walls that have become yellowed over time, metal bars for doors and a lone bulb on the ceiling. All the stories that Haleh has heard about jail describe it as a smelly dark place. They got the smelly part right but at least the dark part is blissfully wrong. Thank the gods for small favours.

"Please tell me that one of you have family who's going to come looking for you and hopefully get us all out of here?" Pari asks, her voice taking on that cheery quality again. But this time, it sounds genuine. Haleh looks at her face, surprised that she isn't freaking out or even looking worried like the rest of them are. Of all of them, she is the outsider, thousands of miles away from her country, friends and family. Oh wait, Pari already said that she doesn't have much of family.

"My parents are dead." Delnaz announces. Haleh notices that all of them stiffen at the mention of Delnaz's dead parents. Pari's smile dims a little before recovering its full wattage.

Haleh however accepts the refreshing honesty. "Rule Delnaz's parents out of the situation. We're down one womxn." She deadpans.

For the second time that hour, all eyes found their way back to her. She smirks and waves her fingers.

A second later, Toman snorts. "That was actually kind of funny."

"Not kind of, honey, I'm hilarious." Haleh says.

"And humble too." It's Javid this time.

Haleh ignored the urge to roll her eyes. "I can't tell you the number of times I've heard this line. You're definitely not creative." She says but there really isn't any bite to her words.

"Okay, parents are out of the question." Pari cuts in, her face a little apprehensive as if she expects a fight to break out between Haleh and Javid. If only she knows that Haleh rarely gets physical; she rather hires someone to beat someone else rather than get her hands dirty. Plus, it's all just banter, even though Haleh has known her less than five hours, she already likes Javid and the classical Haleh way of showing affection happens to be bantering and sarcastic comments.

"Does anybody have siblings?" Pari asks.

Haleh is a little surprised when none of them raise their hands. No wonder they're all headstrong womxns who don't back down; children who grew up without any siblings tend to be that way.

"Mine died too." Delnaz says, this time her voice does waver a little.

"You always ask the traumatic questions, Pari," Haleh drawls in a bid to break the ice.

Javid laughs and Haleh relaxes in the slightest. She never has to play the role of comedic relief and yet, here she is willingly playing that role for a bunch of womxns she only met a few hours ago.

Pari raises her hands in mock surrender, "Sorry for trying to get us out of here." She says and snickers when Haleh shoots her a playful glare.

"There's no need to be worried. A few people would have gotten away and if there' s one thing I know about queer people – it's that we never leave one of our own behind." Javid says and Haleh has to admit that she is right.

"I didn't imagine that my first pride event in Tehran would end this way," the tall womxn, Javid says. She lets out a breathy laugh.

Haleh understands what she's trying to do; not exactly make

light of the situation but trying to make sure that nobody was drowning in self loathing of anger. It was a little too late for Javid to be playing therapist though, Haleh has been swimming in anger for most of her adult life, she's a pro at the sport.

Haleh thinks that Toman might be the most like her; she doesn't have Haleh's superior quirky fashion sense — usually, nobody does — but she is quiet and calculating in the way that Haleh is, also without all the sarcasm and snark.

She doesn't like being similar to someone else. Haleh takes great pride in being one of a kind, the kind that makes a long lasting impression, leaves a burning imprint behind.

"I live in Berlin." Haleh hears herself say. "So this isn't my first pride parade, but surely the one I ended up in jail." Haleh finishes.

Haleh has already zoned out of the conversation, fixing her eyes on Delnaz who is sitting on the floor, her back resting against the jail bars. Other than offering the tidbit about her dead parents, she has been otherwise quiet and not because she wants to, Haleh has noticed her lips part several times in the past few minutes as if she wants to say something but she quickly clamps down on her lips, deciding against it.

***

Delnaz notices that everyone is watching her. The truth is that all the high from performing earlier has faded, leaving her exhausted in the most inconvenient dress and with a splitting headache.

Still, it could be worse. Sure, she's sitting in jail with four strangers but they're some of the funniest people that she has ever met. They all have cool stories to tell, funny experiences to share and then there's her. Although, she can't fault them for her quietness, Javid keeps trying to force her into the conversation and with every monotone reply that she gives, she can see Javid grow more confused, no doubt wondering where the hell the confident girl from the coffee shop was.

Javid is relentless though, a trait Delnaz both admires and despised, she cuts into the conversation with a determined etched in the smile on her face. "So, what's your story, Delnaz? Quiet as a mouse, it seems."

Delnaz bristles; the last thing she expected was to be spending forced time with four strangers she is growing irritated with as the night grows. How dare this womxn call her a mouse? She is not afraid of standing up for herself as the nickname suggests. When she sings, her voice commands the attention of everyone listening, a modern siren's call. Didn't she already prove that back in the bar?

"I'm not a mouse," She grounds out forcefully, glaring daggers at Javid.

Haleh chortles rudely but even she quiets when Delnaz sends her the force of that glare. "Damn, it burns." Haleh mutters under her breath. She doesn't seem afraid of Delnaz though, just curious. Delnaz will learn later that Haleh's curiosity is a wicked thing that nobody should ever wish on themselvcs.

Javid is still been smiling easily though, despite being the full recipient of Delnaz glare. "I'd give mice more credit, small things those bastards. But they're smart creatures, silently assessing and capable of causing damage."

Javid's gaze sweeps her form, purely assessing. "But you're not a mouse though. I was wrong, I saw glimpses earlier in the coffee shop."

Haleh snorts from the corner of the room, managing to look glamourous even leaning against the dirty white wall. "Is she the only one who gets a spirit animal analysis? I'm starting to feel a little bit unloved here."

Javid casts her a brief look. "You're a shark."

In true Haleh fashion — even though Delnaz has only known her two hours, she lifts her hand and touches it to her chest as if she is touched, as if she hasn't been watching Delnaz too with a look that makes Delnaz understand why she has been dubbed a shark. Haleh has the tendency to pretend to be nothing but a pretty face but Delnaz knows that a much darker story lies beyond the femme fatale persona.

"Oh, do me next." Pari chirps in, she goes ignored though.

"I'm not an animal." Delnaz finally says when Javid continues to stare, gaze long and probing.

"The story, love. We've been in here for over two hours now and we've each taken turns to spill out our guts. But you, you've been silent, watching but I've been watching you – seeing your lips part as if to speak and close firmly as if you want to swallow your words and keep them to yourselves. You want to talk, the stage is yours."

It is then that Delnaz knows that Javid is more observant than given credit for. Although, casting a swift glance at Haleh tells her that the other womxn had observed the same thing, she just chose to be quiet about her discovery. Delnaz doesn't know whether to be mad at her for it. Every time she tried to speak in the past two hours, she noticed that it was when Haleh would cut in to announce something sarcastic and cutting. She thought it was mere coincidence but not again. Haleh had been challenging her silently, daring to speak.

"I'll give you a refresher on where we stopped, in case you tuned out," Haleh cuts in again, gesturing at Toman who is standing still, arms crossed over her chest. "She's just got the most tragic story, police career gone wrong."

It is the perfect opening Delnaz had needed – a link to the conversation so her input wouldn't be random.

"I thought cops didn't have hearts." Delnaz begins, licking her lips and locking eyes with Toman, silently sending her a look of apology – she doesn't want to invalidate the other womxn's pain.

Pari takes the words as a jab either way and lets out a loud, "Burn!" she's more playful than the rest of them, Delnaz isn't sure what to make of her yet; if the playfulness is a front for something much darker.

"You'd be surprised," Toman says. "Want me to take off my

shirt and show put your hand over my chest?" Later, Delnaz would learn that Toman wasn't the biggest joker but she'd made a joke then, to let Delnaz know that she wasn't offended. Toman is easy to like and Delnaz likes her first.

"The police were the first people I went to when my whole family was murdered. I'd been naïve, foolish even – they certainly hadn't done a single when my brother was murdered years before. Although, our side of town was crime ridden. Still, a shitty thing to tell a girl who'd just seen her family murdered before her eyes."

"What did they say?" Pari is the one that asks, Delnaz found her constant peppiness annoying at first. But when she asked that question, her gaze was sober and serious.

Delnaz gives a shrug and to others it may have look like she was feigning casualness but the cop she spoke to had shrugged, while her family's bodies were covered just few distance from them, he patted her shoulder in a condescending gesture.

"Shit happens at this side of town, gang related murders are always a dead end. You're on your own, kid." She spoke the words in the same careless swagger. She shrugs again, this time feigning casualness. "I ended up in the same gang, singing for a living at their brothels to pay off the debt my family supposedly owed them and when I paid off every last debt, I left and went to make a name for myself. No sad story here." As if she hadn't spoken the saddest story.

Delnaz hates to be stereotypical, but she expects the ladies to gather around her, hug her and murmur useless words of comfort as other people do when Delnaz mentions her family – or even worse, stare in awkward silence as their eyes sweep her form, searching for visible forms of her scars.

The ladies did none of that, Haleh continues to look disinterested. Pari swears loudly. Toman was Toman, just standing and observing. Javid however, shakes her head.

"I was definitely wrong." She said much later when they were out of that room, walking side by side while the others were ahead and arguing very loudly. Even then, Pari had a thing for pushing Haleh's buttons and calling it flirting.

"You're not a mouse, you're a lion."

***

"Since we're telling our life stories, I would like to go next." Javid says. She pretends not to see the worried look that Toman sends her. Because this may just be the crazies thing that Javid has done and she's done plenty of them in her lifetime.

"Hear hear," Haleh says mockingly, miming raising up a glass.

"My mum and I immigrated to England when I was a tween." Javid says. "My dad died as a result of the terrible healthcare in the country. My mum didn't want her only child to grow up in the same country, so she made the necessary arrangements and within a year after my dad died, we were in England. It was a whole new way of living, my mum never failed to tell and remind me how privileged we are." Javid continues. "She tried to teach me the Iranian side of our culture but it's not the same thing. As I grew older, I felt more British than Iranian. I would watch the news and Iran would appear but never for good, only for bad. I began to feel as if I'd betrayed my own country, living a much better life when countless of others didn't."

"Once I hit it big, it was my chance to do something meaningful for my country, I donated a lot in charity."

"Hold up a second," Pari cuts in, "Just how rich are you?"

Javid gives a modest shrug. It is Toman that answers for her, "She's pretty fucking rich."

"All these British people." Pari says as if all British people are wealthy.

"They have a thing for reaping where they did not sow." Is all Haleh says, she looks at Javid as if expecting her to challenge this. Haleh doesn't understand that Javid could care less about being wealthy: sure it's nice being able to afford the things she wants and she won't lie and say that she doesn't enjoy pampering herself or flying her plane or vacationing wherever she wants in the world. But she is also pretty sure that she would be content with less.

"Charities didn't fill the void. Sure, it helped knowing that I donated to a couple of charities and that my money was being used to transform the lives of other Iranian people. But I thought that there had to be something I could do, more instead of throwing money at everything."

"I agree." Haleh says with a curt nod of her head.

"So I found something that could potentially change our worlds, for the better."

"So, what are you waiting for, tell us all about it." Delnaz said.

***

The present

"You didn't just give us hope, Javid, you changed our lives and we dedicated it to this cause. It doesn't matter what happens in the end. We have a fighting chance and best believe that we're going to fight as hard as we can." Toman finished.

CHAPTER TWENTY THREE
The Last Supper

The headgear was lighter than Javid had anticipated, it fit like a perfect crown on her head and she couldn't help but smile a little. She took it off and set it back into the backpack that the rest of her gear was inside. Those had arrived yesterday morning, Javid had taken it upon herself to make sure to provide her team with the best gear they would need while they were in the cave. Shirin had been true to her word and Javid had received the map of the route that led to from the cave to underneath the Damavand mountain. She'd duplicated it, creating a waterproof copy. There were several copies of it too, the rest of her friends were getting copies.

There were a few other maps. They would be driving to the Gol-e-Zard Cave early tomorrow morning. They were as prepared as they could be; early this morning, they'd gone over the specifics of their plan. If Javid was being honest, she was still a little nervous, there were a million things that could go wrong, a million things to hyper focus on but she was determined not to do that.

She was going to enjoy a nice dinner with her friends and her team and they were going to get some sleep before tomorrow. It had been Pari's idea for them to have a proper dinner like family the night before they left.

Surprisingly, despite the crazy rollercoaster of the past few days, they still weren't opposed to dressing nicely to eat at the hotel's restaurant.

"You know, you could have showered with me and saved water." Toman's voice came from the bathroom.

Javid couldn't help the grin that spread on her face, couldn't tamp it down even if she tried — and she didn't. She and Toman weren't the type of people to put a label on what they were. Javid loved Toman and Toman felt the same way. It was as clear as night and day and easy the same way for them. She heard Toman's footsteps and turned around to face the very naked womxn standing in front of her and dripping wet on the tiled floor.

"You're going to get my clothes all wet." Javid said, even though she was the one closing the distance between them, her arms wrapping around her curves.

Toman's reply was a wicked grin. "That's not the only part of you that I want wet." She said.

Javid was well aware that she would likely end up teased by their friends the moment they stepped out of the comfort of their room. She couldn't bring herself to care, only pressed her lips against Toman's.

***

"And this is why you don't date your coworkers, people." Pari announced when Toman and Javid reached their table..

Javid was impressed by the interior of the restaurants, hotels tended to go a bit overboard with their restaurant interior design but this one gave off a warm ambience. The decor was muted colours; brown seats enclosed in booths, cream walls and well lit chandeliers; not too dim and not too bright. The whole setting was intimate and Javid was charmed by it.

She watched Toman say something to Pari and half nodded; mostly to herself.

Dinner went by in a blur of tasty food and dessert. The food was good and the drinks flowed easily. Javid didn't do much talking, she let her friends talk and she just listened, happy to be involved in their happiness, to watch their faces; the smiles, the thoughtful frowns and of course, the way their faces lit up whenever they prepared a joke. Whatever happened to them at the Gol-e-Zard Cave, Javid tried not to think of, she tried to bottle up the feeling of satisfaction that she felt.

Something was telling her that it wouldn't last.

***

That night, after everyone had gone to sleep, Haleh crept from her room to Pari's, knocking on the door as quietly as she could and eyes darting around as if she was a thief wanting to rob their penthouse suite.

When she got no immediate response, she knocked again, this time the action was more insistent. She waited a few beats and raised her clenched fist in the air, preparing to knock again when the door opened silently; thank goodness for nice hotel suites and soundless doors.

She smirked at Pari who was dressed in a tank top and teeny tiny shorts. From the looks of it, Pari hadn't been sleeping, her face was devoid of makeup and she was clear eyed, there was something like frustration swimming in the depths of her gaze as if she'd tried and tried to fall asleep but failed. Kinda like Haleh.

"Can't sleep?" Haleh asked, she didn't wait for a reply from Pari, she pushed past her and strided into the room. "I brought gifts." She added, raising up the half full bottle of whiskey she'd snuck from the stocked bar in the living room area.

The room was bathed in dim yellow light that caused Haleh to squint in order to sleep. The sheets on the queen sized bed were rough as if Pari had tossed and rolled in them, desperate for sleep.

"Could you turn up the lights in here? I can barely see you

well." Haleh asked.

Pari made something of a snorting noise, sounding very deeply irritated and for a brief second, Haleh wavered. She didn't like to go where she was not welcomed and even though she might have stopped anywhere else, she's chosen to come here, but if Pari didn't want her, then she would leave.

Just as she was thinking of doing so, the lights became brighter, not too bright that Haleh winced at the glare but bright enough that she could see the whole room clearly. There was a book on Pari's bed, laying face down. She walked to it and picked it up, mouthing the title to herself and reading the blurb written on the back. She glanced at the book and up at Pari who was waiting, arms on her hips like a stern, disapproving mother.

"You read horror to fall asleep?" Haleh asked.

Pari barked a sudden laugh, the sound breaking through the weird tension between them. "You come in here and ask me at least three questions and you don't even wait for me to answer one before moving on to the next." She said, shaking her head almost fondly.

Haleh sat down at the foot of the bed, she patted the space beside her expectantly, glancing at Pari pointedly to make sure the message was gotten.

"Come sit next to me, and you can answer all my questions." She said, offering a smile, genuine.

Pari looked taken aback by the request but she obliged and sat down besides Haleh, putting a little space between them. Haleh snickered a little and rose a brow in a dare that Pari chose to ignore.

"Yes, I can't sleep and yes I can turn on the lights. And yes, I read horror to fall asleep." Pari sighed.

Haleh pretended to think very deeply. She wasn't yet ready to ask Pari why she couldn't sleep, afraid that their answers would be too similar. "How does that even work? Aren't horror books supposed to scare you to stay awake? Back when I was studying to join the police force, I read a lot of horror books to keep awake at night — just when I would begin to doze off, I'd hear some random sound in the house that would scare me awake."

Pari giggles a little at that. "I didn't know you read."

Haleh shrugged. "Well, you don't know much about me."

Pari scoffed. "That isn't true, and whose fault is that?"

"Definitely mine," Haleh agreed easily.

Was that surprise that made Pari blink slowly? Haleh almost laughed, she really should share tidbits from her past more often, if only to shock a chattering Pari into silence.

"Are you always this honest at night?" Pari asked jokingly.

Even though the words had been made as a joke, Haleh couldn't help but consider them seriously. The truth was that she was not. The nighttime back in Berlin had been her most active part of a day; she could stay awake from midnight to the late hours of the morning. She usually spent the afternoons sleeping.

"No. I'm rarely ever honest." It was the truth, she'd carved out a life of lies for herself in Berlin and she'd gladly lived it because it was better than the truth.

"Oh." Pari said softly. "Why couldn't you sleep?"

Haleh shot Pari a look, "I didn't say that I couldn't sleep."

Pari rolled her eyes, a hint of her rare sass peeking through. "Please, Haleh. You're sitting right here with me. Don't lie."

"I guess my body is tuned to being awake at this time." Was what she said, it was the truth, it just wasn't the entire thing and Pari seemed to know it.

"But that's not the only reason." Pari prodded gently.

Haleh rolled her eyes, but there was no malice in the action. She was pretending to be pissed off so that Pari would back off the topic. Pari didn't seem like she was going to stop quizzing her though and in the end, Haleh relented.

"I'm a little scared of tomorrow. I kept lying there in my bed, thinking that this might be my last night alive. It's not that the thought of death scares me, per se." Haleh quickly added, although Pari was the last person who would judge her and call her a coward, Haleh still felt the need to justify herself.

"Not to be depressing but I've never really been frightened of dying. I know that it'll come and I've always been prepared for it. I've even come close to it several times in Berlin." She laughed, thinking of all the enemies she'd made, of Cash who wanted her dead so bad that he must have been sniffing around the place, must have realised that she was out of the country and was very likely putting in place plans that would destroy her when she returned.

Haleh was in no way at all scared of dying. When death came, she would embrace it with open arms.

"It's just that my whole life feels pointless, I've done nothing I should be proud of. I left this country and ran as far away as I could just so I could avoid my past and pretend to be a whole new person— one that doesn't give a single fuck about anyone and anything. That was who I was in Berlin."

She inhaled a deep breath, "do you ever feel like that, darling? Like you've lived the most meaningless life and there will be no legacy you leave behind."

Pari was silent for the longest time and Haleh was beginning to wonder if she'd actually managed to silence her up for once.

"You're part of the team that will find the sword."

Haleh cut in with a harsh laugh, "There's no guarantee of that."

Pari gave Haleh a flinty gaze. "Shut up and listen to me."

Haleh obliged, even though the moment between them was serious as sin, she couldn't help but be a little turned on by Pari's bossy tone.

"I believe that we'll find the sword." Pari affirmed and Haleh

wanted to ask if she believed it herself. Pari could be blindly opti-
mistic, choosing to see no other way but sunshine and rainbows.
Haleh was usually the opposite, saying things as she saw them.
Who would have thought? The pessimist falling for the optimist?

"But even though we don't. Haleh, what you've done, what
we've all done, willingly put ourselves, our lives and our chances
at a future on the line for our countries — that is a real fucking
legacy to leave." Pari said. "It doesn't matter that nobody knows
it, it doesn't matter at all."

Somehow, during her spiel, she'd closed the distance between
the two of them. Haleh was sitting so close to her that she saw the
light of the room reflected in Pari's eyes. Her eyes flicked down to
Pari's lips but before she could make a move, or even run away and
end this connection she felt to Pari — she had always been scared
of how easy she related to Pari, how easily she wanted to be the
one making her smile, to defend her when it was necessary. That
was really scary, Haleh hadn't felt this way in years.

Haleh was going to move away, going to break Pari's heart by
being a coward again. But Pari didn't let her, before Haleh could
blink, she was leaning in and kissing the hell out of her.

Haleh pulled away a few seconds into the kiss. Pari's face fell,
thinking that she'd been rejected.

Haleh raised up a hand, "I just need to put this bottle down. I
need to be able to touch you with both of my hands."

And Pari blushed, her cheeks stained bloody red.

Haleh set the bottle of whiskey on the rug clad floor and pulled
Pari in for another crushing kiss; she was done being cowardly.
This time, she wasn't going to run, because she'd found some-
where she belonged.

CHAPTER TWENTY FOUR
The Necklace

Javid paced her room, perplexed. She was anxious. Anxious about a decision she had made and how she was going to come back from it remained a mystery to her. She glanced down at her watch and time seemed to have noticed her little panic attack. It was moving so fast. Faster than it should have and it only caused Javid to grow more unsettled. She made her way out of the room to the living room, her fingers trembling and the confidence she had in herself wavering. Still, she remained on her feet, knowing there was no way to turn back from all she had put her and her friends into.

The night before, she had spent hours planning the whole day and most of it, she was busy coming up with a pep talk. She planned to give it to her friends that morning and perhaps, it might do a great job to help ease the tension between them. Their journey for the day was a major one and they probably needed to be motivated.

She reached for the bottle of water that had been left on the table the night before, opened up the bottle, and gulped down the content as she felt dehydrated. The one thing that bothered her the most was giving the speech she had made. She dreaded it so much that she made a little whisper something underneath her breath that she won't need to give it. Still, it didn't help clear the expression on the faces of her friend that she had imagined in her head.

Javid had expected a downcast face that morning, probably accompanied by a bit of fear embedded in it. The journey they had the plan to make was not going to be an easy one and the very fact that someone could die in their midst had been established. They could have easily turned down the mission and forgotten about the whole thing, thereby prolonging their lives a little longer, but they had refused to do that.

Not that Javid didn't care about her friends. They were daring to her and the more reason for her to panic. She felt unstable having to bear such information in her heart. She had even looked for signs of reluctance from the ladies but she had found none the night before. They were all just hiked about the adventure and they completely just ignored the fact that it had consequences. She did promise herself that the slightest reluctance she sensed in anyone's voice or expression that morning would mean cancelling the whole trip.

As she sat on the couch and waited impatiently, tapping her legs against the board of the floor, she began to hear footsteps coming down from the stairs towards the living room. She adjusted herself and tried to get herself ready for what was coming but was flabbergasted when she first heard soft giggles from a distance.

She was confused, wondering if it was coming from the friends she was worried about. The giggling increased and turned into a chuckle as it got closer. When she could no longer take it, she got up to her feet and went round the corner of the corridor to see what was going on. She was stunned to see Pari bent over, laughing hysterically at something someone had said. The rest only had genuine smiles on their faces.

"Good morning people," she called out to them, drawing their attention.

The words rolled off her tongue as though she was telling them to let her in on their joke, but instead when they all saw her, they all burst into another round of laughter. Except if it was the worry they were all facing from their imminent visit to the cave that was causing them to go nuts, Javid had no other explanation.

Still, the laughter they had shared had felt so genuine that it crossed out every doubt in her mind that these ladies were worried about the adventure they wanted to embark on. They all walked past her and made their way into the kitchen to fix themselves a quick meal, leaving her with her thoughts.

She had expected wrinkles on their faces, bags underneath their eyes, and a nervous glance at every corner they turned to but they had shocked her completely with something entirely different. Something that got her thinking was if she was the only person worried on her team of five about the possible outcome after they visited the cave.

As she sat with them and they ate, there was such calmness in their eyes and attitude that put Javid on edge. It was strange to think that she was worried and they were not. She could have even called for a postponement of the whole engagement, but it looked like she was the only one at ease. Even still, she was going to be responsible for five lives, excluding her own.

"Hurry up ladies, time waits for no one. I'm pretty sure we all had a good rest. It's written on all our faces. Let's finish up and get going soon." Javid finally said to the ladies who seemed to be cool with her as they listened with so much respect on their faces it started to become awkward.

Javid got to her feet quietly and picked up her now empty plate before she ended what she had to say. "Like I said yesterday, we need to be at the cave way before nightfall."

"Yes, boss. We will hurry up," said Haleh with a mouthful and a big smile.

Javid nodded back at her and headed straight into the kitchen. She was immediately followed by Toman who stuck close to her as chicks do to a mother hen. There was an awkward stare and giggling between the two of them.

Toman leaned closer to her and placed her mouth close to her ear to murmur something.

"Can you believe after all the drama, they're together now," she said with some glee in her voice.

Javid frowned in slight shock, confused as to what that was supposed to mean.
"Uh?" she exclaimed at first. "What do you mean by saying now? Weren't they together previously? I thought they were."

"Oh, Javid! You never cease to amaze. It can be lonely sometimes being the only observant person in the room."

Javid gave a soft chuckle as she cleaned her hand with the towel that was right within her reach. She looked straight into the dining room at the two ladies now acting like a couple freely in front of everyone and could tell that Toman was right all along. Javid watched as Haleh tried to feed Pari and instead of eating from the spoon already, the lover bird was taking about a minute to giggle before accepting the food. Javid remembers having mentioned that time was a resource they had to cherish and she didn't hesitate to call out the couple.

"Haleh and Pari, I believe I did mention that we don't have that much time, didn't I?" she asked, her voice rebounding with so much authority that the two shrank, and the whole group broke into another round of laughter.

"We'll hurry up now," Pari said, the smile on her cheek stressing her cheekbones more than the chewing of her food.

After they had all finished eating their lunch, they cleared the dining table and moved back into the living room for one more run through the plan. It was a simple one even though they knew that if they disobeyed the slightest of rules that had been made, they would be made to pay costs for it. Then, they headed for the driveway. Javid shut the penthouse door behind her and led them downstairs toward the new car she had rented for this particular journey. It was big and more spacious than the one she had originally and that just made the journey a little easier for her. "Has everyone gotten their backpacks?" Javid asked as she was about to close the truck of the car.

There was a scattered response amongst the ladies, affirming that they had all packed their backpacks into the trunk.

"Are we going to have to carry those backpacks though? They are so effing heavy" Haleh pointed out, rubbing shoulders with her partner's shoulder.

"Yes," Javid responded rapidly and without hesitation. She was the one who had created a list of all they would need and she had also taken time to go through them just to ensure that the contents were right. In each backpack, it contained an individual safety suit, helmet, ropes, flashlights, and a small first aid kit.

"Alright, let's get this over with," said Javid as she entered the car. The rest of the ladies filed into the car and just like Javid had wanted, it contained them all with little space to spare. She wanted them all to be in the same vehicle as they travelled toward the cave.

They were only forty minutes drive away from the cave, but still, it felt like two hours drive for some. They talked and ranted about a lot of things, especially things they would do with the sword when they got it. "I never knew we would get to play Arthur and the magical sword in real life," Delnaz commented and they had all laughed about it.

The drive was lit except for the one time when someone mentioned something about wishing everyone a safe trip that they all returned safely. That had struck a chord of worry in Javid's heart again, but they had quickly covered it up with more lovable and laughable memories. Javid knew for sure that she loved her team and would do anything she could to protect them all.

Finally, they pulled up near the field's yellow flower that surrounded the cave and when they could no longer go further with the car, they pulled over and all got out. Javid looked down at the map in her hand and she could tell they were just walking distance from the entrance of the cave now.

At that time of the year, the area was always closed to tourists and locals who wanted to go hiking. They gave them strict warnings to stay away from the area, but then, the ladies were going to be going against the law.

"Alright now," Javid called out as they took their first few steps into the forest. "We keep our wits with us and we don't do anything stupid, understood?"

She got a scattered yes across the group and then continued, saying, "stick close to each other, don't stray, remain focused, and listen to simple instructions," said Javid, sounding like a military officer that was spitting out orders.

"Oooh! Sir yes sir," Toman said teasingly and they all giggled at the comment made. As they walked up the trail, they began to encounter more rocks and fewer flowers. The path turned into a rocky terrain quickly and they were climbing rocks in a moment.

"Is it me or this stuff is getting heavier?" asked Pari, turning to face Haleh.

"I was going to say that too," Haleh supported, pulling at the straps of the backpack.

Javid was also feeling the weight of the backpack but she had decided to act like the leader between them all. She realised it would do them a lot of good if they could reduce the weight of the backpack and instantaneously, an idea popped into her head.

"All right everyone, listen up," Javid began, stopped in her tracks, and turned back to look at all the ladies. "I think it is only wise if we choose to change into our suits here. That way, we can reduce the weight we carry."

"Yes! Brilliant." Pari said and without even hesitating, dropped the backpack from her shoulder and started unpacking it.

"Slow down babe," Haleh said with a grin on her face. "The cave ain't running nowhere."

"Yeah, that's true, but time is," Pari said, completely fixated on her backpack.

The rest gave off a light chuckle but then got on with dropping the backpack and taking out their suits. They began to undress themselves and Javid could see Haleh's eyes peering against Pari's skin. Pari had caught her and bit her lips in a quick reaction to the gaze. She noticed that both of them were getting distracted and decided to step in.

"Okay, hurry up people!" Javid ushered them. She slipped into the black with green vertical stripes suit faster than any of the ladies and fastened her helmet safely over her head. She then went around to help the others with wearing the gear the right way.

By the time they were done, all the things they could need were inside a single backpack. She then assigned Haleh and Delnaz to be in charge of carrying it. They kept the rest of their things behind a rock and continued their journey, climbing up the rocks.

"You know, in the movies, this is the part where they start to sing cave songs," Pari called from behind.

Despite herself, Javid laughed, feeling a little of the worry in her shoulders leave.

"Go ahead and sing, by all means," Javid said aloud.

"I don't know any cave songs," Pari replied, sounding a little peeved as if she really ought to have put some time into learning songs.

Their whole group roared in laughter.

"It sucks being the only single one in the group," Delnaz said randomly.

'Farzaneh is single too, aren't you, far?" Javid heard Pari say not so subtly. She imagined Farzaneh giving Pari her usual look of patience.

'Yes." She answered warily.

"You know who else is single, Far?" Pari continued saying. Javid imagined that dopey grin on her face. it was almost scary how well she knew her friends, their mannerisms down to the last T.

"Who?" Farzaneh asked, this time with some amusement. At least she was taking all the teasing like a good sport. She fit right in with them.

"Delnaz!" Pari beamed.

"Real smooth, babe," Haleh said, she was probably rolling her eyes.

"Pari, I swear, I'm going to kill you." She heard Delnaz's growl. Pari yelped a second later as if she'd been pinched.

Meanwhile, as the group carried on with their little chit chat Javid looked ahead in the distance, the Damavand Mountain was so close, looming ahead ominously. Javid looked at it and swore in her mind, I'm coming for your heart.

Not long after she had made yet another promise to this one mountain, they appeared at the mouth of the cave, a small opening that Javid had anticipated. She had not been there before but she had gotten a pretty impressive imagination of the whole thing and she just wasn't far off course.

The group grew silent, knowing for sure that finally, they were there. Getting into the cave seemed to be pretty easy at first from the outside. Javid pulled out her flashlight and turned it on. Gesturing with her hand, she asked them to stay out first and let her have a quick look at what was happening down there.

Javid's heart gradually began to race and she just tried to contain herself. She placed her glove hand against the wall of the cave and then walked in slowly, her eyes narrowed, ensuring that she was able to see every corner of the room. The air in the cave was different and it felt chilly even though she was thrown into a baggy suit. She hadn't gone more than five steps when she thought she was staring into a wall.

"That's impossible," she muttered under her breath.

"Guys! Get in here," she said in a hurry, worry gripping her heart. "Surely it must be here somewhere."

"What is it?" asked Toman as she closed in on her. "Oh no!"

They were all flabbergasted at the sight of the wall in front of them and it turned out that they had only walked into an opening in the cave. Though according to the map, they've been following, that was the only opening and surely must be the cave.

"Hold up guys. Can we all hear that?" Delnaz asked, trying to tell them all to stay put and keep mute.

There was a faint sound of water drop against the surface of water coming from underneath the rock they were standing on.

"Is that coming from…"

"There's an opening underneath us," Javid said, an iota of hope surfacing again in her heart.

"I mean, are we supposed to break through this… arghhhhh!" Pari was still saying when she stepped forward and all of a sudden found herself almost getting swallowed by the ground.

The cave was thrown into pandemonium as everyone rushed to save her as she struggled to hold on tight to the loose sand that was all over the place.

Javid got her hands on Pari's wrist first and as Haleh closed in, Javid screamed for her to stop.

"Don't get too close or we are all going down this hole," she said, her voice calm and her breath controlled.

"Please don't let me go," Pari said, her voice breaking.

"I won't let you go," Javid assured her.

Slowly, with the rest behind, looking on and definitely praying within themselves, Javid put her out of the hole that had been made in the ground. As she did, she gave off a heavy sigh of relief. What had been bothering her all the while was now here—the looming danger at every corner they turn, looking for a way to zap out the air that they breathe.

Pari and Haleh hugged for a long while before breaking up and all the while, Javid was busy inspecting the hole. It turned out that they would have to climb down to a whole new ground level than they had anticipated.

"Can I get a rope?" asked Javid as she turned towards Delnaz.

Delnaz reached into the backpack and pulled out rope. They engineered the rope to a rock on the outside of the cave, tying it firmly and then tried their best to open up the space that had almost swallowed their friend.

"Who's going to go first?" asked Delnaz.

The hole wasn't too big and for the first few distances to be covered deep into the ground, there was no luxury of space. It was like passing through a thin pipe that was only large enough for your body to pass through and then, it was only made of dirt. "I can go down the hole first," Farzaneh said but Javid only turned to her and gave her a kind of glare that said she shouldn't even think about it.

"I brought you all into this place and I am going to take the lead role of risking my life first. Get me the flashlight."

Javid had made it so clear that no one dared challenge her. In truth, they respected her for that, but then none of them would have willingly agreed to do what she did.

The flashlight was passed to her by Toman who held on to the end just as Javid was about to pull it from her grip. "Are you sure you will be safe?" Toman asked, looking straight into her eyes.

The lightning in the cave was poor, but Toman could still see the light in her eyes. Javid gulped hard. She knew the weight of her responsibilities and she was still going to go for it head on.

"I'll be fine. Give me a walkie-talkie too just in case you don't hear me."

After she had gotten the walkie talkie, she began climbing down the rope through the narrow hole that they had managed to create. Javid had a lot on her mind as she claimed it, more importantly, she hoped she found what she was looking for. By the time she was out of the narrow hole, she looked down to be confronted by a rocky floor. She found herself in an underground cave, every nook and cranny covered in stalagmite and stalactites from the reaction of limestone and water.

As she got down from the rope, she felt the chill in the air get stronger. The sound of water drops clashing against the surface of a water pool was louder. Everything seemed normal though, there was hardly a glimmer of light aside from the one that came from the flashlight. After scanning and checking to confirm if all was well, she then brought out her walkie talkie and spoke to the ladies above.

"It's safe. You can all come down."

Minutes later, they all came through. They walked forward towards the path that opened up in front of them and were confronted with another wall, only this time, it had a hole in it like a vent, suitable enough for someone to fit into it.

"We should be able to squeeze in." Haleh said as she approached Javid's side.

"That's exactly what she said." Pari cracked a weak joke. Delnaz politely laughed, but no one else did.

"Let me go first." Javid made the announcement. They should have known that; they'd gone over the plan numerous times. "Haleh, bring your backpack."

Haleh placed it on the ground and drew out the thick red rope. Javid was the first to wrap it around her, followed by Toman, Haleh, Delnaz, Pari, and Farzaneh.

Javid lay down flat on the ground and began to shimmy into the open cave mouth. "Put on your head lights." She shouted at her friends, right before she turned hers on.

And so it began, Javid kept her breathing even and calm just as she'd practised. She wasn't claustrophobic by any means but she could feel the walls around her, clamping in a manner that was discomfiting. If she didn't know any better then she might say that she thought the walls were closing in on her. That wasn't true, she forced herself to remember. She heard the distant sound of roaring water – there was a fountain outside at the end of the cave; it was that path that they would be taking to the Damavand Mountain. For what seemed like forever, she continued to crawl, she didn't dare call out any of her friends' names; she needed to conserve strength and air. She felt something sharp on the wall slash her cheek, felt the skin break open and something wet slide down that side of her face.

Still, she kept on going, after what seemed like forever, the mouth of the cave began to widen, giving more space and making for easier crawling. Javid allowed herself one teensy sigh of relief before continuing on.

***

After a few minutes - or was it minutes? It was becoming increasingly difficult to tell how much time had passed in here. She had a pocket watch, but it was hidden inside her suit, along with the cave's waterproof map - the cave became a more impressive sight, a vast space spread out before her, a mammoth of a cave, tall, jagged pillars of limestone had formed around resembling ice.

Javid waited until she felt the tug of the rope behind her before standing up; the water levels were still low at this point, barely reaching Javid's ankles. For the others, it may have reached their ankles, but at least they hadn't reached the cave's swimming area yet.

"Wow," Haleh said, her voice echoing. "It is bigger than I imagined."

"I don't think any of us expected it to be this big." Toman responded by turning around and taking in the sights of the cave. As she spun around, her helmet light beamed and bounced off the walls.

Javid felt a surge of pride at having made it this far. She allowed herself to feel the hope that was pressing against her chest.

"Are we all okay?" Javid inquired, surveying her companions. They nodded in different ways.

"You have a cut on your cheek, Javid." Toman took a step closer to her. "You're in pain."

Javid had forgotten about it, the adrenaline coursing through her veins numbing whatever pain she should have been feeling. "I'm fine, love," she said with a smile. "I moved too quickly and scratched my cheek against the rough wall."

Toman wasn't one to make a fuss, so she lingered for one more second over Javid's face before nodding.

Javid took out his pocket watch and frowned at it. That couldn't be right, an hour had passed. They couldn't have spent the last hour crawling through that dark space. Before she could tamp it down, a shiver snaked down her spine. She took out the map and angled the helmet light so that it shone down on the map.

"All right, Farzaneh, your call." Javid stated. They needed to keep waddling in the water until they reached a two-headed way, according to the map. That could have been the most difficult part of the mission, but they had Farzaneh, and she was the pathfinder. Javid couldn't help but wonder if this was the same location where Nazanin Hesami had died. She shivered once more at the thought. It was too soon to fail, and she had to make sure they all got to the sword.

Farzaneh began to take the lead, walking first. When the water levels were low, it made for easy treading through it, with water splashing as they stepped. They had to avoid the occasional jagged limestone tip, and they couldn't put their hands on the walls for extra stability because the walls were rough with limestone.

Javid kept her gaze ahead and would occasionally check her watch; she wasn't sure if she was hallucinating, but time seemed to move faster inside the cave.

The closer they got, the higher the waters rose, and it was almost up to their waists. And Javid wasn't lying when she said she was becoming concerned. She'd planned on them swimming, but the cave seemed to stretch on forever, as if the distance would never end; sure, they could swim, but how long would they have to hold their breath under water, wearing suits that weren't ideal swimming attire.

Javid had never believed in the existence of a deity, but for the first time, she found herself praying to Gordafarid, the only thing she believed in. Please allow us to bring it to life.

"Walking is becoming increasingly difficult!" Delnaz yelled.

It was also becoming increasingly difficult for her to hear any of her friends.

"Just keep going, we're almost to the two-way path." When Javid responded, she felt Toman reach out from behind her and squeeze her hand.

Javid forced herself to concentrate on what lay ahead; they'd soon arrive at the fork in the road, and Farzaneh would point out the correct path to them. So Javid trod on and on until her leg muscles ached and she felt like if she took another step, her legs would give out. She took deep breaths in and out. She occasionally turned to shout encouraging words to her friends.

"We're nearly there!" When Pari complained about not being able to keep up, she would yell.

For the second time, Javid understood why Shirin had stuck to a two-man team. She may not admit it, but she was forced to slow down so that her friends could catch up. Time was not on their side, and Javid's heart sank in her chest with every glance at the pocket watch. She didn't want to consider what might happen if they missed the sword.

The cave split into two wide paths just as Javid was about to give up, the roaring of the distant waterfall rushing harder and drowning out even the hopeful voice in her head.

They were literally inches apart!

They stood in the centre, waiting for Farzaneh to decide where they would go. Farzaneh, on the other hand, was immobile. "What's wrong?" Javid asked awkwardly.

Farzaneh returned her gaze, her face flushed. "I'm not sure."

Javid's heart sank to the pit of her stomach. "What do you mean you're not sure?"

Farzaneh shook her head, and Javid noticed tears streaming down her cheek. "The voice that guides me has vanished. In my head, there is only silence."

Javid grabbed her shoulders and shook her. "You can't say that because you're the trailblazer."

"What exactly is going on?" Their friends had gathered around them, terrified. "How come we aren't walking?"

"I can't—" Farzaneh paused, not saying what she couldn't.

"Fuck!" Javid yelled.

"Javid, would you mind telling us what the fuck is going on here?" Haleh exploded.

"Farzaneh, has no idea which path to take," Javid indicated the two options in front of them. "...That's what we're supposed to do. This is not a good sign."

"Fuck," Toman yelled. "What should we do now? We've come a long way."

Javid was well aware of the situation. "We're going to split up; three of us will go this way, and the rest will go the other."

None of them seemed pleased with the new plan, but there wasn't an alternative. "You're with me, Farzaneh and Delnaz." Javid stated. "Toman, Pari, and Haleh, you three are on the right track."

"That sounds foreboding!" Pari stated.

"That way, it ensures that someone will find the sword. Whoever gets out first, take the sword and follow the map to Damavand's heart; stab the sword into it, and bring light back to our countries."

Calmness was the opposite of what her friends were expressing right behind her.

They had been together since and having to separate into two groups was ominous. They were muttering to each other, saying that everything would go on well if they just stuck to the plan. More like the backup plan as none of them ever thought their pathfinder was going to lose her ability.

Still, Toman didn't understand why she was calm. While her friends were wondering if they would be the ones to find the sword, she was just quiet. Naturally, she would have freaked out just like how she cursed when Farzaneh realised that she was lost and there was no way she could help.

They had all panicked but now that they were divided, Toman was calm. There was no persistent beat in her chest which was a sign of her fear but she wasn't. She felt everything would end fine.

Still, she couldn't pretend that a little part of her wasn't frightened for her friends.

Being separated meant there was no way they could know if they were all alright or not. Something could happen to both teams and they would only be lost in the cave. She hoped nothing of that sort would happen. Also, there was a certainty that filled her mind.

She couldn't lay a finger on it or really detect the source but she knew that something worth it was going to come out of it. There was no way she could confirm, but she knew she was going to find the sword and then come back for Javid and the rest of her friends.

Still, she didn't say it out loud. If Farzaneh hadn't been able to point in the right direction, what gave her the certainty that they were on the right track? As a result, she shut her mouth and only focused on her surroundings. "Come on guys, let's move forward," she said to the rest.

"Do you think we are on the right path?" Pali asked.

Toman didn't want to sound like she did. "I don't know but if we find it, I think it will be a good thing."

"I hope we find it," Haleh said. "I really want to be out of here."

They all seemed to agree as they trudged on. Toman was filled with excitement and anticipation, as the sound of the water crashing down seemed to be a beacon of hope, a guiding light out of the darkness and towards their destination and subsequently out of it towards Damavand. The noise seemed to be a sign that they were nearing the top of the cave. Soon, they would know if they were on the right track or not.

Toman could see the worry in Pari's eyes, her small frame quivering with each step. Deciding to help, she put her arm around

Pari hoping it would give her the courage to continue. Haleh also followed suit, and the three of them trudged on and waddled through the rising water, the waves lapping at their chests. If she had to estimate, she would guess that the water was up to four feet and Pari was the shortest only two inches past five feet, so they held on to her. Finally, she felt her heart swell with pride when she saw Pari's face light up with determination. With their combined courage, they stuck close to each other.

Sometimes, Toman had to look at them to make sure they were on the same pace. When she did it the third time, she realised something. Haleh seemed to have issues of her own. She held onto Pari's hand with a grip of steel, as if her life depended on it. Her eyes were wide with desperation, almost like she knew something Toman didn't. The womxn was so focused on keeping Pari afloat that she didn't seem to notice the ripples of water.

Toman had noticed it but now the ripples were getting bigger and bigger, and she thought there was a problem. She was about to say something about it but it was too late. Toman felt something slimy and cold brush against her ankle beneath the murky water and she instinctively kicked her leg out in an attempt to rid herself of the strange sensation. Her heart was racing as it happened again, and she let out a blood-curdling scream.

"Swim!" Toman shouted, panic lacing her voice. Haleh's face paled in fear.

In the darkness of the cave, their only source of light had flickered out; the helmet light of Pari's had already fallen off her head before they had reached the two-headed way. With only Toman's helmet light providing some light, they were surrounded by inky blackness and had no idea what was lurking beneath them.

Toman dove into the water, her heart pounding as she swam with all her might, not daring to look back. She felt a deep sense of guilt, knowing that she had left Haleh and Pari behind, but her survival instincts told her to keep going. If she didn't, there was a high chance that whatever happened was going to happen to her too. She couldn't allow that to happen.

Suddenly, she heard a loud scream, and against her better judgement, she stopped and surfaced for air. She peered into the dark, her heart pounding as she heard strange and eerie noises. The other two seemed to hear it as their eyes went wide. As Toman looked closer, she saw something that made her heart stop. A giant sea monster emerged from the depths of the cave, its huge tentacles writhing and its eyes glowing with a sinister light.

It was right behind Haleh and Pari and paralyzed with fear, she could only point to it. She watched as the monster lunged forward and with a powerful swipe of its tentacles, tried to get Pari into its arms. However, Haleh was quick to push Pari into the water. The tentacles caught her instead.

In a matter of seconds, the entire lake was engulfed in blood. Toman's heart shattered. Gone were the days of joy, laughter, and of friendship. Pari's cries echoed through the air like a raging waterfall, her anguish more painful than any Toman had ever experienced.

***

The crescent sword pendant Toman wore glowed a steady rhythm at her neck. Javid was wrong about the emerald's ability could foretell the future and save them all, the black sword pendant was saying something. Toman thought the necklace—with a pendant that resembled the shape of Gordafarid's sword—would protect Toman and lead her to the Sword.

It was an omen of sorts, giving Toman the courage when she needed it. It was why she felt a sense of serenity in her chest. Maybe it was telling her that she was close?

As she neared the end of the path, the vast expanse of the cave opened up before her. Looking up, she saw two holes carved into the roof of the cave, showing her a night sky. She was taken aback at the sudden darkness that had descended.

Memories of the battles fought, and the lives claimed, rushed through her mind. Gordafarid's sword had achieved victories, yet the price was always paid in blood. As she thought of Haleh, her knees gave way, and she collapsed on the rocky ground, weeping into her hands.

Toman glanced up, her gaze resting on the light of the moon that shone through the right hole in the cave's roof. Like something out of a dream, the sword materialised out of thin air. Its hilt and blade were a shining black. Towering above her head, it was far bigger than Toman had realised.

Suddenly, Toman had a change of heart. She could no longer bear the thought of the sword being used for bloodshed and pain.

"You can't do that," Pari's voice spoke from behind her, her voice wavering from all the tears and screams. Miraculously, the sound of rushing water was absent in this part of the cave— it was as if time had stopped.

"I want to but—"

"There are no 'buts.' Haleh gave her life for this. Do not let everyone's sacrifices be in vain— their legacies cannot go to waste. So, stand the fuck up and pick up this sword."

Toman stood up and took up the Sword despite her aching knees and bleeding cuts. A blinding light and a gust of wind blew past her, forming a white, snowy heart shape, revealing Damavand Mountain as its background.

Instantly, she pointed the Sword to the heart - as if she was pricking it to awaken the spirit of their nation. A vivid blast of colours immediately filled the cave.

A warrior ready to usher her people into salvation.

There was no sign that a snowstorm had recently plagued the city of Tehran, the sun was high in the sky, there seemed to be an extra skip in everybody's steps. The truth was that there was nothing special about that day; it could have been like every other day, the sun shining, people going about their daily businesses. But little did Iranians know that their lives had been changed that very morning, by six brave womxns whose names they might never know, might never be able to thank for the joy in their hearts, the skips in their steps and the positive changes that were no doubt soon to come.

In a matter of days, the value of Iranian currency would skyrocket to become one of the most valuable in the world; alongside Afghanistan and Tajikistan currency. Who would have thought?

In a year to come, these three countries will have superseded the highest ranking countries in terms of GDP per Capita. Iran would rank as the country with the happiest people in the world, Afghanistan would be a close second and Tajikistan would be third. In five years, this feat would stabilise, these three countries would come to be known for good things; the past few decades would be a long distant memory, almost like a fuzzy nightmare.

All these things would happen because of one powerful relic and the sacrifice of six courageous womxns.

Acknowledgements

There may only be one name listed as the author of this book, but this work of passion and aspiration could not exist without the following people:

Thank you, Melinda, for teaching me that there is more than one way of doing things or telling a story. Thank you, Peer, for reminding me that my insecurities and life journey as an introvert have given me perspective. Therefore I should cherish the struggles. Thank you, Peniel, for telling me that the final chapter is a farewell, so I should decide how to say it.

My Farsi is way better than my English, so I am forever grateful to Edi, who has taken the time to transform my story into proper English for a smooth read.

Finally, yet most importantly, my sincere gratitude goes to those who read this novel. Thank you for making time to live in my world of words and images.

Xx Kiana

9 781915 557087